THE SECRET SOLDIER

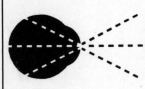

This Large Print Book carries the
Seal of Approval of N.A.V.H.

THE SECRET SOLDIER

ALEX BERENSON

WHEELER PUBLISHING
A part of Gale, Cengage Learning

.Detroit • New York • San Francisco • New Haven, Conn • Waterville, Maine • London

GALE
CENGAGE Learning

LIBRARY OF CONGRESS CATALOGING-IN-PUBLICATION DATA

Berenson, Alex.
    The secret soldier / by Alex Berenson. — Large print ed.
        p. cm.
    Originally published: New York : G.P. Putnam's Sons, 2011.
    ISBN-13: 978-1-4104-3499-9
    ISBN-10: 1-4104-3499-0
    1. United States. Central Intelligence Agency—Fiction. 2. Intelligence officers—Fiction. 3. Saudi Arabia—Fiction. 4. Large type books. I. Title.
    PS3602.E75146S43 2011b
    813'.6—dc22   2010049548

Published in 2011 by arrangement with G. P. Putnam's Sons, a member of Penguin Group (USA) Inc.

Printed in the United States of America
1 2 3 4 5 6 7 15 14 13 12 11

For my wife

PROLOGUE

Manama, Bahrain

JJ's had cold Carlsberg on tap and a dozen flat-screen televisions on its dark wooden walls. It was an above-average bar, generic Irish, and it would have fit in fine in London or Chicago. Instead it occupied the ground floor of a low-rise building in downtown Manama, the capital of Bahrain, a small island in the Persian Gulf.

By eleven p.m., JJ's would be packed with men and women pressing their bodies together in search of pleasures great and small. Now, at nine, the bar was crowded enough to have a vibe, not too crowded to move. A skinny kid with bleached-blond hair spun Lady Gaga and Jay-Z from his iPod as a dozen women danced badly but enthusiastically. The crowd was mostly European expatriate workers, along with American sailors from the Fifth Fleet, which was headquartered in Bahrain.

Robby Duke had gotten to JJ's early. The best girls were taken by midnight. Robby was twenty-eight, built like a rugby player, squat and wide, with long blond hair and an easy smile. Plenty of girls liked him, and he liked plenty of girls. Expat birds were all more or less the same. British, European, whatever, they came to the Gulf for adventure, and adventure usually meant a few easy nights.

Dwight Gasser was Robby's wingman. He was soft-spoken, almost shy. He wasn't much use as a wingman, but some women liked his curly hair and sleepy eyes. "Them two," he said, nudging Robby toward the corner. A blonde with a round face and nice thick lips. The other skinnier and darker. Spanish maybe. They sat side by side, facing a table with two empty seats.

"Yes, Your Highness." Robby squared up and headed for them. Once he'd decided to go for it, he didn't see the sense in mucking about.

"Room for two more?"

The blonde sipped her drink and looked at him like a copper who'd caught him pissing in an alley and wasn't sure whether to give him a ticket or wave him on.

"All yours," she finally said.

Robby extended a hand. "I'm Robby Duke."

"Josephine."

They shook. Robby sat. Robby looked around for Dwight, but he'd disappeared, as he sometimes did when an introduction didn't seem to be going well. Annoying bastard. Though he'd be back soon enough, might even have a beer for Robby by way of apology.

"Josephine. A fellow commoner. Where you from? If you don't mind my asking."

"London."

"The center of the universe." He'd bet his right leg that she didn't live in London.

"Slough, really."

Slough was a suburb west of London, just past Heathrow Airport. Slough was more like it, Robby thought. He could line Slough up and send it into the right corner and the keeper wouldn't do anything but wave.

"Slough sounds like London to a Manchester boy like me." He turned to the dark-haired girl. "You from London, too?"

"Rome."

"Rome. The city of —" Robby couldn't remember what Rome was the city of. "Anyhow, the plot thickens. What brings you ladies to JJ's?"

"We're cabin crew," the Italian girl said.

"For Emirates" — the biggest airline in the Middle East, known for its shiny new planes and equally shiny flight attendants.

"Emirates. Have you flown the A-three-eighty, then?"

"It's a beast," Josephine said. "Who thought a plane with eight hundred seats was a good idea?"

"Not glamorous, then?"

"About as glamorous as the Tube."

"I like it," the Italian said. "I know it's stupid, but still, there's something amazing about it. How something so big can fly."

Robby turned to face the Italian. She had a big nose, but she wasn't bad. Those dark eyes and that long black hair. And the accent. Most important, she looked happy to talk to him, unlike Josephine. "What's your name, Italiano?"

"Cinzia." Beside her, Josephine sighed. Have fun with Dwight, Robby almost said. You two will get along great. Instead, he raised his glass. "Here's to Italy."

"To Italy."

"And to Bahrain on a Thursday night." He took a long swallow of his beer. *And we're off.*

The black Mercedes E190 rolled down the King Fahad Causeway, the ten-mile bridge between Saudi Arabia and Bahrain. Below the asphalt was the water of the Persian Gulf, warm as a bathtub and nearly as flat.

Omar al-Rashid sat behind the wheel. His younger brother, Fakir, slept beside him in the passenger seat. A line of drool curled into Fakir's pure white *thobe,* the long gown that Saudi men wore. Fakir had the soft bulk of a high school nose tackle. His *thobe* draped his round stomach like a pillowcase. He was eighteen, two years younger than Omar.

"Fakir."

Fakir grunted irritably. "Let me sleep."

"You've been asleep since the Eastern Province. And you're drooling."

"I'm relaxed."

"You're as stupid as a donkey."

"Better to be stupid than scared."

"I'm not scared." Omar punched Fakir, his fist thumping against Fakir's biceps. And then wished he hadn't, for Fakir didn't complain, didn't even rub his arm.

"It's all right, brother. If you want to back out. We can do it without you."

"I'm not scared." For the first time in his life, Omar hated his brother. He was scared. Anyone would be scared. Anyone but a donkey like Fakir. But now he'd gone too far. The humiliation of quitting outweighed

11

the fear of death. And maybe the imams were right. Maybe virgins and endless treasures awaited them on the other end.

Though he didn't see the imams lining up to find out.

Three minutes later they reached the tiny barrier island that marked the border of Saudi Arabia and Bahrain. A bored guard checked the Mercedes's registration. A hundred meters on, an immigration agent swiped their passports and waved them through without asking their plans. Everyone knew why Saudis went to Bahrain. They went for a drink, or two, or ten. They went to hang out with their girlfriends without being hassled by the *muttawa,* the Committee for the Promotion of Virtue and Prevention of Vice. The Saudi religious police. They went to watch movies in public, movie theaters being another pleasure forbidden in the Kingdom.

After Bahraini immigration, they were waved into a shed for a customs inspection. An officer nodded toward the blue travel bag in the backseat. "Open it, please." Omar unzipped the bag, revealing jeans, sneakers, and black T-shirts. The clothes were hardly suspicious. Saudi men often changed into Western-style clothes in Bahrain. "Enjoy your visit," the officer said, and waved them on.

"We will," Fakir said.

At JJ's, Robby was off his game. Dwight had won Cinzia's attention, leaving Robby with Josephine. He decided to go the tried-and-true route of getting her drunk.

"Time for another round. What's your pleasure?"

Josephine raised her glass, still half full. "No thanks, Frodo."

"Frodo!" Robby said, in what he hoped sounded like mock horror. In reality the joke cut a bit close. "Hope I'm bigger than he is."

"I hope so, too. For your sake." She glanced at Cinzia.

"Figuring the odds you'll be stuck with me?"

"Exactly." She swallowed the rest of her drink. "All right, then. Vodka and tonic. Grey Goose."

Of course, Grey Goose, Robbie thought. *Top-shelf all the way, this one. And thin odds I'll get more than a peck on the cheek.* "One Grey Goose and tonic coming up."

Five minutes later, he was back with fresh glasses. "Thanks."

"My pleasure."

"What about you? Live here?"

"Indeed." Even this one would melt a bit when she heard his next line. "I teach." Robby grinned. "I know what you're thinking. How could I teach? You probably think I barely made my O-levels" — the basic British high school graduation exams. "But these kids are special."

"Special how?"

"Autistic. Developmentally disabled, we call it."

"That must be hard."

"I feel lucky every day." Robby wasn't lying. He did feel lucky. Lucky he wasn't one of the monsters. Half of them spent their days spinning and screaming *whop-whop-whop* every ten seconds like they were getting paid to imitate helicopters. The other half punched you when you asked them to look you in the eyes like they were actual human beings. Once in a while, Robby felt he was getting through. Mostly he could have been playing video games in the corner for the good he did. Lucky, indeed.

"My cousin's son, he's autistic." Josephine's mouth curled into a smile Robby couldn't read.

"Are you close with him?"

"Hah. Real little bugger, inn't he? Talk to him, he runs off and bangs his head against

14

the wall. Pick him up, he claws at you like you're about to toss him out the window. Six months of his mum telling him, 'Pick up the spoon, Jimmy, pick up the spoon.' And he picks up a bloody spoon. And we're supposed to pretend he's solved cancer or some such. But come on, the kid's basically a vegetable with arms and legs and a mouth for screaming. Pick up the spoon already and be done with it."

Robby was speechless. Of course, what she'd said wasn't that different from what he'd been thinking, but *you weren't supposed to say it.* It wasn't civilized.

"I wish you could see the look on your face. Like I'd suggested putting the darlings in the incinerator."

"Is that what you think we should do?"

"Only if they misbehave." She smiled. "My. I've shocked you again. I'm pulling your leg, Robby. Honest to God, I don't have any idea what to do with them. Do you?"

"They're people. Could have been any of us."

Josephine took another sip of her Grey Goose. "Could have been, but it warn't. Why should we all run around and pretend that the facts of life aren't so?"

"Maybe sometimes pretending is the only

15

way to get by."

Omar and Fakir had grown up in Majmaah, a desert town in north-central Saudi Arabia. Omar's father, Faisal, was a big man who wore a red-and-white head scarf and kept his *thobe* short around his thick calves, the practice followed by conservative Muslims. He saw Omar and Fakir — the youngest sons of his third wife — only rarely.

By the time Omar reached puberty he understood that he was a spare, to be watered and fed in case his older brothers died. The knowledge hollowed his insides, but he never complained. His brother was simpler and happier than he. They were best friends, their strengths complementary. Omar helped Fakir with his lessons, and Fakir pulled Omar out of his doldrums. They spent their teens in a *madrassa,* a religious school, where they learned to recite the Quran by heart.

When Omar was seventeen and Fakir was fifteen, the *madrassa*'s imam brought the boys into his office to watch *mujahid* videos. Helicopters crashed into mountains, and Humvees exploded on desert roads. "One day you'll have the chance to fight," the imam said. "And you may give your life. But you needn't fear. You will be remembered forever. In this world and the next."

The imam couldn't have chosen a better pitch for a boy who hardly believed he existed. Omar offered himself to the cause, and Fakir followed. A few months later, they were blindfolded and taken to a date farm tucked in a *wadi* — a desert valley whose low hills offered faint protection from the sun. A man who called himself Nawif trained them and two other teenagers for months, teaching them how to shoot and take cover. How to clean and strip assault rifles, to wire the fuses on a suicide vest.

One day Nawif said, "Each of you must tell me you're ready." And one by one they pledged themselves to die for the cause. Then Nawif outlined their mission. Allah had smiled on them, he said. Their targets were Christians. American sailors. Drinkers and drug-takers. Any Muslims in the place were even worse, guilty of apostasy, forsaking the faith, the deadliest of sins.

They spent the next week walking through the attack. Just before they left the farm, Nawif announced that Omar would be the group's leader. Omar wasn't surprised. He was the oldest of the four, the best shooter. Despite his vague doubts about the mission, he was proud to be chosen.

On the night they left, the stars were as

17

bright as they would ever be, the desert air cool and silent. A van waited, its exhaust burbling. Nawif held a blindfold. Omar submitted without complaint. He felt like a passenger in his own body.

Ten hours later, they stepped onto a Riyadh street filed with two-story concrete buildings. Nawif led them past a butcher store, flies swirling over the meat, to a dirty two-room apartment with a rattling air conditioner. Nawif handed them passports with their real names and photos.

"How —"

"Don't worry about it. You'll need this, too." Nawif tossed Omar a car key. "There's a Mercedes outside. You'll take a practice run this afternoon."

The highway to Bahrain was flat and fast. They reached the border post in five hours, just after sunset. A Saudi immigration officer flipped through their passports.

"Just got them last week, and already you're on the road."

"We didn't want to wait."

"Enjoy yourself." The agent handed back the passports, and they rolled ahead.

In Manama, they found the apartment easily. Curtains covered the living-room windows. When Omar peeped out, he saw only an air shaft. Beside the couch was the locked chest Nawif had told them to expect. It held two Beretta pistols. Four short-stock AK-47 assault rifles, wrapped in chamois and smelling of oil. Extra magazines. Twelve Russian RGD-5 grenades, rounded green cylinders with metal handles molded to their bodies. They were the simplest of weapons, metal shells wrapped around a few ounces of explosive, triggered by a four-second fuse. Omar picked one up, fought the urge to juggle it.

"Let me see," Fakir said. Omar ignored him. Fakir grabbed a Beretta, pointed it at Omar. "Let me see."

"Put it down. You know what Nawif said. Treat them with respect. Next week you can have all the fun you want."

Now next week had come. Omar steered the Mercedes down the eight-lane avenue that led into downtown Manama. Skyscrapers loomed ahead, glowing in the dark. In the cars around them, women sat uncovered. Across the road was a building hundreds of meters long, with a giant LCD screen displaying brand names in Arabic. A mall. Omar wondered what the inside looked like. A traffic light turned yellow in front of them, and he stopped for it, ignoring the honking behind them.

"You shouldn't have stopped," Fakir said.

"No need to rush."

"You know, you hide it well. How scared you are. If I weren't your brother, I wouldn't see it."

"What is it you want? Tell me. Or I won't go any further."

"I want you to *believe*. Otherwise, you shouldn't be here. Because you'll chicken out at the last minute."

"Don't worry about me, brother. I'm ready."

Fakir squeezed Omar's shoulder. "Good."

"Good."

The light dropped to green, and Omar steered them toward the apartment. Fifteen minutes later, they parked outside. Omar grabbed the blue bag and climbed the building's narrow stairs as Fakir huffed behind. Omar didn't know who had rented the place, just as he didn't know who had bought the Mercedes or arranged his passport. Nawif had said they would be kept in the dark for their own protection. Omar didn't even know why Nawif had told them to attack this particular bar. He saw now that he had been treated all along like a disposable part. But Fakir was right. The time for questions had passed.

At the apartment, the other two jihadis, Amir and Hamoud, waited. Omar unlocked the chest, splayed the weapons on the floor. He stripped off his *thobe,* put on his Levi's and T-shirt and hiking boots. In the bathroom, he shaved and gelled up his thick black hair and sprayed on his cologne. He brushed his teeth, too, though he wasn't sure why. A knock startled him, and he dropped the brush.

"Come on, brother. It's almost midnight. It's time."

Omar looked himself over in the mirror. He wondered whether he could back out. But the other three would go ahead regardless. He would be proving only his own cowardice. "All right. Let's pray, then." They faced west, to Mecca. Together they recited the *Fatiha,* "The Foundation," the first seven lines of the Quran's first verse. *"Bismillahi-rahmani-rahim . . ."*

In the name of Allah, most gracious, most
    merciful
Praise to Allah, Lord of the Universe
Most gracious and merciful
Master of the day of judgment
You alone we serve and ask for help
Guide us on the straight path
The path of those you have favored, not
    of those deserving anger, those who
    have lost their way

"We have nothing to fear tonight," Omar said. "When we wake, we'll be in paradise." The justification was predictable, ordinary. Yet its very familiarity comforted Omar. He wasn't alone. So many others had taken the same journey.

Fakir tucked a pistol in the back of his jeans and stuffed the grenades and AKs and spare magazines into a black nylon bag. Amir and Hamoud took the other weapons. They slung loose-fitting nylon jackets over the rifles. Anyone looking closely would see the telltale curve of the magazines, but no one would have the chance to look closely.

On his disposable phone, Omar called Nawif. "We're ready."

"Go, then. And remember that Allah is protecting you."

Omar wanted to keep talking, to invent a conversation that would end with him telling the other three that the mission had been called off. Instead he hung up. "It's time," he said.

They didn't bother to wipe down the apartment. Nawif had told Omar that it couldn't be traced to them. Further proof of their essential disposability.

JJ's was barely five hundred meters away. They trotted through the narrow streets, following the path they had traced the week before. They didn't speak. No one stopped them, or even noticed them. At this hour the neighborhood was largely deserted, the guest workers who largely populated it home for the night.

They turned a corner, and Fakir saw the bar's sign shining green and white just a block away. JJ's Expat. Music filtered through the windows. Fakir took his brother's hand. "I'm sorry I said you were scared."

"It doesn't matter. I'm not anymore, though." A lie.

"That's good, brother."

A few meters from the bar, Omar slowed his pace. "Remember, don't start until you hear us open up," he said over his shoulder to Amir and Hamoud. He wanted to add something else, but he had nothing left to say.

Covering the last few meters took no time at all. The noise rose. He heard people talking in English, a woman singing. He was dreaming and couldn't wake. He had two grenades in the front pocket of his windbreaker. He had a sudden urge to blow one now. Only he and his brother would die.

He didn't.

JJ's main entrance was inside the building that housed the bar. A corridor connected it to the street. Fakir stepped into the hallway, Omar a step behind. Two bouncers, big men in red T-shirts, stood just outside the entrance. Fakir walked confidently toward them, his chubby body jiggling under his T-shirt. When he was three steps away, he reached behind his waist and pulled the black 9-millimeter pistol.

"Hey —"

"Allahu akbar," Fakir said. He pulled the trigger, and the pistol sang its one true note. The shot echoed in the corridor, and the bouncer touched his chest and looked down at his hand. Fakir shot him again, and he screamed and fell. The other bouncer tried to turn, but Fakir pulled the trigger again. The bullet caught him under his arm, and he grunted softly and collapsed all at once.

Robby Duke was on his sixth Carlsberg and feeling no pain. After his last trip to the bar, he'd scooted next to Josephine. She'd made way without protest. A soft glaze had slipped over her eyes and she'd squeezed his arm a couple times, always a good sign.

Her eyes drooped. He leaned in for a kiss, but she raised a finger and pushed him off. "Not a chance, Frodo." The fact that she was still calling him Frodo was definitely *not* a good sign. He didn't argue, though.

24

She had the kind of knockers he loved, big and full, a real handful.

"Hey. Quit staring at my breasties. They're available to first-class passengers only." She smirked. "Notice anything about this place, Frodo?"

Robby turned his head. He felt like he was looking through a snorkel mask. Six pints would do that. JJ's was hopping. Three tall black blokes — American sailors, no doubt — towered above the crowd. On the screens overhead a new soccer match had begun, Manchester City and Tottenham. He couldn't tell what she wanted him to say. "You mean that girl in the corner? The one with the lip ring."

"Not her. She is cute, though. I mean the whole place. Notice anything?"

"It's pretty chill. Wouldn't expect it in Bahrain."

"But you would, see. You know, Emirates, we fly to New York. Tokyo. Buenos Aires. Sydney."

"You've been all those places."

"Not yet. But a bunch."

"I've been to New York," Robby said proudly. "It was awesome. Times Square and all that."

"Shush. And everywhere we go there are these Irish bars with DJs and tellies playing

25

live football. I swear, even in Dublin it's just like this. Even in Ireland the bars have lost whatever made them authentic and turned into replicas of themselves."

"Dublin. Fantastic, innit?"

"I give up. You're missing the point."

"I *get* your *point.* People like the same stuff everywhere. So what? We're all the same in the end. A few drinks, have a good time, a few shags. More if we're lucky. Settle down with the missus, get old, piss off. Remember that song, got to be twenty years old. 'Birth! School! Work! Death!' "

"The Godfathers. But that's what you don't get. We're not all the same. Not everybody wants this stuff. We think they do because it's what *we* want —"

Robby was sick of hearing deep thoughts from this flight attendant who was nowhere near putting out for him. He stood on the bench, threw his fists in the air: "Birth! School! Work! Death!" Around him, Beyoncé sang: 'All the single ladies . . .' The girls danced and raised their arms, and the bar descended into the beautiful drunken majesty of Thursday night.

And then — weirdly — Robby was sure he heard the quick *snap* of a pistol shot. A branch breaking cleanly. Over the music pumping, over his own voice yelling. He

26

looked around, sure he was wrong.

Then he heard two more.

Fakir reached into the nylon bag, came up with an AK. Omar grabbed the second rifle. Amir and Hamoud opened up outside, firing long bursts. Omar couldn't see them, but he knew they were standing on the street, firing through the windows at the bar.

The bar's front door popped open and four women in T-shirts and jeans ran toward them. Fakir unloaded a burst on full automatic. Two of the women flopped down in the corridor a couple steps from the door. The third tripped over a bouncer and started to scream in English before Fakir blew her head off.

The fourth kept coming, screaming. Omar raised his rifle. His first shot spun her, and his second and third went through her back. She reared like a frightened horse and fell.

It's happening, Omar thought. *It really is.*

Inside JJ's, pandemonium. Robby Duke felt himself falling before he even knew he was hit. The round caught him in the left shoulder and spun him off the table. He sprawled on the ground and grabbed his shoulder, feeling the blood trickle under his fingers in steady pulses, not enough to be life-threatening right away.

Bizarrely, the speakers were still pumping Beyoncé: ". . . shoulda put a ring on it —"

The music broke off. Screams and shouts tumbled through the room.

"I can't —" "My leg —" "Call 119 —" The Bahraini equivalent of 911.

Above Robby, Josephine was screaming. He knocked the table aside, spilled his Carlsberg. Even in this madness, a tiny part of his mind regretted the loss of a good cold beer. He reached up, pulled Josephine down, covered her mouth with his hand.

"Are you hit?"

She shook her head.

"Shut it, then. There's enough shouting already. Right?"

She nodded. He lifted his hand.

"The police —"

"These bloody camel jockeys aren't going to wait for the police."

The lights were still on. Robby rolled to his knees and looked left. He didn't see Dwight, but Cinzia was lying face-first on the table. Her brains were all caught in her pretty brown hair. A round had peeled off the top of her head. Lucky shot. Not for her. Robby wondered if he could get to the entrance. He peeked up as the doors opened and a group ran out —

And a burst, full auto, echoed outside, and a woman screamed, *"No, don't —"*

Another burst ended her plea.

"Jesus God," Josephine shouted.

He squeezed her lips shut. "We have to move —"

"I can't."

"Then you'll die here."

He'd been to JJ's enough times to know that the place had only two exits on the first floor. These twats were obviously covering both of them. But the balcony that over-looked the dance floor had some narrow windows that Robby was guessing opened onto an interior airshaft. If he and Josephine got up there, he could try to break them. Then they could shimmy to the roof and wait for the cops.

It wasn't much of a plan, but they didn't have time for a better one. Robby had been in the British army for four years after he turned eighteen. He'd served in Basra. Not too far from here. He knew the men outside. He'd seen what they did to their own, much less to foreigners. They wouldn't stop shooting until everyone was dead.

The firing started again. Bottles smashed open, and the pungent smell of whiskey filled the room. Most people had gotten under tables now or hidden in corners.

Robby heard a dozen panicked calls to the police. He grabbed Josephine's arm and tugged her, but she wouldn't move.

He couldn't wait longer, not for this woman he'd just met. He let her go, crab-walked toward the stairs. And then he heard it. The hiss of a burning fuse. *"Grenade!"* he yelled. He dove forward, flattening himself on the floor. The training for grenades and mortars was simple. Get low and hope the shrapnel goes high. He heard it land, its metal shell bounce along the floor. It didn't blow straightaway. It was an old one, then, with a time fuse —

"Christ, throw it back —" he yelled.

And then it went. The bar shook with the impact. His ears turned inside out. For a couple seconds, he couldn't hear anything at all. The grenade was maybe fifteen feet from him, too close. The shrapnel shredded his jeans, cut his thighs into ribbons, hundreds of needles stabbing him at once. He couldn't bear to look back. He had tried, he'd tried to get her to move, and she wouldn't —

He looked back. He shouldn't have. It must have landed practically on top of her. She was even worse than he expected, her breasts and belly pulped open, half her jaw gone —

Another grenade exploded, on the other side of the bar. Robby could barely hear this one. His eardrums must be blown. The room shook. Part of an arm slung across the room. *Jesus. A hand.* A woman's hand, red nail polish and rings. It hit the bar and knocked over a glass of beer. *Guess we won't be needing that one,* Robby thought wildly. *The beer or the hand, either.*

The game was obvious now. Pin them with rifle fire and then lob in grenades. With proper gear and a few mates from the 7th Armoured, he would have torn these bastards to shreds. But he didn't even carry a knife anymore. He couldn't do anything about it. Nothing at all.

Still. He had to try. Plenty of people were still alive. In another three minutes they'd all be dead, these idiots singing to Allah all the way. He pushed himself to his knees and crawled for the stairs as another grenade, this one behind him, shook the room. Fortunately, he was wearing his favorite moto boots, thick leather and heavy rubber soles. They had a couple inches of lift, which in another life five minutes ago had come in handy picking up girls. His calves and feet weren't too badly cut. But his thighs felt like they were on fire and he didn't know if he could stand.

The room around Robby was smoke and blood and bodies. He couldn't put together a coherent picture of what was happening, only snatches, as though he were watching through a strobe light. One of the American sailors stood and threw a bottle at the main doors. He ran along the bar, crouching low, grabbing bottles and whipping them blindly as he went. "Go on," Robby yelled. "Get there." But the guy didn't. Four steps away from the door, he went down, grabbing his chest, his legs still pumping.

The stairs to the balcony rose behind a filigreed wall that divided the dance floor from the rest of the bar. Robby reached them, pulled himself up. He saw he'd gotten lucky. The guys at the main entrance couldn't come in while their buddies outside were lobbing grenades. They waited by the door, shooting at anyone who moved and tossing in their own grenades.

Robby guessed that when the police showed, the bastards on the street would turn to hold them off. Then the ones at the door would come in, mop up everyone in the room who was still alive. Maybe set the place on fire to boot. For now he had a few seconds to move. Move or die. Like Josephine, like Cinzia, like Dwight Gasser, the worst wingman ever. Dwight had never

liked JJ's. Robby couldn't blame hi
more. Maybe God was punishing h
what he had said about his students. H
truly sorry. He closed his eyes. He w
to rest. He was going into shock. He ha
pull himself out. He grabbed his woun
shoulder and squeezed, jolting him
awake. Before the pain faded, he grabb
the banister and pulled himself up the stair
ignoring the agony in his legs.

Step, step, step. Rounds dug into the wood
around him, but he kept moving. He
reached the top step and saw, too late, the
table laid sideways as a barricade. He
lowered his head and drove his strong,
stubby legs forward and smashed his undamaged shoulder into it. The table gave a
foot. He reached an arm forward and yelled,
"I'm English!"

The table slid aside. Two men grabbed his
arms, pulled him onto the balcony. He felt
his wounded shoulder tear as they dragged
him. It should have hurt, but it didn't. He
looked around. About ten people. No one
seemed injured. These were the lucky ones.
He was safe. For now.

PART ONE

CHAPTER 1

MONTEGO BAY, JAMAICA

"One-forty-nine . . ."

John Wells felt his biceps burn as he reached full extension. He held, held, lowered himself again. Beneath him, the world narrowed to a few square feet. The cigarette burns speckling the dirty green carpet were as large as canyons.

"One-fifty."

Up Wells went, slow and sure. Outside, a spring breeze rolled off the Caribbean. In here, the air was humid, almost murky. Sweat puddled at the base of his neck, dripped off his bare chest.

The room's door swung open. Afternoon sunlight flooded in. Wells raised his left hand to shield his eyes and decided to see if he could get away with a one-armed push-up. Down he went, balanced on his right arm. He hadn't tried one in years. Harder than he remembered. Or he was getting old. He tensed his chest, felt his triceps and biceps quiver, held himself steady.

Brett Gaffan stepped into the room, flipped on the light. "Trying to impress me, John?"

Wells ignored Gaffan, pushed, rose. Stopped. Found himself stuck. Sweat stung his eyes. He slipped sideways —

And with a final convulsive effort forced himself up. Once he passed halfway, he felt the power coming from his biceps rather than his triceps and knew he'd be all right. He stood as soon as he finished, before his arm could give out.

"You look like you're gonna have a stroke."

"I could do those all day." Wells tried to stop panting.

"Uh-huh." Gaffan tossed Wells a paper bag. Inside, a liter of cold water.

"Thankee." Wells sucked down half the bottle. As part of his cover, he had to drink. And though he was careful to nurse his Red Stripes, he couldn't be too careful. He'd gone through five or six last night. He wasn't used to drinking so much. Or drinking at all. Every morning he woke to a cotton-filled mouth and a shrunken skull.

Until a few months before, Wells had been a CIA operative. He'd had a long and successful career at the agency. A few years before, he'd played a highly public role in stopping a terrorist attack on Times Square. But his missions since then had been kept quiet, and the public's attention was fickle. He was still a legend among cops and soldiers, but civilians rarely recognized him.

Wells would admit that part of him had loved working for the agency. The CIA and its cousins in the intelligence community could arrange a new identity in a matter of hours, get him anywhere in the world in a day, hear any call, open any e-mail, track any vehicle. But the power came with a price, one Wells could no longer pay. He had always been allergic to the Langley bureaucracy, the way the CIA's executives put frontline operatives at risk for their own gain. After his last mission, the tension had grown unbearable. Vinny Duto, the agency's director, had used Wells to win an intra-agency power struggle. Wells felt what was left of his honor boiling away in the cauldron of Duto's contempt.

He saw no choice but to quit, make a life for himself in New Hampshire, a land whose silent woods mocked Washington's empty talk. The granite mountains would outlast empires and the men who built them. He rented a cabin in a little town called Berlin. But he and his dog, Tonka, spent a lot of time fifty miles south, in

North Conway, with Anne Marshall. Wells
had met Anne a few months before, before
his last mission. She knew who he was and
some of what he'd done, though he kept
some details from her. He wasn't sure yet
what their future would be.

Now Wells was back in the field. He had
decided to run down a fugitive CIA double
agent. Without official approval. Not for the
first time on this trip, Wells wondered what
he was trying to prove. And to whom.

He dropped the empty water bottle on the
floor, where it joined crushed Bud Light
cans and the remains of a joint that had
rolled under the dresser between the two
queen beds. All left here on the unlikely
chance that a Jamaican drug dealer decided
he needed to check their cover. Gaffan and
Wells were sharing the room, which had
acquired a funky odor after four days.

"Yo. You have to play that way?"

"Did you really just say 'yo'?"

"I did." Gaffan had grown up in northern
New Jersey, a rowhouse town called Ber-
genfield, near New York City. His years in
North Carolina and Georgia had coated his
Jersey accent with a strange sugar. He
seemed to speak fast and slow at the same
time. Wells couldn't explain how.

"Please don't ever again."

Wells pulled a dirty T-shirt on with his cargo shorts, slipped black work boots on his sockless feet. He'd owned the boots barely two weeks, but they were as ripe as the room. He tugged a New York Mets cap low on his head and stuffed twenty twenty-dollar bills in his pocket. Wells was a Red Sox fan, but he couldn't wear the cursive *B* under these circumstances.

"How do I look?"

"The question is not how you look, it's how you smell."

"How do I smell?"

"Like a skeezy pothead dumb enough to think you can buy a few ounces of good shit without getting rolled, mon."

"Exactly right. Let's go."

Gaffan was a former Special Ops soldier who had crossed paths with Wells twice before. They'd stayed in loose touch after the second mission. When Wells realized he would need backup for this trip, he'd called Gaffan, who had quit the army to join a private security firm in North Carolina. Gaffan had happily taken a week of vacation to join him.

At the door, Gaffan stopped. "Peashooters tonight?" Wells's old Makarov and Gaffan's new Glock were stowed in plastic bags

41

in the air-conditioning vent in the bathroom — along with two suits, one for Wells and one for Gaffan. For the moment, Wells had insisted they leave the weapons. They were supposed to be small-time dope dealers. Guns would raise questions, and being unarmed didn't bother him. He'd gone naked on lots of missions. Gaffan obviously didn't enjoy the feeling. He'd asked Wells to reconsider a couple of times.

" 'Son. Don't take your guns to town.' "

Gaffan tapped his temple. "Johnny Cash. Like it, yo."

"Keep this up and there's trouble ahead."

"The Dead. Showing your age."

Wells and Gaffan were chasing Keith Robinson, a former CIA officer who had sold secrets to China. After his cover was blown, Robinson fled the United States on a fake passport. For three years, he turned to smoke. Agents never found a credit card or phone connected to him. His name didn't pop at border crossings. The best guess was that Robinson had altered his appearance and was living in a country that had a mostly cash economy — and enough Americans that he wouldn't stand out. Selling trinkets in Guatemala. Teaching English in Vietnam. Studying at an ashram in India.

The CIA had promised a five-hundred-thousand-dollar reward for information leading to Robinson's arrest. The FBI and CIA websites and U.S. embassies displayed his photo and the reward offer. The agency's best hope was that a tourist would recognize Robinson or that someone who knew him would betray him for the money. Indeed, tipsters had reported spotting Robinson everywhere from Paris to Beijing to Wrigley Field. But none of the sightings panned out.

The investigation had not been closed. It never would be. Robinson's crimes were too serious for the agency and the FBI to give up on him. Officially, anyway. But after three years without a lead, only four agents were assigned to the case full-time. They spent most days asking local police forces to chase tips. They no longer monitored the phone calls or mail sent to his ex-wife, Janice.

So they never saw the postcard that dropped through the slot of Janice's front door in Vienna, Virginia, a few miles from the agency's headquarters. On the front, a photo of a six-foot-long marijuana cigarette on a beach towel. And four words: "Getting baked in Jamaica." On the back, a phone number. No signature, no explanation.

Janice hoped the card wasn't what she thought it was. Suddenly she was thirsty, an itch in her brain as real as a spider bite. She could almost feel the welt. She didn't have any booze in the house, of course. But she knew every liquor store in Fairfax County. Didn't have to be hard alcohol. She could have a glass or two of wine. To relax. A bottle. One bottle wouldn't kill her.

She raised her shirt, looked down at the scar where the George Washington University surgeons had given her a new liver. She'd lost the old one to cirrhosis before she turned forty. *Wouldn't kill her?* She might as well put a gun in her mouth. Be quicker and hurt less. She tore the postcard into pieces so small it looked like she'd run it through a shredder. Her hands ached when she was finished. She threw the pieces into the garbage disposal and went to the first Alcoholics Anonymous meeting she could find.

The second card came three months later. This one had a photo of Bob Marley above the words "Don't worry, be happy." A phone number. Janice couldn't remember if it was the same one that was on the first card.

This time she didn't panic. She made

herself a pot of coffee and sat on her couch and stared at Bob Marley. She couldn't pretend now. It was Eddie. At the agency he'd gone by Keith, but his middle name was Edward. She'd called him Eddie, and she'd always think of him as Eddie. Anyway, it was him. Had to be.

She'd hoped he was dead. A couple of the FBI guys had told her, he's dead. You can't run like the old days. We post his picture on the Web, everybody in the world sees it. If he were still alive, someone would have told us. She never believed them. Eddie was too much of a snake to die. A cockroach. Didn't the scientists say that cockroaches would outlast everybody? He'd dragged her down inch by inch, drop by drop, and she'd let him.

No. She wouldn't blame him. After their son Mark died, she'd stopped caring about anything but her own misery. Every day dawned grayer than the one before until the sun stopped rising and the night was eternal. Eddie seeped away in the darkness like smoke. So she wouldn't blame him for what she'd done to herself. But she wouldn't forgive him, either. He was a whoremonger and a spy. He'd betrayed his country. Four men, at least, had died for his sins.

She'd felt so stupid the night she found

out. How could she not have known? The early-morning walks. The piles of cash. Poor Eddie. Always frustrated with the agency. Stuck in a dead-end job working counterintelligence when he wanted so much to be in a foreign post. Always so sure that his talents were wasted.

She had to admit it seemed obvious in retrospect.

After Eddie left, the FBI moved her to a hotel, a Marriott in Alexandria. And they made sure that she had plenty of wine in the room. They weren't even subtle about it. They brought in Costco bags filled with bottles. For a couple days she was grateful. Then, finally, she realized just how far she'd fallen. The FBI was afraid if she stopped drinking she'd go into withdrawal.

A week later, she quit. She woke up and reached for the bottle on the bedside table and thought, *I can't do this anymore.* She wasn't sure at first whether *this* meant drinking or living, but then some part of her decided she wasn't ready to give up yet. In a day, she had the shakes so bad that the agents called 911. She wound up in thirty-day rehab, and to everyone's surprise, including hers, it took.

A month after it ended, she got another surprise. She woke up vomiting, her eyes a pale yellow. A blood test showed she had hepatitis C, a final going-away present from Eddie. The combination of booze and virus had ruined her liver. The doctors told her that if she didn't get a transplant in a year, she'd be dead. Not that she needed the warning. Her skin was yellow, curdled like milk left out too long.

She didn't expect a transplant. She didn't deserve one. She had done this to herself. But the transplant networks had their own rules, and after eight months her name came up. She never asked about the donor. She couldn't face another ounce of grief.

The transplant took. The immunosuppressant drugs worked. She went to her AA meetings and stayed sober. The months turned into a year, and another. She divorced Eddie in absentia. She started teaching kindergarten again, something she hadn't done since her son died. She knew her life would never be smooth. He ex-husband was a traitor. She was no one's idea of a catch, a forty-year-old woman on her second liver. But she imagined she might make a life for herself. It would be simple and lonely, but it would be hers.

Then the postcards came.

Almost from the beginning, the FBI agents

had told her that she wasn't a suspect. For that, she was grateful. As the investigation wound down, they asked only that she inform them if Eddie ever reached out. A call, a letter, an e-mail. *Even if you're not sure it's him. You start getting hang-ups late at night, let us know.*

Now she needed to tell them. But she couldn't face having Eddie back in her life. She couldn't face a trial, replaying the humiliations of the last decade. The newspapers would portray her as the pitiful ex-wife of a traitor. And they'd be right.

She needed Eddie gone. Forever.

John Wells.

It wasn't so much that she remembered Wells. She'd never forgotten him. He and another CIA agent, Jennifer Exley, had discovered what Eddie had done. They'd come to the house the night after Eddie disappeared. She hadn't seen Wells since then. But he'd taken charge, and part of her, despite her despair, because of her despair, had hoped that he would sweep her up and rock her to sleep. Her knight in bulletproof armor. Maybe he could solve this for her.

Ridiculous. God. Ridiculous didn't even begin to describe her. But Wells had given her his phone number. And she'd never thrown it away. She'd kept it in her wallet all along. Now she reached for it.

Wells came to see her two days later. He was older than she remembered, flecks of gray in his hair, narrow creases around his eyes like a child's drawing of rays coming off the sun. But he still had his hair. His chin was still square, and his shoulders, too. She'd bet he could still pick her up with one hand. Anyway, this wasn't a *date*. She hadn't told him about the postcard, but he must have known that her call had to do with Eddie.

He stepped inside, looked around as if he were trying to match the furniture in his head with what he saw in the living room. Most everything was new. She'd thrown out the heavy, smoke-sodden couches and replaced them with bright futons from Ikea.

"I redecorated. It's probably meant for some college student half my age, but I don't care. I needed the old stuff gone." She realized she was chattering and made herself stop. She couldn't remember the last time a man had visited the house.

"It's nice."

"I'd offer you a drink, but there's nothing in the house —"

"I understand —"

She felt herself redden. Of course he

49

understood. "If you'd like some coffee."

"Coffee's fine, sure."

She came back with two cups of coffee. "Milk? Sugar?"

He shook his head, leaned back, waited. She'd hoped for small talk. She wondered if Wells was still with Exley. She'd been certain back then that they were together. And even as she watched her life collapse, she'd found the energy to be jealous.

But she was afraid to ask Wells about his life. She could see he wasn't much for casual conversation. So she told him about the postcards, how she'd destroyed one and kept the other. She showed the card to Wells. It was creased at the corners. He looked it over carefully, though there wasn't much to see, just the phone number and the stamp, canceled with a postmark from Kingston.

"You think it's Eddie?" she said.

"Any idea why he'd do this now? He knows the risk."

"I think maybe he's lonely. And bored. And thinks I won't tell."

"Why would he think that?"

"Because he believes I'm weak. And that he can manipulate me. And he's right."

"You're not weak. You're —" Wells broke off. She could see he couldn't bring himself

50

to say "strong," the lie was too obvious. "You're human. But what I don't understand is why you came to me on this. The FBI —"

"I don't want them. I want you."

"I'm retired."

"Even better. Because there's something I can't ask the FBI."

Wells shook his head, like he already knew what she was going to say.

"When you catch him. I want you to kill him."

Again, Wells thought. Vinny Duto last year and now Janice Robinson. The director of the CIA and the ex-wife of a double agent. They had nothing in common aside from their shared belief that Wells would kill on command. That he would turn another human being into dust, not in battle but methodically and without remorse. Wells had killed before, more times than he wanted to count, but he wasn't an assassin.

"Not yet," he said aloud.

"Not yet what?"

"I'd love to be the one to bring him in. But it's not my place."

"You don't understand." She told him of the humiliations she feared, the loss of privacy. "Anyway, what he did. Not to me.

51

To the country. He doesn't deserve a trial. He deserves to disappear. Feed him to the sharks."

An idea flickered in Wells. "Look. If we're lucky, and Keith" — Wells couldn't make himself say "Eddie" — "is in a place where I have leverage, what if I get him to come back to the United States on his own? And plead guilty. No trial."

"I know what you're saying. If he plea-bargains, he won't get the death penalty. But I promise he doesn't care. Knowing Eddie, he thinks that life in prison, no parole, is just as bad. If you catch him, he'll want a trial. His moment in the limelight, to tell the world what he thinks. He'll love it. He'll drag it out as long as he can."

"There's things worse than the death penalty."

"I don't get it."

"I guess you'll have to trust me."

From his Subaru, Wells called Ellis Shafer, his old boss at the agency. Shafer was an odd little man, jumpy and brilliant. Sometimes Wells thought that he and Shafer were both too independent to fit inside the CIA's bureaucracy. Yet the evidence proved him wrong. Shafer had survived almost forty years at Langley. And Shafer had stayed on when Wells had quit, even though Vinny Duto had used Shafer as badly as Wells on their last assignment. Wells supposed he understood. Shafer was more cynical, more used to these games. Still, he hadn't entirely forgiven Shafer.

"Hello, John."

"You'll never guess who I just saw."

"Bill Gates."

"What? No —"

"Tiger Woods."

"Stop naming random celebrities."

"You asked me to guess."

"No, I didn't."

"Well, you said I'd never guess, which is the same thing —"

"Ellis. Please stop. You win."

"Who was it, then?"

"I'll tell you when I see you. Which will be in about five minutes."

"Don't hurt me. I promise I'll confess to whatever you like." Shafer hung up before Wells could reply.

The front door was unlocked. "In the kitchen," Shafer yelled.

The kitchen smelled of burnt coffee. Coffee grounds blotched Shafer's jeans, and he was wearing a T-shirt that said "World's Best Grandpa." He raised his arms to hug Wells.

"No hug. Please. And congratulations, Ellis. Why didn't you tell me?"

"Tell you what?"

Wells nodded at the T-shirt.

"Oh. No. There's no grandchildren. Lisa, you know, she's at UVA, and she's got a boyfriend now. It's kind of reverse psychology. I figure the shirt is so lame, she'll be sure to take care when she —"

"You found the shirt for ninety-nine cents, didn't you? At Sam's Club or something."

"Maybe."

"Ellis, you're getting weird in your old age."

"You sound like my wife. But it's good to see you. What's going on?"

"Sit." Shafer sat. Wells recounted Janice Robinson's story, and what she'd asked. By the time he finished, Shafer was leaning forward across the table, his eyes boring into Wells, all the slack gone out of him.

"You know, I hear this, my first thought is you quit," Shafer said. "You live up in the sticks with your dog and your new girlfriend."

"She's not my new girlfriend —"

"Oh, no, no, no. You are some genius at ops, but you couldn't be more emotionally stunted. Especially about women. And please don't tell me we're the same. I've been married thirty years. Thirty years, one woman."

"I didn't come here to talk about this."

"How about this, then? Call the FBI and be done with it."

"Janice Robinson wants me to handle it."

"I'm sorry. I missed the section of the criminal code that says the traitor's ex-wife decides who brings him in. Anyway, she doesn't want you to handle it. She wants you, period. I remember Jenny telling me, back in the day."

"I have a plan." Wells explained.

"You understand that's not a plan. That's five long-shot bets. Even if you're right about where he is, what he's doing, you have to find him. Then you have to get to him. Then you have to hope he doesn't want to go out in a blaze of glory."

"He's a runner. Not a fighter."

"Runners fight when they're cornered. I understand why you're doing this. But nothing's going to make up for what happened last time. Let the Feebs" — Shafer's unfriendly term for the FBI — "do their job."

"Thanks for the advice." Wells stood to leave.

"You're going to be as pigheaded as always, do this on your own."

Wells nodded.

"Then you want some help?"

Another nod.

"All right. But let me make one thing clear. I'm not doing this because I think I owe you, I should have quit with you, whatever. I'm doing it so you don't blow it."

The next afternoon, Janice led Wells to her kitchen. The counter was strewn with red horses, purple cows, yellow sheep, a menagerie of construction paper.

"Decorating?"

She laughed, the sound sweeter than Wells expected. "For my kindergarteners."

"You like teaching?"

"You probably know this, it must be in a file. But Eddie wanted another baby. After our son died. I couldn't do it. Wouldn't. Maybe things would have been different if I . . ." She trailed off.

"Guys like your husband, they find excuses to do what they want. And if they can't find one, they just make it up."

Janice shrugged: *I don't believe you, but I won't argue.* "Anyway, the teaching, it's D.C., Northeast, a charter school. These kids, they don't have two nickels to rub together. You see it in the winter, their shoes, these cheap sneakers that soak through if there's any rain. Much less snow. So I'm trying to show them the world cares about them, even a little bit. Maybe it means something to them. Probably not, but maybe. That's a long way of saying yes, I like it, John. You don't mind if I call you John?"

"Of course not." Wells touched Janice's arm and then realized he shouldn't have. Her face lit like a winning slot machine. "You understand what I want you to do?"

"I don't know if I can."

"It's the only way. Otherwise, I have to tell the FBI."

"All right."

"Good. So tomorrow, somebody's gonna put a tap and trace on your phone. Keith won't know it's there." Shafer had called in a favor he was owed from an engineer who used to work at NSA. "Tomorrow night, you call him. Sooner or later, he'll call you back. Don't ask him where he is. Unless he brings up a visit, don't mention it."

"Don't push."

"Right. You'll make him nervous. Don't be too friendly. Don't forgive him. Don't let him think you're giving in too easily. Deep down he knows this call is a bad idea. You've

57

got to make him focus on you instead of that."

Janice turned away from Wells and opened the kitchen faucet all the way but held her glass a foot above the spout, as if somehow the water could defy gravity.

"He loved me," she whispered to the window, her voice barely audible above the water sloshing down the drain. "It sounds stupid, but it's true."

"I believe you."

"God. I hope you catch him."

The next night, with Wells sitting beside her on her couch, Janice made the call, straight to voicemail. "Eddie. Is that you? I got your cards. Call me."

Wells figured Robinson would wait weeks to call back. If he ever did. But a few minutes later, with Wells still in the house, the phone rang. Janice grabbed it. "Hello."

Through the receiver, slow, steady breaths.

"Eddie. Is that you?" She waited. "Why did you send the cards, Eddie?"

"Are you okay, Jan?" His voice was raspy and deep.

"I had a liver transplant."

"I'm sorry."

"Go to hell, Eddie." She slammed down the phone before Wells could stop her and slumped into Wells's chest. They sat silently for a few minutes as Wells wondered why he'd ever trusted Janice.

"He's never calling back, is he?" Janice finally said.

"I don't know." The phone rang again. Janice reached for the phone, but Wells put a hand on the receiver before she could answer.

"Like I said, he's definitely calling back. Keep cool. Promise?"

She nodded. He let go of the receiver, and she picked up.

"I deserved that."

"Why are you calling me?" Her southern twang thickened when she talked to Robinson.

"I wanted to talk."

"That simple. Like you've been away on business instead of — I don't even know how to describe it —"

"I miss you, Jan. It's hard out here." He sounded close to tears. Wells hadn't understood until now that in addition to everything else, Robinson was simply a spoiled brat.

"Are you sick?"

"Been better. But I have a fine doctor taking care of me. Cuban. Viva Fidel. I'm gonna live forever. I'm gonna learn how to fly."

"You need to turn yourself in."

A hollow laugh from the other end. "Not a good idea."

"What do you want?"

"To talk. To somebody who knows me."

"I don't know you. The day they came to the house, I realized that."

Beside Janice, Wells twisted his hands: *Steer the conversation if you can.* "I hope you're doing something good now, Eddie. Making up for what you did."

Another laugh. "Could say I'm doing a little community service. Helping young-sters in need. I've got to go, okay?"

"Tell me how to get hold of you."

"I'll get hold of you."

"Eddie. Are you still in Jamaica? Kings-ton?" Wells shook his head no, but he was too late.

"Are they there? On the call?"

"No, it's just me. I swear."

"Swear on Mark's grave."

She looked at Wells. He nodded.

"Don't make me do that." She squeezed her eyes shut. Wells wasn't sure whether she was talking to him or to Robinson.

"Do it."

"God, Eddie. I swear. It's just me." Tears

peeped from under her eyelids.

"Yes. I'm in Jamaica. Montego Bay. I'll call you again." *Click.*

Janice swung at Wells, her fist glancing off his chest.

"You shouldn't have made me say that."

Wells was all out of compassion. Her husband was about the most miserable human being alive. She'd just had to lie on her dead son's grave. He was sorry for her. But that didn't mean he was responsible for her.

"You wanted him? We'll catch him now. Between the trace and what he told you, we'll have enough. If he reaches out again, let me know."

She shrank against the couch. "I'm sorry," she said. "Please don't go."

Wells walked out. He wanted to find a fight, make someone bleed. Instead he got into his Subaru and peeled away, promising himself that Keith Edward Robinson would regret sending those postcards. ⟩

Seven hours and five hundred thirty miles later, Wells turned off I-91 at Boltonville, Vermont. He had sped through the night *Cannonball Run*–style. Normally, driving soothed his anger, but tonight he gained no relief from the empty asphalt.

Long ago, in Afghanistan, Wells had converted to Islam. But his faith came and went, pulling away just when he thought he'd mastered it. Of course, no one could master faith. God always hovered around the next curve, the next, the next. The quest to find Him had to be its own reward. Wells understood that much, if nothing more. But tonight the search felt lonelier than ever. He hadn't seen another vehicle for more than half an hour. As though he were the last man alive.

He swung right onto Route 302, drove through a little town called Wells River — no relation. Past a shuttered gas station and an empty general store and over a low bridge into New Hampshire. Then Woodsville, a metropolis by the standards of the North Country, with a hospital and a bank and a thousand people clustered in steep-sided wooden houses against the winters. Wells gunned the engine to leave the town behind.

A few miles on, he swung right, southeast on Route 112, the Kancamagus Highway, impassible in the winter. He was exhausted and driving too fast now, through old forests of fir and pine, the Subaru a blur in the night, sticking low to the road. The next curve, and the next. Wells felt his eyelids slipping. In the dark now, in the night, he began to murmur through pursed lips the *shahada,* the essential Muslim creed: *There is no God but God, and Muhammad is his messenger.* Finally he emerged into the open plain of Conway, a town too quaint for its own good, and turned left toward North Conway.

Anne lived in a farmhouse at the edge of town, run-down and sweet, with maple plank floors and an iron stove in the kitchen. Wells was helping her restore it, painting, sanding the floors, even putting in new sinks — a job that had almost gone disastrously wrong. The place needed new wiring and a new roof, and she couldn't afford the fixes on a cop's pay. Wells's salary had piled up during his years undercover. He wasn't sure whether he should offer to pay, if he'd be presuming too much.

He slipped the Subaru into the garage beside the house and padded into the kitchen through the unlocked back door. Tonka, his dog, a German shepherd mutt, trotted up to greet him, her big tail wagging wildly. She put her paws on him, buried her head in his chest. He'd bought jerky at the gas station, and he fed it to her strip by strip.

"John?"

Anne's bedroom was upstairs. She slept

63

sideways across the bed, stretched like a cat under a down comforter. He slipped under the blankets and hugged her warm, sleepy body and kissed her slowly.

"Flannel pajamas. Sexy." He tried to reach under them, but she twisted away. "You stink of the road. Brush your teeth and come back. I'm not going anywhere."

And she wasn't.

An hour later, she lay beside him, touching the scar on his upper arm, a knuckle-sized knot from a bullet he'd taken long before. She rolled the dead flesh between her fingers like a marble. "Does it ache?"

"No."

She pinched it. "Does it now?"

"I thought we were supposed to be relaxing."

"You never struck me as the cuddling type."

He closed his eyes, and she rubbed his face, tracing slow circles over his cheeks. In seconds he fell into a doze, imagining an endless narrow highway. But he woke to find her hand sliding down his stomach.

"Really? Again?"

"If you can handle it."

"Easy for you to say. I do all the work and you get all the credit."

"Is that so?" She lifted her hand, tweaked

the tip of his nose.

Wells turned sideways so they were face-to-face. "Maybe not always."

Again she dropped her arm. He was eight inches taller than she was, and she had to scoot halfway under the blanket to follow her hand. "I'm looking for something." Her hand was on his stomach now.

"You found it."

"That's your belly button."

He leaned down, and their mouths met.

"There it is." She paused. "You're worn out. But I can fix that."

"We'll see. Maybe . . . Yes. Yes, you can."

Later she nestled against him, her breathing soft and steady.

"You've got a mission coming. An operation. Whatever you call it."

"Why do you say that?"

"I saw it when you came in. In your shoulders. Want to tell me?"

"It's old business." He waited. "Are you mad I can't tell you?"

"John. Please. Do you want me to say I am, so you have an excuse to leave? You don't need an excuse."

He was silent. Then, finally: "I'm sorry."

"It's like you want to reinvent yourself but you know there's no point in trying, because you know that you can only be who you already are."

"Isn't that the same for everyone?"

"Most of us have some give. You're cut from rock."

"Let's go to sleep."

"You want to spend your life with me here, you will. If not, you won't. Just don't ask me to fall in love with you while you're deciding. I have to protect myself, too."

He closed his eyes. He felt that somehow she was accusing him, though he wasn't sure of what. Anyway, everything she said was true.

He slept heavily and without dreams. When he woke, she was gone. She worked the afternoon shift. He padded downstairs to find that she'd left coffee and a tray of freshly baked biscuits. He always wound up with women kinder than he deserved.

Wells drank the coffee as he considered his next move. He was guessing that Robinson dealt drugs small-time. He'd be handy to the local dealers. As a white face, he'd be less likely to frighten tourists who wanted to score.

Wells wondered how long Robinson had been playing this game, and why. Maybe he'd drunk or smoked through his cash and was supporting his habits by dealing. Maybe he had the insane idea that if he put together a big enough nut, he could get back to the United States. Maybe he was hoping to relive the thrills he'd had as a mole. Even he might not know the answer. Guys who listed pros and cons on a yellow pad didn't wind up as double agents.

Now that Robinson had given up his best defense, his invisibility, Wells figured that finding him shouldn't be too difficult. Montego Bay was only so large. Still, Wells wanted backup for the mission, a face that Robinson wouldn't recognize. He thumbed through his phone, found Gaffan's number.

Montego Bay was Jamaica's second-largest city, the hub of the tourist trade. From November to April, cruise ships disgorged clumps of sunburned Americans to buy T-shirts and rum at a heavily policed mall near the port. They were back on board by nightfall to head to the Bahamas or Puerto Rico.

Montego also had a busy international airport. Many wealthier visitors saw the city only on their way to the fancy all-inclusive resorts outside of town. But younger tourists on tighter budgets often stayed in Montego itself, in an area south of the airport called the Hip Strip, a name that immediately proclaimed a trying-too-hard uncoolness. Centered around Gloucester Avenue, the Hip Strip mixed hotels and clubs with shops selling overpriced bongs and bead necklaces. The hotel rooms facing Gloucester were useful for heavy partiers or heavy sleepers only. Until early morning, reggae and rap boomed from beat-up Chevy Caprices, the old square ones, and Toyota RAV4s with tinted windows. Outside the clubs, barkers promised drink specials and Bob Marley cover bands. Wells and Gaffan had rented a room just off Gloucester. Wells figured they would cruise the clubs until they ran across Robinson.

But catching Robinson had proven more difficult than Wells had hoped. Until he arrived, he hadn't understood the scope of the drug trade in Jamaica. Pot and other drugs were technically illegal on the island, but at every corner on Gloucester, dreadlocked men cooed, "Smoke. Spliff. Ganja, man. Purple Haze." After a while, the words blended into background noise. "Spliffsmokeganjaman." The Jamaican national anthem.

The Montego Bay cops were around, too, walking the avenue. As far as Wells could tell, they weren't trying to stop the trade. Their presence was intentionally obvious, giving the dealers plenty of warning. The only people they caught were tourists too stupid or high to hide their smoking. Wells had seen an arrest, a barely disguised shakedown. A young woman — mid-twenties, maybe — passed a tiny joint to her husband when the cops approached. "Come here," one of the cops said. The couple wore narrow wedding rings of bright, cheap gold. "I'm sorry," the woman said. "We're sorry. We didn't mean to disrespect your country."

The lead cop pulled the man into an alley. The other cops stood in the street around the woman. "You know, it's the first time I ever smoked pot," she mumbled. "I don't even feel anything. Just thirsty."

Wells watched from a shop across the street, riffling through T-shirts that read "Life's a Beach in Jamaica" and "No Shirt. No Shoes. No Problem." A couple minutes later, the guy emerged from the alley, an unhappy smile plastered on his face.

The cop in charge seemed satisfied. He patted the husband. "Enjoy your trip, mon. And be careful."

"Yes, sir. We'll do that." The cops disappeared. The husband pulled out his wallet, cheap black Velcro, and opened it wide.

Empty. "Two hundred dollars. Assholes," he said.

"You said it would be okay," his wife said.

"It could have been worse."

A philosophy of sorts, Wells figured. Then the couple disappeared, poorer and wiser. The shakedown had happened the second day, when Wells still hoped to find Robinson on the street. But Robinson was no doubt working carefully, popping up for a few days and then retreating. And the sheer volume of the drug trade meant that Wells and Gaffan couldn't simply hope to bump into him. They would have to search him out, a more dangerous proposition.

Now Wells tucked his wallet, thick with twenties, into his shorts and followed Gaffan out of their hotel room. "Where do we start tonight?"

"Margaritaville." Part of Jimmy Buffett's empire, which stretched over Florida and the Caribbean like an oversized beach umbrella. The Montego Bay outpost featured water trampolines and a one-hundred-twenty-foot waterslide that dropped riders into the Caribbean. Each night it filled with tourists who would prefer to visit another country without seeing anything outside their comfort zone, exactly the type of unimaginative dopers who wanted to score from white dealers.

The night before at Margaritaville, Wells had watched a guy in a tropical shirt work the room. He sat with a table of frat boys for ten minutes before he and one of the guys got up. They came back five minutes later, the frat boy rubbing his nose, his face flushed. The coke must have been pretty good. An hour or so later, the dealer pulled the same trick with another table. But the dealer couldn't have been Robinson. He had blond hair and was a decade too young.

Margaritaville was on the southern end of Gloucester Avenue, separated from the street by high walls. Wells and Gaffan paid their cover and walked past three bouncers, each bigger than the next. They gave Wells a not-very-friendly look, letting him know that his shorts and especially his boots barely passed muster.

"Welcome to the islands," Gaffan said. "Nicest people on earth. Want a beer?"

"Red Stripe."

The inside of the bar was empty. The drinkers had migrated to the decks over the bay, getting ready for another subtropical sunset. The sun had turned the sky a perfect Crayola red, and a satisfied hum ran through the crowd, as though the world had been

71

created solely for its amusement. The dealer stood in the corner, in a different tropical shirt today, his hair pulled into a neat ponytail. Wells edged next to him.

"Nice day," Wells said.

"They all are this time of year."

"Peak season. Business must be good."

The dealer shook his head.

"I saw you last night."

"Looking for something?"

"I might be."

"I'm not a mind reader. Ask away."

"It's more a someone than a something."

"That's gonna be impossible. Something, difficult. Someone, impossible."

"You don't even know who."

The dealer pulled away from the rail, turned to face Wells. He looked like a surfer, tall and lanky, with a craggy, suntanned face. He lifted his sunglasses to reveal striking blue eyes.

"What I know is that you and your bud, you couldn't look more like cops if you tried. Him especially."

Gaffan walked toward them, holding two Red Stripes. Wells raised a hand to stop him. "We're not cops."

"You don't fit, see. There's several kinds of doper tourists. The frat boys, bachelor-party types, they just wanna buy some weed, coke, not get ripped off too badly. You're too old to be frat boys. The old heads, retired hippie dippers, they were in Jamaica back in the day, man, back in the day. Probably once for about a week, but they still talk about it. Now they have kids and they came on a cruise, but they want to get high for old times' sake. That *definitely* is not you."

"True."

"Then you have the true potheads, the guys who subscribe to *High Times* and argue on message boards about Purple Skunk versus Northern Lights. Amateur scientists. At least they would be if they weren't so damned high all the time. They come down here two or three at a time. Mostly they don't look like you, they're fatter and their eyes are half closed. But let's say you two have kept yourself up better than most. Except they don't hang out here. They go straight to Orange Hill, like wine connoisseurs in Napa doing taste tests. And believe me, they're equally annoying. So what are you, then? You look like cops. Or DEA, but why the hell would the DEA be buying ounces on the Hip Strip?"

"We're not DEA. We're not cops. We're looking for someone. Nobody fancy. Nobody like Dudus" — Christopher Coke, a dealer who had run an infamous gang with the unlikely name of the Shower Posse.

"That's good. Seeing as he's in Kingston" — the Jamaican capital. "And seeing as you wouldn't get within a mile of him. Let me tell you about Jamaica. Seventeen hundred murders reported last year, not counting a couple hundred bodies that never turn up. Dumped in *de sea* to feed *de fishees*, mon. Four times as many murders as New York City, and New York has three times as many people as Jamaica."

The dealer stopped talking as a woman splashed down the waterslide and into the bay with a pleased scream. "Watch this. Her top's going to come off. Yep."

Shouts of "Tits!" erupted from the deck. "Tits! Tits! Tits!" The woman happily raised her polka-dotted bikini in the air as the crowd cheered.

"The whole country is a warehouse for coke and pot. From here you go west to New Orleans, east to the Bahamas and Florida. The politicians are owned by the gangs lock, stock, and barrel. They don't even try to hide it. The cops just play along. Don't let the dreads and the Marley songs fool you. This place is Haiti with better beaches."

"So how do you get by?" Wells found

74

himself intrigued.

"These frat boys? They'd pay by credit card if they could. They like a friendly face. And by friendly I mean white."

"And you keep the locals happy."

"I take care of the people who take care of me. In and out of this bar. I understand my place in the ecosystem. I don't have aspirations. And understand, please, that whether it's white or green, it's so pure that I can step on it two, three times and still make my customers happy. In fact, I have to, or they'd wind up OD'ing. And trust me, you don't want to see the inside of a Jamaican hospital, any more than a Jamaican jail."

Around them the deck was filling up.

"It's getting busy," the dealer said. "I appreciate the chance to chat, but I gotta go."

"How do we prove we're not cops? Get high with you?"

"I believe you. You're not cops. But you're trouble. Whatever you want, it's trouble."

The sun touched the edge of the horizon. A long collective sigh went up from the crowd beside them.

"Gonna be a beautiful night," the dealer said. "Do me a favor. Get lost. I see you and your boy hanging around, I'm gonna talk to my friends. You don't want that.

These dudes, they won't care even if you do have a badge. They do sick stuff when they're stoned. Most people get relaxed when they smoke, but these guys, they just dissociate. They won't even hear you screaming."

"We'll be going, then."

The dealer nodded. Two minutes later, Wells and Gaffan were on the street.

"So? He know where Robinson is?"

"He didn't say, but I have a feeling he might."

"And he'll help us?"

"He doesn't think so. But we're gonna change his mind."

CHAPTER 2

MANAMA

The sirens from the street couldn't hide the women screaming from inside the bar, their high voices begging in a language Omar couldn't understand. What had he done? It didn't matter. Nothing mattered. He was in a tunnel with death on both ends, and the only way out was the rifle in his hand.

Fakir peeked through the front door, stepped inside, fired a blind burst to keep the troublemakers down. He hefted a grenade, pulled its pin, flipped the handle. *"Wahid, ithnain —"* he said. *One, two —*

He tossed the grenade high and deep, aiming at the back edge of the bar. It spun end over end and disappeared. The explosion came a half-second later, and the screams a half-second after that, not even words, pure animal keening. Another wave of shooting began outside, the quick snap of pistols against the rattle of AKs. Amir and Hamoud defending their posts. "Time to go in," Fakir

77

said. "Finish this."

Omar's watch read 12:16. They'd walked into the corridor at 12:13. All this had taken just three minutes.

Robby peeked down from the balcony. He could hear again, a little. Outside, an amplified voice shouted in Arabic. The police telling the jihadis to surrender, Robby figured. Good luck with that. The AKs outside were still firing, three-shot bursts, the SOBs conserving their ammo while the ones in here killed everyone who was left. In London the police wouldn't have wasted any time; they would have mounted up and attacked. But these Bahraini cops would take ten or fifteen minutes. Too long.

Two men stepped into the bar, holding AKs. They were young, as young as he had been when he joined the squaddies. But old enough to step in here and kill. The one who'd come in first was bigger and seemed to be in charge. He stepped behind the bar, fired a burst.

Robby squirmed back, pushed himself to his knees. The two men who'd helped him in sat with their backs to the wall, their feet pressed against the table that was barricading the stairs. "They're going to kill everyone down there," Robby said.

"The police are here," the man closer to Robby said. He had a faint French accent. "We should wait. The ones down there don't notice us."

Shouts came from downstairs as the jihadis herded people toward the bar's back corner, almost directly below the balcony. Robby didn't know why no one downstairs was fighting back. He supposed people would do anything for a few extra seconds.

"They're going to put them in the corner, shoot them all," Robby said. "Then come up here. We're gonna die, let's die fighting."

"You have an idea?" the Frenchman said.

Robby explained.

"*Merde.* Not much of a plan."

"It's a start."

Bodies were slumped under chairs, against walls, huddled together behind the bar. At least thirty people were dead. The others couldn't possibly think Fakir had something different in store for them. Still, they obeyed.

Fakir grabbed a wounded woman by the leg, pulled her from under a table. "Move!" he yelled. She crawled for the corner. Omar could almost smell his bloodlust. Fakir was an animal now, not even an animal. *And what am I, then?*

"Enough, brother. It's enough."

"No. All of them."

Outside, an amplified voice shouted: *"Drop your weapons. You are surrounded by the Bahrain Civil Defence Force. Drop your weapons. This is your final warning."*

A few AK shots stuttered from the street outside. Then a single rifle shot, close and loud, cracked the night. The AK stopped.

"Let us out," a man in the corner shouted. "It's over."

"Quiet —" Fakir yelled.

The table smashed his skull wide open.

Omar saw it a quarter-second before it hit, a blocky blur of heavy, round wood, its legs facing up. It caught Fakir's head with a sick crunch. His neck snapped forward and he collapsed, his bulky body falling sideways like a curtain.

For a moment, the people huddled in the corner didn't move, as though they, like Omar, did not believe their own eyes. Then a man shouted something in English and ran for the door. And somehow despite his doubts, Omar didn't hesitate. He turned toward the men and women in the corner and tugged at the AK's trigger —

Just as Robby Duke, all two hundred pounds of him, landed on him, Robby jumping from the balcony with his arms spread wide, berserk from shrapnel and blood loss and everything he'd seen. He crashed into Omar, smashing him onto the bar's wooden floor. The AK came loose from Omar's hand and bounced sideways, firing two shots into the ceiling before the trigger came loose. Omar frothed at the mouth, concussed and barely conscious.

Robby pushed himself to all fours and then his feet and looked over at what was left of Josephine the flight attendant. He very carefully put his boot on Omar's neck, feeling the bones of Omar's larynx under his heel. *"We're not all the same,"* Josephine had said, and sure as death she'd been right. Omar mumbled something Robby didn't understand and wrapped a weak hand around Robby's ankle, and a woman yelled "Don't," and Robby smiled and put all his weight into his heel. Omar kicked against the floor and a terrible wet half-gasp slipped out of his mouth as he tried to breathe through the useless blocked straw of his crushed windpipe, until he finally gave up and died.

Then Robby found a chair and sat and wiped the spit off the side of his boot. Most of the televisions had been destroyed in the attack, but a couple still played, and Robby tilted his head to watch Man City and the Spurs until the cops finally showed. He knew he shouldn't have killed the Arab, but he didn't have the strength to care. He wondered vaguely if he'd go to jail.

But of course the world didn't see it that way. He was a hero, Robby Duke. He'd saved at least twenty lives and killed a terrorist. In the days to come, the BBC and *The Sun* and everyone else would call him a hero. And as soon as the doctors let him out of the hospital, he said no to all the interview requests and the free trips to London and went straight back to work. Robby didn't thank God for much anymore, but he was grateful to be able to work with kids who had no idea who he was or what he'd done.

Yet even with Robby's last-minute valor, Omar and his team did terrible damage. The Bahraini police found the bar so covered in blood and brains that they asked the Fifth Fleet to send a hazardous-materials response team to sterilize it. Forty-one people were killed that night, not counting the four attackers. Six more died over the next two weeks. And the attack on JJ's wasn't even the deadliest terrorist attack on the Arabian peninsula that night. In Riyadh, the Saudi capital, a car bomb tore off the front of the Hotel Al Khozama, killing forty-nine people. And just off Qatar, fifty miles east of Bahrain, a speedboat filled with explosives blew itself up beside a super-tanker loaded with millions of barrels of Saudi crude. Fortunately, the attack failed to ignite the oil. But it killed four sailors, breached the tanker's double hull, and spilled one hundred fifty thousand barrels of crude into the Gulf.

Even before the sun rose on Saudi Arabia the next morning, a claim of responsibility arrived at Al Jazeera and CNN from a previously unknown group — the Ansar al-Islam, the Army of Islam. The group's spokesman wore a mask and gloves, and stood before a black flag painted with the Islamic creed.

"Our warriors protest the endless corruption of King Abdullah," he said in Arabic. "He and his supporters live as infidels. They steal the treasure that Allah has given all Muslims. They desecrate the Holy Kaaba" — the cube-shaped building inside the Grand Mosque in Mecca that served as the center for Muslim prayer. "We reject them. And make no mistake. We will never stop fighting until we drive them from these sacred lands."

CHAPTER 3
MONTEGO BAY

Wells and Gaffan spent two days trailing the dealer from Margaritaville. They didn't know his name, so they were calling him Marley. He drove a black Audi A4 with tinted windows and a roof rack for surfboards. He lived in a gated community in the hills east of Montego, near the Ritz-Carlton and other four-hundred-dollar-a-night resorts. The development, called Paradise East, was still under construction, half its lots empty. An eight-foot brick wall, landscaped with ivy and topped with razor wire, surrounded the property. Two security guards patrolled around the clock with German shepherds.

Given his line of work, Marley had a remarkably stable life. He followed the same routine both days. He surfed in the mornings, had lunch at home. At around three p.m., he drove to Margaritaville and disappeared into the club, emerging at about two a.m. Going home, he headed east on the A1. After about twenty miles, he turned right onto an unmarked road that led up a hill to the gatehouse for Paradise East.

Like the development, the road was unfinished. The first quarter and the last quarter were graded and paved. But the middle stretch was a mix of gravel and red clay. Trees hemmed it in on both sides, leaving it barely wide enough for two cars to pass. It was a carjacker's dream.

Wells intended to take advantage.

Wells had outlined his plan in their hotel room that afternoon. When he finished, Gaffan shook his head. "What if somebody else comes up the road?"

"Hasn't been a problem the last two nights." The fancy neighborhoods outside Montego shut down after midnight. "And it won't get loud if we do it right."

"We don't know if this guy knows Robinson."

"He does. He's smart, and he's been around awhile."

"We don't even know his real name."

"Obviously you're not sold. It's all right. I can do it myself."

"I'm thinking out loud, is all."

"We can't touch him in Margaritaville. His

85

house could work, but if something goes wrong we're stuck inside the compound."

"What about the other thing? The badges."

"I'd rather keep that in reserve. It's high-profile, and we can only do it once."

"We could keep working the town, find Robinson ourselves."

Wells felt his temper surge. Gaffan was younger than he was, less experienced. Gaffan had no right to question his judgment. Was this a glimpse of the future? These ops were a young man's game, and Wells was more middle-aged than young. He wasn't old, not yet, and he was in great shape, but the Gaffans of the world would keep coming. Their suggestions would get louder, until they turned into orders. And eventually he would lose the fight. An old lion forced to give up his territory. The young had no idea how relentless they were.

"How old are you, Brett?"

"Thirty-three. I know you have about a thousand times as much experience as I do. I'm trying to help, John. Work through the options. Didn't mean to piss you off."

Wells was embarrassed. He was fighting with himself, not with Gaffan. He hoped Gaffan didn't know why he had overreacted. "I'm used to making my own mistakes, is all," he said. "And yeah, we can keep cruising the bars, looking for Robinson. But now this dealer has us made. Sooner or later, he's going to see us. I'm always in favor of moving, holding the initiative. Not saying it's my way or the highway —"

"Yeah, you are —"

Wells smiled. "Maybe I am."

"We could always call the FBI in."

Wells didn't feel like explaining what had happened in the 673 case, how Vinny Duto had made a fool of him for his puny efforts to follow the rules. "No."

"Then I'm done arguing. Let's go get us a couple of cars. And whatever else we need."

At 2:15 a.m., with a light rain falling, Marley's Audi rolled past the Esso station on the A1. Wells was hidden in a rented Econoline van with tinted windows. He pulled onto the road and called Gaffan, who was five miles ahead, on a disposable phone.

"I got him. He's alone. Giving him plenty of leash."

Ahead, the Audi pulled away, its red tail-lights disappearing into the mist. Wells stayed back. No reason to make Marley nervous, especially since Wells had slapped a GPS tracker with a radio transmitter on the Audi four hours before.

■ ■ ■ ■

Halfway up the nameless road that led to the Paradise East guardhouse, Gaffan sat in a dented Daewoo minibus that he'd stolen from a McDonald's parking lot four hours before. The Daewoo had seen better days. Its odometer read 243,538, and even in kilometers, that was a long way on Jamaican roads. It was high-sided and square, and had a gash along the left side painted over in beige paint that didn't match the original. It had a manual transmission whose handle was covered with a worn tennis ball. It reeked of stale pot even with the windows open.

Gaffan still didn't understand why Wells was insisting on catching Keith Robinson without help. He didn't understand much about Wells, what drove him. But he trusted Wells. Wells had been everywhere and done everything. Gaffan had been with him the night he'd found the nuke.

Between the two of them, they should be able to handle this guy.

Gaffan saw the Audi's lights moving up the side of the hill, a Cheshire cat smiling in the dark. The sedan itself remained invisible, its black bulk hidden under the trees.

Gaffan put the bus in gear, rolled slowly down the hill, the rosewood and mahoe arching overhead. The Audi came up at him. Behind them, Gaffan saw Wells turning off the A1, maybe thirty seconds behind.

Gaffan heard the Audi grinding up dirt and rock from the unfinished road. Then, at last, he saw the car. The Audi blasted its brights at him, honked, slowed but didn't stop. It swung left, away from the center-line, to make room to pass. In Jamaica, like Britain, cars drove on the left.

Gaffan flipped on his own brights, swung left, but not enough to allow the Audi by, trying to buy enough time for Wells to close the trap on Marley. He didn't want to be too obvious about what he was doing, not yet. Gaffan was wearing a baseball cap pulled low on his forehead. He raised a hand as if he were shielding his eyes from the Audi's brights. In reality, he was hiding his face to keep Marley from recognizing him.

The Audi stopped, honked again. Gaffan put the Daewoo in reverse, backed up, as if trying to make more room. Marley edged forward.

Then Gaffan saw Marley's eyes open wide in surprise and recognition. Marley reached under his seat. Going for a pistol, Gaffan figured. Gaffan put the bus into gear, floored the gas, steamed downhill. The Daewoo jumped ahead, smashed into the Audi, obliterating the interlocking rings on the front of the grille. The whine of tearing metal and the high clink of breaking glass echoed through the rain. Birds poured out of the oaks beside the road and disappeared into the night. Gaffan was thrown against his seat belt. In the Audi, a half-dozen airbags exploded, the white balloons filling the sedan, bouncing Marley harder than the collision had. The steering wheel airbag covered his face like a man-eating pillow. He wrenched back his head to free himself.

Gaffan floored the minibus's engine. The bus ground into the Audi, pushing it backward down the hill. The steering wheel's airbag deflated. Again Marley reached down below his seat. Gaffan laid off the gas, slammed the bus into reverse. Metal shrieked, tore, as the minibus and the Audi separated. Gaffan tapped the gas, backing up as Marley came up with a pistol. Gaffan ducked low as Marley fired blindly through his windshield, the shots high and wild, echoing in the night, scaring up more birds. One flew directly at Gaffan, its breast a shocking iridescent green. A foot from the windshield, it pulled up and disappeared over the minibus. Gaffan raised his head and chanced a peek at the Audi and saw that Marley was scrambling for his seat belt, which seemed to be stuck.

And Wells's van appeared.

Wells had heard the crash not long after he turned off the A1. So had half of Jamaica, probably. Gaffan was supposed to block Marley from getting by for long enough to let Wells get behind him. But Marley had spotted the trap too soon. Wells bounced up the hill, the Econoline sliding sideways on the mud. He took a right too fast and nearly cracked a tree but feathered the gas and the brake at the same time and kept the van on the road.

Now Wells saw the Daewoo's headlights. He was one turn away when the shots started, four in a row, a medium-sized pistol. Finally, too late, Wells skidded around a corner and saw the Audi stopped in the middle of the road, its driver's door opening. The sedan's hood was crumpled, and the minibus looked worse. Daewoos were not exactly built to military specs.

Twenty feet away now. Wells stopped the van, jumped out, ran for the car. Marley pushed open his door and stumbled out, nearly falling. Red dirt smeared his Hawaiian shirt. He focused on the minibus and didn't see Wells. He raised the pistol in his right hand, taking careful aim at the Daewoo's windshield —

Wells tackled him, a linebacker drilling a quarterback from the blindside, a clean shoulder-to-shoulder hit that arched Marley's spine. The gun clattered from his hand and skittered into the drainage ditch. Wells kept coming, driving his legs, finishing the hit, pushing Marley face-first into the mud of the road. Marley grunted and then cursed wildly, shouting into the night. Wells grabbed a hank of his long blond hair and jammed his face into the road to choke the fight out of him.

Gaffan jumped out of the bus and piled on, putting a knee in Marley's back. Together they cuffed his arms and his legs. They turned him over, and Wells slapped a piece of duct tape on his mouth. They picked him up and ignored his wriggling and tossed him in the Econoline's cargo area and slammed the doors.

"What about the van?"

"Let the cops figure it out."

Wells reversed down the hill until the road widened enough for him to make a U-turn. He didn't hear sirens. The incompetence of the Jamaican police might save them yet.

■ ■ ■ ■

At the bottom of the hill, Wells turned right, east, away from Montego. After Rock Brae, the next town, the road opened into low green fields. A billboard promised they were looking at the future home of the Marriott White Bay. Wells pulled over and grabbed a baton and leather gloves from his kit. He nodded for Gaffan to drive and slipped into the back. When they were moving again, he tore the duct tape off Marley's mouth, taking a piece of Marley's lips with it.

"What's your name?"

"You assholes are dead," Marley said. "You have no idea. I'll kill you."

"No one's killing anyone."

"Slice you up."

"We want to have a conversation, that's all."

"You think you're hitting a coke house? Snap off a couple hundred keys and no one's going to notice? You are as stupid as they come."

Wells didn't enjoy beating prisoners, but he had to take some of the fight out of this one. He smashed an elbow into the side of Marley's skull, the soft spot high on the temple. The force of the contact ran up

93

Wells's arm into his shoulder. Marley's head snapped sideways. But when he opened his eyes, Wells saw that he hadn't given up.

"Your name."

"Ridge. Real name's Bruce. But everyone calls me Ridge. Since high school. Ask me what you need to ask. I can answer without getting myself killed, I will."

Wells sat Ridge against the side of the van and offered him three photos of Keith Robinson. The first was a blown-up version of Robinson's CIA badge. The second and third were computer-generated versions, predictions of what Robinson might look like now with long hair — or no hair.

"Mind if I ask why you want him?"

"Yeah," Gaffan said from the front of the van. "We do."

"Robin speaks," Ridge said.

"Focus," Wells said. "He might have different hair. Put on weight."

"Lemme see the third one." Ridge looked for a while. "There's one guy, it might be him. He's maybe fifty pounds heavier."

"He's in your business?"

"Works a couple places on the east side. Nowhere too fancy. We buy from some of the same people. He's got a kid who helps him. I'm not saying it's him. Just that it could be."

94

"He have a name?"

"He goes by Mark. I think."

Mark. Keith Robinson's dead son. Robinson's life had gone off the rails when his son died. Would he be crazy enough to have taken his son's name as an alias? Wells suspected the answer was yes.

"Is he American?"

"I think so."

"Where can we find him?"

"I'm telling you I've met him, like, twice."

"I need you to find out where he lives."

"He's connected, just like me. Come after him, you piss off some nasty boys. I help you, they may take it out on me. Nothing more I can tell you. And if you're smart, you'll catch the first plane out tomorrow and hope the boys don't chase you back to whatever hole you're from."

Wells grabbed Ridge's handcuffed wrists and twisted them back and up until he felt Ridge's shoulders come loose from their sockets. Ridge let out a low moan.

"You think we're negotiating? Get this guy to meet you. Tell him whatever you want. Tell him there's a gang war coming and you've got to talk to him."

"If he's even the guy you want."

"Get him to us. Let us worry about what happens next."

"Then you'll let me go?"

"We're not after you."

"All right. Let me call somebody."

The quick turnaround bothered Wells. But maybe the guy had taken enough of a beating for one night. Wells uncuffed Ridge's wrists, recuffed his right hand to the base of the passenger seat. He put a disposable phone in Ridge's left hand and sat him up against the side of the van. "Do it, then. Whoever you have to call."

"I need my phone," Ridge said. "The people I'm gonna ask, they'll want to see it's my phone on the caller ID."

Wells dug through Ridge's pockets, found a book of rolling papers, a baggie of dark green weed, and an iPhone.

"What kind of phone?" Gaffan said.

"iPhone."

"Don't let him touch it. He could have tracking software on there, some app that signals he's in trouble."

Wells felt his anger boil over. All the frustration of his last failed mission. No more sass from this drug dealer. He reached for his studded baton and lifted it high and watched Ridge's eyes open wide. He swung it in a long whipping arc, getting his shoulder into it, and cracked Ridge just over the left ear. The van echoed with a hollow metal ping. Ridge's skull snapped sideways, and he slumped against the wall and slid to the floor. He gasped and wriggled against the side of the van, trying to put as much distance between himself and Wells as he could.

"Who *are* you?"

Wells met Gaffan's eyes in the rearview mirror. Gaffan didn't speak, just raised his eyebrows, the question obvious. Wells ignored it. He grabbed Ridge and stretched him on his back and straddled Ridge's chest and laid the baton across his neck. Ridge turned his head furiously, tried to rock his shoulders, swiped at Wells with his free left hand. But Wells was two hundred and ten pounds of muscle. Ridge stayed pinned. Wells held the baton in both hands, let Ridge feel the metal against his skin.

"I swear I wasn't going to double-cross you."

"I want you to live, but you're making it hard. For the last time, you are going to help us get this guy." Wells sat back. His heart was pounding and his mouth was dry. This violence came much too easily to him. He could bow his head and pray for peace five times a day, but part of him would always want to pound skulls. Might as well admit the truth. To himself, if no one else.

"You ready to be a team player?"

Ridge nodded.

"Tell me the number."

Ridge did. Wells unlocked the iPhone, dialed, held the phone to Ridge's face.

"Sugah. It Ridge, mon. Need your help. I looking for dis jake snakes at Sandals." Ridge suddenly sounded like a native Rasta to Wells. "Axing on me. Gonna tell him, ease up." A long pause. "No, mon. Do it mi own self. Aright."

Wells hung up. "So?"

"Sugar said yeah, the guy buys from him sometimes. Doesn't have a phone number for him. But he thinks the guy lives on the other side of Montego, this place called Unity Hall. Up in the hills, another gated neighborhood. If I'm thinking about the right area, it's big, like four hundred houses. But Sugar said this guy drives a Toyota Celica with a spoiler. The Jamaicans call them swoops."

Like the name Mark, the Toyota sounded right to Wells. Robinson was car-crazy. The FBI had traced a half-dozen antique cars to him, at a house in Miami that no one at the agency had known about.

"If you can find him, we're even, right?" Ridge's tone was low and wheedling, the whine of a dog exposing his belly to a more dangerous member of the pack to prove that he wasn't a threat.

"Something like that."

"How you gonna find him?"

"We got to you, didn't we?"

Ridge closed his eyes.

Gaffan topped off the van's tank at a twenty-four-hour gas station while Wells bought a gallon of water from the clerk behind the bulletproof counter. Back in the van, he tried to clean Ridge's wounds, but Ridge shrank from him.

They rolled off. A few minutes later, Ridge coughed uncontrollably. He was breathing shallowly, almost panting, his forehead slick with sweat. "I'm not playing, man. I think my skull's fractured. You gotta stop." Wells touched Ridge's scalp. Ridge yelped, and Wells felt the break under the skin. His fingers came back red and sticky.

"Get through this village," Gaffan said. Five minutes later, he pulled over. The van was on a hillside, the nearest building a concrete church a half-mile away. The sweet, heavy stink of marijuana wafted from the fields across the road. Wells helped Ridge out of the van. Ridge leaned over and vomited, a thin stream. "I need a hospital."

"When we're done. You'll live." Wells gave

him some water and a washcloth to clean his face, and bundled him back in the van.

They arrived in Montego as the sun rose. "What now?" Gaffan said.

"We can't leave him, and we don't have much time. We're going in the front door."

"The badges."

At the hotel, Wells waited in the van while Gaffan showered and shaved. When Gaffan was done, they switched places. Wells stank fiercely, his sweat mixed with Ridge's fear. He rinsed himself under the lukewarm shower, and with the help of Visine and a shave, he looked halfway human. Though Ridge might have called that assessment generous.

Wells pulled on the suit that he'd hidden in the bathroom vent. It was lightweight and blue and slightly tight around his shoulders. And it came with a DEA badge and identification card. The DEA operated fairly freely in Jamaica — at least when it was chasing traffickers who didn't have government protection.

Wells looked around for anything that could identify him. He was on a fake passport and had prepaid for the room. Most likely, the hotel wouldn't even notice he and Gaffan were gone for at least a day. Wells tucked his pistol into his shoulder holster, put a do-not-disturb tag on the doorknob, left the room behind.

As Gaffan drove them toward Unity Hall, Wells knelt beside Ridge, lifted the duct tape. "Another couple hours and you're done."

"I don't get it." Ridge's mouth was dry, and Wells could hardly hear him. "You guys aren't DEA. DEA doesn't play like this."

"We're not DEA."

"You gonna kill this guy?"

"That's up to him."

"Either way, I'm dead, man."

"We'll get you to a hospital."

"Not what I mean. Soon as I get out, Sugar will put this mess on me."

"You want to get back to the States, I can help. But I'll have to make sure that the DEA knows who you are when we get back to Miami."

Ridge shook his head. Then winced.

"Then you're going to have to handle it yourself."

"I don't need any morality lessons from you," Ridge said. "I sell people a good time. Nothing more or less. Pot, coke, they're just like booze. Safer, probably. I don't force my stuff on anybody, and I don't hurt anybody. Unlike you."

Wells didn't argue, just slapped the duct tape back on Ridge's mouth. Though maybe the guy had a point. In his years in Afghanistan and Pakistan, Wells had seen a dozen men executed for dealing or using drugs. Mostly heroin, occasionally hashish. The youngest was a boy, no more than fourteen, only the slightest peach fuzz on his chin. He'd been caught smoking heroin by the Talib religious police. His family lacked the money to buy his freedom or his life.

The incident had happened a decade ago, but it was etched into Wells's mind as deeply as the first man he'd killed. The central square in Ghazni, a town southwest of Kabul. The boy's father waited silently as the Talibs tied the boy to a wooden stake, pulling his arms tight to his body. Hundreds of men waited in a loose cluster. Wells stood on the fringes. The binding seemed to last hours, though it couldn't have taken more than a few minutes. The kid didn't say a word. Maybe he was still high. Wells hoped so.

He wanted to step in, raise a hand to stop the slaughter. The penalty might be legal under *sharia,* Muslim law, but Wells couldn't believe that Allah or the Prophet would smile on this scene. But he stayed silent. He had spent years building his bonafides with the men around him, even fighting beside them in Chechnya, an ugly, brutal war where both sides committed atrocities every day. He couldn't risk his mission to save a heroin addict. And he'd be ignored in any case. He held his tongue.

The Talibs finished their binding. The leader of the religious police, a fat man with a beard that jutted off his chin, spoke to the boy too quietly for Wells to hear. A pickup truck drove up. The fat Talib opened the liftgate and stood aside as dozens of stones, baseball-sized and larger, rolled out.

The crowd moved forward, men pushing at one another, reaching down to grab the rocks. Wells had a vision of the last time he'd been bowling, in Missoula with friends on his sixteenth birthday, picking up a ball and squaring to toss it.

Finally the boy seemed to understand what was happening. He pulled at the stake, but it held him fast. "Father, please," he said. "Please, father. I won't do it again. I promise —"

The big Talib raised his arm and fired a long, flat stone at the boy, catching him in the side of the head. The boy screamed, and suddenly it seemed as if the air was full of rocks. The screaming grew louder, and then ended as a softball-sized stone smashed open the boy's skull. His face went slack, and he collapsed against the stake.

That was the Taliban policy on drugs. Zero tolerance. Yet heroin and hashish were everywhere. Men staggered glassy-eyed through Kabul, their mouths open, smiling to themselves even on the coldest days of winter. Once, in a hailstorm on the Shamali plain, north of Kabul, Wells had stepped inside an abandoned hut for shelter and found a half-dozen men huddled in a semi-circle around a low flame, cooking a fat ball of opium. They turned and growled at him like hyenas at a kill. He raised his hands and backed away. Even at the time he'd thought, *If the death penalty doesn't stop this stuff, what will?*

Now he looked down to Ridge, who was pale, eyes closed, an unhealthy shine on his cheeks. "Ridge."

"What now?"

"You want out, I'll get you home. Get-out-of-jail-free card. No DEA or anything."

"You can do that?"

Wells nodded.

"Man," Ridge said for the second time. "Who *are* you?"

"I have friends."

"The original original gangster."

"You want it or not?"

"Maybe." He looked Wells over. "What, I'm supposed to say thanks? After you kidnapped me, bashed my head in? You're a real humanitarian." Ridge closed his eyes. Wells decided to do the same.

"John," Gaffan said. "Ready?"

Wells scrambled up beside Gaffan. "Where are we?"

"About three minutes from Unity Hall. So how do I play this?"

"Show them your ID and tell them as little as possible. Tell them to call the embassy if you have to, the JCF" — Jamaica Constabulary Force. "They won't want to."

"If they ask where we're going?"

"Tell them you can't say."

At the gatehouse, the guard was a small dark-skinned man who wore a blue shirt with a seven-pointed star. "Yes?"

Gaffan flashed his badge.

"Let me see that," the guard said. Gaffan handed his badge and ID over. Wells followed.

"This is Jamaica. Not America."

"The man we want, he's a U.S. citizen."

"What's his name?"

"I can't tell you."

"No name, no pass."

105

"Call our embassy."

"Tell me his name or I call the constables myself —"

Wells leaned across the seat. "His name's Mark Edward. Drives a Toyota with a big spoiler on the back. Celica."

The guard nodded. "That one a cheap bastard. Gwaan, then. You know where to find him?"

"End of the second row on the left."

"Exactly wrong. Right and then left. House one-forty-three."

The barrier rose, and they rolled ahead. "His son's first name and his middle name," Gaffan said. "Nice guess."

"Looks like he should have tipped the guards better at Christmas."

The houses at Unity Hall were a mix of brick mansions on narrow lots and semi-attached town houses. Robinson's was one of the latter. His Celica sat in the driveway in front, black, a spoiler jutting off the back deck. A pink flamingo and three dwarfs in Rasta hats graced the concrete front landing. Gaffan drove past, dropped Wells in front of the house. He walked ahead and rang the doorbell. A chime inside boomed.

"Who is it?"

Wells rang again, heard a man stepping

slowly down the stairs in the front hall. He unholstered his pistol, held it low by his side.

"Yes? Who's there?" The voice was raspy and low. He'd heard it a few days before, on the phone in Janice's house in Vienna. But not in person. Until now, Wells and Keith Robinson had never met.

"Keith."

"You have the wrong address."

"Keith. It's John Wells. It's over."

CHAPTER 4
RIYADH, SAUDI ARABIA

The American embassy compound in Saudi Arabia was a fortress within a fortress, the most heavily guarded building in Riyadh's high-walled Diplomatic Quarter. The Saudi government had built the zone in the 1980s, on a low mesa on the western edge of Riyadh. Unsmiling Saudi soldiers in armored personnel carriers guarded its gates, subjecting vehicles to inspection by explosives-sniffing dogs. Trucks and SUVs faced undercarriage examinations with long-handled mirrors, the bomb-squad version of the reflectors that dentists used to see inside their patients' mouths. Drivers who grumbled about the searches found themselves forced to turn off their engines — and their air-conditioning. With summer afternoons in Riyadh topping one hundred twenty degrees, complaints were rare.

Behind the walls, the quarter stretched three square miles. It should have been a pleasant place, especially compared to the rest of Riyadh. The Saudi government had spent a billion dollars on the district, hoping it would attract executives at multinational companies, and even wealthy Saudis. The quarter was subject to the same strict Islamic laws as the rest of the Kingdom, but it had coffee shops, parks, even a riding club. Date palms lined its boulevards. Its central square had won an award for fusing traditional Islamic architecture with modern design. In 1988, a local magazine had bragged that with its picnics and bicycling children, the zone could be mistaken for Geneva or Washington.

No more. The hassles at the checkpoints had driven Saudis out of the zone, but they hadn't reassured Americans and Europeans. Following attacks on other Western compounds, multinational companies had shrunk their staffs in the Kingdom to a minimum. The quarter felt besieged, its avenues empty, gardens run-down. It had turned into Paris in 1940, with the Wehrmacht approaching. Anyone with a choice had left. The remaining expats huddled in houses with thick steel doors and barred windows, in case a band of suicide attackers penetrated the checkpoints.

The American embassy was the ultimate

target, of course. The embassy occupied six acres near the quarter's western edge, on the oddly named Collector Road M — though its location was no longer disclosed on the State Department's website, as though that omission might stop terrorists from finding it. It had opened in 1986, at a ceremony presided over by then Vice President George Herbert Walker Bush.

At the time, Osama bin Laden was just another young Saudi heading to Afghanistan to fight jihad. Still, the attacks on American embassies in Pakistan and Iran in 1979 had made the State Department aware of the Islamic terror threat. The new embassy in Riyadh had been built to withstand a sustained attack. Its concrete exterior walls were a foot thick. The embassy itself was a modern castle, built around a courtyard, with few exterior windows.

Security had been tightened further since September 11. Today, visitors parked outside the compound and then passed through explosive detectors at a marine-staffed checkpoint. Besides M-4 carbines, the marine guards toted shotguns, their fat barrels projecting immediate menace. Without exception, the guards had seen combat in Iraq and Afghanistan. They were ready for war.

■ ■ ■ ■

Ambassador Graham Kurland hoped they'd never have to use their skills.

Kurland and his wife, Barbara, lived inside the embassy compound in a mansion formally called Quincy House. The name referred to the USS *Quincy,* the cruiser where Franklin Delano Roosevelt had met Abdul-Aziz, the first Saudi king, in February 1945.

The king had never seen a wheelchair until he met Roosevelt, who used one because of his polio-damaged legs. Abdul-Aziz, who was severely overweight, found the contraption fascinating. Roosevelt gave the king his spare chair, cementing the partnership between the United States and Saudi Arabia. That was the legend, anyway.

In fact, chair or no chair, the two countries had good reason to ally as World War II ended. By 1945, vast oil deposits had been found under the sands of the Kingdom's Eastern Province. Having seen oil's strategic importance during the war, neither Roosevelt nor the king wanted the oil to fall into Soviet paws. And the Saudis were predisposed to trust the United States, which had avoided the Middle East empire-building of

111

France and Britain.

To commemorate the fateful meeting, a model of the *Quincy* sat in the lobby of the ambassador's residence. And the United States and Saudi Arabia had stuck to their bargain. Even after the formation of the Organization of the Petroleum Exporting Countries, the Saudis tried to keep oil cheap. In return, the United States made sure that Iran and Iraq never seriously threatened the Kingdom.

But recently the partnership had frayed. Blaming bin Laden for the problems was the easy answer, Ambassador Kurland thought. But bin Laden spoke for millions of Saudis who felt they were living under a dictatorship disguised as a monarchy.

Now the terrorists had struck again. The dead in the Khozama bombing included an American, David Landie, a reporter for the *Chicago Tribune.* The day before the bombing, Landie had interviewed Kurland at Quincy House. The embassy's public-relations officer had warned Kurland to stick to his talking points. Even so, Kurland was happy to talk to an American journalist. Few visited Riyadh anymore, aside from a couple stalwarts from *The New York Times.*

Landie was researching an article about the success, or lack thereof, of the camps where the Saudis "re-educated" former Guantánamo detainees. The camps had gained a reputation as a joke, since so many ex-Gitmo prisoners had returned to terrorism. Now, instead of waiting to see whether Landie quoted him accurately, Kurland had the grim task of helping repatriate what was left of his body. Kurland wondered if the Khozama bombers included any ex-prisoners. He suspected that Landie's family would not appreciate the irony.

The phone on the bedside table trilled. "Yes."

"Mr. Ambassador." The voice belonged to Clint Rana, the career foreign service officer who served as Kurland's personal aide and translator. "Dwayne Maggs would like to meet this morning. Says it's urgent." Maggs was deputy chief of the CIA station in Saudi Arabia, as cool as they came. Kurland couldn't remember Maggs using the word *urgent* before. He checked his Rolex: 8:15.

"Tell him nine. Thank you, Clint."

Kurland looked through his bedroom's bulletproof windows to the embassy's tennis court. His wife was practicing forehands with Roberto, a cook who doubled as her trainer. Roberto favored 70s-style headbands that showed off his long hair, and tight white shorts that showed off his other good qualities. Kurland wasn't worried. He and Barbara had been married longer than Roberto had been alive. As he watched, Barbara banged a line drive into the net and grunted, "Gosh dang."

Kurland couldn't hear the words, but after thirty-six years, he knew. He gingerly made his way down the back staircase, wincing with each step. He'd torn his left ACL skiing five years before. The knee had never fully recovered. Now the first slivers of arthritis had come to his hips, scouts of what would no doubt be an occupying army. Getting old stank. The poets could dress it up all they liked, but the reality was simple: Getting old stank. Though it came with a few compensations, Kurland thought, like knowing what your wife would murmur when she shanked a forehand.

And here she was, in a blue skirt and white top, tall and long-limbed. She still looked exactly like the sophomore he'd seen at his spring formal at the University of Illinois. Well, not *exactly*. But close.

"Morning, darling."

"Morning, dear."

"You looked great."

"Not how I felt." She mimed a couple of

forehands. "Practice, practice."

"Well, you looked great."

"Roberto looked great. As he always does."

"Quién es más macho," Kurland murmured.

"Are we finished for the morning, Mrs. Kurland?" Roberto shouted.

"Indeed we are, Roberto."

"May I?" Kurland took her racket. "Make sure to tell him to wear tighter shorts tomorrow."

"Oh, I will."

"Do you think he gets the joke?"

"I think. I'm not sure."

They walked side by side to the white wicker table at the edge of the court. A jug of ice water and a pot of steaming coffee awaited. Kurland pulled back a chair for his wife and poured water for her and coffee for himself. From the table he could just see the gun emplacements atop the walls around the court. At the moment, they were unmanned.

"Another day in paradise."

"Amen to that." She raised her water glass in a mock toast. "Anything new?"

"They broke up another cell last night." In the wake of the attacks, the classified cables had been even more disturbing than usual. Saudi police had arrested a four-person cell planning an assault on an Aramco compound in Dhahran, home to the foreign engineers who maintained the Saudi oil fields.

"Isn't that good news?"

"Barbara. There's something we need to talk about."

"No, there isn't."

"You don't know what I'm going to say."

"I'm not leaving."

"I don't want you to leave. I want you to *consider* leaving."

"Is there a difference?"

He sipped his coffee. He'd known she would say no, but he had to keep trying. "It's for your safety."

"I've never felt safer. Every time I turn around, I see a marine. And Joshua himself couldn't bring down these walls."

"It seems like overkill, but it's not. Trust me."

"When my book's done, I'll think about it." His wife was writing a novel set in Riyadh and centered on the lives of rich Saudi women. Her second book. "These ladies, the chance to talk to them, it's once in a lifetime." A couple times a month, a black-clad ghost arrived at Quincy House to chat with Barbara. Once the women were inside, their burqas came off, revealing the fanciest designer clothes Kurland had ever seen. He wondered if they intentionally wasted money on Chanel skirts and Dior jackets to spite the regime that made them cover themselves.

"That's at least a year away."

"Problem solved, then." She drained her water glass and stood. "I've got to wash before I start to smell like one of those camels." Months before, Kurland and Barbara had visited a ranch where King Abdullah kept hundreds of prize camels. At the king's urging, Kurland had sat on one. He'd encouraged his wife to do the same. She still hadn't forgiven him.

She kissed his bald head and walked off. He watched her go, amazed, as always, that he still loved her so much after so many years.

His good feeling lasted only until he arrived in his office on the embassy's top floor, where Dwayne Maggs waited. Maggs, who didn't speak Arabic, had gotten the job after an extraordinary tour as a CIA security officer in Pakistan. Kurland didn't know exactly what Maggs had done, and Maggs wouldn't say. But it had turned him into a legend. Maggs and his team were half the reason that Kurland hadn't insisted that Barbara leave. The other half being that he hated fighting with her.

"This came in this morning," Maggs said, handing over a flash-coded cable.

Beneath the usual security warnings, the cable explained that the National Security Agency had intercepted calls and e-mails between Al Qaeda's lieutenants in Pakistan — now called AQM, short for Al Qaeda Main — and the group's cells in Saudi Arabia, called AQAP, for Al Qaeda in the Arabian Peninsula. An attachment detailed the messages, leaving Kurland wishing for a dictionary that translated NSA and CIA lingo to English.

> 02:23:01 GST: TM from mobile phone +92-91-XXX-XXX [Peshawar, PAK] to +966-54-XXX-XXXX [Jeddah, KSA]: *????*
> 02:25:37 GST: TM from mobile phone +966-54-XXX-XXXX to mobile phone +92-91-XXX-XXX: *La. La.*
> 03:01:18 GST: IM from XXXXXXX12@gmail.com [IP address, Karachi, PAK] to XXXXXXXXLION@gmail.com [IP address, Riyadh, KSA]: *What is this?*
> 03:14:56 GST: IM from XXXXXXXXLION@gmail.com to

XXXXXXX12@gmail.com: *Inshallah.*
[God's will.]

And so on, for three more pages. Kurland read the attachment twice, didn't get it. These crazy kids, with their IMs and their TMs and their suicide bombs. "Explain," he said to Maggs.

"TM, that's text message. IM, that's instant message. The bracketed information is the location of the phone or computer where the messages were sent. NSA redacts the precise location, if we have it, and the exact phone number or e-mail address, for OPSEC."

"Operational security," Kurland said, glad to be able to play along at last. "Dwayne, I spent the last thirty years building houses for hicks." In fact, Kurland had run one of the largest residential construction companies in the Midwest. "Help me out here. Isn't there always traffic like this before these attacks?"

"Yes, sir. But the timing, these e-mails, they're all *after* the attacks. Not before. These guys, what you have to remember about them, sir, the dumb ones are dead. We've killed them. The weak ones, they've surrendered. The ones who are left, they're tough. And smart. They're hiding up there in the mountains, and they know the risk they run every time they pick up a phone. They know we're on them, and they don't make these calls lightly. And look, they're not taking credit or congratulating each other. They're asking what happened. It looks like AQM —"

"Al Qaeda Main —"

"Right. The guys closest to bin Laden. I'll try to keep the acronyms to a minimum, sir. Bottom line, looks like they didn't have a clue this was coming. And the ones here, Al Qaeda in the Arabian Peninsula, they didn't know, either. One message, they say they didn't. The other, they keep their options open, like they're waiting to see if maybe they can get credit even though they didn't do it."

"Is it possible they would hide their involvement? Make these calls to trick us?"

"Possible. But that hasn't been their style the last few years. And given the risk of making these calls, they'd need a good reason to play that game."

"I see."

"There's something else. As you can see from these intercepts, we have these guys pinned tight. If they do manage to get an op going, we usually hear about it pretty damn quick. We don't always have enough

120

intel to stop it, but we at least know it's coming. This time, nothing."

"So add it all up; you're telling me this wasn't Al Qaeda."

"I had to bet, I'd say no."

"Who was it, then?"

"I wouldn't even venture to guess. When I get any intel, you'll be the first to know. But right now we don't have anything."

"I understand," Kurland said. Though he didn't, not entirely. The United States spent fifty billion dollars a year on intelligence. He didn't expect all his questions to be answered right away, but he would have liked some idea what was happening.

Maggs seemed to sense his dissatisfaction. "Sir. I promise you there are literally a thousand people in Langley and Fort Meade, and here, too, working on getting the answer. In Qatar, the FBI can examine the tanker, and in Bahrain the FBI will have access to the bar. But from what I hear, it's a real mess, and it's going to take time to sort out. Here, we'll have to depend on the Saudis. They should be able to trace the car that hit the Khozama. If it wasn't stolen."

"And can we expect them to cooperate? Since an American citizen was killed."

"One American, three British, eight Kuwaitis, twelve Japanese, and twenty-five

Saudis, sir. I think we can expect that they'll give us what they choose when they choose."

"What about the cell they broke up last night? That should help."

"I've only heard bits and pieces, but I think that's unlikely. Typically, something like this happens, the *mukhabarat* arrest whoever's on their lists, try to prove they're on top of things."

Kurland had already left a condolence message for King Abdullah. He wondered if he ought to call Abdullah again. Or Saeed, the defense minister. Or even Nayef, the interior minister. But he decided to wait. He didn't have anything concrete to offer, and Abdullah was difficult to reach. He was spending a lot of time in his palace in Jeddah, the Kingdom's second city. Which didn't make sense to Kurland. Shouldn't the king be here, in Riyadh? Kurland had started to wonder if the king, now nearly ninety, was turning senile. Or worse.

Saeed, the second most powerful man in the Kingdom, still seemed sound enough mentally, but Kurland didn't trust him. He was more conservative than Abdullah, and Kurland sometimes wondered what would happen if Saeed became king.

Another question occurred to Kurland. He hesitated, wondering whether he would sound dumb for asking, then decided that he needed an answer. "Dwayne. This kind of operation, is it hard to pull off?"

"Harder than it looks, sir. Three operations, at least twelve guys, timed to cause maximum damage, in two countries and on the Gulf. That requires planning and operational support we haven't seen since — well, since September eleventh. And these came out of nowhere."

"I asked Barbara this morning if she'd go home," Kurland said. Immediately, he wished he'd kept his mouth shut. His conversations with his wife were his own business. But what Maggs had told him weighed heavy. He'd known living here wouldn't be easy, but he hadn't expected the strain to reach this level.

"Sir?"

"My wife. Barbara. She said no." Kurland felt almost as though he'd betrayed some elemental weakness, confessed his own desire to leave.

"I understand your concern, Mr. Ambassador."

"Please. Call me Graham."

"Graham. But trust me, she's safe. With our marines, these defenses, it would take an army to get inside this place. I mean that literally. An army."

"We just have to worry about the rest of the country, then."

"Yessir. Got that right."

CHAPTER 5

JEDDAH, SAUDI ARABIA

Conservative Muslims believe that making images of the world or the people in it is disrespectful to Allah. They don't like having their photographs taken. The only art on their walls is calligraphy of Quranic verses. The billboards on Saudi Arabian expressways don't show people. Clothing brands — including Victoria's Secret, which has stores in the Kingdom — advertise themselves with scarves and bottles of perfume rather than models. Even the happy families eating pizza on Sbarro signs have their eyes pixelated out.

But the prohibition against human images doesn't apply to everyone. The face of the Saudi monarch, Abdullah bin Abdul-Aziz, looms on billboards, posters, even on the Kingdom's pastel-colored currency. Everywhere, Abdullah smiles under his *ghutra,* his white head scarf. His portraitists have been gentle. He is a big man with a heavy black goatee and wide, kind eyes. He is everyone's favorite uncle.

Once, maybe, Abdullah was the man the billboards depicted.

The king sat alone in his third-floor study in his palace in Jeddah, the second-largest city in Saudi Arabia. The palace compound occupied a mile of Red Sea beachfront. A twenty-foot concrete wall separated it from the city. Signs along the wall warned drivers against stopping or taking pictures.

A few months before, a French doctor visiting Jeddah for a conference had made the mistake of ignoring the warnings. In search of a souvenir of his trip to the Kingdom, he snapped photos of the wall and its entrance. Before he got back in his car, a half-dozen unmarked cars and Jeeps screamed out of the palace to surround him and his driver. Only the immediate intercession of the French consulate and the doctor's abject apologies had saved him from a nasty run-in with the Saudi judicial system.

Behind the wall, the compound included dormitory quarters for maids, police, and drivers, a garage with a dozen armored limousines, even a firehouse and helipad. The palace itself contained more than one hundred rooms. From the outside, it appeared squat and thick-walled, like the mud forts that had once protected Riyadh. The exterior was an illusion. Inside, the palace was a modern Versailles, a maze of long rooms with fifteen-foot ceilings, filled with gold saucers, antique wool carpets, and crystal chandeliers. It had four elevators, one capable of lifting a car to the third floor, so the king could come and go without having to step outside. At full blast, its cooling system could chill the entire building to fifty degrees Fahrenheit, even in July and August, when the air outside was seventy degrees warmer.

Abdullah's quarters occupied the third floor of the palace. The royal bedroom took up the entire south end. Besides the obligatory marble-and-Jacuzzi bathroom, it included a separate sauna and a massage room. On the north end of the palace was his study, which included a balcony overlooking the Red Sea, which divided Saudi Arabia and Egypt. In happier days, Abdullah had sat safely behind a bulletproof partition on the balcony and sipped pomegranate juice and watched boats putter along the water. But he couldn't remember the last time he'd been outside.

Abdullah was tired. Beyond tired. Weariness had crept into his bones, joints, even his skin. He didn't understand how skin could be tired. But his was, papery and dusky. His veins tunneled through it. At the mirror, he didn't recognize himself, the puffy bags that had grown under his eyes, the deep cave of his mouth. Once he had been the hardiest of his brothers, a true Bedouin. He loved the desert. In 1953, after his father died, he took servants and camels and made his way south into the Empty Quarter, the *Rub al-Khali,* where hundreds of miles separated the oases and even the scorpions barely survived.

His father and sixty warriors had lived in the Empty Quarter in the winter of 1902, before Abdul-Aziz led the attack on Riyadh that was the first step in creating modern Saudi Arabia. To honor his father's memory, to prove he could survive the desert, Abdullah had lived in the Quarter for a month. Now he could hardly walk. With every step, he felt his legs quiver under his big body. He forced himself to push on, though he wanted to sit and sleep for days. When had this happened to him? When had his flesh lost its vigor?

He didn't tell his doctors, but the world was turning monochromatic, the white desert light fading to gray. Dates tasted like they were wrapped in plastic, their sticky ooze only faintly sweet. He knew what was happening to him. He had all the money in the world, the very best doctors. And nothing could stop it.

If Allah wanted to take him, he would have to succumb. All men did. *The dead are children of the dead,* the preachers said. But while he was alive, no one would steal his kingdom. He imagined the attack on the hotel in Riyadh, his own people killed in their beds, and a fresh fury coursed through his veins. He would raise his sword over the heads of these terrorists and —

A knock startled him. Had he been sleeping? He napped more and more. He wiped his mouth, looked at the gold Patek Philippe clock he'd installed on his desk a month before when he realized that he could no longer read his watch. A quarter past eleven. "Yes."

"It's Miteb. With Mansour."

"Come in, then." Abdullah pressed a button under the desk to alert his steward that he wanted coffee. Miteb, Abdullah's half-brother, stepped in. Miteb was Abdullah's closest adviser and dearest friend, the only man he could truly say he trusted. But Miteb was nearly as old as Abdullah. In the last five years, he'd had two heart attacks.

He could barely walk.

Mansour, the director of the Saudi *mukha-barat* — the country's secret police — followed. Mansour was the son of Saeed, another of Abdullah's many half-brothers, and thus was Abdullah's half-nephew. His mother was a legendary beauty, and Mansour had inherited her round face and light skin. He was nearly fifty, but his eyes were unlined and his robes flowed smoothly over his flat stomach. In truth, Mansour was unmanly, Abdullah thought. He had never understood the desert. He limped slightly, the result of a motorcycle accident two decades earlier.

"You're late."

Mansour knelt, kissed Abdullah's hand. "I apologize, Your Highness."

"Sit, then. Hamoud is bringing coffee." Abdullah pulled himself up from his desk and shuffled over to his favorite leather chair, a gift from the first President Bush. Miteb sat across from him on a yellow eighteenth-century French couch that had cost the Kingdom a few thousand barrels of oil. And Mansour took a low wooden stool beside Abdullah's chair.

A faint knock. "Come, Hamoud."

Hamoud arranged the coffee, keeping his eyes down. In thirty years as Abdullah's steward, he had looked directly at his master only a handful of times. "Anything else, Your Highness?"

"No. Go on." Hamoud left. "Was your flight smooth?" Mansour had flown in this morning from Riyadh, the capital, five hundred miles east.

"Yes, Your Highness, *hamdulillah*" — thanks be to God.

"Good. Tell me you've found these devils." Mansour shook his head.

"Tell me you've found them, Mansour."

"We will find them. In the meantime, may I report what we have discovered so far?" He didn't wait for an answer but pushed ahead. "We've discovered the identities of eight of the bombers. I regret to tell you that they are all Saudi. The four who attacked the drinking establishment in Bahrain, they were from the Najd" — the high Saudi desert in the center of the Arabian Peninsula. "They disappeared a few months ago. We're speaking with their fathers to determine where they might have trained. So far, all the fathers insist that they had no idea what the boys were planning. The local clerics say the same. It's disappointing that they aren't being more honest. If we must, we'll bring them in for interviews in Riyadh" — a reference to the *mukhabarat* headquarters.

"And the other four?"

"All from Taif" — a town in western Saudi Arabia, not far from Jeddah. "The same situation. None on our watch lists."

"You have found nothing."

"Whoever's training these men is canny. These attacks were months in the making. Years. It will take time to unravel this."

"Why do you waste my time if you have found nothing?"

"You asked me to come here from Riyadh, Your Highness." A hint of ice crept into Mansour's voice. "I assure you that all of us are frustrated. We won't let these criminals attack your name. You are the state, Abdullah. We live and die with you —"

"Spare me this recital." Abdullah was fully awake now, his anger quickening him. "If you live and die with me, you won't live much longer —"

"Then let me say. We all want these terrorists caught."

"I wish I were certain of that."

"What are you implying, Abdullah?"

"I am your king, Mansour." Abdullah knew he needed to control himself, hide his anger and distrust from his nephew. But he couldn't. His weakness rubbed him raw. He upended the silver coffeepot, sent a gusher of black liquid onto the antique Persian rug that stretched across the study. "Never again shall you take that tone with me."

Mansour looked sidelong at Miteb and shook his head. Abdullah pushed on, compounding his mistake. *Someday you'll be old,* he thought. *Someday you'll know.*

"I am your king. Say it."

"You are my king."

"Go back to Riyadh, then, and find these men. Whoever they are. Foreign or Saudi. We will cut off their heads and let the world know that we don't stand for this. Do you understand me?"

"Yes, Your Highness."

Miteb left with Mansour but promised to return in a few minutes. In the meantime, Abdullah's steward cleared away the coffeepot and wiped up the stain. Abdullah ignored him until he finished.

"Shall I bring another pot, Your Highness?"

"No."

"Something else?"

"Leave me, Hamoud. Now." Hamoud left. Abdullah sat alone in his study. He wanted to call Saeed, Mansour's father, and scream at him about his son. But he knew losing his temper again would further weaken his position. He would have to go back to Riyadh. He couldn't stay here. He needed to talk to the other senior princes. The conversations would be unpleasant. They'd burn a hole in his stomach. He shouldn't need to beg for support.

But in his heart he knew he'd brought this disaster on himself.

The door opened. Miteb returned. "You mustn't do that, Abdullah," he said without preamble.

"These jihadis, they call us apostates, brother. The world is upside down when these men say they speak for our religion. They won't frighten me. Not in this world or the next. They think the Prophet, peace be upon Him, wants them to attack their own people? I'll pluck out their eyes and pour salt down their throats —"

"My brother. Everything you say, it's true. But we have something else to talk about."

"Don't bother me with this."

"These matters can't wait anymore."

"*You* dare to tell *me* what waits?"

"Abdullah. Listen now. Yes, you to me. You can't treat your nephew this way. He was furious. He told me, 'I am forty-eight years old. I have my own sons and grandsons, and that man insults me like a child. No more, Miteb.' He wouldn't even use your name, Abdullah. 'That man' was all he'd say. And do you know that I was actually glad to hear his anger? Because if he's still willing to complain, it means that he may still be loyal. If he held his tongue to me, it would mean he'd given up on you and was nursing his anger in private."

"You think Mansour is loyal? You're a fool. It's exactly the opposite. He speaks that way only because he knows that if he didn't complain, you'd suspect him."

"If you don't think he's loyal, why do you bring him here?"

"I bring him here because he expects it of me. Just as I know he'll lie to me."

"And I suppose losing your temper is part of your act, too. Come on, my brother. I saw your face when he told you that they hadn't found anything. It wasn't an act."

"Let Mansour complain. Mansour is nothing."

"Mansour is something. And Saeed is more than something."

"I treat Mansour like a child because he is a child. He thinks I don't see that he's mocking me. I should have rid myself of him years ago."

Miteb reached out and squeezed the king's hand. "Abdullah — you can no more rid yourself of Mansour than of these walls."

"They wait for me to die. My brothers and my nephews. So be it. When Allah calls me, put my corpse on the pyre and light the flames and let my ashes join the desert. It makes no difference. Mansour, Saeed, they can say whatever they like. Khalid" — Abdullah's eldest son — "will be king."

"He is your son, but that doesn't mean he'll be king."

"He will be king."

"Say it as many times as you like, but words alone won't make it so. You've stirred the scorpions with this. You know our brothers don't agree. They say the system has worked and why change it?"

The full name of the first Saudi king was Abdul-Aziz ibn Abd al-Rahman ibn Faisal al-Saud. Abdul-Aziz, son of Abd, son of Rahman, son of Faisal, son of Saud. In its length, the name highlighted the importance that Arabs placed on their lineage. Abdul-Aziz had died in 1953, twenty-one years after uniting the Arabian peninsula. He had named the new nation after his own family: the Kingdom of Saudi Arabia.

Today, Saudi Arabia was the only nation still named after a single family. Its Basic Law decreed that "the rulers of the country shall be from among the sons of the founder,

King Abdul-Aziz . . . and their descendants." For almost sixty years, Abdul-Aziz's own sons had been the only rulers the Kingdom had known. Under the system, which had been formalized after Abdul-Aziz's death, the crown passed from half-brother to half-brother, usually following birth order. Because Abdul-Aziz had sired at least forty-three boys by more than a dozen wives between 1900 and 1947, the Kingdom had no shortage of potential rulers. As head of the Defense Ministry, Saeed was generally considered the most likely candidate to succeed Abdullah.

But a year before, Abdullah had secretly told his brothers that after his death, he expected his own son Khalid to be named the next king. So far, the brothers had resisted that demand. For now, Abdullah's successor remained unchosen.

"Khalid is ready," Abdullah said now.

"More ready than Mansour? Or the rest of his cousins?"

"You compare Mansour to my son?"

"It's not only Mansour. Saeed has waited his turn. And our other brothers. And after that, a whole new generation."

"Stand up, my brother."

Miteb pushed himself off the couch,

wheezing, his breath unsteady.

"You want to be king? Is that what this is? Then go ahead. Slake your thirst. Take my crown."

"My brother, don't slander me." Miteb sat down heavily on the couch, which creaked under his bulk. "I know my age. Unlike you. I tell anyone who asks, I don't want the crown."

"Then help me. Tell our brothers. Khalid is ready."

"Abdullah, you don't know how alone you are."

"I listen to my brothers —"

"Your brothers *beg* you to stop. And you refuse. Saeed wants you gone, yes. But the others don't want to oppose you. Because they love you."

"And don't love Saeed."

"Because you've ruled wisely. Until this foolishness. But Khalid is only fifty. You're asking Mansour and all our sons to give up any chance at the throne."

"Only Khalid is strong enough to move against these rejectionists who set off these bombs. These men who want girls to marry their uncles."

"Let me ask you, Abdullah. Has Khalid ever told you he wants this?"

"Of course." Though Abdullah was lying.

The only time he'd ever discussed his plans with Khalid, Khalid had said something like, *If that's what you want, father.* An answer that had been enough for Abdullah. He'd never asked again.

"Admit the truth, Abdullah. To yourself, if not me. Khalid may be a good king, and he may not. None of us know. Khalid is the flesh of your flesh, and that's why you want him to rule. Drop this plan or you'll return us to the days of Ali and Uthman" — seventh-century Muslim leaders who engaged in bloody power struggles after the death of Muhammad.

"Not as long as he has the National Guard."

In Saudi Arabia the force known as the National Guard functioned almost as a second army. The Guard trained and ran separately from the regular Saudi military and existed mainly to protect the royal family from the threat of a coup. Its soldiers were mostly Bedouins whose tribes were considered loyal to the family. Abdullah had controlled the Guard for forty years, long before he became king. A few months before, he had turned the force over to his son.

"You think that giving him the Guard makes him safe, Abdullah. But it's the opposite. It makes the other princes think they have to take power by force." Miteb pulled himself off the couch, sat on the ottoman beside Abdullah.

"Say what you mean, Miteb. You think that our family is working with these terrorists. Against me. And my son. You wish that I reward them for that? For betraying me? Attacking Riyadh? Never, Miteb. The snakes in my court, I'll cast them out. It's time. Time and past time."

"Who, Abdullah? Who are the snakes? You don't even know."

"How can I know? They come to me with their fine words and their smiles, and promise me their love."

"Because you've isolated yourself. Staying in this palace alone. Making the rest of us fly from Riyadh to see you. The ones who love you and believe that you're right, the system must change, they're frightened. Those that oppose you, they're growing more bold. I don't know if you can stop them anymore. You surely can't trust the *mukhabarat*."

"There's always the Guard."

"Promise me you and Khalid won't use the Guard. If you try, then the army will interfere and there will be war."

"I promise you only this, Miteb. My son

will be king. Leave me if you wish."

The two men sat in silence for a minute that stretched to five and ten. Finally Miteb knelt at his brother's feet, his joints popping audibly. He lifted Abdullah's hand and kissed it. "You're a fat old fool. But I can't leave you now."

"Because you know Khalid should be king."

"Enough of Khalid. I'm your brother, and I've always done what you asked, and we're both too old to change. If this is what you want, I'll help. Maybe somehow I can convince the others. But we've got to keep the Guard out of it."

Abdullah stood and pulled Miteb up, and the two old men hugged and swayed back and forth, each braced against the other's bulk, aged sumo wrestlers in long white cloaks.

"Miteb, my friend." But even so, Abdullah felt the darkness creeping close. For the briefest moment, he wondered whether he ought to give up, let Saeed have the crown. And after Saeed, the next generation of al-Sauds could fight among themselves. But he shook his head — *No, no* — and opened his eyes. He wouldn't let the darkness have him yet.

CHAPTER 6

NORTH CONWAY, NEW HAMPSHIRE

"What happened then?"

"I'll tell you in the morning."

Anne arranged herself around Wells, her breasts touching his back, her nose in the crook of his shoulder. "Come on, out with it." She tugged his ear.

"Then . . . then he took off. Sprinted all the way to Montego, jumped on a cruise ship. He's probably having cocktails with some honeymooners as we speak."

"Idiot."

"I told him who I was. He'd never seen me before. He looked me up and down, didn't say anything. I should have worried he was going for a weapon, but I didn't. He walked up the stairs to his bedroom. I followed him. He wasn't running, and neither was I. He reached under his bed, and then I did start to wonder, but he came up with a suitcase. Unzipped it and started packing. Like he was going on vacation."

142

"What I want to know is how he looked. What he said."

Around them, the old house settled, timbers creaking like a sailboat on the open ocean. Tonka roused herself from the rug at the foot of Anne's bed, looked around, sighed, and lay down again.

"He asked me if Janice told me where he was. I didn't answer. Then he got mad. He seemed angrier that she'd broken the vow she'd made on their son's grave than anything else. He started ranting about her. I cooled him off."

"How'd you do that, John?"

"I expressed my dismay. I'm very persuasive, you know." In fact, Wells had given Keith "Eddie" Robinson what kids in junior high called a swirly. Picked him up, dunked his head in the toilet. Lucky for Robinson, the water was clean. "After he was calm, I sat him down and told him he would have to confess to everything, no trial. I told him he owed that much to Janice."

"And what would you have done if he said no?"

"He didn't say no."

"But if he did?"

"Then I would have threatened to tell the dealers he was buying from that he was working for the DEA."

He knew that she wanted to ask him if he would have followed through on the threat. The answer was probably. Robinson was overdue for a reckoning. But she stayed quiet, and after a few seconds Wells went on.

"How he looked? He looked relieved. Maybe not relieved but tired. Like he had been getting ready for somebody to knock on his door. I asked him why he called Janice, and he said he was lonely. He showed me in his closet he had cash, maybe twenty-five thousand dollars in hundreds and twenties. He had another passport, too, a Mexican one that said his name was Eduardo Márquez. He said it was real, that he'd paid somebody at the Mexican embassy in Kingston."

"But he didn't want to go anywhere else."

"I guess not. He said he could have stayed hidden a lot longer. With that passport, he could have gone to Cuba or somewhere in Southeast Asia where there are enough white people that he wouldn't get noticed. But he said it was wearing on him, being alone, never telling anyone who he really was. He said he was scared to death of prison, but that living this way was prison, too. I think there's something else. I think he might be sick. He had all kinds of pill bottles in his bathroom. But when I asked him, he denied it. And choked up. Which was weird, because aside from that, he wouldn't stop talking. But all the things he said, he certainly didn't say he was sorry."

"Did you think he would?"

"I hoped he would."

"You know, I've arrested I don't know how many. Eight years — say, one a week — that's, ah, eight times fifty. Four hundred, give or take. Of course nothing like this. But serious stuff. Domestic violence, assault. Rape. Two murders. And I've never heard a genuine apology. Ever. It's not in these guys." She let go of him, pushed herself away. "I have to say, I don't like what you did, John."

He turned toward her. Her eyes were intense on his. "Say again?"

"You should have just called the FBI. Done it the right way. You almost killed somebody down there."

"He was a coke dealer."

"It's a matter of time before you hurt somebody who's completely innocent —"

"You wanted the story. You got the story. I'm going to sleep."

"God forbid anyone question your judgment."

"I hate to tell you, Anne, but Keith Robinson isn't some DUI you Breathalyze on Main Street."

"And I hate to tell you, John, but you're a grade-A asshole."

"I'm sorry. I shouldn't have said that."

"You believe it, though. Push comes to shove, you think I have no right to express any opinion on this."

Wells knew he should apologize, tell Anne the truth. He'd blown up because he was worried she was right. He had refused to involve the FBI for no better reason than his anger at the CIA and Duto. Over the years, he'd lost his moorings one by one. His wife and child. His parents. Then Jennifer Exley, his lover. Then his faith. He still believed in Islam, but how could he claim to be part of the *umma,* the community of believers? He prayed sometimes, but almost always in private, rarely in mosques. Faith was hard to sustain that way. Only his identity as a CIA agent had remained. But now he'd quit.

He believed he'd made the right choice in leaving. Even so. He'd severed his last connection. He was completely alone. An amnesiac without the consolation of forgetfulness. He knew who he was, what he'd done. After so much violence, killing came to him naturally. He'd always imagined that he could take off the killer's mask as he wished. But he feared the mask had become his face.

He could have said some of this to Anne. Or all of it. Could have and should have. Instead he closed his eyes. "You've got every right to express your opinion," he said. He hated the words even as he spoke them. He sounded like a lawyer. A lousy one.

"I can't even start to imagine what you're thinking," she said. "Are you angry?"

"I'm not angry."

"Are you happy I'm challenging you, then?" He was silent. "Do you have any emotions at all, John?"

"I'll leave tomorrow if you want."

She put her arms around him. "I don't want you to *leave*. I just want to understand you a tiny bit. It's like the longer you stay here, the less I understand you. And that's awful."

He heard her breathing quicken and opened his eyes. She was sitting up, her back to him. *Women.* She left the room and walked downstairs. A few minutes later, he heard the teakettle squealing. She came back holding a cup and lay beside him and put her hand on his shoulder.

"This is why the others left, isn't it? Your wife and the one from the CIA."

"Maybe. My wife, we got divorced because I went undercover. And Exley, my fiancée, someone hurt her and I wanted to find out who did it and she didn't want me to."

"You wanted revenge. She asked you to stay away. And you ignored her."

They lay in the dark and the minutes unrolled, a black carpet stretching to infinity. At this hour, North Conway was as still as a chimney with no fire. He put his arms around her, and she didn't fight him.

"I meant it. If you want, I'll leave tomorrow."

"Please. Have you looked at the quote-unquote eligible bachelors in North Conway? Slim pickings. Anyway, I see hope for you yet. You wonder if all this violence has destroyed your core. And I'm telling you that it hasn't."

"I hope so."

Her laugh was music. "There you go. 'I hope so.' On the John Wells scale, that counts as a soul-opening revelation. You're gonna be okay, John."

He fell asleep feeling something close to peace.

He woke alone, his cell phone ringing. A blocked number.

"John Wells." The voice was soft, cultured,

European. Immaculate as marble. The past was tugging him again. First Keith Robinson. Now Pierre Kowalski. Kowalski was a Swiss arms dealer, a gleefully amoral man who had made a fortune off miserable little wars that no one cared about.

"Pierre."

"I hear you're at liberty. I might have something for you. To supplement that government pension of yours. Nadia, you know, she still mentions you." Nadia was Kowalski's lover, a model, tall and blue-eyed, the most beautiful woman Wells had ever seen. "She's waiting for you to make your fortune."

"Who told you I quit?"

"Word gets around. But I hear also that you're having a hard time staying away."

The intimacy in Kowalski's voice infuriated Wells. As did the fact that Kowalski still had sources at Langley. He shouldn't have known that Wells had left, and he definitely shouldn't have known about Keith Robinson. "Do you think we're friends, Pierre?"

"I would never make that mistake. Your friends have a short life expectancy."

"Soon I'll have no one at all to counsel me. Then I'll decide to settle old scores."

Kowalski sighed. "Please let me know

when that day comes so I can hire more bodyguards. In any case. A friend asked me for a recommendation. Someone who operates with absolute discretion and certainty. Someone not connected to any national organization. Someone who speaks Arabic. I thought of you."

"I have to tell you, if you want an assassination, I'm going to be seriously upset. People keep asking me to kill other people."

"I see. And that makes you angry."

"So angry I could kill somebody, yes."

"Now you are being ironic, Monsieur Wells. It doesn't suit you."

"Do you know what I'm thinking right now? How much I'd like to make you strip naked and pull an oxcart in the middle of Zurich. Give kids rides."

"That wouldn't be much fun. For me or the *kinder.* But all this is a digression, and these international calls are expensive. So let me tell you, this job, it's not an assassination. Undercover work."

"Be specific."

"It's connected to recent events."

The terrorist attacks in the Gulf, Wells guessed. "Who am I working for? And what do they want from me?"

Kowalski was silent. Then: "As for the first question, the answer is complicated. As for the second, I truly don't know."

"Then forget it."

"These people, they will pay you one million dollars just to meet. Say the word and they'll send a plane for you."

That's insane, Wells thought. And then said aloud: "That's insane. Tell me, Pierre. Are they paying you for this introduction?"

"No. But the person who asked for help, I've known him a long time. And — you know I don't care much about these things — but he's on what you would call the right side."

"You know what people say about things that sound too good to be true. One million dollars. To work for the right side."

Kowalski was silent, letting the hook dangle. Wells could truly say he didn't care about money. Yet the thought of being paid a million dollars for a day's work was hard to resist. "All right," he said. "Tell your friends I'm in."

"Oui."

"But I want the money first."

"Spoken like a true mercenary. I approve."

That night Wells told Anne about the offer.

"And who is this guy, Kowalski?"

"Swiss. Lives in Zurich. An arms dealer."

"You're friends?"

Wells shook his head.

"But you trust him."

"Betraying me isn't in his interest."

"Why do it? If the money doesn't matter."

"For someone who doesn't understand me, you understand me pretty well."

"I know what *doesn't* drive you. And I know you're going over there. I can almost feel the energy coming off you. You were like this before you went to Jamaica. You can't wait."

It's the only time I feel really alive, Wells thought. Even unspoken, the words felt like a betrayal. She took his face in her hands, kissed him lightly, her lips just touching his. "I'm not going to say anything dumb, like 'Stay alive,' but stay alive, please."

Wells put his arms around her, pulled her close, kissed her until her mouth opened to him. And without another word he picked her up and carried her to her — their — bed.

CHAPTER 7

NEW YORK CITY

At Kennedy Airport, the limousine turned off the access road short of the main terminals and stopped at a gatehouse whose black-painted sign announced "General Aviation." The driver passed over his license and the gate rose. The limo swung right along a cyclone fence and stopped at an unmarked concrete building.

Wells stepped out of the limo, blinking in the sunlight and wishing for sunglasses. A tall man with close-cropped gray hair emerged from the building, walked toward Wells, extended his hand. "Captain Smith. You must be Mr. Wells. Pleasure to meet you, sir." His accent was English, surprising Wells, who had somehow expected an ex-flyboy.

"Captain Smith. Not Captain Jones."

"Yes, sir. Smith, not Jones. Sorry to disturb you, but I must ask. Are you armed?"

"No." Kowalski had specified no weapons.

"Your passport, please."

Wells handed it over. His real passport. His real name. He wasn't used to traveling under his real name, wasn't used to being a civilian. Smith flipped through it, handed it back. "Do you have any electronic gear with you? Laptop, BlackBerry, phone?"

"Just my phone."

"I'd like to keep it, sir. Only for the duration of the flight."

Wells handed over his phone, a cheap silver Samsung. "This way, please." Smith led Wells to a giant twin-engine passenger jet.

"*That's* my ride?"

"Correct, sir."

"Please stop calling me sir. Is anyone else coming?"

"No, sir."

The jet was a Boeing 777. Normally it would hold about three hundred passengers. "Where are we going, captain?"

"I'm not meant to give you that information until we're airborne, sir."

Three flight attendants waited at the top of the jetway. All women. They wore demure jackets and knee-length skirts, but all three could have modeled on their days off. Wells supposed that anyone who could afford this jet could afford whatever crew he wanted.

"Mr. Wells," the prettiest attendant said. "I'm Joanna. Please come this way."

At the center of the jet, four leather chairs were arranged before a fifty-inch television and a fully stocked bar. Despite its opulence, the interior was studiously anonymous. No books or flags gave away the name or nationality of the owner. The exit signs were in English. The jet seemed to be part of a fleet. In that case, the pool of possible owners shrank even further. The Russian and Chinese governments were the most obvious suspects. But Wells's recent adventures hadn't made him friends in Moscow or Beijing. The Saudi or Kuwaiti royal families. Maybe the French, though in that case this jet ought to be an Airbus. Maybe an oil company.

Nobody very nice. The short answer was that nobody very nice owned a plane like this.

"Mr. Wells," the attendant said, "we have a video-on-demand library with six thousand movies. There's also a live satellite feed. Whatever you'd like to watch." She gave Wells a smile that could be described only as saucy. "If you'd rather sleep, the bedrooms are this way." She nodded toward the front of the cabin.

"And we'll be in the air about ten hours?"

"Less than eight, sir."

Information, of a sort. Eight hours meant Western Europe or South America. "Thank you."

The jet took off fifteen minutes later. An hour after that, Captain Smith walked into the cabin. "Sir. You asked our destination. It's Nice." As in France. "We get in around eight in the morning local time."

"Who's waiting for me?"

"I don't know. Truly."

"When a man feels the need to say truly, he's usually lying. And I told you about calling me sir."

"Yes, Mr. Wells. In any case. We're expecting a smooth flight. But if you need medicine to sleep, Joanna can help."

The bedroom was as pointlessly luxurious as the rest of the jet. Wells lay on the white cotton sheets and closed his eyes. But he couldn't sleep. He found himself thinking of Evan, his son. He wondered how he could be so strong and so weak at the same time. Death hardly scared him, but the idea of picking up a telephone and calling his own blood had paralyzed him for years. Evan was a teenager now, old enough to decide for himself whether to allow Wells in his life. Wells supposed he feared that Evan

156

would reject him, leaving him even more alone. But he had to take that chance. He needed to drop his guard and tell the boy that he'd never forgotten him, not in Afghanistan or anywhere else.

Just as soon as this mission was over. How many times had he made that promise to himself? Too many. He closed his eyes and lay in the dark as the jet crossed the sea.

In the morning, the coffee was strong and black, and the landing was smooth. The jet banked low over the Mediterranean before swinging into the airport at Nice, offering a priceless view of the waves crashing into the Côte d'Azur. Priceless, indeed. In 2008, a villa near here had sold for five hundred million euros, close to one billion dollars. Wells had entered a land of wealth beyond comprehension. He wondered again who had summoned him, and why. As he left the plane, Captain Smith gave him a perfectly correct smile, neither too large nor too small, neither familiar nor dismissive. "Beats coach," Wells said.

"My pleasure," the captain said. Wells supposed that the crew never broke character, never acknowledged that they and the passengers they served were members of the same species.

Outside, a breeze whipped off the Mediterranean. A French immigration agent stood on the runway beside a white Renault minivan. Beside him, a second man wore a blue sport coat that flapped open to reveal a shoulder holster. Neither looked happy to see Wells. Their hostility was a relief after the paid-for, painted-on smiles of the plane's crew.

The agent waved Wells into the Renault, and they sped to the main terminal building. In a windowless office, the agent scanned Wells's passport. "Are you carrying any weapons, Mr. Wells?" That question again. Wells shook his head. "Raise your arms," the man in the blue sport coat said. Wells did and was rewarded with a thorough pat-down before the agent handed him back his passport. "Welcome to France, then. Jean will show you to your car."

Jean, the man in the sport coat, led Wells in silence through the airport's back halls, windowless corridors lined with banged-up baggage carts. Two men in brown uniforms smoked under a poster that warned, *"Défense de fumer."* They reached a door with a simple push-button combination lock. Jean keyed in the code, pulled it open, waved Wells through. They were near the front entrance of the arrivals level. A black

BMW 760 waited at the curb, two men inside. Wells admired the precision of the handoff. Even if he had known he was being taken to Nice, even if he had somehow arranged for a weapon at the airport, he couldn't have picked it up. He hadn't been alone since Kennedy. And whoever was on the other side had plenty of juice with the French government.

Wells slipped into the rear seat of the 760, leaned against the cushioned leather. No point in asking. He'd have answers soon enough.

They drove along the A8, the highway called La Provençale, which tracked the coast to the Italian border. The BMW's driver sliced through the heavy morning traffic as if he were playing a video game in which the only penalty for an accident was the loss of a turn. Wells loved to speed, but this man was at a different level. "You ever race F1?" he said. He didn't expect an answer.

"He never made F1," the man in the front passenger seat said. "Only F2."

"Where are we going?"

No answer. Wells tried to turn on his phone but found the battery had been drained. Nice touch. West of Nice, the sedan swung onto the coast road, two narrow lanes that rose and fell along the hills. They turned back toward Nice. The precautions seemed pointless to Wells. He had no phone, no gun, not even a change of clothes. The tactician in him admired the way these men had cut him off from any possible support.

Outside Nice, they turned back onto the A8, running east this time, and fast, the driver's hands high and relaxed on the wheel. Another racing clinic. Wells would have liked to ask for tips. On an overpass ten miles east of Nice, the sedan pulled over.

"Get out."

Wells didn't argue, just stepped out and watched the BMW pull away. He didn't bother getting the plate number. The last twelve hours had left him sick of tradecraft. He wouldn't have long to wait, he guessed. After going to so much trouble to make sure he was sterile, they'd be foolish to leave him alone for long.

Sure enough, a stretch Mercedes Maybach pulled up almost before he finished the thought. Black? Check. Tinted windows? Check. Run-flat tires and armored doors? Check and double-check. Wells raised a thumb, leaned toward the window. "Anywhere east, I'll take it. I can chip in for gas. Cool?"

The door swung open.

■ ■ ■ ■

The man in the backseat had a heavy square face and wore a white *ghutra* low on his forehead. A neatly trimmed goatee covered his jutting chin like black-dyed moss. From a distance, he might have passed for sixty-five. Up close, his face betrayed his age. His skin was as creased as month-old newspaper. Under his thick black glasses his eyes were rheumy and yellow. Wells didn't recognize him.

Then he did. Abdullah, the king of Saudi Arabia. The richest man in the world. Everything made sense. The overwhelming security. The one-million-dollar fee. The ridiculous opulence of the plane. Everything except the question of why he was here.

"Salaam aleikum," the man in the front passenger seat said. He turned to face Wells. He was almost as old as Abdullah, with swollen cheeks and a quiet, wheezy voice. Wells guessed he had heart trouble.

"Aleikum salaam."

"You are John Wells."

"Nam."

"I am Miteb bin Abdul-Aziz. This is my brother, the Custodian of the Two Holy

Mosques" — the official title of the Saudi kings.

"Prince Miteb. King Abdullah. I'm honored to meet you."

"Please excuse our precautions. They're for our protection, and yours, too." Miteb's Arabic was the most perfect that Wells had ever heard, a smooth stream. Wells's own Arabic was rough and visceral.

"I understand." Though Wells didn't. The king's security team should have been Saudi, not European. And this meeting should have happened at the Saudi embassy in Paris, or in Riyadh. Did the king mistrust his own security detail?

"You speak Arabic," Abdullah said, his first words to Wells. He looked Wells over, a cool appraisal, then broke off, coughed into his hand, a wet, soft murmur. He wiped his mouth with a white handkerchief embroidered with gold thread. When Abdullah put the kerchief away, Wells thought he saw flecks of blood on the fabric. Wells wondered how long Abdullah had left.

"Yes. But I'm American."

"And a spy."

"A retired spy."

"Do spies ever retire?"

"Do kings?"

"My brother Saud, he retired. Because he

was weak. From whiskey. It fogged his eyes and his mind. Made him too weak to rule. And too weak to fight when we told him he wasn't our king anymore. That we could no longer trust him with our fate." The king looked at the front seat, as if waiting for his brother to explain further. But Miteb stayed silent, and Abdullah returned his focus to Wells.

"The fate of the king is the fate of the people. You don't understand this. No American can. We told Saud to leave our land. Go wherever he wanted. Here. Switzerland. We sent him into exile, and he accepted our decision like a child. Oh, he whined, but he never once raised a hand to save himself. He knew he was weak. Do I look weak to you? Answer me, *Ameriki*."

"If you weren't weak, I wouldn't be here."

"You don't lie? Not even to a king?"

"Especially not to a king."

The Maybach turned up a narrow road hemmed by walled villas on both sides. Abdullah closed his eyes. He seemed too old for this, whatever *this* was. "Some of my family is against me," he said, his eyes still closed, his voice low. "I look into their hearts. They have turned." He coughed. His voice vibrated. "They're feckless. Spoiled. All of us are to blame. We drown in our own luxuries. We thought that it was Allah who left us the oil, but I know better now —"

"Abdullah —" Miteb said.

"Hush, brother. My nephews, they'll agree to anything the clerics say to keep their power." Abdullah opened his eyes, waved at the hills around them. "All Gaul is divided into three parts —"

"Caesar —" Wells said.

"Of course Caesar." He dug his fingers into Wells's arm, surprising Wells with his strength. "You think I never learned about Caesar? You think I'm too old to remember? The kingdom is mine, and it will be my son's. No one but his. Do you understand?"

Had old age destroyed Abdullah's reason? Wells wasn't sure. Everything he'd said made a sort of sense, though not as much as Wells would have liked. *It will be my son's. No one but his.* Wells understood that much, anyway.

Abdullah leaned toward Wells. He exuded a bitter mix of coffee and stomach bile. He smelled like a rusty V-8 burning oil from a leaky cylinder. He smelled like an old man who'd scare the grandkids if they got too close. He grabbed Wells's cheek and looked Wells over like an angry lover.

"Ameriki." Abdullah relaxed his grip. He leaned back and grunted as though a stone

164

had fallen on his chest. After a few moments, his breathing slowed. His eyes opened. He touched his goatee as if seeing Wells for the first time. "You've come a long way to see us." His voice was smooth and low, all trace of his madness gone. "Do you know why you're here?"

"I assume it's related to what happened last week, the attacks."

"Yes and no. I don't have long to live, Mr. Wells." Abdullah spoke with an authority Wells wouldn't have expected from a man who'd seemed so unhinged a minute before. "I've lived my life. My bones grind like beetles. The doctors say they can fix me, but they're lying. One day you'll be old, and you'll cough as if your soul means to escape through your mouth, and you'll understand. But for now I still breathe. And before I die, I want to lay my kingdom on its foundation. Do you see?"

"I see you want me to help your son become the next king."

The king waved at Miteb and settled back in his seat, as if this portion of the conversation was beneath him.

"We need someone from the outside to help us," Miteb said. "Someone unconnected with our security forces. A private citizen. Someone Muslim. Someone who can handle the most difficult situations."

"Your enemies are within your family?"

"Yes, but not only. We should never have let the radicals and the clerics get so powerful," Miteb said. "We thought we would give them a few tokens, let them send men to Afghanistan, they'd be satisfied. But these men, once you give them power, you never get it back, not without war."

"Your brothers don't agree."

"Our brothers, our nephews. Some believe what the Wahhabis preach. They want jihad. But the middle, most of them, they just want the oil to flow. Or to gain power. To become ministers, have planes and palaces."

"Their blood is thin," Abdullah said. "When I was a child, there was only desert. To both ends of the sky. We were proud to be Bedouin. We knew we lived where no one else could. In all of Arabia, there were a few hundred thousand of us. Now Riyadh has five millions all by itself. We've forgotten the desert. And it's forgotten us. It won't have us anymore."

"Abdullah —" Miteb said, apparently nervous that his brother would erupt again.

"Some of my brothers, nephews, they don't care about their people. They have their accounts in Swiss banks. Whatever side wins, they'll give their loyalty."

"But I don't understand. Who's on the other side?" Wells was genuinely confused. "These terrorists, it's not like they can be king."

"No. But if Khalid isn't king, it will probably be Saeed. And Saeed will give the jihadis what they want, as long as they don't interfere with him or try to take the oil. He doesn't care if women have to stay covered, if the Shia have no rights. I think he's working with them already."

"Why don't you arrest him, then? You're still king. You have the *mukhabarat*" — the secret police.

"No. Mansour, Saeed's son, is the head of the *muk*. They belong to him."

"If we trusted them, we wouldn't be in this car," Miteb said.

"On the Côte d'Azur." Wells was tired. And not from jet lag. When he looked at Miteb and Abdullah, he saw Vinny Duto and the spy chiefs at the top of the Washington bureaucracy. Using Wells to fight battles that only they could win. "You talk about clerics and jihadis. But this, it's about power. Nothing else. Abdullah, sooner or later he's going to die. Probably sooner."

"You dare speak to me this way?"

"Every king needs his fool, and I guess that's me. So let's call it like it is. The king

167

is dead, long live the king. When that sad day comes, you want Junior to take over. But your brothers don't agree. Especially Saeed." Wells wondered if anyone had ever lectured Abdullah this way. Probably not. So be it. He would fly commercial home.

"Only Khalid has the strength to fight the clerics," Miteb said.

"With you as his closest adviser, no doubt."

The king twisted toward Wells. "You think I want to waste my last days spitting clever words with you? You Americans are all the same. Too cynical and not cynical enough. The poison in my land, it's real."

Wells almost laughed. These two old men, asking him to help them save their people from religious repression. As if their family hadn't ruled Saudi Arabia for eighty years. Abdullah, sitting in a three-hundred-thousand-dollar car and complaining that luxury had poisoned his family. "No wonder you couldn't meet me in Riyadh," Wells said.

"Saeed will set our country back a generation," Miteb said.

"Saeed has a thousand eyes, and they all watch me," Abdullah said.

"I'll bet he's got sons, too."

"His sons are nothing. They scuttle through my kingdom like crabs."

168

"Your kingdom. I suspect our ambassador is too polite to tell you so, but Americans don't like kings much, Abdullah. Not for two hundred years."

"You don't even know what we'd like," Miteb said. "Or what we're willing to pay. I promise, it's more than you can imagine."

Wells was angry now. He should have guessed they would eventually dangle a fortune. "First you appeal to my better instincts. Then you offer cash. Next you'll promise me a woman. The oldest game there is. At Langley, they call it MICE. Money, ideology, compromise, ego. Will you drop me at the airport, or do I have to catch a cab?"

Abdullah leaned toward the driver. "Take him to the airport, be done with it."

"Please," Miteb said. The word seemed directed at both Abdullah and Wells. "We have a villa for you. At the Eden-Roc. Relax this afternoon, and we'll talk tomorrow morning. If we can't reach agreement, you can fly home as you like."

The Maybach crested a hill, giving Wells a view of the smooth, blue waters of the Mediterranean. He hadn't heard of the Eden-Roc, but he guessed its villa would have the same view, or better. And truth be told, his curiosity was piqued. He still had no idea what these two octogenarians wanted from him. He could do worse than spend the night.

CHAPTER 8
BEKAA VALLEY, LEBANON

Hezbollah, Party of God.

Hashish, god of partiers.

The Bekaa Valley has both.

A rocky, hilly plateau that lies between Lebanon's coastal mountains and a lower range on the Syrian border, the Bekaa has had a fierce reputation for centuries. Like Napa Valley, its hot, dry summers and cool winters make it ideal for growing grapes. Unlike Napa Valley, it is controlled by Hezbollah, an Iranian-backed Muslim group that aims to destroy Israel.

Ahmad Bakr hated Israel as much as Hezbollah did. Even so, Bakr did not enjoy coming to the Bekaa. Bakr was Saudi, and like most Saudis, he was a Sunni Muslim. Hezbollah's members were Shia, followers of the other major branch of Islam.

Both types of Muslims agreed that the Quran was the word of Allah. But unlike the Sunni, the Shia revered early Muslim rulers as "imams," nearly godlike figures. They eagerly awaited the return of the twelfth imam, whose arrival would herald the End of Days. To conservative Sunnis like Bakr, the Shia belief in the twelfth imam amounted to idol worship — a serious offense against Islam.

But when he was in Lebanon, Bakr kept his views to himself. He was simply being practical. In the Bekaa, Hezbollah served as judge, jury, and executioner. And Bakr ran a jihadi training camp in the Bekaa that needed the group's approval to exist.

To get that approval, Bakr had met nine months earlier with a Hezbollah general at a farm near Baalbek, the dusty town that served as the group's headquarters. A friendly Saudi intelligence agent arranged the meeting. "I can guarantee you safe passage," the agent said. "After that, it's up to you."

The next day, Bakr flew to Beirut. As he'd been instructed, he rented a car and attached a red strip of tape to the trunk. He drove to Baalbek and parked in the lot beside the Roman ruins that loomed over the town. The site included the remnants of the Temple of Jupiter, a giant Roman shrine. The temple's columns stood seventy feet tall and were mounted on one-thousand-ton stone blocks. But the ruins left Bakr cold. To him, they were just another site for idol worship, like the golden-domed shrines in Iraq where the Shia buried their martyrs. He would have been happier if they were all blown to rubble.

A few minutes after he parked, a black Toyota 4Runner stopped beside him. A man in a long-sleeved black shirt and black pants knocked on his window. The man frisked him and waved him into the 4Runner. Bakr wondered if he'd be blindfolded, but no one seemed overly concerned. These men didn't need to protect themselves, not here. At-tacking Hezbollah in the Bekaa was a fool's errand. The Israelis had tried in 2006. Even with their planes and missiles, they hadn't touched the group's leaders. Hezbollah had come away from that war stronger than ever.

The Toyota headed north. A few minutes later, it turned east onto a rough dirt road with vineyards on both sides. The road dead-ended at a concrete wall that protected a massive beige house, three stories high, with balconies and turrets and a green Hezbollah flag flapping from a pole. A golden-domed mosque, a miniature version of the shrines in Iraq, stood beside the building. The 4Runner stopped at a black gate guarded by two militiamen. They saluted as the gate swung open.

The Hezbollah general was a small man with deep-set brown eyes. In his cream-colored shirt and gray slacks, he could have passed for a Beirut businessman, except for the long white scar that hooked around his neck. He had nearly died in a 1996 car bombing that had been blamed on both the Israelis and the Syrians. He sat on the house's back balcony, looking out over the garden, where an old man tended to scraggly tomato plants and a half-dozen lemon trees. "Coffee?"

"Please."

The general poured them both cups. The sun had disappeared, and the balcony was pleasantly warm. Aside from the scrape of the gardener's shovel on the soil, the house was silent.

"You've come a long way," the general said.

"Not so far. Thank you for seeing me." For the next few minutes, Bakr explained what he wanted. When he was finished, the general put a hand on Bakr's shoulder.

"Where will these men operate?"

"Not Iran or Lebanon."

"Of course not. And not Israel, either. Any

174

action against Israel comes on our own terms."

"Not Israel. Iraq." By the time Hezbollah found out he had lied, it wouldn't matter. "We have the same enemy there."

"Yes. Still, what you want, it's very expensive."

"Tell me."

"Two hundred thousand dollars."

Bakr had expected a much higher price. "That's fine."

"Every month."

These Shia thieves, Bakr thought. Two hundred thousand dollars a month for a broken-down farmhouse and land too rocky even to grow hashish? But he didn't have a choice. He planned to house as many as forty men, and he wanted room for practice with small arms and explosives, and maybe even more important, the high-powered rocket-propelled grenades that could defeat armored vehicles. In all, he figured he had to have at least two thousand acres with an absolute guarantee that he wouldn't be disturbed, which meant he needed government or quasi-government protection. The only other options were the Sudan or maybe the Algerian desert. Lonely, inhospitable places. The Bekaa would serve him far better, and Lebanon and the Kingdom were

175

connected by highways and nonstop flights.

"I can't afford that."

"How much, then?"

"A hundred thousand."

They compromised on one hundred fifty thousand dollars, and both sides kept the bargain. Bakr transferred the money faithfully each month, one numbered Swiss account to another. In turn, the militia never bothered his men and ensured that the handful of Lebanese police and army units in the Bekaa also stayed away.

The camp had taken three months to build. It included a one-story concrete barracks and dirt-covered berms where Bakr's men could practice wiring and blowing bombs without disturbing the neighbors. It lay in the barren northern end of the valley, on the western side, in the foothills of the Qornet as-Sawda, the highest mountain in Lebanon, more than ten thousand feet. At first glance, it didn't look like much, a couple buildings, a couple trailers. But with Al Qaeda's camps in Afghanistan long since obliterated, it was the largest and most sophisticated training center for jihad anywhere in the world.

Ahmad Bakr stood an inch short of six feet. Serving in the National Guard for eight years had given him a soldier's broad shoulders. He was relatively dark for a Saudi, more brown than tan. He'd grown up in Tathlith, a speck of a town in southwestern Saudi Arabia. Even within the Kingdom, the area was known for its religious fervor. Fifteen of the nineteen hijackers on September 11 were Saudi. Of those, eleven had come from the southwestern corner of the Kingdom.

The eldest son of a tribal chief, Bakr had been known for his religious fervor, even as a child. He had memorized the entire Quran before he turned twelve. He woke at dawn to pray and fasted each Ramadan without complaint.

The incident that sealed his belief came just before his seventeenth birthday. A few months before, his father had given him a Toyota Land Cruiser, a monstrous old beast with twenty-inch wheels and a raised chassis. He spent his days rumbling through the desert northeast of Tathlith. Nuri, his cousin and best friend, trailed behind him in a pickup. Bakr raced up the dunes, his wide tires kicking up clouds of sand, the Land Cruiser's engine growling. As he grew more experienced, he changed the Land Cruiser's gearing so he'd have even more torque at low speeds. He sought out the steepest dunes, ones that other boys avoided.

And then, in empty desert one hundred fifty kilometers from Tathlith, Bakr came upon the biggest dune he had ever seen, more than one hundred meters high. It soared out of the desert, its sand glistening. It changed color as Bakr rolled closer, darkening from neon white to a cooler clay. Bakr gunned his engine and rolled up the sandy ridge that formed the side of the dune. Halfway up, he stopped. Beyond this point, the ridge turned too steep to attack directly. To reach the top he would need to cut across the center of the dune, zigzagging across its face. Nuri pulled up beside him, jumped out of the pickup.

"It's too steep, cousin. And too soft. You'll get stuck."

"Then you'll drag me out."

"Don't —"

Bakr gunned the engine, ignoring his cousin's pleas, and plunged across the dune.

He'd gone less than one hundred meters when he realized that Nuri was right. The dune was too tall and steep, its sand too fine. Even with the Land Cruiser's massive tires, he lost his grip. The truck slowed, kicking up clouds of dust. Bakr downshifted into second, floored the engine. His tires caught, and the Toyota lurched forward. Bakr feathered the steering wheel, turned right, cutting across the dune to regain speed. Then he hit another soft patch and sank into the sand and came almost to a halt.

On the dunes, momentum was the only way to survive. On a slope this steep, the sand under Bakr's downhill tires would cave as soon as he stopped moving. In seconds, he would be rolling sideways. He wouldn't stop until he hit the bowl at the base of the dune. By then the Toyota would be a steel pancake, with him as filling. Worst case, he would trigger a sandslide that would envelop him. Neither he nor the truck would ever be found.

The engine knocked. Bakr downshifted again. He was in first now, no more gears left. With no alternative, he slammed the truck into reverse, floored the gas, and spun the steering wheel hard left. His best chance was to point the truck downward and then race down the dune. He'd be stuck in the soft sand at the bottom, for sure. The Land Cruiser would be a loss. No way could Nuri winch it out. But he had no choice.

The engine roared. His tires gripped the sand. The nose of the Land Cruiser pulled right, giving Bakr an extraordinary view down the face of the dune. Rivulets poured down from his tires. Bakr feathered the gas and rode backward up the dune as if Allah himself were tugging him free. *Save me now and I am your servant for eternity,* he thought —

He popped the clutch, grabbed the gearstick, and slammed the truck into first —

But as he did, a slab of sand broke under his front tires and the Land Cruiser's front end lurched down. The back wheels came off the ground —

And even before Bakr registered what was happening, the Land Cruiser began to flip, tail over nose over tail, eight loops in all, before coming to rest right side up.

The back of the truck was crushed. Yet the front somehow survived. The windshield pillars were intact, though the glass itself had popped out halfway up the dune. Sand filled half of the passenger compartment, covering Bakr to his waist. But his only real injury was the broken nose he had suffered when his face slammed into the steering wheel.

Bakr unbuckled his belt and drove his shoulder into the door to pop it open. Sand plunged out of the Toyota and rejoined the desert. Bakr stepped down, took one shaky step, another. Then he began to run, his legs pumping, slipping, kicking up sand, blood streaming over his chin. He looked up at the unbroken blue sky. Still alive. *Hamdulil-lah.* Thanks be to God.

For the rest of his life, Bakr would remember that moment as "the calling." He knew he wasn't a prophet. Muhammad was the last prophet, and only an infidel would think otherwise. But he had no doubt that Allah had saved him that day in the desert. Allah had heard his prayer. Bakr would never forget the vow he'd taken. *Save me now and I am your servant for eternity.*

A promise that left the question of *what* exactly Bakr had been called to do. But he didn't need long to figure out the answer. In August 1990, five years before "the calling," Saddam Hussein had invaded Kuwait. The little sheikhdom was Iraq's nineteenth province, Saddam said. He was putting it in its rightful place. Kuwait had even more oil per capita than did Saudi Arabia, and as a rule, Kuwaitis didn't enjoy manual labor, including the labor of defending their borders. They fled even before Saddam's tanks arrived.

The Iraqi attack terrified the House of Saud, too. The Kingdom's army was hardly more capable than its Kuwaiti counterpart. If Saddam decided that eastern Saudi Arabia was actually Iraq's twentieth province, the Kingdom couldn't stop him.

But the United States could. And the United States preferred the Saud family to Saddam. A half-million American troops headed to the Saudi desert. As he would twelve years later, Saddam dared the United States to attack. The result was a butt-whupping that brought to mind nothing so much as a one-round Mike Tyson knockout. The ground war to force Iraq out of Kuwait began in January 1991. It also ended in January 1991. The hostilities lasted four days before Saddam's supposedly mighty armies fled.

The United States didn't bother to chase them. America would later regret that decision. But at the time it seemed like the safest course. With the war over, oil prices dropped. The Kuwaitis came home from the exile they'd endured at five-star hotels in London. New York City threw a ticker-tape parade. Then everyone more or less forgot that the Gulf War had ever happened. Except for Saddam. And a few million Saudis.

Muhammad died in the Arabian town of Medina on June 8, 632 A.D., two decades after bringing Islam to the world. In the years that followed, the men who had prayed with him wrote down everything he had said for posterity. His words were collected in books of hadith, or narrations. The hadith are not part of the Quran, which Muslims consider the actual word of God. But they are vital nonetheless. One of the most important came on Muhammad's deathbed, when he decreed that "two religions should not exist together in the peninsula of the Arabs."

In practice, the hadith has never been strictly enforced. Tens of thousands of Christians work in Saudi Arabia, although they are not supposed to pray inside the Kingdom. But the flood of American soldiers onto Saudi soil in 1990 was an incitement that conservative Muslims could not ignore. The presence of hundreds of thousands of infidels, including many women, ran against the express wishes of the prophet. Clerics all over Saudi Arabia turned their anger against the United States. When some soldiers remained in the Kingdom even after the Gulf War ended, the clerics grew even more infuriated.

Tathlith lay almost a thousand miles from the American bases. But at Bakr's mosque, the local cleric — a man named Farouk, one of Bakr's eleven uncles — preached about the threat the Americans posed as if their tanks were just over the horizon. Every Friday at noon, he explained that the United States always sided with the Jews against Islam. American weapons enabled the Israelis to control the Palestinians and occupy land that belonged to Muslims. In fact, the Jews ran the United States. Because of them, America had a hundred nuclear missiles pointed at Mecca. Only Allah's divine strength stopped them from vaporizing the Grand Mosque and Kaaba.

Farouk didn't limit his criticism to the United States. Clerics in the Kingdom were not supposed to attack the royal family, which spent billions of dollars supporting mosques and religious schools. To make sure that the clerics were staying in line, the Ministry of Islamic Affairs sent monitors to the Friday sermons. But like many clerics, Farouk had tired of princes who gambled and whored and drank their way across Europe. During sermons, he avoided talking about the royal family. But afterward, in the mosque's back offices, he made sure his followers knew his opinion. The House of Saud failed to follow Islamic law. To preserve their power, the princes had violated Muhammad's hadith and had accepted Crusaders on sacred Arabian soil.

Under these circumstances, jihad to restore Islam to its rightful place was not merely a choice but an obligation. The Saud family, the puppets of the United States, could not be allowed to rule Mecca and Medina forever.

Bakr had heard these sermons for years before his near-death experience on the dune. He never questioned them. Why would he? Aside from a few trips to Mecca and Medina, he rarely left Tathlith. Nearly all his closest friends were also blood relatives. He had been raised to accept the word of his father without question, and to venerate Farouk for his knowledge of the Quran.

The Friday after Allah saved him, Bakr visited his uncle and explained what had happened in the desert. The bridge of his broken nose throbbed as he told the story.

"And you say the car flipped eight times."

"I don't count them, but that's what Nuri said, yes. Is it a sign, uncle?"

"Have you had any dreams since then?" Observant Muslims took dreams seriously as potential signals from Allah. In this, they followed the example of Muhammad, who was often guided by dreams.

"Yes, uncle."

"Tell me, then."

"In one, I'm riding a horse over the desert. I want the horse to turn, but it won't. It rides faster than any horse ever has. Then it throws me. But I'm not hurt. I land on the sand. I'm lost, but I'm not afraid. I see a flock of sheep and follow them. Then the desert turns into a highway. In the distance I see a stone, black like the Kaaba. The sheep run ahead, but a truck smashes them. The driver is made of glass. Beside him is a demon with yellow eyes. The truck bears down on me. And then — well, then I woke."

"You're trying to reach the Kaaba. But the corruption of our rulers stops you. It makes perfect sense."

"So everything that's happened, it's part of a plan?"

"You've been chosen. There's no other explanation."

You've been chosen. The words everyone one day hopes to hear. For a Muslim boy living almost in the shadow of Mecca, to be chosen *by Allah* was a blessing too rich to bear. Bakr's blood avalanched through him.

"Then what's my next step, uncle?" Bakr expected to be told that he should go to Afghanistan, join the jihad there.

Instead, his uncle sketched out a very different path.

At twenty, Bakr joined the National Guard

— the one-hundred-thousand-man militia that served as the Saud family's private fighting force. For the next eight years, he served ably, getting the military training he knew he would need. He kept his fundamentalist views concealed. To his superiors, he was a devout Muslim but a loyal Saudi.

Meantime, he quietly looked for men who might one day prove useful in his quest. The *mukhabarat* closely watched the National Guard. Bakr knew that being identified as hostile to the regime would land him in prison for decades. Nonetheless, he connected with soldiers and officers who shared his views.

Eight years passed. Then, on a spring morning, as Bakr napped in his two-room apartment in the National Guard barracks outside Mecca, a knock woke him. He opened the door to see two military police officers. "Captain Bakr? Please come with us. And leave your sidearm."

"What's this about?"

But they wouldn't answer. And somehow he knew. The *mukhabarat* or the internal Guard police had gotten to one of his men. Lieutenant Gamal, maybe. Gamal was fervent but weak. Bakr didn't doubt he would break. Without another word, he followed the MPs to a Jeep.

They drove along the edge of the base, which stretched over thousands of acres and housed an entire battalion, two thousand five hundred soldiers, plus air support. The Saudi government had built it after the 1979 fundamentalist attack on the Grand Mosque. If terrorists ever again tried to seize the mosque, the battalion's soldiers could reach it in fifteen minutes.

A windowless two-story concrete building squatted near the southwest corner of the base. It housed the battalion's internal security unit. Bakr knew he should be frightened. Yet he wasn't. Whatever was about to happen would be Allah's work. And Allah had guided him since that moment in the desert.

They drove past the security headquarters and parked at a warehouse two hundred meters on. The warehouse had once housed spare parts for the vehicles in the battalion but had been abandoned because of its inconvenient location. Now its front door was open. "Go on," the military police sergeant said.

The warehouse was hot and stank of epoxy. Inside, the overhead lights illuminated a concrete floor. Broken pallets lay at the far end of the building. A man in an officer's crisp olive uniform stood near them. As Bakr approached, he saw crossed swords and three stars on the officer's shoulderboards. Not merely an officer. An *amid* — a brigadier general. Bakr stopped a few feet away, offered his crispest salute.

"At ease, Captain Bakr. Do you know who I am?"

"No, sir."

"General Ibrahim."

Bakr hadn't recognized the face, but he knew the name. Though not a royal, Walid Ibrahim was a cousin of a low-ranking prince. He was also head of internal security for the western brigades of the National Guard. He was rarely seen and much feared. His men handled "political problems" — as they were euphemistically known — with a brutality that would have pleased a commissar for Stalin.

The general stood toe-to-toe with Bakr. He was light-skinned, taller than Bakr, with pockmarked skin and a neatly trimmed goatee. His breath stank of coffee and cardamom. "One of your men has confessed, Captain Bakr."

"Sir?"

Ibrahim slapped Bakr, catching his cheek with all five fingers. "Must I repeat myself? A man in your cell has confessed. Step back. Three steps. And go to your knees."

The concrete was warm through Bakr's khakis. He wondered whether Allah would save him again. Perhaps he didn't deserve to be saved, not after being so stupid as to trust Gamal.

Ibrahim unholstered his pistol. "Lieutenant Gamal al-Aziz has told us that you've recruited a cell of traitors" — Ibrahim spat on the concrete floor, the sound echoing softly — "and you plan to steal weapons from this base."

"He's mistaken, sir."

Bakr found himself looking at the pistol's dark eye. It didn't shake, not even a fraction. He didn't doubt that Ibrahim would pull the trigger. "Hands behind your back, captain. And don't move your head, no matter what I do."

Bakr intertwined his fingers behind his back. Ibrahim disappeared behind him, his clipped steps echoing on the concrete. Now he was just a voice. "It's my business to evaluate men like this. And he's telling the truth. He came to us of his own accord. Says he had an attack of conscience. Probably he got scared. He's hoping for clemency. You made a mistake with him."

Sweat ran down Bakr's chest. He promised himself that whatever happened, he wouldn't betray the men he'd recruited.

"But here's the thing, captain. He only has four names. He says there's more, but he doesn't know them."

"There is no cell."

Crack! Half the sun poured into Bakr's eyes. For a moment, ecstasy filled him, and then the pain came. Pistol-whipped. Still he stayed upright, kept his hands laced.

"Tell me the truth. Or I'll put a bullet through your neck. If you're lucky, you'll die right away. If not, you'll wind up paralyzed for a few miserable years. Then you'll die."

"Sir. Lieutenant Gamal is mistaken —"

"Three seconds. Two —" Bakr bit his tongue so he couldn't speak. "One —" The pistol touched the nape of his neck, settled in. Bakr closed his eyes.

The pistol pulled back. The shot echoed in Bakr's ears — and nothing changed. He felt the concrete against his legs. He opened his eyes. He was still in the warehouse.

"Last chance," Ibrahim said. Another endless pause —

"Stand up and face me." Ibrahim holstered his pistol. "I know that lieutenant is telling the truth. But I've been looking for a man like you. I'm sick of the corruption, too. We're on the same side. I'm going to give you a chance. I've sent Gamal to his barracks. Take care of him and we'll talk."

Bakr didn't trust himself to speak.

"You won't be suspected, captain. For now, I'm the only one who knows what he's said. My men brought him directly to me."

"Sir —"

"You have forty-eight hours. If you don't solve this problem by then, my men will be back for you." Ibrahim handed a handkerchief to Bakr. "And clean yourself up. You're bleeding."

Bakr mopped at the blood dribbling from his skull as he stumbled to his barracks. The day had turned scorching, forty-eight degrees Celsius — one hundred eighteen degrees Fahrenheit. The devils in his head danced. In his quarters, he pulled the shades and draped a wet towel over his skull and tried to think through what had happened. Maybe Ibrahim was trapping him, hoping to make him incriminate himself. Gamal had confessed, but Ibrahim didn't have enough evidence to bring a case.

Then why not just arrest him and the others, and shake out the truth? Ibrahim had brought him to the warehouse to test him. One-on-one, without witnesses.

A trap, or a lifeline? Perhaps he should ask Gamal directly, let the man defend

192

himself. Bakr lay on his bed and closed his eyes. His head ached terribly, and he squeezed his eyes tight. Then, suddenly, the headache passed and he knew what to do.

It was six p.m., the dinner hour. The barracks were nearly empty. Bakr scribbled a note — *The warehouse for spare parts. 11 p.m. Bring this. Tell no one. I.* He took the fire stairs to the fourth floor, where Gamal lived. He checked to make sure he was alone and then slipped the note under Gamal's door.

At 10:55, the warehouse door creaked open. "General? Hello?"

Even before he saw Gamal, Bakr knew his reedy voice. Bakr stepped forward from the wall where he'd hidden himself. He dropped the garrote over Gamal's neck and pulled tight. Gamal tried to scream but managed only a wet whisper. His hands came up and tugged at the wire as he desperately tried to take the killing pressure off his carotid artery.

But Bakr was stronger, and had the surprise and the leverage. With every second, Gamal weakened. Bakr tugged on Gamal's neck until Gamal's hands fell away and his feet drummed a death rattle against the floor.

"Traitor," Bakr whispered. "Infidel. Apostate." Let those be the last words that Gamal heard before the next world. Let him know that he would face an eternity of torment. Finally Gamal's feet stopped their useless clacking and his body slumped. Bakr put him on the floor and flicked on the lights. Gamal's face was mottled, his eyes bulging. The garrote had seared his neck. Bakr leaned close to Gamal's mouth. Nothing. Not a breath.

Gamal still clenched the note in his fist. Bakr slipped it into his pocket, reminding himself to flush it away at the barracks. He had a sudden urge to mutilate the corpse, put Gamal's pistol in his mouth and pull the trigger. Punish the traitor properly. But Gamal was already in hell, and that was punishment enough. Bakr flicked off the lights and left.

Fifteen minutes later, he lay in his bed, reading his Quran. He slept easily that night, and in the days that followed he hardly thought about what he'd done. Gamal had needed to die, and so Gamal had died.

The corpse was found a week later. Rumors blew through the base. A Star of David had been carved into Gamal's chest, his eyes gouged out. His corpse had decomposed so badly that he could be identified only by the name on his uniform. Bakr waited for the police to take him away. But no one came, and Bakr saw that Ibrahim's offer had been genuine.

Two weeks later, Bakr was ordered to report to the National Guard base at Jeddah, the headquarters of the western region. When he arrived, a sergeant escorted him to an unmarked black SUV. They drove north along the seaside road, past a gleaming white mosque that seemed to rise out of the Red Sea. The sergeant left him in a parking lot that looked out over a narrow inlet, told him to wait, and disappeared.

Bakr settled himself on a concrete bench. Nearby, a handful of families played on a public beach a few meters long. Even here the women wore long black *abayas* and burqas, as Saudi law required. Still, the children were having fun, squealing and running and dumping sand on one another. Public spaces such as the beach were rare in Saudi Arabia, and a great treat. Bakr didn't object to the beach, as long as unmarried women didn't pollute it with their presence and married ones stayed covered. As Allah had intended.

Ibrahim arrived a few minutes later. Today

195

he wore traditional Saudi clothing, a *thobe* and *ghutra*. Bakr stood to salute, but Ibrahim shook his head and sat beside him. "Captain. It's terrible what happened on your base."

"Yes, sir."

"It looks like the killer will never be found."

"Then that's Allah's will, sir."

"Lieutenant Gamal was deprived of a proper funeral," Ibrahim said. Under Muslim law, corpses were supposed to be buried or cremated as soon as possible, never more than two days after death.

"Perhaps that's as it should be. If the lieutenant betrayed our faith."

"How long have you been putting your cell together, captain?"

"Sir?"

"Listen now. No more games. If I'd wanted to arrest you, I would have already."

Bakr saw himself tumbling down the dune. Everything had led to this moment. "Three years."

"How many men do you have?"

"Nine. Eight now, I suppose."

"You've done well, captain. No one has ever hidden so much from me. So what is it you want?"

"For the land to be pure, sir. For us to

196

live as Allah intended."

"And you think King Abdullah is failing us."

Bakr was silent.

"You don't have to answer, captain. Every true Muslim knows it's so."

For a general to speak this way . . . Allah had rewarded his faith. For the second time in his life, he asked, "So what's our next step?"

"Nothing can happen now, captain. Abdullah is too strong. But the moment will come when he's weak. When he overreaches. It's then that we'll strike."

Bakr quit the National Guard a year later. His superior officers were surprised, since he'd just received a promotion to major. One by one, his men followed him out. With them as trainers, he built his organization. To find recruits, he relied on a dozen deeply conservative clerics. He wanted a small, elite force. Let other groups make grand pronouncements. His men would strike on their own timetable and cause maximum damage. He saw Ibrahim once every few months. They both knew that meeting more frequently would be dangerous. Ibrahim provided tactical advice — and money. On a day-to-day basis, he let Bakr work without interference.

A year ago, Ibrahim had told Bakr that the time for action was coming. Abdullah had secretly told other princes that he wanted to install his son Khalid as the next king. Khalid was even more liberal than Abdullah, Ibrahim said. He would lead the nation astray, allowing women to drive and to vote, letting Christians and Jews into the Grand Mosque. He had even spoken of making peace with Israel. "Everything we believe in, Khalid hates," Ibrahim said.

But Bakr and his men could stop Abdullah, Ibrahim said. Their attacks would reveal the opposition to Abdullah and Khalid. Many princes didn't want Khalid to be king. The attacks would show them that the future of the House of Saud was at risk. They would force Khalid into exile and make Abdullah step down. A true guardian of the faith would take over.

"Can that really happen?" Bakr said.

"We'll take control. And establish a new caliphate."

With Ibrahim's money, Bakr had built the most powerful jihadi group since the early days of Al Qaeda, before the American response to September 11 forced Osama and his men into hiding. Besides the suicide bombers who had gone through his camp in Saudi Arabia, Bakr had trained almost fifty men in close combat at his base in Lebanon. These were soldiers, ready to attack a well-guarded palace or oil refinery. With surprise on their side, and the willingness to martyr themselves, they had a good chance of overcoming a defensive force three times as large.

His first attacks had proved as successful as could have been hoped. With a dozen men, he'd killed almost one hundred people and disrupted crude oil shipments all over the Gulf. Bakr should have been ecstatic, especially with another attack coming.

Instead he couldn't shake his fear that Ibrahim was using him. Over time, Bakr had realized how little he knew about Ibrahim's plans. Ibrahim refused to tell Bakr which princes were backing them. Nor would he reveal the details of who would ultimately rule. "Too much information is dangerous," he said. "For both of us." Bakr wondered whether Ibrahim simply wanted to replace one branch of the royal family with another. Ibrahim's story about Khalid sounded like palace intrigue, princes conspiring. Bakr didn't want thieves replacing thieves. He wanted the House of Saud uprooted from its foundations.

As bad as the secrecy was Bakr's suspicion about Ibrahim's faith. Certainly the general *seemed* to believe. When Bakr prayed with him, he spoke his *rakat* — prayer verses — easily and correctly. Yet he'd told Bakr that he had only once performed the *hajj,* the annual pilgrimage to Mecca that is one of the five pillars of Islam. The Quran itself said, "*Hajj* is the duty that mankind owes to Allah." Certainly, a Muslim was required to conduct *hajj* only once. But with his wealth and power, Ibrahim could have performed *hajj* many times. Bakr himself had undertaken the pilgrimage three times. He didn't understand why Ibrahim wouldn't have chosen to go more than once.

Of course, Ibrahim was far busier than Bakr. And every Muslim slipped up and broke the ritual laws once in a while. But Ibrahim lacked something deeper. In his heart, Bakr felt the destiny that Allah had chosen for him. He felt Allah's power. Praying was an honor and a pleasure, not a duty. The thought of God warmed him like the sun. He felt the same spirit in other true believers. But not in Ibrahim. Ibrahim spoke the words, but he never sounded convinced. If Bakr hadn't believed so fervently, he might not have noticed. But he did. And so he did.

Bakr knew he might be wrong. Only Allah could know Ibrahim's heart, the ripeness of his faith. But what if he was right? Why then had Ibrahim spared him, instead of arresting him when Gamal betrayed him years earlier? The answer must be that Ibrahim had always planned to use Bakr to seize power. Bakr imagined how Ibrahim saw him. A zealot from the most religious region of the Kingdom. A rabid dog to be unleashed when Ibrahim saw fit. Then tossed aside.

But if that was Ibrahim's plan, the general had miscalculated, Bakr thought. With Allah's guidance, Bakr had devised his own plan. He would use the soldiers that he had trained in a way that neither Ibrahim nor the men behind him would ever expect. He would do more than trade one branch of the Kingdom's ruling family for another. He would free Arabia entirely from the tyranny of the Sauds. And if the strategy worked as Bakr intended — as *Allah* intended — it would draw the United States onto the Arabian peninsula, provoking a final confrontation between America and Islam.

Before that battle could take place, Bakr faced a thousand obstacles. But as he sped north through the Bekaa to his camp, he felt confident, almost serene. For as the Prophet Muhammad — peace be upon Him — had said, "Whoever fights so that the Word of Allah is held high, he is in the way of Allah." Yes, Bakr's enemies were mighty. But Allah was mightier. And as he had since that day on the dune, Bakr knew beyond doubt that Allah was with him.

CHAPTER 9

The villa was as ridiculous as Wells expected, with a private pool and a balcony overlooking the Mediterranean. Wells decided to swim, then realized he didn't have a bathing suit. Or a change of clothes. He called the concierge.

"Give me your measurements. One of my men will pick up what you need." Wells did.

"And how much would you like to spend, monsieur?"

"For a shirt and pants and a shaving kit? A hundred euros, I guess."

A faint throat-clearing told Wells that he had guessed wrong.

"Five hundred?"

More throat clearing.

"Up to you, then. Just put it on the room." Wells hung up, reached for his cell, remembered that the battery was dead. He picked up the room phone again, called New Hampshire. Long distance at the Hôtel du

Cap-Eden-Roc. Another couple barrels of Saudi crude down the drain.

"John?"

"None other."

"I tried to call. Your phone was off."

"I didn't have it for a while."

"But you're okay."

On the slopes below the villa, the cypress trees glowed in the sun like a dream by van Gogh. "Could say that."

"Why are you laughing?"

"I'm in the south of France. The biggest risk I'm running is that I'll slip getting into the pool. And I think I just spent two thousand dollars on a shirt and pants."

"I hope they're nice. The shirt and pants, I mean."

"I expect they will be. I'll take a picture for you."

"Can you tell me who they are, the people you're with? Or what they want?"

Wells looked at the phone. Open line. He ought to keep operational security. "Wish I could, but not now. I'm not sure you'd believe it anyway. I'm not sure I do. How are you? How's Tonka?"

"You put me first. That's sweet. We're both fine."

"Anything happening?"

"I did arrest a couple of drunks on Main

Street last night, but I know that doesn't count for much."

Wells supposed he had that coming. "Anne. I promise. We'll come here one day. You'd like it."

"That would be nice." Though she didn't sound convinced. "Be careful in the pool, okay? Those things can be deadly."

"Noted."

The clothes arrived an hour later, linen pants and a blue silk shirt and pure white swim trunks. They didn't have labels. But they looked expensive. They felt expensive. They even smelled expensive. Wells tried them on and hardly recognized himself. The man in the mirror looked as sleek and shiny as a peacock looking for a mate.

The trunks were even worse. They fit tighter than boxers. When Wells cinched them, he had the odd sensation that he was molesting himself.

The phone trilled. "Are your clothes pleasing, monsieur?"

"Pleasing? They're —" Wells wanted to say *absurd,* but went with "very nice."

"Can I help you with anything else?"

"Actually, yes. A laptop."

"I'm sorry, sir. We have an executive center in the hotel, but we don't keep laptops for guests —"

"Then buy one." *Can't cost more than the bathing suit,* Wells thought.

"Yes, sir. Shall I put that purchase on the room also?"

"You shall."

The Saudi soldiers Wells had met in Afghanistan were undisciplined and lazy, quick to boast but slow to the front lines. Wells had rarely talked to them, and he realized now how little he knew about Saudi Arabia. Before his next meeting with Abdullah, he wanted to learn. If he were still in the agency, he could have gone to the analysts at the Near East Desk or even called to the frontline operatives in Riyadh. Instead he would be reduced to Googling. Like the civilian that he was.

The laptop arrived just as he finished his swim. It didn't come with a receipt, and he didn't ask what it had cost. Heads of state and billionaires must live this way. They never paid for anything. Their accountants settled up later.

Wells booted up, got online. He expected to read for only a couple hours, but the more he learned, the more fascinated he became.

Abdullah's lineage dated back to 1744,

when a fundamentalist cleric named Abdul Wahhab allied with a minor Arabian ruler named Muhammad ibn Saud. At the time, Islam had become an almost polytheistic religion. Many Muslims prayed to spirits, a practice that the prophet Muhammad had banned a thousand years before.

Wahhab demanded that Muslims follow the Quran literally and that lawbreakers face harsh penalties. Around 1743, he ordered an adulterous woman stoned to death. Because of his strict views, Wahhab was forced from his hometown of Uyayna. Looking for protection, he asked Saud if he could live in Diriyah, the village that Saud ruled.

Saud agreed to shelter Wahhab to write and preach. Over time, Wahhab's sermons attracted a growing audience, who called themselves Wahhabis. They pledged allegiance to Saud, forming a potent army. They fought under Saud's flag: a green cloth with the *shahada,* the Islamic declaration of faith, in its center. Beneath the *shahada,* a curved white sword. The flag symbolized Saud's vision, combining the glory of Islam with the might of the state. Wisely, Saud never demanded religious leadership for himself, leaving that role to Wahhab.

With the Wahhabis as his soldiers, Saud

207

conquered the central Arabian peninsula. After he died, his sons followed. By 1810, the Sauds controlled most of Arabia. Then the Turkish army used modern weapons to roll them back. In 1818, the Turks captured Riyadh and brought Abdallah, Saud's great-grandson, to Istanbul, where he was executed. For the rest of the nineteenth century, the House of Saud remained in oblivion.

Then it roared back.

In 1902, Abdul-Aziz, Saud's great-great-great-great-grandson, took Riyadh in a surprise attack. At the time, Abdul-Aziz had only a few dozen soldiers. But over the next two decades, he followed the same playbook as his eighteenth-century ancestors, harnessing religious zeal to conquer Arabia. The *Ikhwan* — Arabic for "brothers" — formed the core of his army. The *Ikhwan* were Bedouin so religious that they disliked even looking at non-Muslims, and they massacred their enemies without remorse. Abdul-Aziz could barely control them, but their brutal reputation helped him. Opposing cities surrendered to him without fighting on the condition that he keep the *Ikhwan* away.

In 1924, Abdul-Aziz's forces took Mecca. The following year, he reached Jeddah and the Red Sea, completing his conquest of the Arabian peninsula. For the second time in two centuries, the House of Saud ruled Arabia. But the *Ikhwan* were not ready to quit fighting. Their leaders turned against Abdul-Aziz, saying that he had allied with the British and was insufficiently religious. But Abdul-Aziz no longer needed the *Ikhwan*. He built a new army from more loyal tribes. Using machine guns and cars from the British, he put down the rebellion. And in September 1932, he officially created the Kingdom of Saudi Arabia. Its flag was the same green banner that Sauds had fought under since the eighteenth century.

Abdul-Aziz died in 1953. His sons had ruled ever since, inheriting the world's biggest fortune. As oil prices soared in the 1970s, Saudi Arabia became one of the wealthiest countries in the world. The princes' wasteful ways became legendary in Europe, but plenty of money stayed inside the Kingdom. A Saudi saying held, "If you didn't become rich during the days of King Khalid" — who ruled from 1975 to 1982 — "you will never be rich." By 1979, the average income in Saudi Arabia was higher than in the United States.

The windfall didn't last. In 1982, a glut of

oil caused the price of crude to plunge. For most of the next two decades, it stayed below twenty dollars. The Saudi economy cratered. The princes still lived richly, but by 2000 the average Saudi made just one-fifth as much as the average American.

Then another oil boom began, as demand for oil soared in China and India. Prices rose and rose, topping a hundred forty dollars a barrel in 2008. Even after the recession of 2009, a barrel of crude traded around eighty dollars. At that price, Saudi Arabia earned almost a billion dollars a day selling oil. Every two months, the House of Saud raked in as much cash as Bill Gates had earned in his entire life. Of course, most of that money went to keep the government running. All Saudis received free education and health care. Gasoline was heavily subsidized. And the Kingdom had no income taxes.

Even so, at least fifty billion dollars remained every year for the family to divide. Every prince received a stipend. Third- and fourth-generation princelings got $20,000 to $100,000 a month. Senior princes received millions of dollars a year. At the top, Abdullah and the other sons of Abdul-Aziz had essentially unlimited budgets. Abdullah's Red Sea palace complex in Jeddah had cost more than a billion dollars.

While the princes prospered, the new boom didn't help average Saudis as much as the original one had. The Kingdom's population had quadrupled since 1980 to twenty-five million. The economy had not created enough jobs to keep pace. Even though almost no women worked, millions of Saudi men were unemployed. Making matters worse, Saudi men considered blue-collar work to be beneath them. Despite the chronic unemployment, five million Indians, Egyptians, and other immigrants worked in the Kingdom as drivers, janitors, and laborers, jobs that Saudis wouldn't take.

The frustration among ordinary Saudis flowed into the only channel that the government allowed — militant Islam. The centuries-old pact between Wahhabi clerics and the House of Saud remained essential to the family's claim to rule. Saudi kings called themselves Custodians of the Two Holy Mosques because control of Mecca and Medina provided their ultimate legitimacy. Without Islam, Saudi Arabia was just another dictatorship.

To keep religious leaders satisfied, the Sauds spent tens of billions of dollars supporting Islam. The princes rebuilt the giant mosques at Mecca and Medina, subsidized the *hajj,* and paid for religious schools around the world. But the clerics wanted more than money. They wanted women in burqas, and strict penalties for anyone caught drinking alcohol or having illicit sex. Like Abdul Wahhab, their spiritual father, they wanted to govern Saudi Arabia as though they were still in the seventh century. They were the most fundamental of fundamentalists.

During the 1970s, the Saudi government had moved away from this vision of Islam. Cigarettes were sold openly. Even alcohol was quietly tolerated. State-run television broadcasts featured female newscasters. Girls' schools were created. Then, in 1979, a Bedouin named Juhayman — Arabic for "the scowler" — led hundreds of rebels in a takeover of the Grand Mosque in Mecca. Ironically, the rebels had defied an important Quranic decree that forbade fighting in Mecca. Juhayman believed that he could ignore the decree because he had found the Mahdi, the true successor to Muhammad. Juhayman promised the Mahdi would establish a new Muslim empire and defeat armies of Christians and Jews.

The takeover staggered the Saudi government. Police and National Guard units tried to retake the mosque, but the rebels repelled them. A siege began. The government imposed a news blackout, but it could not prevent reports of the attack from spreading worldwide.

Besides tactical incompetence, the government had a serious problem: the prohibition on fighting near the mosque. Before the army could attack in force, the Sauds needed approval from a council of Wahhabi clerics. To win them all, the princes pledged that they would roll back the liberalizations of the 1970s. Finally, four days after the siege began, the clerics issued a fatwa, a religious ruling, ordering the rebels to surrender. With that approval, the Saudi army attacked with thousands of men. The mosque caught fire during the ensuing battle — the equivalent of open war inside St. Peter's or at the Wailing Wall. Only the Kaaba, the sacred stone at the center of the shrine, remained undamaged.

The rebels retreated into rooms and corridors beneath the mosque. For a week, soldiers struggled to clear them. On December 3, advised by French special forces soldiers, they dumped potent tear gas into the basement. After a final day of fighting, they captured the last rebels. Two weeks after it began, the siege ended. Witnesses estimated that more than one thousand soldiers, rebels, and civilians died, though an accurate death toll was never released.

Outside of Saudi Arabia, the siege was quickly forgotten. But inside, its effects were profound. The implicit support it had received from senior clerics pushed the House of Saud sharply right. As it had promised, the government restricted women's education, gave new powers to the religious police, and promoted jihad in Afghanistan.

A generation after the siege of the Grand Mosque, Saudi Arabia ran like a medium-security prison. Sex outside marriage was forbidden and dangerous. Questioning the monarchy's right to rule was a crime. Culture and the arts hardly existed. Women couldn't drive, or even have identity cards, unless their husbands agreed.

Since becoming king in 2005, Abdullah had taken small steps to rein in the religious police. But the changes were mostly cosmetic. Political parties were still outlawed, women still couldn't drive, and state-funded clerics still preached war against Israel and the West. Saudi Arabia was among the most repressed places on earth. Its main public spaces were malls, mosques — and the squares where drug dealers and murderers were beheaded.

These rules didn't bother the princes, of course. The Kingdom's laws applied only loosely to them. As for average Saudis, since they couldn't legally protest, no one knew if they were happy with the strictures they faced. The satellite dishes that speckled nearly every house suggested otherwise. So did the angry discussions in Internet chat rooms.

On the other hand, nearly half of Saudis married their cousins, closing ranks against outsiders in the most basic way. Many believed devoutly that the Quran was the word of Allah and that non-Muslims would spend eternity in hell. Even now, the loudest protests in the Kingdom came not from reformers but from fundamentalists.

When he finished reading, Wells could see the Kingdom much more clearly.

But the king remained a mystery. Was he a genuine reformer? Wells couldn't tell. Still, he was glad he had stayed the night to find out exactly what Abdullah and Miteb wanted. By the time he turned off the laptop, the hotel grounds were nearly silent. Miles out to sea, yachts glimmered. A breeze filled his living room with the scent of cypress and pine. Overhead, the stars glowed. Even without the virgins — and Wells suspected that virgins were tough to come by in the south of France — this place was close to Paradise. Here, eternal life seemed not just possible but actually desirable. Wells lay on his five-thousand-dollar-a-night-bed and closed his eyes and wondered at the world that had somehow come to him.

The Maybach picked him up the next morning. This time Miteb sat in back as classical music played. The king wasn't in the car. Wells couldn't help feeling disappointed. He'd wanted to see Abdullah again.

"Good morning, Mr. Wells."

"Good morning, Prince."

"My brother sends his apologies. He's not well this morning."

"Nothing too serious, *inshallah*."

"At our age, everything is serious." Miteb pushed a button, and the music stopped. "Do you think your friends are tailing you?"

"The agency? I doubt it. Out of sight, out of mind. Anyway, they know enough to leave me alone."

"You're used to having your own way."

"Coming from a prince, I don't know whether that's a compliment or an insult."

"Let's say it's both. And what about you? Will you report this meeting to the CIA?"

Wells didn't answer. In truth, he hadn't

decided.

"You're still loyal to your country."

Guilty, Wells thought. *For better or worse.* "If this is a back-channel plea for help from the United States, you'd be better off asking directly," he said.

"It's not. We can't have America involved."

"Prince, I still don't know why I'm here. I assume it's related to the attacks last week, but you haven't even said that."

"My brother and I have a mission for you."

"An entire army reports to you, and you need me."

"We can't depend on the army for this. It's not in our land."

"Your *mukhabarat,* then."

"But as we told you yesterday, that's precisely the problem. The *muk* belong to Saeed and Mansour. Do you think this pleases us? To ask an American we don't know for help?"

"Start at the beginning. Why me?"

"I've known Pierre Kowalski many years. He's supplied the National Guard with weapons. He gave me your name. But he said we'd have to talk in person to convince you."

"How can you and Abdullah come here without anyone knowing?"

"There's a physician in Nice who treats

Abdullah. Saeed thinks he's here for medical treatment."

Wells wasn't so sure. "But don't Mansour's men manage your security?"

"The king chooses his traveling companions. And if he wants to leave his security behind and go for a drive in his Mercedes, he can. Anyway, I think Saeed and his son prefer us outside the country. This way, they can talk to the other princes, campaign against us."

"Is that what's happening?"

"Not openly. But yes. It's complicated and simple at the same time."

"Tell me."

"You heard Abdullah yesterday. He wants Khalid on the throne. His eldest son. It's stuck in his head. He can't let it go. And it's creating a big instability."

"It's not how the system is supposed to work."

"Correct. The first generation should have preference. That means Saeed. And if not Saeed, then the princes should come together to make the decision."

"So how can Abdullah win?"

"Because this problem will come very soon, anyway. Saeed is almost eighty. Even if he takes over from Abdullah, he has only a few years to rule. And once he and Nayef

218

are gone, the first generation will be gone and the country will be just where it is now. The next generation is too large. How can we choose? Two hundred grandsons of Abdul-Aziz can claim the throne."

"Still. Why not let Saeed take the throne, put off the problem?"

"Because if Saeed is king, he'll undo all the good that Abdullah has done."

"You expect me to believe that Abdullah is some great force for democracy."

For the first time, Miteb seemed irritated. "I want you to understand our society. You know what happened in 1979?"

Wells was glad he had read up. "The Grand Mosque."

"Yes. Our clerics, they're very powerful. And most of them, they only read the Quran and the hadith, nothing else. They know everything about Islam, nothing about the rest of the world. Sheikh bin Baz was our most senior cleric until he died in 1999. His most famous fatwa, in 1966, he said that the Quran proves that the earth doesn't go around the sun. The earth is the center and the sun moves around it, he said."

"You're serious."

"Yes. He only changed his mind in 1985, and do you know why? Prince Sultan was on the space shuttle and came to him and said, 'Sheikh, I saw it. The earth rotates and the sun is still.' And that convinced him. This is our society, you see. And Abdullah must move slowly. But Abdullah's a good king. He's a good man, and kind, and he wants more openness. The people trust him. He's moving us in the right direction. Not like Saeed."

"Tell me about Saeed."

"So in 2002, in Mecca, a school for girls caught fire. These schools, they're mainly old apartment buildings, not really schools, because we have so many children and not enough schools. This one, someone was cooking in the kitchen and an electric plate caught fire. It was a small fire, but it spread. There were eight hundred girls inside, more. Not just Saudi, but from Pakistan, Nigeria, everywhere. And there was only one staircase to get out. The girls started to panic. Then the religious police came. You don't remember this?"

"I was in Pakistan at the time, the North-West Frontier. Didn't get much news."

"So the *muttawa*" — the religious police — "came, and you must imagine, this is Mecca, they are even more conservative there than anywhere else. They blocked the entrance to the school. They wouldn't let in the firefighters. And they would only let out the girls who were wearing *abaya*s. They made the other girls go back. The firefighters and the civil defence said, 'This is not the time to enforce these laws.' But while they argued, the school was burning. The girls were stuck inside. Screaming, 'Let us out! Let us out!' They started to jump out the windows. By the time the firefighters got inside, fifteen of them died and fifty were terribly hurt. Little girls. A tragedy. And the newspapers wrote about it. Saudi newspapers criticizing the religious police and calling for an investigation of the school. It had never happened before. And Abdullah and I, you understand, we welcomed this."

"But not Saeed."

"Not Saeed. Not Nayef, the interior minister, either. After a few days, Nayef called all the newspaper editors in. He told them it was time for the investigations to end. And once the interior minister tells you to stop investigating, you stop, or you go to jail. And he said that the *muttawa* had not blocked the gate and that they had behaved properly. He said they were there to make sure that the girls didn't face 'mistreatment' outside the building. And Saeed — Saeed went even further. He called the *muttawa* 'heroes.' "

221

"Abdullah couldn't get involved?"

"At the time, he wasn't the king. And the religious police, the clerics, they don't think this fire is a tragedy. Because to them, the girls shouldn't be in school at all. So the fire is Allah punishing them. And Saeed and Nayef, I'm not sure whether they believe that, but they know the clerics do."

"They sound like sweeties."

"Then, a few months later, Nayef said that the Saudis weren't the ones who hijacked the planes on September 11. The Americans shouted so much that he took it back. But Saeed not only repeated it — he made a big speech about it. He doesn't trust the United States, and he never will. He thinks the clerics are right, that there's only room for one religion. And Saeed, when he dies, he'll be no different than Abdullah. He'll want his son on the throne."

"Mansour."

"Yes. And I've decided that Abdullah is right about Mansour. He believes only in power."

"Is Abdullah faithful?"

"Yes. More than I am. But you don't understand what it's like to be our age. We see death around every corner. We can't pretend that Allah will protect us any longer. But then Allah's kept his bargain with us. We've had our lives. What I mean is that whether you believe matters less at our age. What will be will be. Allah will judge us all on his own scale, heaven or hell. And if it turns out to be nothing at all on the other side — and yes, we all wonder that, too — we can't help that, either."

Wells found himself liking this old man. "You think Khalid will be a good king?"

"I don't know. But it's what Abdullah wants, and I've pledged to help him." Miteb looked Wells over. "I know what you think. You think, *Why help these men? What gives them the right to all this money that comes out of the ground?* But this is our system. Maybe in fifty years, we'll have something different. A constitutional monarchy like Jordan. But it's impossible now. The princes and the clerics won't allow it. And look at Iran, Iraq, Nigeria, Venezuela, Libya. Wherever there's oil, there are dictators and war."

As Miteb had said, Wells was inclined to stay out of this battle for a sticky black throne. Yet Miteb had made a persuasive case. He hadn't pretended that Khalid would be a perfect ruler. He had said only that Khalid was better than the alternatives.

"All right. Let's say I'll help you. Tell me, how do the attacks last week relate to all this?"

"Possibly they don't. Possibly it's co-incidence, Al Qaeda picked last week for more attacks. But I don't think so."

"I don't think so, either."

"So it's a new group. One capable of launching three attacks at once. Avoiding detection from America. Hitting a hotel in the center of Riyadh. They're well-trained and well-financed. They must have had friends inside the *muk.* Maybe the very top, maybe not, but certainly some help."

"Say you're right. What's the point?"

"To create instability. Anger my brother, make him overreact. His temper gets worse every week. I think because he's in so much pain. So he lashes out at his brothers and the senior clerics. Then Saeed goes to the other princes and says, 'We all love Abdullah, but we can't trust him anymore. He needs to step down.' Already they whisper that he's paranoid."

From what Wells had seen of Abdullah, the scenario was plausible. "That's why Abdullah can't strip Saeed and Mansour of their power quietly?"

"If he tries to move openly against Saeed, Saeed will say that Abdullah is losing his mind. Abdullah made a mistake when he said that he wanted his son to be king. We have a proverb, *'Your tongue is your steed.*

224

Guard it and it guards you, abuse it and it abuses you.' My brother spoke too soon. That gave Saeed the opening, set everything else in motion. But what's done is done. Abdullah couldn't help himself."

"What if Saeed has won already?" Wells said.

"It's possible. But my brother has been popular. Especially among ordinary people. And if Saeed and Mansour were sure they'd won, they'd have no need to provoke Abdullah. They would just wait for the succession."

"So. Now that I understand, what is it you want me to do?"

A brown leather satchel lay at Miteb's feet. Miteb reached down and slipped his palsied fingers through the handle. He pulled it up, his wrists shaking. Wells could almost feel him straining.

"Prince —" Wells reached over.

"No. Let me." Inch by inch, Miteb edged the satchel higher, his lips quivering. *I'll never be that old,* Wells promised himself. *Never. Even if I am.* Finally Miteb dropped the satchel on the seat — and let out a giant fart that filled the Maybach.

"Smells like a barrel of oil," Wells said.

Suddenly, both men were laughing. "One day you'll understand."

"Inshallah, I hope not."

Inside the satchel, Wells found a spy's treasure trove.

An Algerian passport, real, with a name and date of birth but no photo. What operatives called a blank. A battered cell phone, its screen cracked. An empty wallet, its brown leather splattered with blood. A Nikon D300, a professional-grade SLR, with a telephoto lens. A second camera, a Canon small enough to be hidden inside a man's palm. A half-dozen flat white plastic rectangles embedded with black strips — passkeys for a hotel or office building. Three architectural maps of a fan-shaped neighborhood that Wells didn't recognize. A plastic police evidence bag that contained a wad of riyals, the Saudi currency, and a money clip of hundred-dollar bills.

"The police in Riyadh found all this a few days ago. We were fortunate. Mansour's men weren't involved. There was an auto accident. A big truck ran through a traffic light, hit a car, crushed it and killed the driver. When the police came, they found the car was stolen and the driver had no identification. When the police opened the trunk, they found the passport and the camera and called their captain."

"Why didn't they tell the Interior Ministry?"

"The head of the police in Riyadh is loyal to Abdullah. He's ordered that this type of material be passed to him so that he can give it to the *mukhabarat* himself. Sometimes files are lost before they reach the *muk.* You understand?"

"Saeed and Mansour don't know you've found all this."

"Correct."

"But you told me the police haven't identified this man. How can you be so sure that he's connected to the men behind the attacks last week?"

Miteb had no answer.

"If this is all you have, you and your brother are really drawing thin."

" 'Drawing thin'? I don't understand."

Wells held up the phone and the plastic evidence bag. "The phone and money were in the driver's pocket?"

Miteb nodded. "The phone doesn't work anymore. But it still has its memory. And it shows three calls from mobile phones with Lebanese area codes."

Which might not have been made from Lebanon at all, Wells thought. "Did he have anything else? Receipts? Credit cards? A map with a big black *X* marking the spot of

227

his hideout?"

Miteb smiled. "No map. As for the rest, I can ask, but I don't think so. Everything the police found is here. You see they even kept the money from the wallet."

"We're lucky for that."

Wells took the money from the plastic bag. He set the clip with the hundred-dollar bills aside and thumbed through the Saudi currency, thirty or so bills, ranging from one-riyal to five-hundred-riyal notes, their edges streaked with blood.

"You don't need to take that," Miteb said. "If you need money, tell me."

"Here's a thirty-second tutorial on trade-craft, Prince. The man who died in that crash was a professional. Or at least professionally trained. He kept almost everything in his head. But nobody can remember everything." Wells thumbed through the hundred-dollar bills, then examined the riyals more closely. "You've got to give yourself help. And even the most careful cops aren't likely to check your banknotes for hidden information."

Wells held up a one-riyal note. Four numbers were written in tiny Arabic script in the upper-right corner: 5421. On the next note, four more numbers in the lower-right corner: 8239.

"See these? I find three more bills like this, I have a sixteen-digit credit-card number with a three-digit pin — personal identification number. Let's say my handlers are giving me a new card once a month. And they don't want me to keep the physical cards. That's a lot to remember, nineteen digits. This way I don't have to. I put the bills together and I have my card. I can use it on the Internet whenever I like. And if the card gets canceled and I need a new one, I spend the money and get fresh banknotes and repeat the process."

"Very good."

"I didn't invent it."

"So now that you have the credit card, what will you do?"

"I'm not planning to *do* anything."

"Please, Mr. Wells. My brother and I, we can offer you whatever you like, but you told us yesterday that money didn't matter, and I believe you. I don't know how to convince you."

"Convince me to what?"

"Find out who was paying this man. Where they're located. What we'd ask our *mukhabarat* to do if we trusted them."

"Even if you're right that the *muk* are involved, the chain won't run all the way up to Saeed or Mansour. At best, I'll find

229

somebody a couple steps removed."

"That's closer than we are now. Then you infiltrate, stop the next attack."

"I don't know what Pierre Kowalski told you about me. But that's not how it works. I can't just find these men and tell them I want to join the war against Abdullah."

Miteb sagged against his seat. Wells saw the prince's exhaustion in the slump of his shoulders. None of this could be easy for a man his age.

"All right," Wells said. He slipped the money into the plastic bag and put the bag and everything else back into the satchel and put the satchel at his feet. "I'll make a few calls, see what I can find."

Miteb put his arms around Wells, kissed Wells's cheeks with his papery lips. His trembling fingers skittered over Wells's back. "Thank you."

"Don't thank me. I haven't done anything."

"But you will."

"Maybe." But Wells knew he was lying. He'd chosen a side already.

At the hotel, Wells called a number that would be burned into his brain even if he lived to be older than Abdullah. The phone rang once. Then: "Shafer here."

"Ellis. I need your help."

■ ■ ■ ■

PART TWO

■ ■ ■ ■

CHAPTER 10

JEDDAH, SAUDI ARABIA

From a distance, the two hundred women in the conference center in Jeddah's Inter-Continental Hotel appeared identical, a dozen rows of black-robed ghosts. Up close, their uniforms varied subtly. Some dressed in full burqa, covering their faces with veils and their hands with gloves. Others, less conservative, wore *niqab*s that allowed their mascaraed eyes to be seen, or raised the hems of their gowns to reveal polished black boots that seemed more appropriate for Paris than Jeddah.

And a few trendsetting women had rejected burqas entirely in favor of *abaya*s, neck-length black gowns. In place of veils, they wore *shayla* — scarves that draped over their hair but left their faces uncovered. In this room, where the only men were bodyguards, a few had even allowed their scarves to slip, revealing tangles of lustrous black hair. Technically, by uncovering their hair,

235

they risked the anger of the religious police.

But no one in this room expected to be harassed. Not today, anyway. These women were the elite of Jeddah, the most cosmopolitan city in the Kingdom. Traders and tourists had visited Jeddah for thousands of years, and until 1925, when Abdul-Aziz took over, its rulers were moderate Muslims comfortable with the West.

Jeddah's liberal tilt could be overstated. The city was part of Saudi Arabia, after all. The House of Saud monitored it closely, especially because it served as the gateway to Mecca, which lay forty miles east. Still, Jeddah's tradition of openness had not disappeared entirely. Religious police were less visible here than in Riyadh. Public discussions were freer. Unmarried women and men could discreetly charter boats and meet on the Red Sea. So Jeddah was the most fitting place in Saudi Arabia for a speech on women's rights from Princess Alia, King Abdullah's oldest granddaughter.

The Quran commanded rulers to seek advice from their subjects. Princes and government officials held meetings where any Saudi citizen could complain or ask for help. Even Abdullah followed the tradition, though his assemblies were largely ceremonial, lasting only minutes.

But the women of the House of Saud were seen rarely, heard even less. And so an air of expectation filled the conference room at the InterContinental as the women inside waited for Alia to appear.

Security for the speech had been planned for months, well before the invitations were sent. After the bombings in Bahrain and Riyadh, the National Guard colonel who managed protection for Alia asked that the princess move the speech to Abdullah's palace on the Red Sea, a fortress that no terrorist could enter. Alia turned him down. She was speaking not just for herself and the elite but for every Saudi woman. Moving the speech into the palace would undercut her message.

"Anyway, you'll protect me, won't you, colonel?"

So the speech stayed, and the colonel did his best to turn the hotel into a fortress. Only registered guests and the women invited to hear the princess were allowed into the InterContinental on the day of the speech. Their names were checked at the hotel's front gate, while bomb-sniffing dogs from the National Guard searched their vehicles. Everyone had to pass through metal detectors. Purses and luggage were x-rayed. Security agents patted down anyone who set off an alarm, their searches thorough and careful. The Interior Ministry checked the names and passports of all 142 hotel guests against national and international watch lists.

A second layer of security protected the conference room. Bomb-sniffing dogs checked the room before anyone was allowed inside. The women had to pass through another metal detector before they entered. Six security agents watched the crowd, two behind the lectern, two on the sides, and two beside the door at the back. They formed a hexagon that covered the room. Another five officers handled the dogs and metal detectors, and three women patted down any women who set off the detectors. All this to watch a handpicked audience of one hundred fifty women. The colonel knew he was being overly cautious, but better safe than sorry.

The princess had arrived at the hotel in her armored limousine an hour before the speech was scheduled to begin. The Inter-Continental's manager escorted her to a suite overlooking the Red Sea. As women slowly filed into the conference room seven floors below, Alia sipped a bottle of water and reread her speech. She wore a black *abaya* and a gray head scarf loose enough to allow tendrils of her hair to swing free. By Western standards, she was a few pounds too heavy to be beautiful. But her eyes were deep and black, her mouth soft and wide. She was twenty-five and had gone to high school in Geneva and spoke Arabic and French and English.

The National Guard captain who served as her personal bodyguard watched her wordlessly. The captain was married, but after three years of watching over Alia, he was half in love with her. He'd have cut out his tongue sooner than admit that truth.

The hour passed, and then another twenty minutes. The captain was just about to ask Alia if she wanted him to call downstairs when his phone rang. He listened for a moment. "They're ready."

Alia flashed the smile he'd grown to adore. "Then let's go."

Before the hour was over, they would both be dead.

"My sisters, my sisters."

Alia looked at the crowd. "Our enemies say we want a revolution. But I don't see any revolutionaries in this room. What about me? Do I look like a revolutionary to you? In my *hijab?* Did I drive a tank to get here?

239

Is that what happened? Did you see my tank outside?"

A few women tittered. Most were silent, too aware of the importance of the occasion even to laugh.

"A year ago, I read a sermon by a famous cleric — I won't say his name — who says what we want is un-Islamic. But we can read the Quran, too. And I ask you, does the Quran say that women can't drive? Hardly, my sisters. The wife of the Prophet — peace be upon Him — we know that she rode a horse with him. The very wife of Muhammad. Why, then, can't we drive? We don't ask for anything that the Quran forbids. In other Muslim nations, we drive freely. And this law, forbidding driving, it's foolish. Male servants must drive us. Does that make sense? I tell you it doesn't. If we could drive ourselves, there would be no need for this.

"I'm proud to be Muslim. I know that Islam doesn't fear women's rights. We should wear our burqas by our own choice. Not because the *muttawa* force us. If we choose to wear an *abaya* and show our faces, the police shouldn't interfere. As to whether we work or stay home, we and our husbands can decide."

The princess paused, looked out at the

crowd. "I know you don't mistake what I'm saying, my sisters. I don't want to live immodestly. But let's not confuse what is *haram*" — forbidden — "with what is allowed. Drinking alcohol is *haram*. Eating pork is *haram*. Eating during the fast, that's *haram*. But driving and working, those are allowed. I know some of our brothers and fathers don't agree" — a few in the audience laughed — "but they're allowed."

Alia went on for another twenty minutes. Her arguments weren't new. But she spoke with a regal authority. And slowly the crowd warmed, lost its fear. The women leaned forward, interrupted her with applause and laughter. She came to her last page knowing she'd won.

"My sisters, this won't be a short fight. In fact, I shouldn't even use the word *fight* to describe it. We're all believers. Let's call it a conversation. It won't be a short conversation. It's going to happen in bedrooms and living rooms and even bathrooms" — more laughter — "all over our kingdom. It will happen one husband at a time, one brother at a time, one father at a time. But it will happen. One day we will drive and work and sit with men in public. I believe with all my heart, as a woman and as a Muslim, that day will come in my lifetime."

241

■ ■ ■ ■

The assassin sat in the third row of the audience, no more than seven meters from the princess. He wore a black burqa with a full veil that covered his face. His hands — small and hairless, with manicured pink fingers — rested lightly in his lap.

The assassin was a short man with sloped shoulders, narrow hips, light brown skin. He had a valid Jordanian passport that didn't show up on watch lists. On his Saudi visa application, he called himself a religious tourist coming to the Kingdom for an *umrah* — a pilgrimage to Mecca that occurred outside the annual *hajj* period.

He arrived in Jeddah eight days before the princess was due to speak and booked a room at the InterContinental, a junior suite that looked east toward Mecca. He left after two days. He'd used a debit card from a Lebanese bank to guarantee his stay, but he settled his bill in cash. No surprise. Arabs liked paying cash. Tax collectors couldn't trace it.

"I hope you enjoyed your visit," the clerk said.

"Jeddah's very pleasant."

"This time of year, yes."

242

"I may be back as early as next week." The assassin handed a fifty-riyal note to the concierge — almost fifteen dollars, enough to be remembered favorably without really being remembered.

"If there's anything I can do for you, let me know."

Sure enough, the assassin returned four days later. Two nights before the princess was due to speak. Again he booked a junior suite. Nineteen hundred Saudi riyals a night, about five hundred dollars. He traveled with two roller suitcases, small enough to fit in an overhead cabin compartment, the kind that experienced travelers everywhere used. The first held men's clothes, Western and Arab. A long gray robe. Khaki slacks.

The second case would have been of greater interest to the security agents downstairs, if they'd seen it. Its top compartment held a burqa, a modest dark blue dress, a full-face veil, a padded bra, pink nail polish, and a cell phone that looked ordinary but wasn't. Beneath the clothes, a second compartment contained what looked like a thick, stiff piece of cardboard in a plastic bag. The cardboard was actually made of two kilograms of RDX, military-grade plastic explosive.

The assassin had spent nearly a year practicing for this day. Long before he learned of the princess's speech, Ahmad Bakr realized the value of having a suicide bomber who could convincingly pass as female. Saudi society was so sexist that women weren't viewed as threats. And though security officers knew that men could hide themselves in a burqa, they had never addressed the threat. The police hesitated even to speak to a woman in full burqa. They would make her remove it only in extreme circumstances.

Bakr had found a man perfect for the task. The Jordanian was skinny, high-voiced, with thin arms. He might have been one of *those*. Bakr didn't care, as long as he passed as a woman. And surely *they* had an easier time passing.

Staying at the hotel allowed the assassin to penetrate the outer cordon of Alia's security. Still, he faced additional defenses, including the second metal detector and a potential pat-down, a disaster he had to avoid. He had learned that the breasts and the hips were the key. Breasts couldn't be too large. A padded 34B bra worked best, with small silicone pads taped to his chest to fill out the cups. For his hips, he favored black spandex stockings that pushed his behind up and out.

While the princess prepared for her speech, the assassin was preparing, too, following a routine he'd practiced a dozen times in hotels in Lebanon and Jordan. He didn't have a heavy beard or body hair, but he shaved himself smooth anyway. After he put on his bra and stockings, he sprayed eau de toilette on himself, Dior, just a few drops, enough to cover him in a light citrus scent.

The next part was the trickiest. He took the explosive plate from its plastic bag, taped it to his stomach, pulled its straps tight around his body. The plate was large, a rectangle fifteen centimeters long, ten centimeters wide, and two centimeters thick at the center. It tapered at the sides, so that its silhouette wouldn't be obvious under the dress. Even so, the assassin would have preferred a smaller plate. But because of the metal detectors, the explosive couldn't be covered with buckshot to create shrapnel. The explosion itself had to be powerful enough to be lethal in a ten-meter radius. Bakr had insisted on two kilograms of explosive.

The assassin made sure the plate was tightly bound and that the holes for the detonators were where he wanted them. Then he pulled the blue dress over his skinny body, making sure the holes he'd cut into it matched the holes in the explosive plate. He strolled around the suite, adjusting his stockings and bra. He stopped in front of the mirror, studied himself. He smoothed the dress over the plate, turned sideways. His hair was too short, and his Adam's apple protruded. The explosive wrinkled the belly of the dress. But his burqa would hide those flaws. He knew it would. He had walked through Baalbek and West Beirut dressed this way without being noticed.

The burqa's veil was made of a thick fabric that looked like black mosquito netting. The veil smudged his features but didn't completely hide them. The outlines of his eyes and nose and cheeks were visible. He needed to be sure nothing about them was masculine. He stroked his cheeks with foundation, plucked his eyebrows until they were pencil-thin. He plumped his eyelashes with mascara, smoothed the circles under his eyes, painted his nails.

He was ready.

He pulled on the burqa, hid himself in its rich, black folds. The fabric was a wool-cotton blend, heavier than usual, the better to hide any trace of his body. He leaned close to the mirror, studied his face. The makeup had done the job. He was a woman now.

The assassin was not a reflective man. He didn't question why he liked dressing this way, didn't question why he felt such hatred for this princess. When Bakr had told him about the mission, he had accepted immediately. Alia couldn't be allowed to spread her lies. She wasn't Muslim at all. He knew that she had lived for years in Europe. No doubt she had behaved shamefully there. Now she would pay for her sins.

He unrolled his prayer rug, faced Mecca. The holy city. Just over the horizon. He'd had the chance to visit it three days earlier, to circle the Kaaba seven times and spend the day praying. A blessing. A vision of the Kaaba filled his mind, and he knew that he'd succeed today.

Dressed as a woman, coated in Dior perfume, more than four pounds of explosive strapped to his stomach, the assassin knelt on his rug and asked Allah for success.

Two officers monitored the metal detector outside the conference room. The assassin handed his purse to one and walked through the detector. It stayed quiet. The detonators and wires, which would have set it off, were in his purse.

The guard picked out the cell phone from the purse, a black leather satchel from Chanel. A very close observer might have noticed that the phone's handset cord looked thicker than normal, or that the headset's earbuds were oddly shaped. The guard didn't. Nor did he see the two metal cylinders that looked like AA batteries at the bottom of the purse. He held up the phone. "Does this take photos?"

"Yes." The assassin's voice was light and breathy, not falsetto, as he'd practiced.

"Photos aren't allowed." The guard handed back the phone and purse. "And once the princess comes, you'll have to turn it off. Go on."

Inside the room, the assassin moved quickly. He'd come early. The room was barely one-quarter full. He chose a seat three rows from the podium, on the right. He'd scouted the conference room the day before, noted the door on the front-right side of the room. She would probably enter there.

No one else was in the row. The assassin sat down and unzipped his purse. He reached inside for the phone and the AA batteries, which in reality were RDX detonators. He kept his hands inside the purse. He uncoiled the cord wrapped around the phone and screwed the earbuds, which were actually electrically initiated blasting caps, into the detonators. He had drilled this move hundreds of times, with his eyes closed, in the dark, with his right hand and his left. Many nights he found himself dreaming the motions.

He armed the detonators in four seconds.

He lifted the detonators into his burqa. The awkwardness of the motion couldn't be avoided, but no one noticed. He leaned forward in his chair and pulled his right arm up his sleeve to his chest. He slid the detonators through the holes in the dress and slotted them into the explosive plate. For a moment, he couldn't find the second hole. He didn't panic. He found it.

And he was done.

He pulled his arm out of the burqa. He'd finished the tricky part. The cord hung loosely down his right sleeve. When he was ready, he would plug it in. Pushing any button on the phone would fire the blasting caps, setting off the detonators and the explosive.

He sat up in his seat and waited for the princess.

■ ■ ■ ■

"I believe with all my heart, as a woman and as a Muslim, that day will come in my lifetime."

The assassin reached in his purse, plugged the cord into the cell phone.

On the podium, Princess Alia smiled. "Thank you, my sisters. Thank you." The assassin turned on the phone. Around him, women applauded. Scattered cries of *"Inshallah!"* — God willing — came from the rows. *"Inshallah,"* the princess said. She stepped away from the lectern, walked to her left, crossing in front of the assassin.

He stood. "Princess." She turned toward him. The crowd stirred. The officers on the podium looked at one another. The colonel, Alia's bodyguard, who had watched the speech from the edge of the podium, stepped forward. They were all too late.

"Inshallah," the assassin said. He squeezed the phone's call button —

Abdullah and Miteb sat in wicker chairs in the sunroom of Abdullah's villa in Cap d'Antibes. Beneath them were the homes of lesser royalty. Beneath those homes, the sea. A chessboard lay on the table between them.

Abdullah was playing white, but he had lost interest. Early on he had moved his knight diagonally, like a bishop, to see if his brother would stop him. Miteb hadn't. Finally, Abdullah looked at Miteb and said, "Are we playing Arabian rules, my brother?"

" 'Arabian rules'?"

"Where the king does what he wants and no one stops him?"

"Aren't those always the rules, Abdullah?"

The sun broke through the high white clouds. Under the room's bulletproof glass, orchids and ferns rose to greet the rays. The heat baked the pain from Abdullah's bones, and for a few seconds he imagined himself young.

"What did the American say?" Abdullah said. "Will he help us?"

"As if you don't know."

"What do you mean?"

"My brother. You made your point with the chess. Don't pretend you don't remember."

"I don't know what you're talking about. Didn't you meet him this morning?"

Miteb cleared his throat. "I met him yesterday, not this morning. And I told you about it yesterday." Quietly, now: "You really don't remember."

Abdullah didn't. Not a word. Yesterday

251

had disappeared. Yesterday was today, and today was never. *Is this what happens? I know I lose the future, but must I give up the past, too?* He grabbed Miteb's arm. "I know. Of course I know. But pretend I don't. Repeat it, then. What did he say?"

"He's suspicious, but I think he'll help us."

The conversation came to Abdullah in pieces, a book with half the pages torn out.

"He said . . . something about a credit card? And numbers on money?"

"That's right. You remember."

The pity in Miteb's voice infuriated Abdullah. "What do you mean he's suspicious? He dares judge me? He's insolent. I don't want him."

"We need him."

"Did he ask for money?"

"No."

The answer surprised Abdullah. Everyone asked for money. Some asked slyly, some directly. But they all asked sooner or later. "He will."

"I wouldn't be so certain."

"It would be best. . . ."

Abdullah trailed off. Miteb waited. Abdullah pushed back the hem of his *thobe,* shook his arm, scowled at his pruny, withered skin. "I wish it was five hundred years ago. Back then you would have left me in the desert." Abdullah coughed, spat a glob of phlegm flecked with blood onto the sunroom's red tile floor. "No doctors. You would have left me behind, and I would have walked until I died. It wouldn't have taken long. Only a few days. There'd be none of this."

"Abdullah —"

"Tell me that this is better."

A knock on the sunroom door stopped Miteb from answering. Hamoud, Abdullah's servant, entered. "Your Highness —"

"Out. Now!"

"Sir." Hamoud tried to hand the king a cell phone. Abdullah ignored him, and he gave it instead to Miteb, who listened silently. "You're sure. In Jeddah. Yes. I'll tell him." Miteb's face hollowed like an empty house. "We need to go back. It's Alia."

"What's happened?"

Miteb told him. Twenty-three women were confirmed dead at the InterContinental. Including the princess.

Abdullah grabbed the phone, threw it down. It shattered on the tiles, and Hamoud hurried to collect the pieces. The king ignored him. The king looked through the glass and into the sun until his eyes burned and he couldn't see anything at all.

"Saeed will burn for this." A terrible new

thought raged through his ravaged mind. "You wanted me to come here. To distract me. You're part of it, too."

"Abdullah. Never again accuse me of betraying you. Never again."

Apologizing was beyond Abdullah. But he nodded.

"As for Saeed and Mansour —"

"I know."

"Even if you're right, this is what he wants, Abdullah. Don't fall for this. Leave it to the American."

"All right. For now. But if he can't help us —"

"I understand, my king."

"If you don't, you'll learn." Abdullah pushed himself up, knocking over the chessboard. He stumbled toward the door that would take him to the car and then to the plane and then home. His home. His Kingdom. All he knew.

CHAPTER 11

NICE, FRANCE

Shafer hadn't been happy to hear from Wells.

"Tell me again why I'm helping you?"

"This isn't like the Robinson thing."

"You don't work for us anymore. You can't come running every time you have a problem. Not how it works. Even for you. Even with me."

Wells had no answer.

"I need to know who's paying you. Especially on this. This is no such business and they like knowing their clients." By *no such,* Shafer meant the National Security Agency. The nickname dated from the Cold War, when the United States denied the NSA's very existence.

"I can't."

"Give me *something,* John."

"It goes back to the attacks two weeks ago."

"Who hired you?"

Wells was silent. Shafer was silent. A transatlantic pissing contest.

"All right," Shafer said finally. "I'll see what I can do."

"Faster would be better."

"Give me more and it'll be faster."

Shafer was right. Wells had asked for a favor he didn't deserve. He didn't like being in this position. But only the NSA had a chance of tracking the phones and credit card.

The card was a better bet than the phones. Before an online purchase could be completed, retailers had to get approval from the bank that had issued the card. Banks stored that data in "server farms," windowless, high-security warehouses stacked with neat metal rows of computers and hard drives. The farms themselves were impregnable, but the NSA tapped the Internet connections into them to copy credit card numbers and purchase orders.

In the United States, the taps were legally questionable. The Constitution required warrants for searches. The Bush Administration had decided that the taps were legal, as long as NSA made its "best efforts" to discard purchases made by American citizens. The rule had a massive loophole. "Best efforts" had never been defined. No one outside the NSA knew exactly how much data the government had collected on American citizens. Yet the program hadn't ended on January 20, 2009. The new president had found it, like Guantánamo, too useful to give up. Expanding national security programs was always easier than scaling them back.

Even so, the card monitoring wasn't foolproof. The NSA couldn't always get access to data lines, especially in China and Russia. It estimated that it caught fewer than half of all credit card purchases worldwide. And the feeds were encrypted, so after it stole the data, the NSA had to decode it.

Nor were credit cards the only concern. The NSA monitored phone calls, e-mails, instant messages, Facebook updates, a digital tidal wave. Tens of billions of messages, open and encrypted, were sent every day. The NSA spent massive energy just figuring out which ones to try to crack. At any time, one-third of its computers were deciding what the other two-thirds should do. Inevitably, credit card transactions didn't get much attention. The vast majority were routine purchases.

But they couldn't be entirely ignored, because both the NSA and CIA believed that terrorists now had to have credit cards to pull off major attacks on American soil. Since September 11, living a cash-only existence had gotten tricky. Paying cash to fly set off automatic red flags in airline and Homeland Security databases. Car-rental agencies wouldn't rent to drivers who didn't have cards. Trying to buy industrial chemicals or lab equipment with cash raised even louder alarms.

So the NSA hadn't given up on credit cards, especially from banks based in places like Egypt and Pakistan. The CIA's analysts believed that jihadis would avoid multinationals like Citibank. Local banks would be more willing to open accounts and issue cards, and fervent Muslims might stay away from Western banks on principle.

So if the credit card number Wells had found came from a bank in Lebanon or Turkey or Pakistan . . . and if the NSA had tapped the connection to that bank's servers . . . and if its software algorithms had decided that the feed was worth trying to crack . . . and if the bank hadn't installed the most advanced 256-bit security on its feed . . .

Then maybe the NSA would have a card in its database that matched the number Wells had found. Complete with name, address, and purchase data. The name and address could be faked, but the purchase information couldn't. If Wells was supremely lucky, the NSA might even be able to link the card with others still in use. All this from nineteen digits on five Saudi one-riyal notes.

So Wells knew he had no choice but to ask Shafer's help. But he didn't like it.

After Shafer, Wells called Anne, asked her to FedEx an envelope from their bedside table. The envelope held two passports, one American, one Canadian, both with his photo, neither with his name. Both should work anywhere in the world. Unless the CIA had shut them down. Which was unlikely. Duto and Shafer probably wanted him to use passports they could track. Even if the agency hadn't been paying attention to him before, he'd put himself on its radar by asking for help. He seemed to be playing under Hotel California rules. *You can check out anytime you like, but you can never leave.*

"What's in the envelope?"

"See for yourself."

The envelope rustled open. "Are these real?"

"Depends on what you mean by reality."

"Cool."

"Never admitted that before, but yeah. I

259

guess they are."

"I guess this means you're not coming home anytime soon."

"Looking that way. Listen. Will you do something else for me?"

"Depends."

"An honest answer."

"I'm an honest girl."

"Buy a disposable cell phone. Pay cash. Set up a new e-mail account. Not from the house. I'll set one up, too. Mine will be the name of the mountain where we met, followed by the name of the bar we went that first night, followed by the drink you bought for me. No underscores. Got it?"

"Mountain, bar, drink. Got it."

"Don't say it."

"Like Rainier-redlion-cosmo."

"You have me drinking cosmopolitans?"

"You can be a little bit girly, John. I like that about you."

"How's that again?"

"Tell you next time I see you."

"Something to look forward to. When you're done buying the phone, e-mail me your number. I'll call you when I can."

"You don't seriously think someone's monitoring my phone."

"Possible. And getting more possible."

"Anyone else, I'd be calling a shrink about

now." She paused. "I'll get the phone. Tell me you miss me."

"I miss you."

"I miss you, too." Click.

The day passed with no call from Shafer. Wells wanted to move but had no place to go. He fought the urge to book a flight for Karachi or Cairo, motion for motion's sake.

He prayed that night, properly, for the first time in weeks. Perhaps if this mission went off, he'd have the chance to see the Kaaba. The thought cheered him more than he would have expected. When he closed his eyes, he could see the great black cube, imagine walking around it. He supposed talking to Miteb had stirred him. The old man's acceptance of Allah's judgment and death's inevitability felt like wisdom.

In the morning, he sent the concierge for more clothes and a bag. Wherever he went, he'd be well dressed. The passports arrived, courtesy of FedEx. And just before noon, the phone trilled.

"Ellis?"

"Hold for Prince Miteb," a man said. A moment later: "Princess Alia is dead. A suicide bomb in Jeddah."

"Slow down, Prince —"

"This is Abdullah's granddaughter. His

favorite. If the others are involved —"

Miteb fell silent. But Wells understood. Suicide bombers had gone after the royal family before. But if Miteb and Abdullah were right, this wasn't just another suicide bombing. The king's own brother might have ordered this attack.

Wells wondered how Abdullah would respond. Under normal circumstances, Saeed and Mansour had the edge. They had the secret police. But in a war, Abdullah's National Guard could reduce the *muk* to rubble. Except that open war would be desperately risky for both sides. The regular army would get involved, pick a side. Or its mid-level officers might try to overthrow the royal family entirely, take the country's oil for themselves. Saeed and Mansour couldn't take that chance. They had to believe that Abdullah wouldn't order the Guard into action, or that if he tried, the order would backfire because it would make him look unhinged. In other words, they had to believe their conspiracy was airtight.

Assuming they were involved at all, and that Wells hadn't simply fallen for the ramblings of two old men.

"What happened?" Wells said.

"She was speaking. An audience of women. At a hotel in Jeddah. It was a man dressed as a woman."

"How many dead?"

"Too many." Miteb's voice was steady but weak, his age showing.

"I'm sorry, Prince."

"I must go. Our jet —"

"Before you do. I need money."

"A fee? Of course, of course —"

Wells was embarrassed. "Not a fee. For things I need to buy." Plane tickets. Kevlar. Sniper scopes.

"How much?"

"More is better. And one other thing —" Wells explained.

"I think that's possible. Have you found anything yet, Mr. Wells?"

"I'm still working."

"Please try. My brother, you understand, he's very angry."

"When I get something, how can I reach you?"

"Call Pierre. He can pass along the message, even if Saeed's men are listening."

"All right. Please tell your brother I'm sorry."

"Your sorrow won't help him. Only revenge."

And not even that, Wells thought. As Miteb no doubt knew. "Safe journeys, Prince."

"Safe journeys. *Inshallah.*"

■ ■ ■ ■

The knock came thirty minutes later. A valet handed over a black leather briefcase. When Wells popped the latches he found it stuffed with one-hundred- and five-hundred-euro notes and hundred-dollar bills, new and crisp and held in pale blue paper bands that read "Banque Privat — Credit Suisse." Wells didn't bother counting them. Miteb had sent over millions of dollars. In a briefcase that he hadn't even locked. A reminder of the men Wells was dealing with. As if he needed one.

Atop the money, a pistol in a clear plastic bag. Wells's second request. A Beretta 9-millimeter, from one of Miteb's bodyguards. Given the choice, Wells would have preferred a Glock. But he knew that the guys who worried the most about muzzle velocity and trigger pressure were the guys who'd never shot to kill. Up close, a pistol was a pistol. Past forty feet, the Glock was superior. But if he was shooting from that far away, he was already in trouble.

Wells popped the clip, racked the slide to be certain the chamber was empty, squeezed the trigger. The Beretta's previous owner had taken good care of it. It was freshly oiled, its action smooth. It would do. He reloaded it, slipped it into the briefcase.

The phone trilled again. "Mr. Wells?" A woman with a rich Irish brogue. "I'm Sandra McCord. With the American Express private client division. Mr. Azari asked me to call you."

"I don't know that name."

"He works for the prince." Her voice fell to a whisper, as if even saying the title was blasphemy. "He said you would need a credit card."

"Then I'd better get one."

Sandra agreed to messenger over two cards, one in Wells's name, the other under the pseudonym Tom Ellison, matching his Canadian passport. Both would be basic AmEx green cards, less likely to attract attention than fancier varieties.

"How soon can you get them to me?"

"Two hours. We have an office in Nice."

"Of course you do."

"I'm sorry?"

"Tell you what. I'll pick them up in an hour. And what's the limit?"

"A half-million euros. That's our standing agreement with Mr. Azari. I hope it's acceptable."

Miteb had supplied two of the four essential tools of the trade, money and a weapon. Wells still needed a clean passport and an untraceable phone, but those could wait. He had to move. He took the briefcase and folded his expensive new clothes in his expensive new bag and left. No reason to check out. Let the front desk believe he was staying another day.

At the train station, Wells bought a disposable cell and a handful of SIM cards and a first-class ticket for a Eurostar to Milan. He wanted to head east. And to avoid airports as long as he could. Train passengers could pay cash, and passports weren't checked within the European Union's borders.

He arrived in Milan five hours later, just as the evening rush was starting. The station had opened in 1931 and was a creature of its era, enormous stone blocks and vaulted arches. Mussolini had no doubt been proud. Near the entrance, Wells glimpsed an Italian news channel reporting on the bombing in Jeddah: *"Terrorismo nell'Arabia Saudita."* He stopped to watch, but the report lasted only a few seconds. Just another bombing in the Middle East. It had killed a member of the Saudi royal family, but Alia wasn't exactly Princess Di.

Outside the station, Wells found a grimy two-star pensione and slipped a hundred-euro note to the clerk for a room, no passport or registration needed. He flipped on the television for background noise and called Shafer. "Tell me something."

"You're lucky. The card hit. Where are you?"

"Milan."

"Who'd you meet in Nice?"

"Friend of a friend. This thing in Jeddah —"

"It's bad."

"Incisive analysis, Ellis."

"Thank you."

"What happened over there?"

"Nobody knows. We offered to send a forensics team, but they turned us down. They're not in a caring and sharing mood. But they had real security at the hotel. Metal detectors, bomb dogs. They're saying the bomber was dressed as a woman. Which would make it easier, but still."

"AQ?"

"I don't know, and I couldn't tell you over this phone if I did. But we think no. Who gave you that credit card, John?"

"It's from a guy the Saudis picked up last month in Riyadh." An explanation that wasn't quite true and evaded rather than answered the question, in any case.

"He's connected to this?"

"They think so."

"They still have him?"

"He's dead now. They found a body, no ID. They wanted help in making him."

"And came to you?"

"Some people think I'm helpful. What's on that card, Ellis?"

"Tell me again how you got involved in this."

Wells had no choice but to lift his skirt. A little. "The Saudis are worried about their security and thought I could help. They wanted somebody who isn't connected to them."

"Who?"

"Can't say."

"Inside the family or out?"

"Inside."

Shafer was silent. Then: "The card was activated four months ago. First used at an electronics store in Beirut. Based on the size of the purchase, probably for cell phones. Then for flights from Beirut. On Middle East Airlines. The Lebanese carrier. One to Jeddah, two to Riyadh. Only one was round-trip. Then hotels in Riyadh. A rental car. Restaurants. Nothing exciting."

"What's the name on the card and the plane tickets?"

"Not until you give me more and not on

this line. But I have a bonus for you. We think there's a connected card. Used in the same store for more phones. Still active. Somebody's been buying gasoline with it. Something from a gas station, anyway."

"In Beirut."

"No. A town called Qaa. In the northern Bekaa Valley. The plane tickets were bought on an Internet connection from the same place."

The Bekaa. Hezbollah country. Wells didn't get it. Miteb and Abdullah seemed certain that Saeed was behind the bombings. But what if Iranians were orchestrating all these attacks, trying to destabilize the Saudi monarchy?

"You should find an embassy so we can talk on a secure line."

"Not now."

"John. Who'd you meet in Nice?"

"I'm getting a feeling you already know. Who's having this conversation, Ellis? You and me? Or is Vinny on speaker?"

"I'll help you, but you've got to play, John. It can't go one way."

"Answer one question. You guys have anybody on me?"

"Truth. I'm not sure. But I don't think so. You popped up too fast for that. Can I give you some advice?"

269

"Can I stop you?"

"Leave this one alone. Let us handle it. These Saudis, they'll use you and toss you."

"Lucky I can count on you, then." Wells hung up, pulled the SIM card out of the phone, and flushed it away. A roach dropped from the showerhead, crawled along the tub. As if it knew it was in Milan, the creature was strangely stylish, black with brown stripes. Even so, Wells decided to move on.

He sat at a coffee bar just inside the train station's center entrance and considered his next move. The conversation had gone too easily. Shafer hadn't just given him a tip. He'd answered every question Wells had asked and demanded next to nothing in return.

Wells wanted to believe he'd outsmarted Shafer. Or that Shafer was helping him from respect for their history. But he knew better. *Leave this one alone. Let us handle it.* The truth was the opposite. Shafer and the agency wanted Wells to chase this lead. Because the CIA didn't have sources it could trust in Saudi Arabia, certainly not at the top of the royal family. And it couldn't commit operatives to the Bekaa without knowing more about what was on the other end. Vinny Duto couldn't risk losing a team to Hezbollah. Duto wanted Wells to run re-con until he decided what to do. He figured the agency could track Wells, and that even if Wells lost the watchers, he'd have to ask for help when he got in trouble.

The ugly part was that Duto was probably right. Even worse, Wells couldn't be sure Duto would come through if he asked for help. After all, Wells didn't work for the CIA anymore. He was on private business. Getting used by two countries at once.

So be it. At least he understood the game. And he was fairly sure that Shafer had wanted him to see how he was being played. Which was a minor comfort.

Wells didn't think the agency had put anyone on him in the last twenty-four hours. But he needed to be certain. Even on MATO — monitor and track only — orders, watchers would make trouble.

No need for fancy moves tonight, Wells thought. He had enough money and alternate routes to Lebanon to make tracing him a chore. He bought a first-class sleeper ticket for the train from Milan to Bari, on Italy's southeastern coast, the back heel of the boot. The train left at 8:20 p.m. At 8:17, he headed for the platform, shouldering through the dwindling crowds of Milanese

271

commuters on their way home to the sub-
urbs. He didn't run. Anyone or no one
could have been trailing him.

At these moments, Wells always remembered Guy Raviv, the CIA operative who'd
trained him in countersurveillance at the
Farm. Near the end of training, Raviv
brought Wells to the Washington Monument. An agency team was watching them,
Raviv said. Wells had thirty minutes to lose
them and report back. He had to stay within
one block of the Mall.

"These are the pros," Raviv said. "Not the
schlubs we use down in Virginia. I had to
beg them to waste an hour on you. Told
them you were the class stud. Every class
has a stud, you know. Most of you make
damn poor ops. You fall in love with the
moves and forget the rhythm."

"I have no idea what you're talking about."

"If you're lucky, one day you will. Now
go."

Wells wandered east, toward the Capitol.
The day was sunny, warm, not too humid, a
treat for D.C. in July. Thousands of families
and students and twentysomethings hung
out, playing Frisbee on the lush, green lawn
and picnicking under the trees. Wells
couldn't figure who was on him. The heavy
woman in a too-tight T-shirt and a red Car-

dinals hat? The two Asian students kicking a soccer ball past each other?

Wells bought a ticket to the National Air and Space Museum, took the big escalator upstairs, jogged down. The soccer players drifted in his direction. He walked east, found himself standing at the foot of the Capitol, looking up at its great white dome. Two joggers were making suspiciously slow loops. Or maybe they were just slow. The woman in the Cardinals hat huffed toward him. Any of them could have been watching, or all of them. He had no idea how he could lose this team under these conditions. The mission was impossible. Maybe that was the point. Raviv was always making a point.

Raviv was sitting near the base of the monument when Wells trotted back. "I saw you coming two blocks away. Very subtle."

"It was an impossible assignment."

"Don't whine."

"Sorry."

"And don't apologize. Did you lose them?"

"I don't know."

"Who were they?"

Wells nodded at the soccer players. "Maybe these guys."

"Anyone else?"

273

"A couple joggers looked good to me, but they're gone now. I get it, Guy. Real CS is a lot tougher than training."

"There was no one. No team. This idea that any of us have a sixth sense that lets us take three steps in a crowd and know who's watching, there's a word for that. Paranoia. You can't make a team in a place like this unless you have more than thirty minutes. And space to disappear. Or unless they're completely amateur. Or unless they want you to know. The lesson today is sometimes there's nobody to lose. Sometimes you're running from something that doesn't exist."

Sometimes you're running from something that doesn't exist. Later, Wells understood that Raviv wasn't just talking about countersurveillance.

Wells's compartment had a single narrow bunk, barely long enough to fit him but cool and clean and comfortable, its white sheets softer than he expected. Italy. He locked the door and napped fitfully as the train chugged through tunnels carved into the northern Italian mountains. It arrived in Bologna at 11:20 for a three-minute stop.

Wells waited two minutes and thirty seconds, grabbed his bag and briefcase, and trotted off. The station was low-ceilinged and tired, nothing like the grand hall in Milan. At the taxi stand, a half-dozen white sedans waited. Wells walked around to the driver's window of the first taxi. "You speak English?"

The driver was small and round and stank of cigarettes. "Pretty much."

"How much to go to Rome?"

"This is Bologna."

"I know it's Bologna. I want to go to Rome. The airport."

"Fiumicino. Three hundred kilometers. Three hours each way. At this time of night, a thousand euros."

Extortion, but Wells didn't care, thanks to the magic briefcase. "Done." He opened the front door. "What's your name?"

The driver raised a hand. "Before you come in, I like to smoke, okay?" He nodded at a packet of Marlboros on the dash.

"All right."

"And you pay now."

Wells peeled two five-hundred-euro notes from his wallet. The driver inspected them, nodded. Wells could read his mind: *Should have asked for more.* Wells slipped in and shut the door, and they headed out.

"I am Sylvie."

"Sylvie. My pleasure." Wells closed his eyes. If Sylvie didn't smoke too much, he might even sleep a little.

Then he heard the engine behind them. He looked in the passenger-side mirror to see another taxi, this one a Mercedes minivan, following them from the station. It matched them turn for turn through the city's winding streets. The driver looked over his shoulder. *"Signore."*

"I know."

"I don't agree to this."

Wells handed him another five hundred euros. "Drive."

So they'd tracked him from Milan, probably all the way from Nice. But he'd bumped them with a simple trick, forced them to chase him in a taxi. Which meant they weren't pros — not A-level pros, anyway. And they probably didn't plan to hurt him, or at least had no orders either way. If they did, the train would have been the logical spot. Still. Wells reached into the briefcase, pulled the Beretta.

Sylvie spewed a torrent of Italian. Wells could understand only one word: *polizia.* The Fiat slowed. Wells grabbed Sylvie's shoulder, squeezed.

"You stop when I say. Not before." He pulled another five hundred euros from his wallet, put them on the dash. "That's two

276

thousand euros already for three hours' work. Get me to the airport and you get two thousand more. No police."

"All right, all right."

The ramp to the A1 was a few hundred yards ahead. "Get on." Sylvie hesitated, then spun the wheel hard left, onto the ramp. The Fiat's tires squealed. The second taxi followed.

"Who are they?"

"I don't know."

"Who are you?"

"It doesn't matter."

In response, Sylvie reached for a Marlboro and lit up. He smoked daintily, twin chimneys streaming from his nostrils. For an hour, he drove in silence, sticking to the center lane and the speed limit of one hundred thirty kilometers — about eighty miles — an hour. The lights behind them neither closed nor faded. An oddly restful chase. But Wells intended to lose his pursuers before Rome.

"How far to the next rest stop?"

"Maybe fifteen kilos."

"Pull over there."

"You want a cappuccino? Gelato?"

"Witty." Still, Wells couldn't help but like this roly-poly driver.

Ten miles later, a blue sign announced the

Montepulciano rest stop. A wide, brightly lit building rested on a platform that spanned the highway. Atop it, a sign proclaimed "Autogrill" in white letters ten feet tall.

"Here?"

"Here. Go to the end of the parking lot."

They pulled off the highway, drove past rows of gas pumps, bright and yellow in the night, past a parking area where big rigs dozed, toward a run-down building that might have been the original rest stop. The other taxi pulled off, too, keeping well behind them. "Stop here. Turn off the engine."

As soon as the engine was off, Wells grabbed the key, ignoring Sylvie's complaints. He stuck the Beretta into the back of his pants, flared out his shirt to hide it. "Don't go anywhere," he said.

He hopped out of the car, popped its trunk. Amid empty bottles of antifreeze and crumpled cigarette cartons, he saw what he'd hoped for — a tire iron. He grabbed it, strode toward the second taxi, his feet crackling on the asphalt, his hands high and visible in the headlights. The minivan churned ahead a few yards, then stopped.

When he was fifteen yards from the taxi, its back door opened. A man stepped out.

He was Arab, with a neatly trimmed mustache. His hands were empty, and Wells didn't see a holster. Wells set the tire iron on the asphalt. "Let's talk peacefully," he said in Arabic. He walked closer to the guy, confidently, his hands high and empty, making clear he didn't have a weapon. He stopped ten feet away.

"All right." The man's Arabic was as smooth as Abdullah's. Saudi, almost certainly.

"Who sent you?"

"You're John Wells?"

"I don't know that name."

The Arab shook his head. "I tell you, stay out of this business. It doesn't concern you."

"I understand," Wells said, his voice low and soothing. "That makes sense." He turned as if to walk away, and in one fluid motion reached behind his shirt and pulled the Beretta. On the *autostrada* the eighteen-wheelers rumbled by heedlessly. "Kneel."

The man went to his knees unwillingly, an inch at a time.

"Who do you work for?" Wells said.

"The DGSE" — the French intelligence service.

"The French don't like Arabs. Who?"

"I tell you, the DGSE."

"If you work for the DGSE, then so do I.

Lie down."

"Don't do this."

"I'm not going to hurt you, but I don't want you following me. Lie down, face on the pavement, hands over your head."

The man lowered his face to the asphalt, extended his arms. Wells patted him down, pulled a wallet from his back pocket. He'd check it later.

"You'll regret this," the man murmured.

"I'll consider myself warned," Wells said. He walked over to the Mercedes.

"I swear I didn't know," the driver said. "He hired me, told me to follow."

"Turn off your engine, give me the key."

The driver did as Wells said. Wells wound up and flung it onto the roof of the abandoned building at the edge of the lot. He grabbed the tire iron, walked back to the Fiat. Sylvie leaned against the sedan. He tossed his cigarette and whistled quietly as Wells approached. *"Che stile."*

"Say again?" Wells threw the tire iron in the trunk.

"It means 'What style.' "

Wells flipped him the Fiat key. "Let's go."

"That's it?"

"What else were you hoping to see?"

As they left the rest stop behind, Wells

relaxed. He was off the grid for now. He flipped through the wallet he'd taken and found eight hundred euros, a credit card, and a Saudi driver's license, both in the name of Ahmad Maktoum. He'd ask Shafer if the name showed up anywhere. He pocketed the card and license and handed the money to Sylvie.

"A bonus."

"Grazie."

Sylvie dropped him at Fiumicino at three a.m. A few travelers, unlucky or too cheap to book a hotel room before an early-morning flight, waited outside the locked terminals. Inside, janitors swept the floors halfheartedly. At this hour, the airport was asleep in an almost human way, alive but hardly moving.

Wells took advantage of the quiet to dump his pistol in a trash bin. He'd have to get a new one in Lebanon, but for what he was facing, he would need more than a pistol. He had to assume that he was looking at more than one or two jihadis. A training camp seemed likely. And even with surprise on his side, he needed help. Preferably an Arabic speaker who could pass for local.

He reached for his cell. The East Coast was six hours behind. "How do you feel about another vacation?"

281

Gaffan didn't answer.

"This one isn't personal. I promise."

"You don't do partners very well, John."

"It's gonna be interesting. And it's not volunteer this time. Quite the opposite."

"We have a sponsor? Anyone I know?"

"Yes and no."

"I need more."

"Tell you when I see you. Get the first flight you can to Larnaca tomorrow morning. Rent a room at the Hilton in Nicosia."

"Where?"

"Cyprus."

"Another island. Is this going to be wet?" Wet, in this case, referring to blood, not water.

"Eight ball says yes."

Silence. Then: "I don't think I can get there before tomorrow night. And I reserve the right to back out." Gaffan sounded like nothing so much as a teenage girl who had theoretically agreed only to coffee with her ex-boyfriend while knowing she had committed to much more.

"Tomorrow night works."

The counters at Fiumicino lit up at 5:30 a.m. The workers appeared out of nowhere, as if they'd slept in the belly of the airport. Wells found the Cyprus Airways counter

282

and bought a ticket — first-class, of course — to Larnaca. He used his Canadian passport, hoping it might take a little bit longer to pop in the CIA's database.

Nicosia, the Cyprus capital, was a boxy city stuffed with low-rise white apartment buildings and banks, shiny five- to ten-story glass-and-steel towers that were designed to project honesty and rectitude but somehow sent the opposite signal. Eastern European and Russian money took vacations on Cyprus. Like its owners, it didn't plan to stay forever, but it was happy enough to stop for a couple weeks and get a tan.

Wells found a Citibank and rented two safe-deposit boxes. He took $200,000 and 200,000 euros, all he could comfortably carry, from the briefcase. He left a million dollars loose in one box, and the briefcase, which had another million or so in euros, in the second. He FedExed the key to the second box to Anne and called her to explain.

"So this briefcase, what's in it?"

"Money."

"I don't need money, John. And I definitely don't need your money."

"It's not my money."

"I still don't need it."

"Give it away, then. Start a no-kill shelter

or something."

"That's not a bad idea," Anne said finally. "But you know what I'd rather have? I'd rather have you start that shelter yourself."

"I'm not very good at no-kill."

She didn't laugh. "This is going to get messy, isn't it?"

"It could."

"Just be sure you're on the right side, then."

"I'm trying."

A message from Gaffan: *Plane late. Missed connection in London. Expect me in a.m.* Two full days after the bombing in Jeddah. Wells hated to wait, but he didn't see an alternative. He took a room at a hostel and rented a Fiat and drove south toward the coast. Cyprus was a jumble of poverty and wealth, run-down cottages and new mansions. Wells puttered slowly along the south coast road, looking for a fishing village that would suit his needs.

Gaffan arrived as promised the next morning. Wells picked him up at the airport, and on the way to the coast explained everything that had happened in France and Italy. Gaffan listened, didn't ask questions. When Wells was done, he handed Gaffan the key to the first safe-deposit box.

"This is yours. A million dollars."

"And if I say no?"

"Either way."

"You trust these men, John?"

"I think so."

"Not exactly a ringing endorsement."

"They beat the alternative. And if these guys in Lebanon are connected to those bombings, we'll be doing everyone a favor by getting rid of them. No matter who's behind them."

"All right." Gaffan tucked the key into his pocket. "I'm in."

Near Zygi, in the center of the south coast, Wells stopped at a fishing village that hadn't gentrified, probably because of the cement factory on the hill above town. Two hundred run-down houses with red-tiled roofs clustered around a narrow harbor. The ships were small, their hulls rusty. Except for one, a sleek white cruiser, seventy feet long, at the end of the pier in the center of the harbor.

Wells parked next to a man scraping barnacles from the hull of a trawler that looked barely seaworthy. "Speak English?"

"A little."

Wells nodded at the cruiser. "Whose is that?"

The man went back to scraping. They

285

walked up the pier, slimy with fish guts, kelp, and jellyfish. Up close, the ship was impressive, low and fast, with big twin engines. A shirtless, burly man, early forties, shoulders covered by dull green tattoos, sat in a folding chair by the gangplank. A knife dangled from a leather scabbard on his hip. He looked at Wells and yawned. Wells couldn't remember the last time someone had yawned at him. The gesture seemed particularly disrespectful.

"We want to talk to your captain."

"I am captain."

"No, you're not."

"He's busy. No tourists on this boat."

"We're not tourists."

The guy shooed them away, closed his eyes. Wells stepped forward and, before the guy could reach for the knife, grabbed his arms and tugged him out of the chair and onto the deck. Gaffan grabbed his legs.

"On three —"

They swung him sideways and pitched him into the oily water behind the cruiser. He came up sputtering and shouting in Greek —

And then Wells heard the unmistakable *ch-chock* of a shotgun being pumped. He turned slowly, hands raised, to see a small man with curly black hair standing at the back of the cruiser, pointing a sawed-off at them. "You are looking for the captain?"

Wells and Gaffan followed the man into a spotless café and up a narrow set of stairs to a terrace overlooking the harbor. In the corner, a gray-haired man drank coffee and studied what looked like *People* magazine. As Wells got closer, he saw that the magazine was, in fact, *People.*

"Sit, please," the gray-haired man said. They sat. "Is this your first time in Cyprus?" His English was excellent. Wells nodded. "And you're American. What's your name?"

"Jim."

"Jim. I'm Nicholas. It's a beautiful day here," the man said. "Why would you disturb it? Throw my friend in the harbor."

"I need a ride to Lebanon. I look at your boat, I see a man who does business."

"MEA flies nonstop."

"Flying makes me nervous."

"Strangers make me nervous."

"I need to carry some supplies. The kind that don't fly well."

"Most of the time, those supplies leave Lebanon. Not the other way."

"I mean the kind that go boom."

"What, specifically?"

"Two pistols. Two silencers. Two AKs.

287

Four hundred rounds. Two grenades. Two pairs of handcuffs."

"That's a lot of supplies."

"I have a lot of money."

"Stand up, both of you."

They did. Nicholas carefully patted down Wells and Gaffan. "Who do you work for?"

"Does it matter?"

"This is a very stupid request. Yet you don't look like stupid men."

Wells took the *People* and jotted down a cell number on Céline Dion's face. Then pulled ten one-hundred-dollar bills from his pocket. He laid the money on the magazine like an open-faced sandwich and slid it to Nicholas. "Thanks for listening," he said. "You want to do business, let me know. But decide soon."

"How much will you pay?"

"You tell me."

Nicholas called the next afternoon. He would provide the weapons and carry Wells to Lebanon. Gaffan wouldn't be on the boat. He would fly into Beirut instead, insurance against Nicholas changing his mind halfway across and dumping Wells overboard.

"How much?"

"A hundred twenty thousand."

His greed impressed Wells. The trip would take less than eight hours each way. And one hundred twenty thousand dollars was probably more than the boat was worth. Wells had to haggle a little bit, if only to prove that he wasn't a complete sucker. "For that I can buy my own boat and ditch it."

"You told me name the price."

"Make it eighty thousand."

"One hundred. Last offer."

Wells couldn't waste more time. "Done. But it has to be tonight."

"Then tonight it will be. Nine p.m. Be sure to wear black. Shoes, gloves, jacket, pants."

"Why?"

"You'll see."

When Wells arrived at 8:55, Nicholas stood waiting beside his ship. Wells walked up the pier, picking his way through the fish guts and trash, and saluted Nicholas. Nicholas saluted back. And without a word, Wells stepped on board.

CHAPTER 12
RIYADH

In the days after Princess Alia's assassination, life behind the walls of the U.S. embassy seemed unchanged. The consular officers rejected visa requests. The cultural affairs secretary moved ahead with his long-shot plan for a visit to Riyadh by four lesser-known *American Idol* finalists. Barbara Kurland played tennis with Roberto, whose shorts were as short as ever.

But the façade of normality went only so far. A permanent scowl twisted the lips of Dwayne Maggs, the embassy's head of security. And Graham Kurland, the ambassador, understood why. Kurland had grown only too familiar with the acronyms in the CIA's internal cables.

The OPFOR, opposing force, was probably not AQAP — Al Qaeda in the Arabian Peninsula. No, the OPFOR was UNK, unknown. But it appeared HT/HC, highly trained and capable. The SIM, Saudi Interior Ministry, had not asked for TECH/ LOG, technical or logistical help. The CIA and NSA judged that the SIM was not close to catching the OPFOR.

The reports made Kurland's HH, head hurt. But no acronym was needed for the last bit of bad news, which landed two days after Alia's death. "MORE ATTACKS JUDGED HIGHLY LIKELY. RECOMMEND MAX SECURITY POSTURE."

"Thought we were at max posture already," Kurland said.

"We are."

"They want us to put up a force field?"

Maggs didn't smile. "The women who visit your wife are going to have to take off their burqas before the marines go near them."

"We'll get them a tent or something."

Along with the warnings, the State Department, CIA, and White House kept asking the same questions: *What's happening? Why these targets? Is Abdullah still in charge?* Kurland was short on answers. Abdullah and Saeed responded to his condolence messages with brief thank-yous sent through their offices. Even Prince Turki, a third-generation royal who was pro-reform and friendly to the United States, had stopped returning Kurland's calls.

At least the folks in Washington were too polite to ask *What's the mood on the ground? What's the average Saudi thinking?* They knew full well that Kurland didn't have a clue. On the fourth night after the bombing, Kurland found himself venting to his wife. They were watching television in bed, a day game at Wrigley, nine hours behind. Barbara was snuggled in the crook of his arm, eyes closed, her face covered in the white wrinkle cream that he'd learned not to joke about.

"You know, for all the good we're doing, we might as well be there."

"Where?"

"There. Chicago."

Her eyes blinked open. "I told you, I'm not going home."

"I don't mean you. I mean us. Useless as tits on a bull."

"You know I hate that expression."

"Sorry. But we're stuck in this cage, pretending we have some idea what's happening here. When we go home, everybody asks, 'What's it like? What are they really like?' I hope those ladies are giving you some idea, Barb. I know they're not a representative sample, but they're something. 'Cause I don't have a clue."

"You're doing the best you can, Graham.

Not like you can drive through Riyadh in the back of a convertible, dressed like Uncle Sam and waving the flag."

Kurland had to smile. "Wouldn't that be great? Bring in a Sting Ray and a fire truck and some cheerleaders and have a real parade. Wave our pom-poms on the way through Justice Square" — also known as Chop-Chop Square, the courtyard in downtown Riyadh where public executions were carried out.

"That's a wonderful idea." She closed her eyes, nestled into the gray hair that covered his chest. "Good night, sweetheart."

"Good night."

That night Kurland imagined his Memorial Day parade. But the dream turned into a nightmare. Instead of a convertible, he stood on an old tanker that leaked Saudi crude into the desert. The cheerleaders and firefighters disappeared, and he was alone. Except for Barbara. She was driving. But when he called out to her, she didn't answer.

He woke tired, ready to dress down his staff just to clear his throat. As he was showering, his phone rang. It was Clint Rana, Kurland's personal aide. "Mr. Ambassador. Prince Saeed's office called. He'd like a meeting."

"When?"

"Today. Didn't say why."

Even so, the call lightened Kurland's mood. At least he'd have something to tell D.C.

The meeting was set for 12:30 at the prince's offices in the Defense Ministry, in the center of Riyadh, two miles from the embassy. A five-minute drive. Even so, Maggs insisted on a "hard armored" convoy — two vans and three Suburbans, all retrofitted to survive ambushes. Their doors had been replaced with inch-thick steel plate, their windows swapped for smoked Plexiglas that could stop a .50-caliber sniper round. To protect them from roadside bombs, their chassis had been reinforced and raised three inches. Not all the modifications were defensive. The welders had cut narrow ports in the skin of their armor to allow the marines inside to fire out without opening windows or doors.

Four Marine guards traveled in each van, three in each Suburban. In all, the convoy had seventeen marines, locked and loaded with enough firepower to level a village. Kurland, Maggs, and Rana rode in the lead Suburban, while the convoy's communications officer and the marine captain in charge of the squad followed in the second.

At 12:15, the convoy cleared the north exit gate from the Diplomatic Quarter. Two Saudi police cars and an unmarked Mercedes waited just outside. Lights flashing, the eight vehicles rolled south, then made a quick left onto a six-lane divided highway that ran through the center of Riyadh.

Outside, the muezzins were calling midday prayers. Riyadh had thousands of mosques, ranging from one-room boxes to giant shrines. It needed even more. Through the Suburban's smoked-glass windows, Kurland glimpsed men bowing to the west, toward Mecca, in a parking lot. They looked African, with dark black skin. "Why are they praying outside?"

Rana glanced over. "Immigrants. Probably don't have a mosque."

Immigrants in Saudi Arabia couldn't become citizens and were generally considered disposable. Employers often confiscated their passports and travel documents, and the police jailed them for being in the country illegally if they complained. If they were caught selling or using drugs, they faced the death penalty. Saudi Arabia chopped off an average of one hundred heads a year, and more than half of the executed were noncitizens. American and European workers avoided the worst harassment, but even they were monitored. If they failed to renew their visas, they found their ATM cards blocked, a good way to ensure that they didn't overstay their welcome.

"Nasty place, isn't it?" Kurland said. It wasn't a question.

"Like they say in West Texas, there's no oil in paradise."

The Defense Ministry was housed inside Riyadh's strangest building, an oval office tower, widest at its midsection with a relatively narrow base and roof. At night, the building was lit a faint yellow. Saudis and foreigners alike called it *the egg.*

Kurland had visited the egg once before, for his welcome-to-Saudi round of introductions. He'd listened to Saeed mouth platitudes about the importance of the Saudi relationship with the United States. Saeed was a small man with heavy jowls, bulging eyes, and a trim mustache that looked to Kurland like it belonged on a Colombian cartel chief. Though, to be fair, many Saudis favored mustaches.

Unlike King Abdullah, Saeed had been distinctly cool to Kurland. Despite his age and infirmities, Abdullah had talked for hours and invited Kurland and his wife to see his stable of camels and his prize falcons.

Saeed had stayed precisely thirty minutes and then checked his watch. "I must go, Mr. Ambassador," he said. "I'm sure we'll meet again."

Back at the compound, Kurland asked Rana if he'd somehow offended the prince. "That's just how he is," Rana said. "Plays it close." *And makes sure we know who's a child of Allah and who's an infidel visitor,* Kurland thought.

Now, as the high steel gates to the ministry compound opened and the upside-down building loomed, Kurland wondered why Saeed had asked for him — and whether the king knew of the meeting.

Saeed's top-floor office looked north and west to the two skyscrapers that dominated downtown Riyadh, the Kingdom Tower and the Faisalia Tower. He and his son Mansour, the head of the *mukhabarat,* stood at the window as Kurland and Rana walked in.

Saeed wore a crisp white *ghutra* and a smooth golden *thobe.* He smiled at Kurland as though they were best friends. They settled themselves, and after greetings and offers of tea, Saeed leaned in and grasped Kurland's arm. "These are difficult times for our kingdom, Ambassador. These terrorists have dealt us a great blow."

"America is prepared to provide whatever assistance you need," Kurland said in English, as Rana translated.

"And we thank you. But our security forces are capable of handling the situation. We have a photo of the assassin, as you know. He was traveling under a Jordanian passport. Unfortunately, it wasn't his real name. But the Jordanian GID" — General Intelligence Directorate — "is working with us to trace him."

"Is your assumption that he was Jordanian? Or Saudi?"

"We don't believe any Saudi would commit such a vile act. Of course, we're examining our files, comparing the photograph with known terrorists and criminals, to be certain. But we haven't found anything yet. And if such treason occurred, we're certain that the evildoer's family would come forward."

"That's reassuring." Kurland wondered if Saeed and Mansour would pick up the irony in his voice. If they did, they ignored it.

"Meanwhile, we've sent a dozen agents to Amman," Mansour said. "And I've told Prince Nayef that if he needs help, he's not to hesitate to ask."

"That's a great relief. And when you speak to Abdullah, please tell him I'm sorry I haven't been able to express my condolences to him personally."

"Of course you know he hasn't been well."

Kurland wondered why Saeed had brought up the king's health, a taboo subject in Saudi Arabia.

"It may be nothing to worry about. Abdullah is a lion. But what happened to Alia upset him terribly. She was his favorite."

"She sounds like she was a wonderful woman."

"Certainly," Saeed said indifferently. "Though not everyone agreed with her views."

Sounds like you'd care more if your favorite pet camel died, Kurland wanted to say. He settled for: "The United States did. And does. We believe that Saudi Arabia needs a full dialogue on women's rights."

"Unfortunately, what you believe is irrelevant. The laws pertaining to women, what they can and can't do, Allah has given those to us. Our kingdom is guided by the Quran."

"The Quran has many verses. And even your brother doesn't necessarily agree with the strictest interpretations."

Rana looked at Kurland, silently cautioning him against arguing about Islam with Saeed. Kurland didn't appreciate the warning. He would have to remind Rana that Rana's job was to translate. Not to second-guess him in front of the other side. But the lesson would wait until the ride back to the embassy.

After an awkward few seconds, Rana went ahead. When he was done, Saeed waved a hand dismissively, as much as saying: *Save your opinions about women's rights for Hillary Clinton. I couldn't care less.* "Abdullah has his views, you have yours, I have mine," Saeed said. "These issues, let's not let them sidetrack us. I won't say they aren't important. But I hope you remember that our kingdom has always been a partner to America."

"And vice versa."

"We do everything we can to keep oil at a reasonable price. We know what that means to your economy."

Kurland hid his irritation at this lecture. "Of course, Prince."

"Abdullah and I want you to know that our family will always be a friend."

"You and Abdullah."

"And those who will follow us. Just as Abdullah followed Fahad, and Fahad followed Khalid. All along, the oil flowed. One day, my brother won't be here. It's foolish to pretend otherwise. One day I won't be, either. But whoever's king, the House of Saud will always be loyal to America. And the oil will still flow."

At least now I know why I'm here, Kurland thought. "I wish I didn't have to be so blunt, Prince, but is Abdullah seriously ill?"

"There are many kinds of illness. Some more obvious than others."

Was Saeed saying that his brother was losing his mind and could no longer govern? Abdullah hadn't struck Kurland as demented when they'd last met. Kurland didn't see how he could ask, and anyway, he wasn't sure he could trust Saeed's answer. Instead he stalled. "Abdullah's been a great friend to the United States. As you say."

"Of course. But whatever happens, I want to reassure you that our oil will always be our gift to the world."

Ambassadors were supposed to be diplomats. Even so, Kurland couldn't let that last sentence pass. "Not exactly a gift, though, is it, Prince?"

When they'd left, Saeed looked at Mansour.
"Do you think they understood?"
"Yes."
"They'll reach out to Abdullah."
"They already have," Mansour said.

"We've logged the calls. But he's not talking to them right now. Or anyone. He's too angry."

Or he's planning a counterattack, Saeed thought. "Sooner or later, he'll talk."

"If he raises his suspicions without any evidence, the Americans will think him a rambling old fool. Especially after the hints you've given them. There's no need to worry, father."

Mansour's reassurances grated on Saeed. His son increasingly treated him as a nervous old man who needed to be managed rather than obeyed. In truth, Saeed was already Abdullah's equal. Besides the Defense Ministry, he oversaw the Ministry of Transport, which distributed tens of billions of dollars in contracts every year, and headed the Supreme Hajj Committee, a job that kept him close to the Kingdom's senior clerics. Only Abdullah's control of the National Guard kept Saeed from dominating Saudi Arabia. The Guard, and the genuine affection that tribal chiefs and ordinary Saudis felt for Abdullah. Saeed knew that he and Mansour would never generate such feelings. He didn't care. Better to be feared than loved.

But still he wanted the throne, for the power and the title both. When Abdullah took power in 2005, Saeed knew he was next in line. He imagined his brother would last only a couple years. Age and time had visibly worn on Abdullah. Saeed didn't like waiting, but he was a decade younger than Abdullah, and orderly successions were the Saudi way.

But Abdullah had proven stronger than Saeed expected. And last year he had told the senior princes that he wanted his own son, Khalid, to be the next king. Foolish old man. Saeed and Abdullah rarely spoke anymore, but when he learned of the plan, Saeed called Abdullah himself. The conversation was short and blunt.

"You can't do this."

"You think our family wants you in power, my brother? Now that they see an alternative? You know what they call you? A scorpion."

In the weeks that followed, Saeed waited for his brothers and nephews to tell him that they were against the plan. Some had. But not enough. Most, including Nayef, the third most powerful prince, had remained silent. They were canny, too cautious to choose a side until they knew the winner, Saeed thought. But he was realistic enough to admit other possibilities. Maybe the other princes disliked him too much to give him more power. Maybe they believed that as king he would install his sons as heirs. Maybe they simply were showing their love for Abdullah.

Saeed knew that he shouldn't have cared. All his life, his ability to control his emotions had served him. But age seemed to have softened his iron will. An unceasing rage overtook him when he realized that his brother might keep him from his prize. The sun boiled his blood. *I will be king. By right and custom.* And even more elementally: *Mine. Mine. Mine.* A bell rang in his head morning until night. Even his ultimate relaxation, swimming laps in the Olympic-sized pool in his palace, failed to calm him.

Saeed believed he'd hidden his anger. But Mansour knew. A few weeks after Abdullah revealed his plan, Mansour arrived at Saeed's palace. "This won't stand, father."

"Nothing's certain yet."

"I can stop him."

"How?"

Mansour explained. For a moment, Saeed was almost frightened of his son. Of the vision that had led Mansour to create this private squad of killers. And then Saeed realized: *This is how the world sees me.*

"You've been building this for years, and you never said?"

304

"Putting the pieces in place. I wasn't sure I'd ever use it."

"What if the Americans found it?"

"I could roll up these men tomorrow. And no one can connect them to me."

"The funding —"

"Goes through a dozen different places. It's airtight. I hid it from you, didn't I?"

"And how do you propose to use these men?"

Then Mansour had sketched his plan, the step-by-step process of provoking Abdullah, of ratcheting up the Kingdom's instability until Abdullah would have no choice but to overreact.

Five years before, or even one, Saeed would have stopped his son. *This is madness,* he would have said. *There's no need.* But his patience was exhausted. And the bell rang: *Mine. Mine. Mine.*

Now the attacks had begun.

On at least one level, they had succeeded. Abdullah was furious. At Princess Alia's funeral, he hardly spoke. He sat beside Saeed, fists clenched, his legs twitching under his robe. Saeed didn't believe Abdullah would be able to control himself much longer. Already, he'd nearly accused Mansour of treason. And when he exploded to the other princes, his accusations would rebound against him. Without evidence, he would sound insane. The family would have to rally around Saeed.

And yet . . . Saeed wished he hadn't chosen this path. Mainly because of Mansour. When he'd agreed to rely on his son, the balance between them had shifted. The irony was not lost on him. In his quest for absolute control, he'd given power to his son. And overconfidence was Mansour's great weakness. He was nearly fifty but had a young man's arrogance. He had grown up in a world of supreme luxury and privilege, protected by Saeed's power. He didn't realize that even perfect plans could come apart.

A thought that reminded Saeed of another potential complication.

"What about the American? Wells?"

"We've lost him for now. Abdullah and Miteb can't possibly have told him anything. And he doesn't even work for the CIA anymore."

Saeed knew about John Wells. Years before, Wells had stopped a nuclear bomb from going off in America. The incident was never publicly disclosed, but Saeed had heard of it because a jihadist Saudi princeling had financed the operation. Afterward, the CIA had given the Saudis proof of the prince's involvement. To quiet the Americans, Mansour's men had killed him in a staged car accident. But it was Wells who had found the bomb and killed the men who'd built it. Wells spoke Arabic, and he'd fought in Afghanistan. Saeed didn't want him within one thousand kilometers of this operation.

"You need to find him," Saeed said now.

"All right, father. We will."

Five miles south, Ahmad Bakr sat against the wall of a mosque that was really nothing more than a one-room box with suras stenciled on the walls. Midday prayers had just ended.

Day by day, he was closing his camp in Lebanon and bringing his men to Saudi Arabia. Some flew from Beirut. Others drove overland through Syria and Jordan. In a few days, he'd have everything he needed for the third operation. This time he didn't expect any congratulations from the general. No, this operation would come as a surprise to Ibrahim — and whoever was behind him.

Bakr's phone buzzed. A blocked number.

He stepped onto a crowded street that stank of baked sewage and week-old meat. The buildings around him were only a few years old and already crumbling, rusty re-bar poking from their concrete. This was Suwaidi, a gigantic slum in southern Riyadh, home to hundreds of thousands of immigrants and unlucky Saudis. The Riyadh police rarely ventured into Suwaidi, never at night.

Bakr flipped open his phone. "One hour. The gold souk."

The gold souk sounded glamorous. It wasn't. Wealthy Saudis shopped for jewelry in Dubai or London. The souk was a run-down warren of shops selling gold-plated necklaces and silver earrings. Bakr arrived early and wandered the stalls, making sure no one had followed him. The sergeant showed up five minutes late. He wore a plain white *thobe* and a nervous smile. Bakr put an arm around him and steered him to an empty café two streets from the souk's rear entrance. They sat in a corner at a bruised Formica table. The room smelled of burnt coffee, and flies buzzed over the sugar bowls.

"Show me," Bakr said.

The sergeant passed over a palm-sized digital camera. He worked on the north entry gate at the Diplomatic Quarter. "These are from today."

"No one saw you take them?"

The sergeant shook his head.

"Tell me again how it works."

"We get a call ten minutes before. Maybe fifteen. Telling us to be ready for a special convoy."

"Always the same gate?"

"Not always. But mostly they prefer my gate. There's less traffic. Then they give us another call a minute in advance. They're so arrogant. Like it's our only job. We clear the cars, make sure they have a path, and they come through. Fast. They're very concerned about getting hit on the way out."

"Then?"

"Police cars wait outside, and the convoy picks them up and then they go."

"And how can you be sure it's him?"

"If he's involved, it's five vehicles at least. Big ones, thick armor. Today it was a van at the front and the back and three Suburbans. You'll see in the pictures. And like you told me, I made sure I was on the gate when they came through. And I saw him. You can't see it in the pictures, not through the glass. But I did."

Bakr waited, but the sergeant didn't give him the last, vital piece of information. So, finally, he asked: "Which car?" Mentally adding, *You fool.*

"Sorry. Second vehicle. The first Suburban. Middle row, left side."

"You're sure."

"A thousand percent."

CHAPTER 13
BEKAA VALLEY, LEBANON

The Bekaa was really two valleys.

The southern half, nearer Beirut, was densely populated and fertile. A half-dozen rivers supported farms and light industry. On day trips, tourists visited vineyards and the ruins at Baalbek. In Zahlé, which had eighty thousand people and was the largest town in the valley, Muslims and Christians lived together, their churches and mosques practically side by side.

North of Baalbek, the valley looked different. Water was scarce and precious. The people were entirely Shia, and mostly poor. The twin mountain ranges, the Lebanon and Anti-Lebanon, pulled away from each other. The land between grew dry and wild. Herds of sheep wandered across rocky hummocks. Roads turned to gravel without warning.

In the north, Wells felt very much at home.

311

His ride from Cyprus had gone smoothly. Wells sat on the deck as Nicholas and his men smoked in the cabin and argued in Greek. At one a.m. Wells called Gaffan on Nicholas's satellite phone, confirming that Gaffan had arrived and passing along the GPS coordinates for the landing.

Two hours later, five miles off the Lebanese coast, Nicholas cut the cruiser's lights. "You're captain the rest of the way." Nicholas nodded at the rubber raft tied loosely to the deck.

The raft was six feet long, five feet wide, with a rusted outboard engine at its back. It was made of black rubber, with a yellow patch sewn onto its right tube. Someone had drawn a smiley face on the patch. The smiley face failed to reassure. Wells felt a flutter in his stomach. He wasn't a great swimmer. He hadn't had much chance to learn, growing up in Montana. Was it possible he was . . . scared?

But nothing scared him. Not bullets or grenades or nuclear bombs. And since nothing scared him, he couldn't be scared now. So, good, he wasn't scared. He was irritated. Because drowning would be an irritating way to die after everything he'd survived, and if this raft sank, he'd probably drown. Not scared. Irritated.

Wells was glad to sort that question out.

"Don't be frightened," Nicholas said. "If I wasn't sure you'd make it, I wouldn't let you go. You think I want you to drown, your boyfriend bothering me? It's simple. We drop it in. You get in, push the red button, the engine starts." Nicholas handed Wells a plastic yellow Garmin GPS, the landing position flashing a black X. "Aim at that."

"Simple."

"And one more piece of advice." Nicholas pointed at the dim lights along the coast. "See that red light? On the left? That's Syria. Stay away from the Syrians. They're not nice. Otherwise, no problem. Smooth water. A big bathtub. It takes about an hour. Very flat coast, low draft, you ride right to the beach."

"And when I get there I leave the raft?"

"For a hundred thousand dollars, I can buy a new one."

Wells spent the five-mile ride promising himself he would take swimming lessons when this mission was done. But Nicholas was right. The trip was easy. The eastern Mediterranean was as dull as a lake, the waves no more than two feet. The raft rocked lightly as Wells navigated toward the X, keeping a hand on the wooden box where his weapons were packed.

An hour later, he was a half-mile from shore, close enough to hear the occasional hum of engines on the coast road. The beach ahead was empty and unlit. Even so, Wells was exposed. The moon was low in the sky, but starlight shone off the water. The shore was flat and ran straight north-south, no nooks or crags to hide behind.

No wonder Nicholas had insisted on staying out to sea. Three hundred yards out, Wells revved the outboard, trying to close quickly. He needed a muffler. Fortunately, this stretch of coast was lightly developed, probably because of its nearness to Syria, which had a habit of invading Lebanon.

Fifty yards from shore, Wells cut the engine to just above idle, let the waves carry him in. He didn't see Gaffan. But as he reached the beach, a Jeep pulled off the road and flashed its headlights. Gaffan stepped out. Wells hefted the crate from the raft. "I brought you a present."

They loaded up, headed south. After a mile, Gaffan turned left, inland, passing between citrus groves. "Hit a checkpoint on the way up," he said.

"Army or police?"

"Couldn't tell. Either way, we should ditch that crate." Gaffan parked beside a building that looked like a garage for farm equipment and cut the headlights. Wells stepped out, listened for dogs or traffic, heard neither. He popped the trunk, pried open the crate, pulled out their arsenal: AKs, pistols, grenades, ammunition, silencers.

"Nice."

"I checked it on the boat. It'll do." Wells transferred the weapons to a canvas bag, stowed the bag in the Jeep's spare tire compartment, tossed the tire and crate in a ditch behind the garage.

He checked his watch. Five a.m. Another night gone. Working for the agency had downsides, but it meant quick access to vehicles, safe houses, and identification. Wells would have gotten from France to Lebanon on a fresh passport in hours instead of days and had a pistol and sat phone waiting.

"It's a lot slower when you're on your own," Gaffan said, as if reading his mind.

"Yes and no. On a government ticket, we'd have to check in with the head of station, get an in-country brief —"

"I know you're supposed to do those things. But did you ever actually, John?"

"I didn't always."

"Ever?"

"I can't remember."

315

"I'm picking up some bad habits from you."

"Yeah, maybe."

They headed south toward Beirut on the coast road. The checkpoint was south of Tripoli. The paramilitary police looked them over, waved them through. "If they ever stop us, play the stupid American," Wells said. "Touristico. They are always ready to believe it. Definitely don't let on you know Arabic."

"Roger that. So when we get to the Bekaa, what are we looking for?"

Wells had spent the ride from Cyprus mulling that question. "We know it's a big operation, a bunch of guys. It's been going a while. That credit card's four months old. And it's got to be more than just a crash pad. The logistics don't work. These ops are happening two countries away."

"So a full-on training camp? A base?"

"At least a house where they plan missions. Maybe just a few guys, maybe a couple dozen."

"All Saudi."

"Hezbollah run the Bekaa. They're Shia, and Iran's behind them. Maybe Abdullah and Miteb have it wrong and this is an Iranian operation to destabilize the Saudi government."

"But you don't think so."

"Abdullah, he's old, angry, but he's smart. His brother, too. If they think this is coming from inside their family, then I believe them. And the guy I saw in Italy, he was Saudi, not Iranian."

"Anyway, what would the Iranians get out of it?" Gaffan said. "They've got their own problems."

"True. Figure it's Saudi-run. Even so, they can't operate here without Hezbollah. They must be paying for protection. Which means if we make too much fuss, we'll have a problem."

"Will your friends help?"

"Don't count on it." Wells recounted his last conversation with Shafer. "Duto probably wants to see what we find before he decides to bail us out."

"He'd do that?"

"He'd enjoy it. Any case, we'd best find them quick, before Hezbollah figures out we're looking."

"Then hit them?"

"Depends on the target. If it's fortified, no. But if we can get in and out without waking the neighbors, maybe."

"So how do we find them?"

"That's a very good question."

Beirut looked like a cross between Miami,

San Francisco, and Baghdad, a hilly, densely packed city with a waterfront promenade — and every so often a bombed-out building as a reminder of the civil war that had raged from 1975 to 1990. Wells and Gaffan rented two rooms in a Sofitel in East Beirut, the Christian quarter, to shower, shave, and nap.

By noon they were up, following a highway that rose into the mountains. The Bekaa's farms and vineyards were closer than they seemed. Lebanon was a bite-sized country, one hundred fifty miles from tip to tail but less than fifty wide.

At the crest of the highway, uniformed soldiers manned a checkpoint, backed by an armored personnel carrier under camouflage netting. A soldier waved the Jeep over. "Identification," he said in Arabic.

"Excuse me?" Gaffan said in English.

"Identification. Passports."

Gaffan handed over his passport, Wells his driver's license.

"Your passport, please," the soldier said in English.

The passport was a problem. Specifically, the lack of a border entry stamp in the passport was a problem. The agency specialized in handling these details.

Wells tried to look sheepish. "I'm sorry,

318

captain, I left it at the hotel."

"Which hotel?"

"The Sofitel. In East Beirut."

"And why do you come to Lebanon?"

"Tourists. We're headed for Baalbek."

"You should —"

"The ruins —"

"Shh! I know. You should have your pass-port."

"I'm sorry, sir. I wasn't thinking."

The officer flipped through Gaffan's passport again, held Wells's driver's license close to his face. "Next time make sure you bring it," he said. "You're not in America. This doesn't mean anything here." He handed back the passport and license, waved them on.

They were halfway down the mountain before Gaffan spoke. "*Captain* was a nice touch."

"Yes, but. This is going to be a problem, these checkpoints. Best travel separately, so if I get taken out, you don't."

In Zahlé, Wells bought the first motorcycle he saw, an air-cooled Honda CB650, old but in good shape, worth maybe one thousand five hundred dollars. Wells paid twice that without blinking, another two hundred dollars for a helmet. Then he and Gaffan

319

rolled northwest, toward Baalbek.

Hezbollah territory started east of Zahlé. Yellow and green flags hung from streetlights and telephone poles, proclaiming the group's slogan: "Then surely the party of God are they that shall be triumphant." Ten-foot-tall posters displayed larger-than-life photographs of Hezbollah's leaders, heavy, scowling men wearing long black robes. On billboards, a pale white horse danced across an oddly lunar landscape. The horse symbolized the twelfth imam, and the billboards called the Shia to the festival of Ashura, which commemorated the death of Hussein Ali, the grandson of Muhammad and the third Shia imam. In the Bekaa, party, state, and religion were one.

Baalbek lay almost halfway up the valley. The town had grown around the remains of the Temple of Jupiter, built by the Romans about two hundred years after the birth of Christ. Its size was actually a sign of weakness, a futile effort to stop the new religion: *Look at this shrine and know that our gods are stronger than your Messiah.* But the majesty of a single God had overwhelmed the Roman pantheon. Wells wondered why Hezbollah had based itself here. Probably the group's clerics viewed the temple as a simple tourist attraction, acres of meaningless stones.

North of Baalbek, traffic on the road thinned. The vineyards disappeared, replaced by scruffy farms of tomatoes and lemons. Here and there, Wells saw concrete mansions, set hundreds of yards off the road and protected by high brick walls. The homes were three and four stories high and garishly painted in yellow and green. Mc-Mansions, Lebanese-style. Wells assumed they belonged to hash farmers and Hezbollah leaders. Any of them could have served as the safe house he and Gaffan were looking for.

Farther north, the farms vanished. To the east, gray-brown hills rose toward the Syrian border. To the west, the Lebanon Mountains disappeared beneath low clouds. Qaa, the last village before Syria, was really just a mosque, a few houses, a small grocery store, and the gas station that had shown up on the credit card that the NSA had traced. Wells rode until a blue sign announced, "Syria 1 KM," then made a U-turn and waited for Gaffan to follow.

At the gas station, Gaffan filled up the Jeep. "What are we doing, John?"

"They don't teach recon in the army anymore?"

"This is Jamaica all over again. Worse. This

valley is fifty or sixty miles long, twenty wide. A thousand square miles. We're looking for one house. No way do we find these guys without comint" — communications intelligence — "or imagery. Even with a helicopter we might miss them."

"Wrong. First. The camp's around here. Not in the south."

"Why are you so sure?"

"Because the credit card was used here. If you're in Zahlé, you wouldn't drive up here. And if they have a camp, they need space."

"What if it's just a house?"

"Then why did somebody put five hundred gallons of diesel on a credit card? For the miles?"

"Even if you're right, we're talking hundreds of square miles."

"Wherever it is, once we get close enough, anybody within a couple miles will know."

"You can't be sure."

Wells controlled his frustration. After the near disaster in Jamaica, Gaffan had the right to be gun-shy. "Think it through. Everybody's everybody's cousin here. You think they don't notice if a bunch of Saudis come in? At least the neighbors would have called the paramilitaries, made sure it's okay."

"So. Assuming your instinct is right, and

they're somewhere close, and the locals know where, how do we find them?"

"We ask."

The gas station was a concrete shed with a tin roof and a plywood counter. A middle-aged man in a dirty red shirt sat by the register. He barely looked up as Wells entered. He was focused on the television blaring out a call-in advice show from Beirut. The Lebanese loved these shows. They loved to give one another advice.

"Salaam aleikum."

"Aleikum salaam."

On screen, a woman in a head scarf and a pound of makeup listened to a man complain that his brother had borrowed his car, dented the bumper, and refused to fix it. "First of all . . . are you sure it wasn't your wife who dented the bumper?" the woman said. The audience chortled.

"Good show," Wells said.

"Very funny."

"Yes. I need another delivery. More diesel."

The man shook his head. "I don't know what you mean."

"For the camp."

"What camp?"

Wells couldn't tell if the guy was hiding what he knew, had no idea what Wells was

323

talking about, or was just slow. The third seemed likely. He couldn't push too hard, risk rattling the guy, but he thought he could get away with one more try. "The one in the hills."

"You want it, come with your truck and pick it up. Like before."

"Of course. Like before." He'd hoped to catch a break, trail a tanker truck to the camp, but that would have been too easy. Still, he had confirmed that the camp was somewhere close. Within ten miles, twenty at most.

"What's your name?"

"Jalal." Wells had used the name for a decade in Afghanistan and Pakistan. By the end, he had known it as well as his own. Maybe better. "I'll come back tomorrow. For the diesel."

"As you wish." The man turned back to the show.

Wells rode west, onto a road barely wide enough for two cars to pass. Over a rise, he stopped to make way for hundreds of sheep picking their way across the pavement. Two boys on donkeys and a single mangy collie herded the flock.

The older boy, maybe ten, shouted, "Vroom, vroom," and grinned and waved the stick he was using to prod the sheep along. He wore a tunic and a freshly laundered red-and-white kaffiyeh that contrasted sharply with his dark skin.

Wells hopped off the bike. "What's your name?"

"Hamid," the boy said shyly. The sheep marched around them, as slow and implacable as time itself.

"I'm Jalal. These are your family's sheep?"

"My father's."

"How many?"

"Two hundred and eighty-one." His pride was obvious.

"That's a lot of sheep."

"Next year we'll have even more, my father says. Is that your motorcycle?"

"I just bought it."

"Do you ride fast?"

"Sometimes."

"Do you ride in the dark?"

"Yes. Do you study the Quran, Hamid?"

"Of course."

"And are you Shia?"

"Of course."

"Do you know what Sunnis are?"

"Muslim, but not like me."

"That's right. I'm Sunni."

Hamid pinched his nose, apparently uncomfortable with the turn the conversation had taken.

"Do you know if there are other Sunnis around here?"

"Yes."

"Do you know where they live?"

"That way." Hamid pointed west with his stick, toward the mountains.

"Do you know how far?"

"Closer to the mountains. My father says to stay away from them. They make noise sometimes." The last of the sheep had dribbled past them. Hamid kicked a donkey's flank. The animal grumbled and trudged forward. "Good-bye, mister."

Wells waved good-bye. Gaffan pulled up, lowered his window. "What was that?"

Wells explained. "You've got to be kidding," Gaffan said.

"Don't you know by now that sometimes it's better to be lucky than good?"

They passed a one-lane bridge over a dry streambed. Until now the land had been open and unfenced. Ahead, both sides of the road were fenced with strings of rusting wire that hung between wooden posts. Wells was a child again, on a road trip with his dad, east through Montana and Wyoming, on the way to Kansas City. His first big-league baseball game. He was six.

326

He rarely got to spend much time with his father, who spent most waking hours in the operating room at the hospital in Hamilton. More than once along the way, he'd told himself to remember, remember the diners where they ate and the gas stations where they stopped, as though he could make the trip last forever if he burned it deep enough into his brain. Of course, now the details had vanished. Wells remembered only being obscurely disappointed that his father didn't seem more excited to be with him. But this landscape, so unexpected and so familiar, stirred an emotion stronger and purer than nostalgia.

He slowed. Gaffan stopped beside him, ending his reverie. "See something?"

"Nothing at all." They moved on, approaching the flanks of the Lebanon range. The hills rose and the land crumpled and the road turned to gravel. Wells imagined lines tightening on a topographic map. He rode slowly, his legs spread wide for balance, feet off the pegs. The road turned along the base of a ravine and was blocked by a gate topped with thick strands of razor wire. Behind the gate, the road swung left and disappeared behind a hill. Wells clicked on the GPS in his pocket to save the location, then turned to Gaffan and twirled a finger: *Let's get out of here.*

For the rest of the afternoon, they repeated the drill. Wells saved three more possible locations, fenced areas or walled houses that looked suspicious.

The sun had disappeared behind the mountains by the time they rented rooms at the Palmyra Hotel in Baalbek. Directly across from the temple ruins, the Palmyra had a long and glorious history. The Germans had occupied it during World War I, the British in World War II. The hotel still had a certain faded glamour, with stained-glass windows and overgrown trees in its yard. But its rugs were threadbare and its showers offered only cold water.

Wells and Gaffan cleaned up and sat in the back garden, drinking lukewarm, too-sweet coffee. As far as Wells could tell, they were the hotel's only guests.

"You think we found it?"

"Could have. I already called Ellis. Asked for fresh day and night overheads" — satellite photographs. "For all four locations, but especially the first."

Wells had also asked whether the agency had any new information on the Jeddah bombing or the earlier attacks. The answer was a predictable and dispiriting no. The agency was so focused on Al Qaeda that this new group had caught it wrong-footed. Wells had kept Abdullah's suspicions about Saeed to himself. Wells trusted Shafer, but it was always possible that Duto or someone even higher up would decide that the United States would gain by leaking information about Abdullah's problems to MI6 or the Mossad. Wells preferred not to take that chance.

"So will they help?"

"He wouldn't promise, but I think so. It's in their interest. Waiting will hold us up for at least one night, maybe two, but I don't care. I want to know what's on the other side before we go over that fence."

"Then how do they get the overheads to us?"

"Gmail."

"You really think they're going to send Keyhole imagery to you on Gmail." The Keyhole was the National Reconnaissance Office's finest toy, able to read license plates from space.

"They may degrade them, but yes."

"Because they want us to go in, even though Shafer told you not to."

"Correct."

"Hell of a game."

"The best," Wells said. "And the worst."

CHAPTER 14

LANGLEY, VIRGINIA

The satellite shots filled the wall-sized flat-panel screen in Shafer's office, as clear as life. Maybe clearer. Thanks to mirrors and lenses machined to ten-millionths of a meter, the fifth-generation Keyholes could take daylight photos from low earth orbit at five-centimeter resolution — about two inches.

With five-centimeter resolution, the photos revealed not just the number of men in a unit but also fine tactical details, such as the weapons they carried and whether they wore beards. The NRO promised that the next generation of satellites would reach one-centimeter resolution, enough to distinguish individual features. "Face from space," the program was called.

Shafer remembered when one meter had been state-of-the-art. And he remembered when the overheads had been couriered around Washington in armored vans. These days the process was digital, start to finish. Data and imagery moved between the CIA and other three-letter agencies at the speed of light on an encrypted fiber-optic trunk line that circled Washington.

Shafer felt he'd made the transition pretty well. Technology didn't scare him. He'd watched the agency go from analog to digital, watched it suffer through Aldrich Ames and Wen Ho Lee, watched its top targets move from walled palaces in Moscow and Beijing to nameless caves in Pakistan. He didn't count himself as overly nostalgic. In truth, the CIA was probably more effective now than it had been during the 1990s, when the collapse of the Soviet Union had left it without a mission. The chaotic years after September 11 had been worse. George Tenet, the director at the time, proved to be the ultimate kiss-up and kick-down manager, never letting the facts get in the way of what the White House wanted to hear.

But since Tenet's resignation in 2004, the agency had slowly rebuilt itself to face the new threat. The clandestine service hired as many Arabic speakers as it could find and pushed toward the front lines in Pakistan, Afghanistan, and Iraq. At home, the intelligence directorate encouraged debates, fighting the groupthink that submerged unpopular positions.

Yet the CIA's new vigor had come at a price. In the short term, drone strikes and coercive interrogations disrupted Al Qaeda and contained attacks. But as long as average Egyptians and Pakistanis believed that the United States was their enemy, Muslim extremism would thrive. "The guerrillas are the fish, and the people are the water," Mao had said. Drone attacks that killed civilians were fish food. So was support for repressive and undemocratic governments. The agency was doing a good job tactically. Strategically, not so much.

But then the agency didn't set strategy, despite what the conspiracy theorists thought. The ultimate decision-maker lived five miles away on the other side of the Potomac. And whichever party he represented, he could never plan too far ahead. Not with elections every two years. So the strategy became: Stop the jihadis today, and let tomorrow take care of itself.

Though Shafer didn't have too many tomorrows left, either. His mandatory retirement was fast approaching. The clichés were true, too. Time did fly. The days were long, but the years were short. Shafer still remembered the wonder he'd felt on his first morning as he drove onto the campus in his Oldsmobile, a brand now extinct.

More and more, Shafer found himself thinking of bonds made and broken. He and Jennifer Exley and Wells had known one another for fifteen years. Shafer would trust either of them with his life. And he knew the other two felt the same way, even if Wells was angry about what had happened on their last mission.

Yet the three of them had splintered. Wells and Exley had quit the agency. Wells had an uncontrollable thirst for action — a rage, really. Exley had left him because she was sure he would eventually get himself killed. And she was probably right. Wells was both lucky and good. But luck couldn't last forever, and skills inevitably eroded. Yet Shafer couldn't imagine reining in Wells. He belonged in the field like no one Shafer had ever met. After everything he'd done, he had earned the right to die with his boots on.

But not this time. Not this mission.

With that thought, Shafer focused on the satellite shots, resolving to glean every detail he could. He would send the overheads to Wells, of course, but they wouldn't be nearly this sharp when they arrived. The agency would have no choice but to degrade them, in part because the file sizes were far too large for a civilian Internet account. And Wells wouldn't have a display panel as good as his, either.

Shafer knocked out two locations quickly. They were nothing more than well-guarded hash farms, complete with tractors and pesticide sprayers. The third, in the northern foothills of the Lebanon range, was trickier. Mysterious tarp-covered mounds and half-buried concrete sheds were scattered across it. Still, Shafer thought he was looking at a Hezbollah arms depot, not a jihadi camp. Only two cars and three unarmed men were visible. The mounds and sheds most likely held howitzers and missile launchers — or possibly decoys to siphon Israeli air attacks from Hezbollah's real depots.

Which left the fourth farm, the first that Wells and Gaffan had spotted, the one Wells believed was correct. Two different Keyholes had taken overhead passes, one just before noon and the second at about two a.m. the next day. Noon was the ideal time for satellite shots. Direct overhead sunlight minimized shadows and shined brightly off metal. The reflections helped the image-processing software that searched for half-hidden bits of steel and aluminum, pipes that might be bunker vents or coin-shaped disks that could be mines. Shafer was looking for more obvious features. From what Wells said, this camp would have been recently built and only semipermanent, with privacy and size as its main considerations.

Wells's instincts looked on target. A one-story barracks sat in a rocky valley a mile south of the gate that seemed to mark the property line. Shafer judged it would be invisible from anywhere outside the property. Its concrete was white and new, but the construction was shoddy. A small generator at the back of the barracks powered a string of bulbs. Three SUVs and a ten-wheel panel truck were parked in front. A blue tarp covered the truck, though Shafer could faintly make out Arabic letters in the back corner, where the tarp had come loose.

Just past the barracks, the road turned west, toward the mountains. It dead-ended a quarter-mile up at a two-story concrete house, cheap and gaudy in hash-farmer style, with balconies and filigrees. But the house's yellow paint was faded, its concrete cracked. Shafer guessed that it had been abandoned a few years back, long before the barracks was built. Two satellite television receivers sat on the roof. One was old, its wires disconnected, the other new.

No transmission equipment, though. A new diesel generator and a half-dozen barrels sat beside the house, presumably fuel from the gas station in Qaa. Next to them was a small shack.

The road between the barracks and the house was well-trod. Shafer guessed they slept in the barracks, trained and ate in the house. A couple other details struck him. A deep pit had been dug near the barracks. Given the hardness of the Bekaa's soil, excavating the pit would have required backhoes. It would have been dug only for a good reason. Maybe live explosives training.

Behind the house, he spotted what might have been a makeshift helicopter pad, flat ground with a small white *X* painted at its center. He might have been wrong. No helicopter was visible, and he didn't see anywhere to hide one. Still. A helicopter pad. *Ambitious.* Shafer clicked back to the first image, the barracks, to take another look —

His phone interrupted him. Vinny Duto. The DCI.

"Can you come up?"

"Love to," Shafer lied.

Duto's office was on the seventh floor of the Original Headquarters Building. The view was nice, but the company wasn't.

Duto had tightened his control over the intelligence community in the last year, thanks in part to Wells and Shafer. In their last mission, they had unwittingly helped him topple his biggest rival, the director of national intelligence, a job created after September 11 to serve as a check on the CIA.

But Duto might have regained control on his own. Technically, the director of central intelligence reported to the DNI. But the DNI didn't have any clandestine operatives of his own, only analysts. Analysis was nice, but power came from the operational side. And operations belonged to Duto. With the DNI neutered, Duto had no real rivals for control. But power hadn't mellowed him. Not even close. Wall Street bankers never had enough money, and men like Duto never had enough power. Shafer knew that Duto found him — and especially Wells, who couldn't be controlled and who lived by a set of principles that Duto would never understand — deeply irritating.

Though Duto had certainly outsmarted them both last year.

Shafer walked into Duto's office to find it nearly dark, the electrically controlled shades down, as Duto examined the Lebanese overheads on his own flat-panel. Shafer sat. Duto ignored him for a couple minutes, flicking through the images. When he turned off the screen, the shades rose automatically. "Pretty pictures. What's Wells going to do with them?"

"Hi, Vinny. Good to see you. You too. How's the wife? The kids?"

"Yeah, yeah. What about the overheads?"

"Wells hasn't told me, but I imagine he's going to raid that camp. As you know."

"And you signed off on sending satellite shots over the Internet?"

"Is there some plausible deniability thing happening here? Aren't we past that? It's just overheads. You can find them on Google Earth."

"Not at five-centimeter resolution."

"We'll degrade them. Anyway, if we're gonna use him, we should help him."

Duto nodded, conceding the point. He'd given in way too easily. Shafer wondered why he'd bothered with this meeting at all. The next sentence provided the answer.

"Is Wells talking to Abdullah, Ellis?"

Shafer couldn't see the percentage in lying. "Not sure, but I think so. The jet that picked him up in New York belonged to the Saudi government. And the DGSE" — the French intelligence service — "say that Abdullah and Miteb were in Nice when he was there. So probably yes."

"So Abdullah is actively involved here. The king of Saudi Arabia. What's Wells doing that his security services can't?"

"Maybe Abdullah doesn't trust the *muk* anymore. Or maybe Wells is working with them to get inside this camp."

"Maybe you should ask your boy for a straight answer."

"My boy doesn't work for us anymore. In case you haven't noticed."

"We're helping him."

"And he's helping us. And if I push any harder, he'll go dark."

"All right. But you need to understand something, Ellis. Across the river they're pulling a strat rev on the KSA" — a strategic review on the Kingdom of Saudi Arabia. "Us, State, NSC" — the National Security Council. "Joint Chiefs sitting in but don't have a brief. They're focusing on our relationship with the House of Saud."

"I love it when you lift your skirt and show me your access."

Once, Duto would have snapped at Shafer's bait. Now he wore handmade suits and pressed white shirts and pants that stretched his legs and smoothed out his rooster walk. Powerful men walked differently than other people did. They flowed. Or maybe Shafer was projecting. Or jealous. He didn't flow. He never would. He wondered if Duto dreamed of higher office. Possibly. The senior George Bush had been CIA director, after all.

"Want to know what they're going to decide?"

"Tomorrow's news today. Inform me, wise one."

Again, Duto didn't bite. "They're going to decide that the stability of the Kingdom is paramount. That Abdullah is expendable, in other words. Because when it comes to Saudi Arabia, we only care about one thing, Ellis. And it's not whether they're making women wear blankets. I'll spell it out for you. Starts with *O,* ends with *L* —"

"You love these realpolitik lectures. Like you're the only one who gets it. Having Abdullah standing up to the clerics is what we need long-term. Strategy, not tactics."

"You still don't get it, Ellis. Abdullah isn't going to be standing up for anything much longer. Prince Saeed called in our ambassador to tell him that."

"Saeed's no friend."

"As long as the oil keeps coming, he is. And the betting across the river is that he can manage that place better than Abdullah. The clerics like him. They think he's on

340

their team. The smart money says the attacks will stop quick once he takes over. And if they don't, he'll chop necks until they do. If there are any downstream effects, we'll manage those."

"Downstream effects. Like planes hitting buildings. Tell me something. Why are we pretending to be so sure we know what's happening here when we have no idea? We don't know who's behind these attacks, or what they want, or whether Saeed is speaking for Abdullah or not."

"We want a calm, orderly succession; Saeed gives it to us. Everybody wins."

"I don't think it's that simple."

"That's what the review's going to say. Everyone's on board. It's nice."

As if the words on a paper in Washington would change the reality in Riyadh. "Tell me again what this has to do with John," Shafer said. "Who last I checked was in Lebanon, trying to figure out who's behind four terrorist attacks."

"As long as that's all he's doing. But it's in nobody's interest for him to get involved in Saudi politics. Especially not his own. He gets sucked down in this, we're not sending a lifeguard."

"You think he'll care?"

"Just make sure he knows, Ellis."

Shafer saluted and walked out. He had only one consolation as he stepped into the elevator that would take him away from the seventh floor. Wells wouldn't need to be warned he was on his own. He already knew.

CHAPTER 15
BEKAA VALLEY

Gravel kicked up under the Honda's tires as Wells rode west, keeping the bike in third gear at twenty miles an hour, risking a stall to minimize engine noise. He wore dirty green cargo pants and a thick black windbreaker and cheap gray sneakers and four days of beard, camouflage that had gotten him past a checkpoint north of Baalbek. His heart was slow and steady. His hands were loose and relaxed.

He hadn't killed anyone in two years. But he expected to kill tonight.

Under other circumstances, Wells would have preferred to carry out this mission under thick clouds, or even better, rain. But the Bekaa's dry season was starting. And he and Gaffan risked attracting attention if they stayed much longer. Already the desk clerk at the Palmyra had shown an unwelcome interest in their plans. This morning he'd asked how many more days they expected to stay. Wells worried that Hezbollah would mistake them for Israeli intelligence officers.

They had another reason to move. Shafer had sent them four sets of photographs of the property that was their top target. Between the second and third, the panel truck had vanished. A week had passed since the bombing in Jeddah. The jihadis seemed to be leaving Lebanon, readying another attack.

So he and Gaffan were going in, despite the half-moon and cloudless sky. Wells wondered now if they'd miscalculated. The low hills hid him from the barracks and farmhouse. But if the jihadis had posted a sentry higher up, on the flanks of the mountain to the west, Wells's approach would be obvious. He could only hope they hadn't bothered. He didn't like having to hope.

Two days before, as Wells prowled around the northern Bekaa to look for other potential targets, Gaffan had driven to Beirut and bought a laptop and a satellite dish that would free them from local Internet connections. By midnight they'd received the first batch of overheads from Shafer, along with a message to call on a secure line.

Which Wells didn't have. He called anyway.

"I have good news and bad news," Shafer said. "Which first?"

"The good. And FYI, you're on Skype. Which may not be your definition of secure."

"Fair enough. You got the pictures?"

"Yes."

"Still thinking the most likely candidate is the first place you found?"

"Yes."

"The good news is that our friends from the No Such" — the NSA again — "agree. They found text messages to one of the phone numbers you gave them sent from a cell tower a couple miles from the camp."

"What'd the messages say?"

"Our friends don't know. The texts are a month old. The database shows they exist, not what they said."

"How can they do that?"

"Don't know. But the key is, you seem to be looking in the right place."

"That is good news. Since we're going in soon."

"Before you do. The bad news." Shafer paused. "We're hearing your friend is done. That there's gonna be a new sheriff in town."

"My friend who asked me to take this trip,

you mean?" If Shafer wanted to keep Abdullah's name off the air, Wells wouldn't argue.

"Yes. And what you need to know, even more important, people over here aren't crying over it. They think all those sheriffs are pretty much the same. Long as the gas station stays open. 'Cause you know we like our gas cheap."

"What if the new sheriff blew up the old sheriff's granddaughter?"

"You'd need good evidence. The kind that would be embarrassing if it went public."

"Still looking for that."

"There's your answer."

"This is coming from your boss?"

"His bosses, too. The ones across the river. So if you feel otherwise, if you want to take a position on this, get involved, you're on your own. Not nudge-and-wink on your own. Really on your own."

"I understand."

"Don't shoot the messenger —"

Wells pushed the red "end call" button on the virtual keypad. The down-the-drain electronic chime of a Skype hang-up didn't offer the same satisfaction as slamming down a phone, but it was the best he could do.

After what had happened with the Midnight House, Wells knew he should be immune to the stench of Washington cynicism. And maybe they were right, Duto and the national security adviser and whoever else was making this decision. Maybe Wells was a sucker for thinking Abdullah was different from Saeed. Maybe a stable oil supply was all the United States could expect out of Saudi Arabia.

Even so, Wells hated the fact that the mandarins in Washington could walk away from a man who had just lost his granddaughter to a terrorist bombing. Abdullah wasn't Lech Walesa or Nelson Mandela. His top concern was passing power to his son. But at least he was trying to make his nation freer, more tolerant. The United States theoretically wanted him to succeed. But not at the risk of a single barrel of oil.

The same attitude had led America to leave Saddam Hussein in power in 1990. Once Saddam had been evicted from Kuwait's oil fields, he was no longer a threat to the United States, whatever his crimes against Iraq's Shia and Kurds.

Even after everything he'd seen and done, Wells believed that the United States was generally a force for good. But the truth was that when oil was involved, American principles got fuzzy. So be it. Wells didn't need Duto to authorize this mission. At least

Shafer had given him the courtesy of letting him know where he stood.

"What'd he say?" Gaffan said. Wells explained.

"So if we go in, we're on our own," Gaffan said.

"That's it."

"What if Duto, somebody back home, knows something we don't?"

"They know plenty we don't. But none of it's got anything to do with this."

"You're so sure of yourself, John. It's not that easy for me. These guys get paid to make the tough calls. Chain of command. I look at you, I think of that line from that television show *The People's Court.* Remember it? Judge Wapner. 'Don't take the law into your own hands. You take 'em to court.' "

"The tough calls? Let me tell you Vinny Duto's priorities, in order. First, more power for Vinny Duto —"

"Power meaning what?"

"Meaning face time with the president. Operational control in Afghanistan and everywhere else. A bigger budget. Bigger voice on strategy. Bigger payday when he finally quits to run Lockheed Martin or whatever. Second, keep the lid on the disaster of the day — and if the lid comes off, make it SEP, somebody else's problem. Third, and this is a long way back, do the right thing."

"You're pretty cynical, John."

"I guess so. Arrogant, too. Duto says the same. The saddest part is he might even be right in the short run," Wells said. "The United States might be better off for a year or two with Saeed running Saudi Arabia. But in the long run, the jihadis will be happy to have him. And Duto knows it, but he doesn't care."

Gaffan rubbed his forehead. Wells thought he was about to back out.

"I won't hold it against you, you want to go home. Money's yours either way."

"No. I gave you my word, and I'm in."

"A two-man chain of command."

"Never been this close to the top."

So Gaffan was still on board. But Wells had another problem: Should he caution the king that the United States no longer supported his reign? Even under normal circumstances, telling a foreign government about a secret American policy decision was illegal at best, treason at worst. This situation was even trickier. Abdullah was old and angry. What if he reacted to the warning by going public, denouncing the White House, cutting off Saudi oil? What if he arrested Saeed and gave the throne to Khalid? Plus, Abdullah and Miteb had given Wells millions of dollars. Wells was sure the money hadn't affected his judgment, but others would surely disagree. Vinny Duto, for example.

On the other hand, Abdullah deserved to know that someone — almost certainly Saeed — had told the American government that he wouldn't be king much longer. Wells decided to pass along that part of the message and to advise that Abdullah see the American ambassador in person to prove he wasn't on his deathbed. Nothing more. With any luck, Abdullah would be smart enough to ask at the meeting if the United States planned to support him. He could judge the ambassador's response for himself.

A reasonable compromise, Wells thought. He reached for his handset to call Kowalski, get a message to Miteb.

On the third day, Wells stayed in the Palmyra, examining the overheads and planning the attack. Gaffan made another run to Beirut. For seventy-six thousand dollars in cash, he bought a used thirty-one-foot Cranchi from the friendly folks at Chehab

Marine. The Cranchi was a speedboat disguised as a pleasure cruiser, with a sharp prow, a narrow white hull, and a spiffy racing stripe. Its cockpit sat four. Belowdecks, it had a cabin where two people could sleep as long as they didn't mind getting to know each other. Its twin engines had been upgraded to put out two hundred thirty horsepower, enough to get the boat to forty knots on full throttle. Equally important, it had a one-hundred-forty-gallon fuel tank, for a range of three hundred miles, easily enough for Cyprus. The boat would be valuable insurance if they had to leave Lebanon fast. Better safe than sorry, especially since they were spending money that came out of the ground. Wells had gotten into the habit of thinking about prices in terms of oil. The Cranchi ran one thousand barrels, give or take.

The dealer at Chehab didn't ask why an American had showed up at his showroom to buy a speedboat with wads of cash in rubber bands. He didn't ask what Gaffan planned to do with the Cranchi. And he was more than happy to recommend a quiet harbor south of Tripoli where Gaffan could dock the Cranchi, no questions asked. He even sent a driver to pick Gaffan up from the harbor and bring him back to Beirut after Gaffan piloted the Cranchi there. The Lebanese were known for their friendliness, especially to anyone who paid list price.

Gaffan came back to Baalbek at around ten p.m. An hour later, Shafer sent the overheads with the truck missing. The next morning, the desk clerk got nosy, and Wells realized they needed to move.

At night the Bekaa showed its teeth. The tourists went back to Beirut and the hash farmers got to work. Hashish was marijuana's more potent cousin, made from the resin of cannabis plants, nearly pure THC — the active ingredient in marijuana. To make hash, farmers threshed cannabis leaves and stems through wire screens, separating a sticky resin. They dried it into a moist powder and pressed the powder into sweet-smelling bricks and wrapped the bricks in thick blue plastic to keep them fresh.

During the Lebanese civil war, the Bekaa became the world's top hash supplier. Lebanese Red was famous in Amsterdam cafés. The government cracked down during the 1990s, but the trade never disappeared entirely. It had surged since 2006, when the Israeli invasion strengthened Hezbollah. Publicly, the group claimed that it didn't support hash farming, but that it couldn't stop poor farmers from growing cannabis to survive. In reality, hash was second only to payments from Iran as a source of income for the Party of God.

Under the watchful eyes of Hezbollah militiamen, the trade ran smoothly. Farmers brought bricks to warehouses in Baalbek and Hermel, receiving three hundred to five hundred dollars per pound. Black-clad soldiers guarded the depots and monitored loads. Growing hash in the valley without Hezbollah's approval was a crime punishable by death. The hash was hidden in crates of tomatoes and hauled to the coast for shipping to Europe — or flown to Turkey and Cyprus on eight-seat prop planes from the bumpy airfield at Rayak. Some even went south to Israel. The Israeli army and police hated the fact that their stoners enriched Hezbollah. They ran television ads showing the group's leader, Hassan Nasrallah, popping out of a bong, an evil genie made of smoke. Still, the trafficking continued.

The hash trade complicated Wells's plans. A late-night firefight would make the local farmers twitchy. They'd call Hezbollah's militia or show up on their own, locked and loaded. To keep the raid quiet, Wells and

Gaffan would have to use their silenced
pistols on anyone they came across. They
couldn't offer warnings, so they ran a real
risk of killing civilians if Wells and the NSA
had made a mistake and this farm turned
out to be the Lebanese equivalent of a Boy
Scout camp.

A half-mile from the front gate, Wells left
the Honda in a ditch and grabbed his gear
from the cardboard box on the back of the
bike. He slung the AK over his shoulder and
tucked a spare magazine and flashlight into
a long pocket inside his windbreaker. He
threaded the silencer onto the pistol and
slipped it into his belt. With the silencer attached, the pistol would be a slow draw, but
Wells had no other way to carry it. He
tucked wire clippers and plastic handcuffs
and a butterfly knife into the top pockets of
his cargo pants. The bottom pockets were
already stuffed with clothesline and electrical tape. A trainer at the Farm — his name
lost to Wells now — had made a mantra of
clothesline and electrical tape. *They're civilian items, you can buy and carry them easily,
and you can use them one thousand different
ways. Make that one thousand and one.* The
trainer's nickname, inevitably, had been
"one thousand and one."

Finally, Wells pulled off his sneakers and replaced them with steel-tipped boots Gaffan had picked up in Beirut. Close-quarters fighting was called hand-to-hand, but aside from a knife, a solid pair of boots was the most important weapon within three feet. He walked west along the road, his boots crunching gravel.

Gaffan was coming in from the south side of the farm, two miles away. The satellite maps revealed a gravel road that ended in a dry streambed. Gaffan should be able to bring the Jeep in most of the way.

Their cell phones were no good here, and they didn't have sat phones. Gaffan did have a flare gun in the Jeep, and they'd agreed he would fire it if he hit trouble. But if Gaffan ran into Hezbollah, he'd have bigger worries than warning Wells.

If this had been an agency-sponsored op, they would have had real communications gear. Bulletproof vests. Gas grenades. Most important, a ride out. Wells had e-mailed Shafer that they were going in and received a simple "Okay" in response. Especially after what had happened a year before, Shafer knew better than to make promises he couldn't keep.

Even so, part of Wells enjoyed running this way, simple and low-tech. American soldiers hated roadside bombs, called them cowardly because they didn't offer a target for return fire. But whenever possible, the United States used higher-tech versions of the same tactic, killing its enemies at a distance with helicopter gunships and drone-fired missiles. Rightly so. War wasn't meant to be fair. But Wells knew that a whites-of-the-eyes fight like this offered a psychic release that killing at a distance did not. *One of us is going to die. Better you than me.*

The road narrowed into the ravine, the gate just ahead. Wells stopped, listened to the night. He heard only the faint grinding of a truck on the central valley road behind him. The gate was made of heavy metal bars topped by razor wire and was kept shut with a steel padlock and chain. It had been placed at the narrowest point in the ravine and stretched to the steep slopes on either side. It had no signs warning against trespassing. It didn't need them. It was ominous enough.

Wells flipped on his flashlight, shined the beam low through the bars. He saw nothing metallic, no trip wires or mines, just a shiny piece of plastic. Wells looked hard at it before it resolved into a water bottle. Trash. He stepped onto the bottom bar of the gate and pulled his clippers. He trimmed at the razor wire as carefully as an apprentice at a fancy hair salon. After the first couple cuts, the tension in the wire relaxed. Wells pulled on the ends of the wire gently with one gloved hand and took bigger cuts with the other.

Sixty seconds later, he was through. He looked at his handiwork. In daylight the hole in the wire would be obvious, but if they were still here in daylight, they'd have bigger problems. He tucked away his flashlight and pulled his pistol and walked along the road as it curved left. According to the overheads, the barracks was a mile down. The road here was hardpack dirt and stone, and Wells moved quickly. It was 1:49 a.m. He'd split from Gaffan twenty-four minutes before.

Then he heard the engine.

It wasn't a generator. It was quieter, smoother. A car or truck. Wells trotted south toward the barracks, still invisible. The top of the farmhouse appeared over the ridge to his right, the west. He heard a man on the far side of the ridge walking up to the farmhouse. Why weren't they sleeping? Had they spotted him? Or Gaffan?

To his left, the ravine was nearly a cliff, too steep to climb. To his right, the slope was flatter and treeless. No place to hide there, either. Wells moved faster. He needed to close quickly. The road angled again. Finally Wells saw the barracks, its lights flickering. He was maybe three hundred yards away. Two black Suburbans were parked nose to tail twenty yards from the building. A third car, a beige Toyota sedan, was farther back. Three men stood around the front Suburban. They had black hair and light brown skin. Probably Saudi. The tallest one wore a long brown gown and looked to be in charge. The other two were dressed Western-style, in jeans and long-sleeved shirts. The tall man pointed toward the farmhouse, then back at the barracks. The other two nodded. Wells was too far away to hear what they were saying.

Wells unslung the AK, threw himself down, crawled ahead. A few scrubby bushes lay between him and the barracks, a few rocks. Not enough. Before he became a spy, Wells had been a soldier. A Ranger. Cover means life, he'd learned. But the land around him was miserly with cover. If he moved too fast, they'd spot him. If he didn't move at all, they'd still spot him eventually. Two hundred yards was theoretically close enough to use the AK, but in reality he had about as much chance of hitting a home run at Fenway.

To say he was in a tactical hole would be an understatement.

The two jihadis in Western dress disappeared, leaving the tall one. He popped the back of the Suburban, pulled out a plastic bottle, took a long drink. Wells used the distraction to pop up and scramble eighty yards closer. He ducked behind a low rock and scraped his left leg hard as he went down, tearing open his sweats, bruising his knee and calf. *Getting too old for this.* But that was a problem for tomorrow.

He steadied his breath, sighted through the AK's hashes. This close, he guessed he had a fifty-fifty shot to take out the tall guy. Then what? The rest would scatter and get under cover. He had to get closer. Another forty yards, at least. He tucked the rifle behind the rock and got as low as he could and waited.

Four men walked out of the barracks and hoisted a duffel bag into the back of the Suburban. Wells heard the clanking of metal as the edge of the bag caught the sill of the truck. Wells wondered why they were moving now. Over the car's engine, Wells caught a snippet of Arabic.

"He wants us there tomorrow night . . . twelve hundred kilometers . . ." *Twelve hundred kilometers.* Wells would map possible routes in the morning. Assuming he got through tonight. The men turned away, and Wells lost the conversation. If the Suburban came this way, he would have to open up. They would see him as they passed. He was facing at least seven guys, plus one or more up at the house. And Gaffan was still missing in action.

A walkie-talkie hissed. The tall man pulled an old-school handheld radio from his pocket, listened. "Are you sure? All right. Stay up there, then, and watch." He turned to the man beside him, square-shouldered and stubby. If Wells had to tag them using American army ranks, he'd make the tall one a lieutenant and the short one an E-6, a staff sergeant.

"Bandar says someone is coming toward us." He pointed south. "That way. He thinks the man has a rifle. You three go and see about it. Remember, don't shoot him unless you're sure. We don't need trouble with the al-Naqbis."

"Why would one of them come here at this hour?"

"I don't know, but *go.*"

The overheads hadn't shown any sentry posts, one reason that Wells had believed they'd be able to pull this off. It was plain bad luck that the jihadis were moving out tonight, more bad luck that one had gone to the house and seen Gaffan. Not one-in-a-thousand bad luck. These things happened. Maybe one in ten. But bad luck nonetheless. On a mission like this, outnumbered and outgunned, bad luck was lethal. They needed absolute surprise. Instead they were about to start a firefight against a larger force on its home territory.

In happier news, they'd found the right camp for sure. No Boy Scouts here tonight.

The jihadis had their backs to him. They were looking at the hill to the south, where the danger seemed to be. Wells dropped the firing selector on the AK to semiauto. He popped up and ran. Sixty yards from the Suburban, he ducked behind a beach ball–sized boulder, the last decent cover between him and the barracks. He could do real damage with the AK from this range. He might even have a chance with the pistol.

At first the barracks blocked Wells from seeing the three jihadis who were going after Gaffan. A few seconds later, he spotted them jogging up the rise behind the barracks in a *V* formation about ten feet wide. The *V* spelled trouble. Amateurs would have moved in a row. Trained soldiers created space.

Wells decided he had only one play. He tugged the silenced pistol from his belt, dropped the safety. He breathed deep, sighted at the center of the lieutenant's back. No head shots. He couldn't afford to miss. He waited for the jihadis who were going after Gaffan to top the ridge. He counted to three. He squeezed the trigger.

The silencer wasn't as good as the ones the agency used, but it was good enough. The pistol burped. A hundred seventy-five feet away, a neat hole appeared in the tall man's gown, halfway up his back, left of the spine. A 9-millimeter round didn't have tremendous muzzle velocity. The silencer cut it further. Even so, the slug pierced the lieutenant's skin, dug through his lats, broke two ribs as it spun sideways into the fat lower lobe of his left lung. It stopped there, not an immediately lethal wound but disabling and agonizing.

The lieutenant put his hands to his chest, scratching at the sudden fire inside him. He dropped to a knee and heaved for air in desperate shallow breaths. The three men beside him hadn't heard the shot and didn't realize the reason for his distress. They turned to him, leaned in, forming a nice tight target for Wells. One grabbed the lieutenant's arm, tried to pull him up. "Talib —"

Wells stood and fired, moving the AK left to right across the men. No speeches, no warning, just cutting down unarmed men. Murder. He pulled the trigger six times, two shots on each man. The first two went down hard. The third dove away and ducked between the Suburbans and ran along the outside of the front one. He pulled open the driver's door and flung himself into the driver's seat and gunned the engine. The wheels spun, then grabbed. The big truck surged forward.

Wells ran into the road and then stopped and raised his rifle as the Suburban accelerated at him, the guy not swerving, risking his own life to run Wells over. *Better you than me.* Wells focused, squeezed the trigger twice, dove into the ditch on the side of the road. The Suburban careened past him, nearly clipping his ankle. He landed awkwardly, gashing his forehead.

Wells thought he'd missed. But he turned his head and, through the blood trickling into his eyes, watched the truck accelerate, its V-8 engine roaring, the man behind the wheel as insensate as the steel that cocooned him. The truck skidded off the road and crumpled sideways into the ravine.

Wells stood, mopped his forehead. Over the ridge to the south, he heard shooting and shouting. Both Gaffan and the jihadis had AKs, so he couldn't guess who had the advantage. He ran for the second Suburban, to put it between him and the barracks. Then he heard footsteps pounding down the ridge —

The farmhouse; he'd forgotten the farmhouse —

He looked over his shoulder to see a man running down the hill, a rifle cradled in both hands. Wells spun, trying to get his own rifle up, but he was too late, the guy had him and was just waiting to get close enough to be sure —

Shots burst from the left. The man screamed and stumbled, dead before he hit the ground, the rifle sliding from his hands and clattering on the hill —

Wells looked left, saw Gaffan. Who said nothing, didn't give Wells a wave or a salute or even a thumbs-up. Just the briefest nod. Which was enough. They both knew that Gaffan had saved his life.

In front of Wells, the lieutenant crawled toward the barracks, coughing wetly, the red-black stain on his gown spreading down

364

his back. "Talib?" a man shouted from the barracks. A rifle poked out of the doorway and fired wildly, blindly into the night.

Gaffan angled down the hill, slid in beside Wells. "Thank you," Wells murmured.

"You're welcome. What happened?"

Wells wiped the blood off his forehead. "I tripped. Looks worse than it is. You got the other three?"

"Yeah."

"Then let's do the barracks. The guy in the gown, don't shoot him. I think he's in charge. I want to talk to him."

"He keeps bleeding like that, gonna be a short conversation." Gaffan nodded at a window at the far end of the barracks. "I'll get them moving."

Wells hid himself behind the high hood of the Suburban, twenty-five yards from the front of the barracks. He fired two shots in the air to distract whoever was inside as Gaffan ran for the barracks. Gaffan smashed the back window with his elbow, tossed in a grenade.

From behind the truck's front tire, Wells waited. The grenade exploded, its blast echoing through the night, blowing out the square front windows of the barracks. Two men ran from the front door, AKs on full automatic, panicked, firing at everything and nothing. Rounds poured into the Suburban, tearing open its windows, splattering its doors with bullet holes.

When the jihadis ran out of ammo, Wells popped up and tore open their chests with twin three-shot bursts. One man died drowning in his own blood from a burst aorta. He frothed at the mouth and muttered incoherently before Wells put him out of his misery with two bullets in his brain. The other was fortunate enough to die immediately and in silence. Wells had no time to comfort them, apologize to them, or pray for their souls. Or his own.

The lieutenant had slipped onto his chest, as though he could breathe through the hole in his back. Gaffan was right. He didn't have long. His skin was ashen, his gown soaked with blood. Wells turned him on his side, pulled up his chin. He was still conscious, barely. Watery hate filled his eyes when he looked at Wells.

"Stay with me," Wells said. "Stay awake. Where were you going?"

"Jerusalem."

"You're lying. Help us and we can help you. You need a doctor."

The man spat weakly, drool settling on his chin. Wells tried again. "Twelve hundred kilometers. That's a long way from here."

The man's eyes widened.

"Yes, I heard you. I heard you say Riyadh. You're going to Riyadh."

The man smiled. Wells wasn't sure if the reaction meant he'd guessed right or wrong.

"We'll find out. We'll stop you."

Death clotted the man's eyes but not his smile. Wells leaned close to hear his last words: "You won't. It's too late."

CHAPTER 16

Wells reached into the pockets of the dead man's gown, came out with sticky, bloody fingers and a ring that held two dull metal keys. A tap on his shoulder pulled him up. Gaffan pointed to the barracks, raised a finger: *One. Inside.*

Wells stepped to the left side of the open barracks doorway. He heard a nervous scuffling, the slow breathing of a man trying too hard to be quiet. Gaffan stood across the doorway. Wells tapped his chest, pointed inside, indicating he'd go in first. He lowered his AK, pulled his pistol and flashlight.

Gaffan nodded: *When you're ready.* Wells stepped inside and —

Dove sideways as a half-dozen rounds studded the concrete above him. He cut the flashlight, crawled beneath a cot, fired twice blindly into the corner. He didn't have much chance, but with the silencer he didn't have to worry about giving away his position. Gaffan tilted his rifle into the doorway and fired three shots.

"Surrender," Wells said. The jihadi fired again, banging shots over Wells's head. "Surrender. Save yourself."

Wells wanted to keep at least one jihadi alive. With the lieutenant dying, this guy looked like their only chance. But they were short on time. The militia was probably already coming. "Grenade," Wells called to Gaffan.

"Grenade?" the jihadi said. He sounded young. And spooked.

"Three seconds. One — two —"

"I surrender." A man stood.

Wells caught him in the flashlight beam. He looked unhurt, aside from minor cuts on his legs. "Raise your hands." Gaffan covered as the man came forward, hands high. Halfway to the door, the man reached up —

And turned on a naked bulb hanging from the ceiling.

The room was simple and spare, with thirty cots, fifteen against each long wall. Each cot had a wooden peg pounded into the wall above it. Most were empty, but AKs hung from four. Wooden shelves at the back held a mix of Western and Arab clothes, along with several pairs of the heavy leather

369

sandals that Saudis favored. One shelf held a half-dozen copies of the Quran and other books that might have been infantry manuals in Arabic. Four photos of the Grand Mosque and the Kaaba were taped up, no other decoration.

"Lie down. Face-first."

He did. Gaffan threw handcuffs on him, and Wells pulled him up and tugged him out. Up close, the guy was young and pitiful, with tiny acne scars, a flat, wide nose, and a scraggly beard. He wore plain white underwear and a dirty gray T-shirt. His arms were scrawny and his legs nearly hairless. The runt of the litter. Probably the reason he'd stayed in the barracks.

Outside, he licked his lips nervously as he saw the lieutenant's body. Wells dragged him away from the carnage, pushed him down, waved Gaffan over. "Guard him," Wells whispered. "See if he'll talk. And we only use Arabic when he's around."

"What are you doing?"

Wells nodded up the hill at the farmhouse.

"John — listen."

Wells heard a diesel engine, distant but growing stronger. He nodded. And ran.

He found the front half of the farmhouse turned into a makeshift classroom, a dozen desks arranged before twin whiteboards. Wells turned them over, but they were blank on both sides. He imagined lessons about weapons, basic infantry tactics.

A door at the back led to the kitchen. Inside, two refrigerators hummed. The counters were spotless, and so were the glasses and plates that filled the rough wooden shelves. These guys handled KP duty themselves, no need for Halliburton. So far, Wells had found nothing but proof of a well-run camp. The person who'd created this place had been through advanced infantry training and served in a real army for years.

Upstairs, three doors came off the landing. The first led to an empty bedroom. The ubiquitous poster of the shrine at Mecca filled one wall. Shirts and jeans and two *thobe*s hung in the closet. But the room smelled faintly musty, as if it hadn't been used for weeks.

The second door was locked. Wells tried the larger of the two keys he'd found in the lieutenant's pockets. It slid in smoothly, and he stepped inside. The bedroom was smaller than the first. A thin black blanket was piled at the foot of the bed, the only sign of mess Wells had seen in the house. A green duffel sat on the floor. Wells reached in and found a dark blue uniform. The uni didn't have name tags or rank insignia. But on its right biceps, it had a black patch with the words "Special Forces" stitched in Arabic in gold. And on the left, a triangular version of the Saudi flag.

He flipped over the duffel bag. Shiny black leather boots clattered to the floor, followed by a black leather belt, elbow and knee pads, goggles, heavy plastic gloves, and an open-face ski mask. Wells wasn't sure if he was looking at a real Saudi Special Forces uniform or just a very good copy.

The rest of the room was unremarkable. The closet held more gowns, two shirts, two pairs of pants. A wooden desk was empty except for a Quran, a pocket-sized green notebook, and a Saudi passport in the name of Talib al-Majood. Wells stuffed the notebook and passport in his windbreaker.

He checked his watch. Two-twelve. He'd been up here five minutes already. He peeked out the bedroom's narrow window, which looked east toward the center of the valley. The diesel engine was closer now, though he couldn't see any lights. He was putting a lot of faith in the gate. Too much, probably.

He hustled for the third door. It was locked. Neither key worked.

Wells pulled his pistol, fired two shots at the doorjamb. He raised a leg and kicked through the door, tearing it from the lock. He twisted against the wall of the corridor, away from the door, in case someone was inside, though he hadn't heard anything, and anyone in the house would probably have joined the firefight long ago.

Inside, a simple office. Two steel desks sat back-to-back. A black Ethernet cable was coiled on the floor, but Wells didn't see a computer. A black-painted supply cabinet sat beside the door. Wells pulled the handle. Locked. He tried the second, smaller key. After a moment's hesitation, it fit.

The cabinet had four steel shelves. Weapons and boxes of ammunition cluttered the top two: AKs and two partially disassembled M-16s. On the third shelf, two shoe boxes. The first held credit cards, cell phones, and two car keys, one Chevy and one Toyota. The second was filled with wads of one-hundred-dollar and twenty-dollar bills held with tatty rubber bands, along with a dozen passports — all Saudi, except for one Jordanian. Wells took the car keys but left everything else.

A nasty-looking short-barrel assault rifle with a wide, angular stock lay on the bottom shelf. Wells thought the rifle was a

Heckler & Koch. Gun nuts loved H&K. So did Deltas. Which meant that the Saudi Special Forces units probably used them. These men had gone to great lengths to impersonate Saudi soldiers. Or else, even worse, they really *were* Saudi soldiers.

In the desks, he found an engineering textbook in Arabic, a copy of a helicopter operations manual, detailed maps of Mecca and Medina and Riyadh, uniform name tags and patches, and what looked like day passes for a Saudi military base. He scanned the place once more, hoping for a laptop, but it was gone or hidden too well for him to find.

He grabbed the duffel bag from the second bedroom and threw the shoe boxes and the junk from the desk inside it. He took a last look around the office. If he had another hour, or even more a few minutes . . . But he didn't. He heard faint shouts, men's voices cutting through the dry night air.

The militia must be at the gate.

Time to go.

As he loped down the ridge toward Gaffan, Wells remembered how he'd once thought that a firefight in Afghanistan belonged in a Goya painting, a vision of hell on earth. The scene below him was less obviously violent but more surreal. Gaffan stood next to the Suburban, holding the arm of the jihadi they'd captured. His touch might have seemed almost friendly, brothers getting ready for a road trip — if not for the thick black hood that Gaffan had pulled over the kid's head. Five bodies were sprawled behind them. To the north, the crashed Suburban lay on its side, an elephant felled by an unseen dart. Norman Rockwell, as commissioned by the Devil.

Around the corner, metal tore at metal, a heavy groaning sound.

Wells reached the Suburban, handed Gaffan the duffel bag and the key to the Toyota. "See if it'll start. Take the bag and him with you." He grabbed an AK from one of the dead jihadis, then unlocked the Suburban and slipped the key in the ignition. Despite the bullet holes in the engine block, it started smoothly.

Wells turned on the Suburban's lights, put the truck in gear, angled it so it faced up the rocky ridge that led to the farmhouse. The ridge stretched at least two miles past the house, ending only at the flanks of the Lebanon range. He grabbed the clothesline from his pants, ran it through the steering wheel, behind the driver's headrest, back through the wheel. He knotted it tight to minimize the play of the wheel.

On the other side of the hill, another collision. Then an orchestral crash that could only be the gate going over. The militia wouldn't need long to move it out of the road. Wells checked that the AK's safety was on. He jammed the butt of the rifle against the gas pedal and shoved the muzzle against the front of the seat. The pedal flexed down and the truck took off, heading up the hill.

Wells dove out of the truck, landing hard on his right shoulder, which had taken more than its share of abuse over the years. A bolt of lightning exploded down his arm. He guessed he'd dislocated his shoulder again. He ran for the Toyota, pulled open the front passenger door, slid inside, his arm loose at his side.

The jihadi they'd captured wasn't in the car. Wells heard a faint banging coming from the trunk. Gaffan drove silently, heading over the ridge south of the barracks, the same way he'd approached. Wells peeked back at the Suburban. The truck was headed up the hill. The militia would naturally chase it first.

They topped the ridge, and the Toyota thumped over one of the men that Gaffan had killed a few minutes before. Wells banged his shoulder against the passenger door. Another bolt of lightning down his arm. Wells gritted his teeth.

"You think that'll work, buy us extra time?"

"Let's hope."

"You think we left intel back there?"

"Probably."

"This turned into a real shitshow. A Delta crew would have done it right. Or your guys."

Wells didn't want to argue. He wanted to sit in the dark with his eyes closed and count the seconds until he could pop his shoulder back in place. But he needed Gaffan to understand. "You still don't get it. Nobody but us was going near that camp. DoD or the agency wouldn't send men in unless they were sure of finding an active cell on the other end. Too risky. Too many lawyers saying no. And in a couple days, a week at most, there wasn't gonna be any place to raid. They were moving out."

Gaffan didn't answer. Wells didn't know whether he'd accepted the truth or was just tired of arguing.

Three minutes later, they reached the Jeep. High on the ridge to the northwest, Wells saw a low fire. The SUV had crashed. The militia would have found it was empty by now and would be figuring out where to go next. No doubt they would reach the logical conclusion: south. Wells and Gaffan had a decent head start, but they would probably radio ahead to their units in Baalbek. They wouldn't know exactly what they were looking for, but they would block the main valley road anyway.

Wells and Gaffan had to get out of the valley before daybreak, back to the coast. Fortunately, the mountain checkpoints were manned by the Lebanese army, which ran independently of Hezbollah. Or so Wells hoped.

Gaffan stopped beside the Jeep, but Wells put a hand on his arm. "No." Switching cars would take time they didn't have, and they were better off leaving the jihadi in the trunk.

They left the Jeep behind, headed east on a low gravel road that was shielded from the mountains. "Where to?" Gaffan said.

"South, then west, when you can. We'll take the road that runs up high on the ridge."

"Then south again?"

"North."

"Back toward the camp."

"Yeah, but west and above it. There's a pass that cuts through the mountains north of here. We'll get to the other side, close to the coast, ditch the car." Wells left the next question unspoken: *Then what?*

"Then what?" Gaffan said.

Wells wanted to find a place to hide, talk to the kid and then to Shafer about what they'd found. But the militia wouldn't need long to trace the Jeep. Wells was on a fake passport, but Gaffan wasn't. By sunrise, every militiaman in Lebanon would be after them. Maybe the cops, too, if Hezbollah decided it wanted the government to be in on the search. If the militia captured them, it might execute them on the spot. Being arrested wouldn't be much better. Wells wasn't eager to spend the rest of his life in a Lebanese jail. And they wouldn't get any help from the agency, not without firm evidence that connected these jihadis to the earlier attacks. Which they didn't have.

"Back to the coast. The boat. Unless you want to stay in Lebanon."

"I'll pass." Gaffan turned right along a narrow gravel road and right again at a silent village that was no more than a few concrete shacks at a four-way intersection. They were on pavement now. They rose through three switchbacks and intersected a narrow two-lane road that ran north-south along the flanks of the range. Gaffan made a right, taking them north. Wells saw head-lights along the valley floor to the east, but the escape plan had worked for now. The road through the village was quiet. It was possible that no one was after them because the militia were trying to figure out what had happened at the camp.

The ridge road had no guardrails, not even a white line to mark the edge of the pavement. It simply broke into gravel and fell away. Gaffan had no choice but to flip on his headlights and slow down. Wells checked his watch again. Two fifty-eight a.m. A long night behind, a long night ahead. And six more bodies to add to his inventory.

"You bust your shoulder again?" Gaffan had been in Afghanistan when Wells dislocated the joint the first time.

Wells didn't want to think about his shoulder. "You get anything from the kid?"

"His name. Meshaal. Other than that . . . He's scared out of his mind. You saw him. Not exactly the first team. I don't think he knows much."

"We'll see."

Soon after they crested the pass at Qam-mouaa, Wells saw houses to the west. Farm-ers and tribesmen had lived in the valleys between the Lebanon range and the coast for thousands of years. Fortunately, the road stayed empty as it swept northwest, curving around a hillside. Beneath them, villages glowed in the dark all the way to the Mediterranean. To the right, a gravel road led to an unfinished mansion, rebar poking from its second floor. Three forty-five a.m. Even the most dedicated fishermen wouldn't be up for at least another hour. Wells tapped Gaffan.

"Up there."

Gaffan swept the wheel right and bounced them up the road, which circled behind the mansion to a half-built garage. "Nice and quiet. First smart move tonight."

"Chain-of-command, please. No back-talk."

Outside, the air was cool and dry. Wells relaxed enough to feel just how exhausted he was. And how dirty. Sweat curdled on his skin. Dried blood covered his forehead. A steady fire burned from his biceps to his fingertips. If he didn't fix his shoulder soon, the nerves would be permanently damaged.

"Help me," he said to Gaffan.

Gaffan looked doubtful.

"I'll show you." Wells put Gaffan's left hand on the outer edge of his shoulder, the right on the meat of his biceps. He put his own left hand between them.

"On three, you push up and forward. I'll guide it."

"Don't I need an M.D. for this? At least a nursing degree?"

"Hard. On three. One. Two. Three —"

Gaffan pushed. Wells closed his eyes, and the world was nothing but pain — and he guided his arm up, up, and —

Into the socket and relief. He leaned against the Toyota, tears flaring from his eyes.

"Didn't hurt a bit," Gaffan said.

A thump from the trunk spared Wells from having to reply. They popped the trunk and tugged the jihadi — Meshaal — out. He started to crumple, but Gaffan put a shoulder under him. Wells pulled off the hood, and Meshaal blinked in the moonlight, his lips blubbering. Wells wondered how the jihadis had planned to use Meshaal. Maybe as a suicide bomber. He wouldn't be much of a soldier. But he wasn't screaming, and he hadn't tried to take off. He might be manageable.

"Can you stand, Meshaal?"

The kid nodded, not asking how Wells knew his name.

"Stand, then." Meshaal firmed his knees.

"How old are you, Meshaal?"

"Twenty."

"Really, how old?"

"Eighteen."

Nobody senior would have told him anything, not intentionally. But he'd surely picked up information. Wells needed to shake it out — without hurting him. Torture was off the table. Lie, steal, kill, no problem. But no torture. Not after what had happened in Jamaica. And especially not after the Midnight House.

Then he had an idea, a way to use the fact that they spoke Arabic and had come in without helicopters or fancy equipment or uniforms. The lie would work only if the kid wanted to believe. But Wells thought he might.

"Take off Meshaal's handcuffs. We can tell him now."

"Tell him." But Gaffan made the words a statement, not a question, and uncuffed Meshaal.

"Meshaal, do you know who we are? We're from" — Wells pointed over the mountain, east — "Pakistan. Do you understand?"

Meshaal shook his head.

"Sheikh bin Laden sent us to find you."

"Sheikh bin Laden."

"These men you trained with, they're not part of his plan. You are."

383

"Those were my brothers."

"They said they were your brothers, but they were traitors to the cause. That's why they treated you so badly."

Meshaal stepped back. "You know about that?"

"Of course. We've been watching."

A unit this size had to have an outcast. Put twenty men together — whether at a frat house or a training camp — and group dynamics demanded a pariah. A zeta male. Meshaal fit the role perfectly.

"But you killed them."

"We had to. We talked to them, but they wouldn't listen. And this mission that they're on, the sheikh doesn't want it. Do you understand?"

Meshaal bobbed his head slowly.

"But you put me in the trunk. You put a hood on me!"

"There wasn't time to explain then. We did this to free you. All of it. Now we have to go. And you're coming. So you need to put on the pants and shoes we have for you" — the blue uniform pants and boots, which Wells hoped would fit — "and then you sit with us in the car. We're going to the coast, and we have a ship to take us away. After that we're going to have a lot of questions for you."

"Then where are we going?" Meshaal was suddenly enthusiastic. He could choose to believe he was with two men who had killed everyone he trained with and were going to kill him, too — or two men who had rescued him from his misery at the orders of Osama bin Laden, the ultimate jihadi hero. Soon enough, the holes in the story would become too obvious for him to ignore. But for now he was rolling with it, and Wells wanted to encourage him.

"I'm not supposed to tell you that. But can I trust you?"

Meshaal nodded.

"Swear to Allah that I can trust you."

"I swear to Allah. You can trust me."

"We're going to Gaza. A special mission."

"Gaza."

"Yes. Let's go. But no more questions until we get out to sea. No talking at all."

Without another word, Meshaal pulled on the boots and the pants, which were a size small and made him look even sillier than before. He slid in next to Gaffan. Between the three of them the Toyota smelled so bad that Wells could hardly breathe. But no matter. They lowered its windows and rolled down the hill toward the coast. Toward the sea. And escape.

CHAPTER 17
EASTERN MEDITERRANEAN

The sun glowed red and belly flopped into the sea, fading with a flourish that the drinkers seven thousand miles away at Margaritaville would have appreciated. Wells didn't mind seeing it go. Gaffan had stocked the Cranchi with extra fuel and water, and even a few bags of dates. He'd forgotten sunscreen, and the motor for the Cranchi's cockpit cover wasn't working, a detail that the dealer in Beirut hadn't mentioned. The glare off the water had burned Wells's eyes and basted his brain.

But they'd had to stay off Cyprus until darkness came. Without a sat phone or Internet link, they couldn't know if the Lebanese police had connected them to the camp. Wells was assuming the worst, that they were wanted from Beirut to Gibraltar. They needed to make contact with the agency before the Cyprus police found them. Their best bet was a night landing.

Fortunately, their time at sea hadn't been wasted. Thanks to Meshaal, Wells had plenty to tell Shafer.

Fifteen hours earlier, the sky hinting at dawn, Wells sat beside Meshaal and offered him a handful of dates. Meshaal shook his head almost shyly. Wells reminded himself that the kid was only eighteen. If he pictured this trip as an adventure rather than an ordeal, he'd be more likely to talk. "Can you swim?"

"I've never even seen the ocean until now."

"One day you'll learn. Where did you grow up?"

"The Najd" — the high desert in the center of Saudi Arabia. "A village called Qusaibah. Maybe three hundred kilometers from Riyadh."

"Do you miss it?"

"Not too much. Where are you from?"

"I grew up in Lebanon, but I trained in Afghanistan."

"You don't sound like you're from Lebanon." Meshaal looked sidelong at Wells and then at the bubbly white wake behind the boat as though he wondered whether he could walk to shore. He was exhausted and scared, but he wasn't going anywhere, and

Wells figured that threats would shut him down.

"If my accent sounds funny, it's because I spent a few years in Germany."

"Where in Germany?"

"Hamburg."

"My cousin went to Hamburg to study. He said the Germans drink too much alcohol and the women are immodest. But still he liked it. But he said the weather is bad."

"It never gets hot like the Najd. But in the winter it snows. Have you ever seen snow, Meshaal?"

"No."

They were silent for a few minutes as the sky lightened around them.

"Are you ready to tell me about the camp?"

"I don't know."

"I think you should. The sheikh wants to know." Wells still couldn't believe he was using bin Laden's name.

"Have you met him?"

"A long time ago," Wells said truthfully. "He has to hide now. Because of the Americans, the drones. But he's in charge. And he wants to know about the mission you were training for. He's worried it will interfere with his plans."

"I don't believe you, but even if it's true, you're wasting your time, because I don't know anything." Meshaal let out a world-weary sigh, a sound that teenagers from London to Los Angeles would have recognized.

"You know more than you think. Start with something easy. How many men were at the camp?"

"It changed."

"At the most."

Meshaal counted slowly on his fingers, his lips moving. No wonder his fellow jihadis had picked on him. "Thirty-four," he said finally. "Or thirty-five."

"There were only thirty cots. Don't lie, Meshaal. I won't get mad at you, but you have to tell me the truth."

"I *am.* Some slept at the house."

"And how many men in all passed through?" The finger counting began. Wells quickly added, "You don't have to tell me exactly — just guess."

"Fifty-five, maybe."

"Who was in charge?"

"You don't know? You told me you watched us."

"But not all the time. So tell me."

Meshaal seemed to realize that whatever his reservations, he had no choice but to talk. "He called himself Aziz. I don't think that was his real name."

"He was in the Saudi military." Wells guessing now.

"I think so. He liked to be called Major."

I think so. Meshaal was drawing distinctions between what he'd seen firsthand and what other people had told him. Whatever his tics, he might be a good witness. "But Aziz wasn't there all the time." Wells guessing again, trying to move the conversation forward.

"He came every few weeks."

"From where?"

"I don't know."

"Riyadh? Jeddah?"

"I don't know."

"How old was he?"

"Old. Maybe your age."

Ouch. "If you saw his photo, would you recognize him?"

"Of course. I saw him lots of times. He lived in the house upstairs."

"In the front room?"

"Yes. Mostly he stayed there or in the office at the back. A few times he spoke to us in class. He said the men against us were strong soldiers, and if we weren't careful they'd kill us. Sometimes he prayed with us. He knew the whole Quran by heart. He never made a mistake."

"Did he say the soldiers would be American?"

"Yes. Sometimes he watched us train. He yelled at me once for holding my AK the wrong way. He told me to respect it."

"He was right. Did he tell you the mission?"

"No. I thought maybe it would be attacking a place where the Americans live, but he never said."

"You mean a housing compound. Like in Riyadh or Dhahran."

"Yes."

"Why did you think that?"

"We practiced with car bombs. How to make them. Twice we blew them up. What do you need such a big bomb for? Only to attack a place that's very well guarded."

"But he never said the target?"

"I told you. He never talked to me. Only yelled at me for the AK. And one time when I made a mistake at dinner and spilled date juice. He said to me, 'This camp is expensive, and the people who are paying, they don't want to waste money, so be careful.' You could see he wasn't nice. And that was even before —"

Meshaal broke off.

"Before what?"

"Nothing." But Meshaal wouldn't meet Wells's eyes.

Wells decided to let the question go for now. "That time in the kitchen, Aziz didn't say who those people were, the ones paying for the training?"

"No. But one of the men — his name was Talib, he was one of the ones you killed — he said something like, 'Even though they might not like what you learn.' I didn't know what he meant, but Aziz didn't like him saying that. He looked at Talib like he wanted to slit his throat."

Wells pulled out the Saudi passport he'd taken from the upstairs bedroom at the farmhouse. "This was Talib?"

"Yes."

"Did you ask Aziz why he was mad?"

"Of course not. I was just happy that he wasn't mad at me anymore."

"Did he ever say anything about King Abdullah?"

"He hated Abdullah. He told us Abdullah makes peace with the Jews and lets the infidels into Mecca."

"Do you hate Abdullah?"

"I don't know."

"Did Aziz say he was planning a revolt against Abdullah?"

"Not really. No."

"Besides Aziz, were there other Saudi soldiers in camp?"

"Yes. Plus one from Iraq. I didn't like him. He was crazy. He punched me when I couldn't do enough push-ups. It wasn't my fault."

"How many push-ups can you do?"

"One time I did twenty-eight. How about you?"

"A few more," Wells said. "And how did you get to the camp?"

"I drove through Jordan —"

"I mean, how did you find out about it?"

"My cleric at home asked me if I wanted to fight in the jihad. I said yes, and he said he would help."

So Aziz — whoever he was — had recruiters who reached into the Saudi heartland and plucked off teenagers in ones and twos. Between the passports Wells had found, the paper trail that the camp must have produced, and Meshaal's testimony, the Saudi *mukhabarat* should be able to roll up the network. But if Abdullah and Miteb were right, the *muk* —or at least Mansour and Saeed — already knew about the camp.

On the other hand, Duto and the CIA would have to pay attention now that Meshaal had confirmed that the jihadis were targeting American soldiers. The United

States couldn't ignore that warning, no matter how much it wanted to stay out of the fight between Abdullah and Saeed.

Which led to the obvious question: If Saeed and Mansour were focused on Abdullah and succession, why would they target the United States? Why wake the dragon? Maybe Talib had blurted out the answer that day in the kitchen. Maybe Aziz — whoever he was — had grander plans than his paymasters knew.

For hours, Wells asked Meshaal about his recruitment and training, what weapons he'd used, what tactics he'd practiced, the other jihadis. The biggest surprise came when Wells asked about Princess Alia's bombing. He didn't expect Meshaal would know anything, but Meshaal told him that one jihadi had frequently dressed in a burqa.

"He slept in a little room behind the farmhouse, because no one liked him. They hated him even more than me. But Talib told us to be nice to him. He left a while ago, and when we heard that Alia blew up, we all knew it had to be him."

Eventually Meshaal's energy flagged, and he went below and lay in the narrow bunk where Wells had stowed the duffel bag from the farmhouse. He lay beside the bag and closed his eyes and fell asleep almost immediately. He looked very young.

Wells came back up, sat beside Gaffan at the helm. The sun was strong now, the glare high off the water. Gaffan had run them west-southwest to get away from the main shipping lane between Lebanon and Cyprus. Still, the waters were busy with diesel-belching trawlers from Beirut and container ships that ran between Tel Aviv and Istanbul.

"You were talking to him awhile."

"He knows a lot. He was there five months, and he's not stupid. And because they didn't care about him, they talked in front of him. He already told me he's sure that someone from the camp assassinated Alia. And he says the commander talked about targeting American soldiers."

"I still wish there'd been another way to do it."

"There wasn't."

"This is the place where the numbers don't add up."

"You think chain of command makes it easier. The last thing I was involved with, some good soldiers, they did some things I'll bet they wish they could take back. But they had a colonel in charge, and authorization. They told themselves it was okay. Just following orders."

"And what happened to them?"

"They died. Most of them."

"You saying what I think?" Gaffan said.

"No. It wasn't me. It's complicated. But what I'm trying to say, you operate the way we do, you can never lay it on somebody else. You answer to yourself."

"And if you answer wrong?"

"Then you pay. One way or another."

Gaffan was silent for a while.

"John."

"Yeah."

"You mind if I ask you about religion? Islam?"

"Ask away." Though Wells didn't like talking about his faith. Too often, Muslims saw him as an impostor, and non-Muslims a curiosity.

"I just don't understand how you say you're Muslim when all the guys we go after — it's not like they're Buddhists."

"World War Two. We and the Germans were both Christian."

"Yeah, but the Germans weren't quoting the Bible when they attacked us. This is a religious war. That's the way *they* see it, anyway. I don't have to tell you. You know the Quran better than me. Jihad, killing unbelievers. It's all in there."

"Brett. You're Christian."

"Sure."

"You pray."

"I'm kind of a Christmas and Easter guy, but yes."

"Do you really, truly believe that Jesus Christ rose from the dead?"

Gaffan looked away from Wells and onto the Mediterranean, as if the water might have the answer. "I don't know. I'd like to."

"There's plenty in the Quran that I don't believe. But all those years in Afghanistan, I accepted the brotherhood of Islam. I learned the words, and at some point I started to hear the music. Maybe because there was nothing else for me over there, maybe for my cover, but I did. And I believe in one God. As far as I'm concerned, putting those two things together makes me a Muslim. And most Muslims don't want suicide bombs and jihad. They want to live their lives like everybody else."

"They have a funny way of showing it."

"You know better than that. Back to World War Two, the Japanese and their kamikaze pilots. Suicide for the emperor. We killed them, and they killed us. Now Japan's one of our closest allies. It's situational."

"I hope you're right, John. But I don't think either of us is going to be out of work for a long time."

"Then we better get to it."

Wells spent the next three hours examining the notebook and helicopter manual and engineering textbook and other papers and passports he'd taken from the farmhouse. Nothing jumped at him, but he did notice a few subtle points. The passports had been recently issued and looked genuine. The men in them were in their teens and twenties, from Saudi towns Wells didn't know, presumably similar to the village where Meshaal had grown up. The passports had hardly been used. The only entry stamps Wells found were from Lebanon, Syria, Jordan, and Dubai. He saw no visas from Europe or the United States — or from Pakistan, Afghanistan, or Iran. The lack of travel to those countries was more proof that this group operated independently of Al Qaeda and the Iranian government.

Wells's Arabic wasn't good enough to let him fully understand the engineering textbook. But it seemed to focus on building infrastructure, heating, ventilation, and air-conditioning systems. Inside, Wells found two folded-up pages that held detailed schematics for truck bombs. The third was covered with what looked like a hand-drawn map of a highway. A section near the top was circled. But the map lacked any description or heading, and Wells couldn't figure out where it was.

As for the name tags and patches, they were either genuine Saudi military badges or very good replicas. If the jihadis were as well trained as they seemed, they had a real chance of successfully breaching security at a Saudi military base, maybe even one of Abdullah's palaces. Again, though, Wells found no evidence of a specific target.

Finally, he looked at the notebook he'd found in Talib's room. It was filled with neat Arabic script, to-do lists that appeared routine. *Buy three hundred gallons diesel . . . Liban Telecom mobile phones . . . send F for B at airport 17 March.* Toward the back the phrase "42 Aziz 3" was circled in Arabic. *Aziz.* That was what the man who'd run the camp had called himself. A code, Wells imagined, but for what? With any luck, the NSA or the analysts at Langley would find a connection that he had missed.

Downstairs, the Cranchi's air-conditioning had given out. The cabin was as stifling as Bourbon Street in July. Wells hoped the engines were more reliable than the boat's other mechanicals. Meshaal's face was slick with sweat. When Wells walked in, he jerked awake, lifting his hands protectively. He lowered them as he realized where he was. "How much longer before we get to Gaza?"

"A while."

"How come we haven't prayed yet today? At camp we prayed five times a day."

Wells didn't want to pray now, with a dead man's blood under his fingernails and Gaffan wondering about his faith. "There's a special rule about being at sea. You don't have to."

"I don't think that's true."

"We're not praying, Meshaal. Come on, let's go up. It's too hot here."

The interrogation continued topside.

"Did you ever see the office in the farmhouse? The room with the computers?"

"A few times," Meshaal said. "I brought food to the pilot."

Meshaal hadn't mentioned anything about a pilot before. "How do you know he was a pilot?"

"It was my job to take lunch to him. Once I came in and he was playing a flying game on his computer, turning the plane upside down. I asked him if I could play. He said, 'No, you have to be a real pilot to play.' I asked him if he was a real pilot, and he said yes, a helicopter pilot. Then Aziz came in and told me to get lost. I didn't talk to him again."

"What was his name?"

"I don't know. And he left — I don't know when, exactly — maybe a month ago. After he left, other people started to leave. Before that, if someone left, someone else usually came, but not anymore."

"The people who left, did they say they were leaving for good?"

"They didn't say, but yes. They didn't leave any of their clothes behind. They left in twos and threes. They were going to Riyadh, and some to Jeddah and even a few to Mecca."

"They told you?"

"No, but I heard."

"Did they take weapons?"

"Some did. The ones who were flying didn't."

"Did Aziz ever say anything about Mecca? Attacking the Grand Mosque?"

"I told you a bunch of times. He never said anything to me."

"When was the last time you saw him?"

"Ten days ago. He told us the mission was coming soon."

"Do you know what he wanted, why he came back?"

"It had to do with the special room."

The kid was full of surprises.

"Meshaal. You never said anything about a special room."

"You never asked. It was next to the little cabin behind the house. It was dug into the ground, made of concrete. Maybe three meters square, four meters deep."

"A cell."

"Yes. We dug it and put a metal roof on it and covered it with dirt, so it was hard to see. It had a special pipe with an engine to blow air inside so it wouldn't get too hot and someone in it could breathe. The night Aziz came back, he made me and some others dig up the pipe and the engine and put it in a truck. Then two men drove it away."

"Did they hold anyone in the cell?"

"One time they put someone in for four days." Meshaal shook his head as if trying to rid his mind of the image. "His name was Ayman."

"This is what you didn't want to talk about before."

"Yes."

"He was a friend of yours?"

"Not a friend, not really. But we looked out for each other. People thought he was stupid. Like me. They said he was a traitor. He wasn't a traitor. He asked if he could leave, and they said no, and he left anyway.

They caught him the next day and brought him back."

"And put him in the cell."

"Yes."

"And didn't give him any food."

"No food, okay. He had no *water.* On the third day, Aziz made us watch. This is what I didn't want to say before. We lifted the lid, and Ayman was begging for water. Begging and promising he would tell. Whatever Aziz wanted. His face. His lips. They were black. And his eyes —" Meshaal stopped. "And Aziz told us, this is what happens to traitors. Then we put the lid back on."

Aziz had been testing the ventilation equipment. Wells was certain. He needed to make sure the cell wouldn't suffocate the captives he planned to hold. By running away, deserting, Ayman had made himself the test case. But Aziz hadn't needed to kill him. He could have provisioned the cell, plucked Ayman out a week later, lesson learned. Death from dehydration was pure cruelty, a dark fire far worse than the slow twilight of starvation.

Wells wondered if Aziz had prayed the night he'd put the lid back on. Probably. Probably with special fervor. Like the Bible, the Quran was filled with tales of man's

403

cruelty to man. And yet Wells couldn't believe that Allah wanted the prayers of a psychopath.

Wells had never met Aziz, never seen the man, didn't even know his real name. But for the first time in years, a righteous fury burned his blood. He wanted to strike down this man who had amused himself by torturing one of his own soldiers. The word was *smite.* He wanted to cast lightning upon Aziz.

"Stop the boat," he said to Gaffan.

Gaffan brought the engines to idle. They were about fifty miles south of Cyprus, out of the main shipping lanes, no other ships within five miles. Wells stripped down and dove into the sea. The water was cool and dark and briny, almost medicinal, and Wells scissors-kicked and then dove as deep he could. With the boat beside him, he was a fearless swimmer.

Far below the surface, he rubbed his fingertips together until the last scarlet traces disappeared in the murky water. He'd find blood enough in the days to come.

Meshaal went below again, curled up, slept. Wells let him. Eventually the interrogators in Guantánamo would take another pop at him, but Wells didn't think they would hear much more. He'd gotten what the kid had to give.

For now he tried to think through the questions the kid's story raised. The answers were disturbing. Why did Aziz need to move the ventilation equipment? Because he'd built another cell in Saudi Arabia, and he didn't want to buy more gear because he feared it could be traced. Why did he need an underground cell? For a captive. For a kidnapping. The obvious target was a Saudi royal. But Aziz had told his men that they'd be fighting American soldiers. Maybe he'd said that to motivate them. Maybe he was aiming at a Western housing compound, as Meshaal thought. The compounds had private American security forces along with official Saudi protection.

Or maybe . . . maybe Aziz thought he could get at the ambassador. But Wells couldn't see how. The ambassador rarely left the American embassy, and when he did, a small army protected him. But Aziz had close to sixty men, a small army of his own. Their training wasn't up to American standards. But their willingness to use suicide attacks was a huge tactical advantage.

Now the United States had to send a team to search what was left of the camp — and quickly, before Hezbollah decided to demolish it and the evidence it held. Raiding the camp now would be easy. Even so, a raid might not happen quickly. Before it could, the most powerful officials in Washington — Duto and the secretary of state and the national security adviser — would have to admit that they should have hit the camp already instead of leaving the attack to Wells. Then they would have to reach the obvious conclusion: The United States needed to go in now. And if Hezbollah and the Lebanese government didn't agree, Langley would have to commit a CIA team with enough backup firepower from the Deltas to convince the militia to stand down.

Wells hoped Duto and the other big names — they liked to call themselves "principals" — would move quickly. Even so, Wells couldn't see how a raid could happen in under forty-eight or seventy-two hours, which was already too long. If Aziz had been dismantling the camp for a month, he had to be close to striking. And the Saudis weren't going to stop him, though they might be surprised when they saw his target.

Wells wished for a sat phone. But wishing was useless. They simply had to wait for darkness and then ease their way into the coast. The Cranchi could run in very shal-

406

low water, more proof of its speedboat roots. They didn't need a harbor, just a quiet beach far enough from a village that they could ditch the boat and wade in. They'd sleep on the ground, and in the morning buy a phone or an Internet connection and get to Nicosia.

They could even leave Meshaal if he slowed them down. They'd get him back. He didn't speak Greek and didn't have a passport. He wasn't getting off Cyprus on his own. Their first priority had to be making contact and getting to a safe house before the Cyprus cops found them and started asking unpleasant questions.

After sunset, the sea glowed, streaks of white and black mating with every wave. They were ten miles south of the southwestern tip of Cyprus. The island glowed faintly through the night's humid haze. "Land ho," Gaffan said.

"Bring us in, then."

"Aye-aye, cap'n." Gaffan was trying for an English accent, not very well. "We'll drink a pint o' grog, have our pick of the lassies."

Suddenly, Wells realized that they weren't speaking Arabic. Hunger and heat and fatigue were making them sloppy.

"What are you saying?" Meshaal yelled.

Wells grabbed Meshaal's skinny biceps, dug his fingers in tightly enough to feel the tendons flex. "Quiet."

Cyprus wasn't quite the cradle of civilization, but it was close. People had lived on the island for at least five thousand years. In other words, the coast didn't have a lot of empty beachfront left for a landing. Hotels and villages speckled the shoreline, their lights glimmering. A mile out, Gaffan cut the engines. They floated silently, listening to cars on the coast road and a party at a hotel that sat behind a wide beach.

"Now what?" Gaffan said.

"Maybe we ought to find a slip, a real harbor, and dock there and walk away. Dare somebody to stop us."

"Are you sure?"

"No. But if they see us wade in like we're crossing the Rio Grande to pick peppers, how's that gonna look?"

"They didn't teach this at the Farm?"

"They did, but I forgot."

"Too bad. Would have come in handy."

At least Gaffan got the cosmic absurdity. They'd successfully raided a terrorist training camp. Now they couldn't figure out how to ditch a speedboat without getting caught. Wells pictured stepping off the Cranchi, walking through a sleepy village. If they

408

were dressed better or spoke Greek or didn't have the kid, maybe they could pull it off. But not this way.

"Find a stretch where the houses look empty, and we'll just have to go for it."

Gaffan chugged slowly east. Then they caught a break. The lights disappeared as the coast road swung behind a hilly ridge covered with scrub and cypress. The ridge sharpened into low bluffs too steep for houses. A wide white sand beach lay between the bluffs and the sea.

"We're not going to do better than this," Gaffan said. "Protected, no houses, smooth water."

Wells looked at Meshaal. "We're going to land there, and then we're all getting out. You're going to have to walk through the water."

"Is this Gaza?"

"You've got Gaza on the brain. Forget Gaza. This is Cyprus."

"You said —"

"We're stopping here first. Then Gaza. Quiet, now."

Gaffan cut the engines to just above idle and swung the ship toward the shore. The sea slopped against the hull, and the inboards grumbled. They closed to five hun-

409

dred yards, four hundred —

And then heard the unmistakable sound of a woman in full cry, moaning as if all the world couldn't contain her pleasure.

"We're not the only ones looking for a romantic hideway," Gaffan said.

Now Wells saw them — or to be more accurate, him — a few hundred feet west, where the beach was narrower and the bluffs made a sort of natural amphitheater. They must have had a blanket or an air mattress. A battered Kia 4×4 was parked on a narrow track along the side of the hill. The Kia gave Wells an idea. The idea wasn't very nice. But it shouldn't hurt anyone, and it might give him a chance to talk to Shafer before the end of the workday in Washington, six hours behind.

"Go. Get as close as you can. Fast."

"That's what she said." Gaffan pushed the throttle, and the boat surged ahead.

Wells ran below and pulled the shoe box out of the duffel bag, left everything else. He emerged to see that they were about one hundred yards from the shore. The guy was still pumping away, but now he wagged a finger at them in warning. The water was nearly still, and the bottom rose smoothly and steadily, just fifteen feet deep, ten —

The moans stopped. The guy stood, his

410

erection obvious. The woman sat up, her breasts full, nipples visible even from the boat. The guy said something to her, and she pulled on her top. The guy pulled on his shorts and shouted at them in Greek. Wells didn't understand a word, but the meaning was clear enough. The guy was short, swarthy, muscular, late twenties, more hair on his chest than on his head. He was swimming in enough testosterone to fight rather than run. A mistake.

Wells grabbed the siderail as the boat scraped bottom and dug itself in. He jumped off the side. The water was only four feet deep and the sand firm. He ran for shore, pushing himself through the low waves. Gaffan followed him over. The Cypriot looked at them in shock. Wells came out of the water and dropped the shoe box and ran toward him. Suddenly, the guy seemed to realize that Wells might be dangerous. He said something to the woman. She stood and pulled on her panties and reached for her skirt. Before she could pick it up, he grabbed her arm and pulled her toward the Kia.

But though Wells wouldn't see forty again, he still moved like the linebacker he'd once been, eating ground with powerful strides. The woman screamed, and Wells knew what he had to do. "Take him down," he yelled back to Gaffan.

The guy tried to cut him off, but Wells spun around him and went for the woman instead. He wrapped her up and covered her mouth with his arm, muting her screams. She bucked and kicked, but Wells held her tight. Her boyfriend punched wildly, but Wells swung the woman around to put her between them. No points for chivalry. He just wanted to get through this without getting any more seriously hurt. Gaffan reached them and punched the guy low in the stomach with a solid right and doubled him over and hit him again in the jaw. The guy went down hard, and Gaffan jumped him and rolled him over and sat on him.

Wells pulled the electrical tape from his cargo pants and wiped it dry and tore a foot-long piece and slapped it over the woman's mouth. He flex-cuffed her wrists and pushed her down. Then he and Gaffan repeated the process with the guy. Their eyes were wide and terrified.

"We don't want to hurt you," Wells said. "Just your car." They shook their heads in bewilderment. Wells reached into the guy's pants and found a cheap black leather wallet and two condoms and the keys to the

412

Kia. Somehow the condoms made Wells feel worse than anything else. He'd ruined their fun tonight.

Meshaal stood at the edge of the water, his mouth open. He'd surely never seen a naked woman before, much less anything like this. Wells waved him over. He picked up the shoe box and walked to them with his feet dragging like a dog on its way to the vet.

Wells dropped two wet stacks of hundred-euro notes on the sand. When they dried, they'd be worth more than the Kia. "I'm sorry," he said. "We have to go."

"They'll be all right," Wells said fifteen minutes later. They were on the A6, heading east to Nicosia, the Kia's heater on high to dry them out.

"Best night of their lives. They'll tell the grandkids."

"They'll be fine."

"You're always so sure. Must be nice."

They reached Nicosia an hour later, ditched the Kia, and walked through the town's quiet streets to the hostel where Wells had stayed a week before. Then Wells found an Internet café and called Shafer, who got Wells into the American embassy so they could talk on a secure line.

"It's gonna be messy," Shafer said, when Wells was done explaining. "And you're right. It may take a couple days to sort out."

"Not too long."

"If the cops get close, call me back. I'll do my best to get you out."

"That's not it, Ellis. You didn't see the camp. These guys have big plans."

■ ■ ■ ■

PART THREE

■ ■ ■ ■

CHAPTER 18
RIYADH

"My brother says I'm dying. Is he a prophet? Does he see the future? What a gift it must be. I wouldn't wish it on anyone. Not even Saeed. To see your own death. And then what do you do? Sit in your bed and count down the days? And your wives and your children and your children's children? Shall you watch them die, too? Better to gouge your eyes and live in darkness than see all that."

Abdullah's rant began even before Kurland reached his chair, the Arabic pouring out of him as Rana struggled to keep up with the translation. They were in Abdullah's massive palace in the desert just north of Riyadh. The king had summoned Kurland that morning, telling him only that they needed to meet immediately.

Abdullah finished his speech and coughed into his hand as if he'd just run a marathon. Kurland settled himself in his chair, a leather recliner that didn't match the room's eighteenth-century French furniture. He wondered what he was meant to say. When they'd met at Abdullah's desert ranch, Abdullah had shown Kurland the spotless cages that housed his prize falcons, proud, long-feathered birds. The king had been smiling, almost playful. He'd laughed when a big brown camel — an ill-tempered beast that had won two races in Dubai — nipped at Kurland.

Abdullah was still alive, but the smiling man from the ranch was gone. The king's face had melted into itself, crumpled like crushed wax paper. His body was heavier, and yet he seemed smaller and weaker. Kurland thought of Humpty Dumpty. *All the king's horses and all the king's men . . .* And the biggest surprise of all, he was alone, though two guards and two translators waited in the gilded corridor outside. Abdullah must have forbidden them.

Kurland tried to deflect the king's rant with a joke. "I don't know any prophets. Maybe I need new friends."

"Are you asking me to smile? After what's happened to my granddaughter?"

"I'm asking — I'm thanking you for giving me the chance to offer my country's condolences about Alia's death."

"Is that why you think you're here?"

"I'm here because you wanted to see me, King."

"You're here because of my brother. The prophet. King Saeed. Abdullah is dead and long live Saeed. Did you bow to him? Did you kiss his hand? Kneel before him to tie his shoes?"

Kurland thought back to his conversation with Saeed. Saeed had implied that Abdullah was too ill to govern. Though he hadn't explicitly said that he planned to take over even before Abdullah died, the implication was clear. The Kingdom had gone through similar transitions before. Abdullah himself had governed as crown prince after King Fahad suffered a stroke in 1996.

Kurland wanted to reassure Abdullah. But he couldn't choose a side in this battle. Two days before, he'd received instructions from Washington: The United States would take no position on succession in the House of Saud. Not officially, not unofficially. "You're still king," he said. "That's how I see you, and that's how America sees you."

Abdullah ignored Kurland's watery words, set off on another journey in Arabic. "I must be jealous of Saeed. He lives in the future, I don't even see the past anymore. Did he flood the room with tears when he told you

419

of my fate? Did he tell you the throne would be his? That he would mount it like a whore even before my corpse cools?"

"The United States respects the process by which your kingdom picks its leaders," Kurland said. "We expect that other nations won't interfere with our elections. Similarly, we don't interfere with yours."

Even to him the words sounded dry, mechanical. No surprise. But when he'd practiced them on the ride up, he hadn't expected them to be so misaligned with the king's mood. Abdullah was unfurling an epic of tragedy and betrayal. Kurland was reading from a position paper drafted by GS-15s in Foggy Bottom.

"Say what you mean. Whether I'm king or Saeed or someone else, the United States doesn't care."

"Of course we care. But our relationship with the Kingdom is long-standing, and whoever is king, we will respect Saudi interests." Whoever had written these words should be flogged, Kurland thought. He quickly added, "King, I don't know what's passed between you and Saeed, but for what it's worth, your brother didn't say you were dying."

"No?"

"He said you weren't well. And that

420

whoever ruled Saudi Arabia, the Kingdom would be a great friend to the United States."

" 'A great friend to the United States.' " Abdullah's voice was steady now, the madness in his eyes gone. "He's as honest as a snake, my brother. Did he tell you about his other great friends? The clerics who preach jihad every Friday. The men who blow themselves up in Iraq and Afghanistan. Does that sound like a friend?"

"Is Saeed funding the insurgencies?"

"He's too keen for that. He closes his eyes while imams shovel money to these men who kill your soldiers."

"You don't stop him?"

"You think I haven't tried."

Abdullah closed his eyes, slumped in his overstuffed chair. Rana reached for him, but Kurland shook his head and they waited in silence. After a minute, the king opened his eyes. "I've forgotten my manners. Would you like some coffee? Or juice?"

"If you're having something."

Abdullah picked up the handset of the antique phone beside him. Almost before he'd hung up, his steward emerged with a tray of coffee, orange juice, and French pastries. Kurland sensed that the king needed a few minutes to gather his strength.

"What do you think of my country, Mr. Ambassador?"

Hardworking would be too obvious a lie, as would *friendly,* Kurland thought.

"I haven't seen as much of it as I would have liked. The security situation. But the people I've met, they're polite, thoughtful. Hospitable. Pious, I suppose. Like certain Americans. Mainly Southerners."

"You think you understand Saudi Arabia?"

"No, sir. I wouldn't say so. Sometimes I don't even think I understand America."

"America's easy to understand. America is on the surface. Here everything is buried. You don't have any idea what's happening."

"Tell me, then."

To Kurland's surprise, Abdullah did. About his plans to make his son king, the fury he had stirred in Saeed and Mansour. About the split in the family he caused.

"This has been going on since last year and we haven't heard of it?"

"You do need new friends, Mr. Ambassador. But most of the princes feel it's in their interest to hold their tongues. Once they've made a decision, they'll want a strong king, and that will be impossible if the world knows our house is divided."

"But you've broken that secrecy. You've

told me."

"My reasons don't matter."

"Even so, I'd like to know them."

Abdullah didn't answer. The silence stretched, and Kurland sat back and waited. Pressing the king to speak would be a terrible mistake, he thought. Beside him, he sensed Rana's breathing change, heard Rana's fingertips drum against his legs. Kurland tilted his head fractionally, trying to catch Rana's eyes and convey the message: *Not a word. Not a sigh. He's got to talk on his own. And if you screw this up —*

"When they attacked Alia, they went too far," Abdullah said suddenly.

Kurland needed a moment to parse the words. "You think your brother was behind the bombing in Jeddah?"

"I think it's possible."

"What would he gain?"

"Look at me!" The words were a plea as much as a command. Abdullah lifted his right hand and watched it quiver. "If Saeed sees my death, he's not far wrong. He's stronger than I am. More ruthless."

Abdullah squeezed his fingers together to hide their trembling and rested his hand on his lap. "Saeed is more ruthless than I am, and more ruthless than you could ever be, and he's going to win. And there's nothing

423

you or I can do about it." His voice had fallen to a whisper. He seemed to have lost interest in the conversation.

"Can you prove he was involved? Because if you can —"

"Of course I can't."

"But she was his grandniece, too —"

"Americans always believe in kindness. When you leave here, drive back to that prison you call an embassy, take a detour. Drive into the desert. Tell me what kindnesses you see there, Mr. Ambassador."

Kurland knew he shouldn't be angry at this half-mad man. But he couldn't help hating Abdullah a little. "That's what you called me here to say."

"And to ask you a question."

"Whatever you like."

"Suppose I could prove that Saeed had killed my granddaughter. Would it matter? To the United States of America?"

"It would matter."

"Would it?" the king said again. "Would it mean anything at all?"

"Yes." Kurland hoped he was right.

"So I guess we're not following the king's advice?" Rana said, as the convoy swung south onto the highway that ran from the palace toward downtown Riyadh.

424

"Hmmm?" Kurland was still trying to understand what Abdullah had said about Saeed. Would the prince use terrorists to attack his own family? These men had everything to lose from a civil war, everything to gain from keeping the Kingdom stable. Maybe Kurland was naive, but he thought they'd be rational enough to make the compromises necessary for a peaceful transition.

"Going into the desert. His object lesson."

In fact, they were heading back to Riyadh and the embassy. Kurland, Rana, and Maggs rode in the second Suburban, the third vehicle in the convoy. Maggs had moved Kurland out of the lead Suburban, explaining that he didn't want to be predictable. Maggs and Kurland sat side by side in the middle seat. Rana and a marine corporal were in back, with two more marines up front. Two Saudi police cars cleared traffic ahead of the convoy, sirens screaming, while an armored Jeep from the king's private security detail brought up the rear. Saudi drivers were famously aggressive, but even they stayed away from this rolling mass of iron.

"Yeah, we'll skip the desert," Kurland said. Though part of him wanted to see what the king had meant. Walk in the heat until he collapsed.

"I have to say attacking Alia was brilliant. Shows the princes nobody's safe. And takes out a progressive voice, a woman, someone who can speak to America and Europe. And it's pushing Abdullah over the edge at this moment when he's fighting with Saeed for control. Three for the price of one."

"Could Saeed have been involved?"

"You're not serious."

"I'm not saying directly. But he's the defense minister. He's got intel on her protection. Maybe he or Mansour gave that to somebody who didn't like her. When we saw him, he didn't seem too upset she was gone."

"Okay. Abdullah's furious that Alia died. Wants someone to pay. He and his brother, they're rivals, hate each other. And Abdullah's blaming Saeed. But why would Saeed take that risk? I don't see it. And I promise you that's what Foggy Bottom will think. They'll say this proves that Abdullah is too old and we can't trust him anymore."

"What if we're looking at it backward?" Kurland said. "What if Saeed is just crazy? What if he's waited forever to be king, and he can't stand the idea that Abdullah wants to skip him?"

"You're letting your dislike for Saeed color

426

your thinking."

"Maybe. But there's something I don't get. The family's kept this to themselves. We didn't have a clue."

Rana hesitated. "True."

"So Al Qaeda probably doesn't know, either. Or Hezbollah. Unless they have better intel into what's happening in the monarchy than we do."

"Which is unlikely, sure."

"And when was the last time the Sauds had this kind of internal struggle?"

"Not since the early sixties," Rana said. "When King Saud was drinking himself to death and his brothers exiled him."

"Almost fifty years ago. So *why now?* The other bombings, sure. But Alia? Like you said, that was a surgical strike at Abdullah. If the terrorists aren't getting tipped from inside, how could they know exactly the right time and way to hit him?"

"Coincidence," Rana said. "They'd planned awhile, and they had a chance at Princess Alia and they took it."

"I hate coincidence."

The convoy passed a massive construction project, hundreds of cranes working on half-finished apartments and office towers, part of the campus of Princess Noura University for Women. The royal family was spending more than eleven billion dollars on the school, part of its effort to funnel oil wealth into creating a sustainable society. Past the campus, northern Riyadh came into focus, concrete houses and mansions and mosques jumbled close behind high walls. In a city where summer temperatures topped one hundred twenty degrees, outdoor space was not a priority. The houses were built nearly to the edges of their lots. Kurland tried to imagine living inside one. He couldn't. *"You think you understand Saudi Arabia?"* Abdullah had almost sneered when he said the words. *No,* Kurland thought. But maybe that was his own failure —

The ambush began with what seemed to be an accident.

A panel truck sliced across the highway right to left, tires squealing, leaving streaks of rubber across the asphalt. It smashed sidelong into the van leading the convoy, pummeling it against the center divider, putting a foot-deep gash in the van's armored frame. And then it blew up —

A half-second later, a Toyota 4Runner pulled up beside the first Suburban, eighty yards ahead of Kurland's vehicle —

And disappeared in a bright orange fireball that cut through the Suburban's armored windows and twisted it onto its side and incinerated the marines and embassy staffers inside —

Through the Suburban's smoked-glass windshield, Kurland saw the truck hit the van and explode. Then everything happened at once.

Twin shock waves came at them up the highway, and the Suburban reared back like a horse trying to buck and then landed hard, its massive shocks rattling, and sped through the intense heat of the 4Runner's fireball —

And accelerated, pushing Kurland into his seat, and swerved into the center lane and then halfway into the right lane as the driver, who'd been through three roadside bombs in Iraq, tried to get them out of the kill zone —

The sergeant in the passenger's seat grabbed the tactical radio mounted to the Suburban's dash. "Charlie Four, this is Charlie Six —"

Metal clacked on metal, and Kurland looked back to see the lance corporal in the back jamming his M-4 through the firing port in the truck's liftgate with one hand while shoving a shotgun into the port over the left rear wheel well with the other, as yet another SUV closed in on them —

Maggs yelled "Down!" and pushed Kurland's head onto the seat, and Kurland couldn't see what was happening anymore — and the shotgun exploded from the seat behind them, both barrels —

The Suburban shook with a crash that snapped Kurland's head into Maggs's body armor, the contact coming from the front, the passenger side, and pushing the truck left into a skid —

The sergeant whispered, "We are hit —" And Kurland didn't understand why he was whispering and then realized that the shotgun had temporarily deafened him —

Kurland squirmed up, needing to see if he couldn't hear, and saw Maggs grab the pistol on his right hip and shove it through the port on the door beside him and fire at the Toyota that had crashed into them —

Two neat round holes appeared in the Toyota's metal skin and a third in the driver's-side window, and the driver, a small man in a white *thobe,* ratcheted forward and his arm came off the wheel and the first spurt of blood flowered on his shoulder —

The marine behind them muttered, "RPG incoming," and Maggs shoved Kurland down — and this time the explosion happened behind Kurland, a searing wave of heat and glass —

The Suburban lurched sideways and down, and Kurland felt as much as heard a terrible grinding as its back half scraped along the pavement —

They ground to a stop, and in the silence Kurland heard another sound, a low grunting from the backseat, not even human, a dying animal, and he tried to sit up, but Maggs was holding him down, and Maggs said to someone, "Chase units, tac team, gotta get him out —"

And Kurland forced himself up. Whatever happened next, he wasn't going to his slaughter with his eyes closed.

To save weight, the steel armor at the back of the Suburban was only a half-inch thick. The rocket-propelled grenade ripped through the plate like tissue paper. Its next stop was Lance Corporal Ray Wade. The grenade shattered his Kevlar body armor and tore open Wade's ribs and poured lightning into his heart and lungs, killing him instantly.

By taking most of the explosion, Wade saved four of the other five men in the Suburban. Rana, his seatmate, was less lucky. Shrapnel tore open his face and neck, and one jagged piece chopped through his skull and cut into the arteries around his brain, causing massive internal bleeding. He died, but not soon enough. For thirty seconds he lay guttering in agony, whispering in words beyond translation, a language only he could understand, until a merciful unconsciousness took him.

Kurland saw all this as he sat up. Saw the bodies behind him. Saw that the jihadi in the Land Cruiser was dead. Saw that they had stopped on the highway, smashed against the center median.

He unbuckled his belt, stepped out of the Suburban. He stood between the truck and the median. The road was strangely empty. A few hundred yards back, the carcasses of the first two vehicles in the convoy smoldered. Behind them, two panel trucks formed a *V* that blocked the highway and the breakdown lane. A Jeep sat in front of the panel trucks.

As his hearing returned, Kurland picked up horns honking and shots rattling. The noise was coming from behind the trucks, which he realized now had intentionally created a roadblock to split the convoy.

He turned the other way, south. Not far ahead, the two Saudi police cars that had been their escorts burned wildly. Kurland had never been a soldier, but even so, he could see how carefully the attack had been planned. Nearly a dozen vehicles must have been involved, and at least twice that many jihadis. And they seemed to want to take him alive. Otherwise, they would have blown up this Suburban like the others.

Maggs pushed out of the Suburban and grabbed Kurland's arm. Kurland twisted away. "Enough. I'm a big boy."

"I am trying to save your life. Get down. Now." Maggs pointed at the roadblock, and Kurland saw that the Jeep was heading toward them, two jihadis standing, bracing themselves on the roll bar and holding automatic rifles. The two marines scrambled out of the Suburban. One took a knee at the back corner of the Suburban and braced his rifle against his shoulder. The other pulled himself onto the SUV's roof.

"Have to sit tight," Maggs said. "Take these guys out and wait for the cavalry."

Kurland nodded. He heard sirens now, distant but closing. The Saudi police had faced terrorist attacks in Riyadh before. They would be here soon, first in ones and twos, and then by the dozens. So Kurland followed Maggs forward and hid beside the Suburban's wheel. Maggs squatted low himself and reached for his cell phone, as the marines started to fire short bursts.

Kurland closed his eyes and prayed for the chance to see his wife again.

The lead Suburban had carried the radio and satellite uplinks that provided secure connections to the embassy. But everyone inside the lead Suburban was dead. Maggs was stuck trying to call embassy security into his cell phone.

Twice he punched *55, his pre-programmed speed-dial for embassy security. Twice he got an Arabic voice chirping at him. Either the Saudis had already shut down the network or the volume of calls had overwhelmed the local towers.

Even so, the deputy chief of security should be getting the embassy's Black Hawk up and putting the tactical response team together. All the vehicles in the convoy were equipped with GPS transceivers that continuously broadcast their locations to the embassy. Even without a distress call, the ambush would have been screamingly obvious from the fact that the convoy had suddenly stopped in the middle of a highway.

But the security team would need at least ten minutes to get the bird in the air, and another five to get here. Maggs checked his watch. The ambush had started just five minutes ago. They were going to have to defend this position awhile. He drew his pistol and edged a few feet up the median so he cleared the front of the Toyota, whose wrecked grille formed an open jaw with the Suburban. From here he could cover the Jeep if it drove past them and looped back from the south. With the two marines covering to the north, they'd finally established a defensible position.

Maggs looked over the median. Astonishingly, on the other side of the highway, the northbound side, the traffic was still flowing. But it was slowing by the second as drivers stopped to gawk at the apocalypse across the road. Then he heard the sirens screaming north up the other side of the highway, saw blue lights flashing in the distance. Maybe the Saudi cops would get here quicker than he had expected.

When the Jeep got to two hundred yards, the marines opened up, short, controlled bursts that dug holes in its windshield and hood. The Jeep accelerated, and the two men in back stood and braced their AKs on the roll bar and fired on full automatic. The Jeep blew by as the marines kept shooting. Nobody hit anybody. No surprise. Shooting at a vehicle moving obliquely past a static

435

post was next to impossible. A quarter-mile south, the Jeep slowed and began a tight right turn across the empty highway.

Maggs squeezed his Glock between his hands, wishing he had something more potent. The Jeep stopped, came forward two car lengths, then stopped. Maggs didn't understand why the jihadis were hesitating. They had planned the ambush brilliantly. But they seemed to have run out of momentum. Maybe they hadn't counted on facing three armed men at this point and didn't have enough guys left to make the final assault.

The sirens on the other side of the highway got louder. So did the explosions behind the two panel trucks. If the jihadis wanted Kurland, they'd have to move soon, Maggs thought. As if the jihadis had suddenly reached the same conclusion, the Jeep accelerated toward the Suburban. Maggs retreated behind the corner of the Suburban's armored grille. The marine on the roof twisted himself around so he was now facing south, toward the Jeep. "Wait!" Maggs yelled. "Let 'em close!"

The Jeep closed to two hundred yards, one hundred fifty, one hundred, the jihadis firing high and wild, rounds dinging off the

Suburban's armored windshield and grille
—

At eighty yards, the marine on the roof opened up, full auto this time, a burst that shattered the windshield. The driver was low in his seat, and Maggs couldn't tell if he'd been hit. The Jeep skidded to a stop, its tires squealing. The driver jumped onto the pavement, holding his stomach.

Maggs took his time and squeezed off three shots that caught one of the guys standing in the back in the chest. His arms came off the roll bar as though he was trying to do a jumping jack, and he fell off the Jeep and thudded against the pavement. The guy next to him jumped down and crawled behind the Jeep and fired three shots that banged off the median a couple feet from Maggs.

Then the cavalry showed up, in the form of two white Chevy Tahoes on the northbound side of the highway, blue bar lights flashing, sirens screaming, their front doors carrying the open-eyed logo of the Saudi police.

The Tahoes stopped across the median from the wreck, and their doors opened and four officers wearing body armor over their blue uniforms poured out. One yelled something in Arabic, and two of the others

437

pulled out a pair of over-under double-barreled shotguns from the second.

Maggs turned, wishing he spoke Arabic, wanting to avoid friendly fire. "Hold your fire —" he yelled, wondering as he did how they'd had time to get into their body armor — and realizing too late that these weren't cops at all, that they were terrorists, part of the ambush —

As one of them jumped onto the median and fired twice at the marine on top of the Suburban. Even the marine's Kevlar couldn't protect him from the shotgun's fury, which nearly split him in half at the waist. Almost simultaneously, a second terrorist fired at the marine on the back corner of the Suburban, catching him in the neck and dropping him instantly —

And the third turned his shotgun at Maggs. Maggs lifted his pistol and fired wildly, his shots catching the jihadi in the neck and twisting him sideways —

But the jihadi was already pulling the trigger. A torrent of steel tore through Maggs's arm and shoulder, a left hook from a giant wearing razor-studded gloves. Maggs fell against the Suburban and tried to raise his hand to return fire. Nothing happened. He looked down to see his arm hanging limply from its socket and his blood pouring down the side of his Kevlar vest. He knew he was dead, had to be, weaponless and useless, and he couldn't do anything but watch as the jihadis reached for Kurland, who had been hiding like Maggs told him and was just now realizing what was happening —

Maggs was slipping to his knees, filling not with pain or even fear of death but with *fury,* fury at himself for getting played, fury that these murderers had taken out a convoy, beaten a squad of marines, and were kidnapping the man that Maggs had sworn to protect —

Maggs tried to stand but couldn't, he could barely hold himself on his knees, and all he could do was watch as the two fake cops, *un*cops, pulled a hood over Kurland's head and jammed cuffs on his wrists and shoved him across the median —

Even as he watched, the light faded from the world. And the pavement rose up to meet him, and the darkness poured down his throat at a million miles an hour until Maggs didn't feel anything anymore.

But the ambush didn't end there, not for Kurland. Men grabbed him and pulled a hood over his head and threw him into the back of the Tahoe. He tried to scream, but the hood muffled his voice and he felt someone cutting at his suit and the creamy white shirt he'd worn to meet the king, a shirt Barbara had chosen for him, Brooks Brothers, one of her favorites. *Barbara.* Something jabbed into his arm, a pinprick at first and then deeper, an angry bite. Kurland yelped, but soon the pain faded and he felt the liquid warmth spreading up his arm and into his chest and neck, and though he tried to fight, he couldn't.

As he slipped into twilight, he found himself back in Abdullah's stateroom, and the king shook his head and said, "I warned you. Saeed, Saeed, Saeed" — the words sounding oddly clipped, as if the king were one of the Three Stooges, King Stooge, funny, the warmth spreading through him now like a blanket. And Kurland wondered idly who would report on the meeting. Who would tell Barbara what Abdullah had said? Because she needed to know. No, not Barbara, Barbara wasn't his boss, Barbara was his wife, his boss was —

But he couldn't remember. And so he slept.

CHAPTER 19

The world had paid only glancing attention to the attacks in Bahrain and Riyadh. Even Princess Alia's killing received just a few minutes on CNN.

Graham Kurland's kidnapping provoked a very different reaction.

The ambush took place at two p.m. in Saudi Arabia, six a.m. in Washington. Within three hours, Arab news channels reported that terrorists had attacked a highway in Riyadh with multiple car bombs. Western news outlets rapidly picked up the story, though no video was available, only a few grainy photos from cell phones. Then, at eleven a.m., Bloomberg News sent a flash note to its terminals: "PENTAGON SOURCES CONFIRM AT LEAST TEN MARINES DEAD IN RIYADH AT-TACK." In three minutes, the price of oil rose two dollars a barrel and the Dow Jones Industrial Average dropped one hundred and fifty points.

At 11:20, the Associated Press reported that the attack had targeted an American embassy convoy. Just past noon, Fox News reported that Graham Kurland, the American ambassador to Saudi Arabia, was in the convoy. Asked for a statement, the White House declined comment but said the president would hold a press conference at one p.m. In two minutes, oil rose another five dollars a barrel, and the Dow dropped three hundred points more. Wall Street traders knew that presidents didn't interrupt their schedules without good reason. And a good reason rarely meant good news.

Of course, as America and the world would learn at one p.m., the reality was even uglier than the rumors. Among the government officials who already knew, Vinny Duto summed up the prevailing sentiment: "The fuck just happened?"

The words both question and statement.

At the time, Duto was in his office with Ellis Shafer. Duto wasn't surprised that Shafer and John Wells were smack in the middle of this mess. He knew he shouldn't blame them, but he couldn't help himself. They brought doom wherever they went. Like that old joke about how lawyers were like nuclear missiles.

"You know how lawyers are like nuclear missiles?"

"The other side has theirs, so you have to have yours. They sit in their silos, doing nothing all day except costing you money. And once you use them, they destroy the world."

Typical of Shafer to step on the joke, not even let him tell it. "That's you and Wells right there. A couple of lawyers."

"That doesn't even make *sense*, Vinny. On any level —"

"Why did you get involved with this?"

"I remind you. Since it's all in writing, anyway. Wells called me from Cyprus three days ago. Soon as I hung up with him, I called you. And gave you his strong recommendation that you put a team into Lebanon. You should have put it together, swallowed your pride, gotten everybody on board."

"It would have been easier if he hadn't hit the camp already under the orders and pay of the Saudi government."

"Be sure to rehearse that speech before you give it to the inevitable congressional commission that investigates this nightmare, Vinny. Get it just right. Because you're gonna be under oath. And your version is so far from the truth that even you may have a hard time selling it. Did you call me to help you prepare your defense? Early for that, methinks. Since we don't even know if Graham Kurland is alive or dead."

"I hope he's dead. For his sake."

"He's not dead. They went to a lot of trouble to get him alive."

Duto knew Shafer was right. Knew also that he needed to focus on the problem at hand and not the fallout, which was months, if not years, away. But he couldn't let it go quite yet. His reflex for blame avoidance was too well developed.

"If State had used a chopper —"

"Black Hawks get shot down, too. Convoys are daytime protocol. As you know. Why don't you stop wasting time and get me up to speed?"

So Duto choked down his considerable pride and told Shafer what he knew. At least fifty Americans, ten Saudi police officers and civilians, and fourteen terrorists were dead. Dwayne Maggs, the embassy's head of security, had barely survived and was in surgery at a military hospital outside Riyadh. At best he would lose the use of his right arm.

Worst of all, Kurland was gone. Saudi cops were canvassing the homes and streets around the highway, on the off chance that he had escaped and was hiding. But more than six hours had passed since the ambush. No one believed they'd find him. He'd been kidnapped.

The secretary of state had already asked Saeed and Abdullah to let FBI into the Kingdom to aid the investigation. Neither man had responded yet, but the bureau was flying agents to Dubai on the assumption that the Saudis would soon agree. Meanwhile, the *muk* was providing hourly updates to the CIA station chief in Riyadh.

The *muk* reported that witnesses had seen Saudi cops drag a hooded man from Kurland's Suburban into a police vehicle on the northbound side of the highway seven to eight minutes after the attack began. Cell phone photos confirmed the timing. The problem was that no Saudi officers had reached the Suburban for fourteen minutes. The obvious conclusion was that the cops who'd taken Kurland were fake.

But the Saudis had no cameras on the highway north of the ambush site. No one knew what had happened to the SUVs. The *muk* figured the kidnappers had stowed them and transferred Kurland to another vehicle. *Muk* officers and National Guard soldiers were setting up roadblocks across

Riyadh and highways around the Kingdom. The checkpoints had created massive traffic jams, but the police hadn't found anything yet. Riyadh had been placed under an eleven p.m. to five a.m. curfew that night, with the curfew to be widened to other major Saudi cities by the next night if Kurland wasn't found.

"What about helicopters? The kid told Wells that there was a helicopter pilot at the base."

"I think they've shut down civilian air traffic." Duto punched a text message into his BlackBerry. "I'll have Lecaine double-check."

Meantime, the embassy was in lockdown, Duto said. Barbara Kurland, the ambassador's wife, had tried to leave the compound — destination unknown — when she was told what had happened. She became hysterical when the marines stopped her. The embassy doctor had sedated her. She was resting in the infirmary for now. The president had spoken with her, promising to do everything he could to rescue Graham. He'd asked her to fly out so she could wait in Dubai or Berlin, but she'd refused. The president had ordered that she not be moved against her will.

The president had also ordered the army

to transfer two Delta squads from Baghdad to the embassy. They would arrive by midnight. They didn't need Saudi permission to enter the Kingdom, because they were technically coming in as a defensive replacement for the marines killed in the attacks. They wouldn't be legally allowed off the embassy grounds. The White House counsel was trying to figure how many laws the squads would be breaking if they left the grounds to rescue Kurland, but for now the consensus was that they should be used only as a last resort. If they killed Saudi civilians in an attempted rescue, they'd worsen the situation. And they had no armored vehicles and only one Black Hawk, so as a practical matter their range was limited to Riyadh.

The CIA and the other three-letter agencies were combing their databases for sigint, comint, humint, geoint, or just plain int that might lead to Kurland. But the kidnappers appeared to be operating independently of Al Qaeda and every other known terrorist group, and the attacks in the last month had come as a surprise. So no one expected much, not right away.

"We'll find them," Duto said. "It's too big an operation to hide. Too many vehicles. Too many guys, and they didn't all get blown up. Some of them will talk, whether they want to or not. Hopefully the bad guys will milk Kurland for a while, try to build the tension, work the press. Give us a chance to catch up."

"I don't think so. He's a depreciating asset. They're smart, they turn up the pressure quick. Make it ugly."

Duto didn't want to argue the point. They'd find out soon enough. "What about Wells?"

"Far as I know, he's still in Cyprus."

"He hasn't called you?"

"I'll remind you. He no longer works for us. And we've dealt with his efforts to work *with* us ham-handedly. By 'we,' I mean you. By 'ham-handedly,' I mean —"

"I know what you mean. We gave him the overheads, didn't we?"

"And told him to use them at his own risk. And you've been stringing him and Gaffan along about covering them with the Lebanese. I wouldn't be surprised if they made other plans before this happened. They may be in transit."

"Find him, will you? Tell him the situation has changed, and if he's got any intel on this we'd like it. And that of course we've got his back with the Lebanese."

"Sure you don't want me to threaten him? Tell him he's been a bad boy and if he doesn't help, he'll get a warning letter?"

Duto wanted to reach across his desk and grab Shafer by his dandruff-specked collar. "I recognize the reality of the situation. You're smart, you won't rub my face in it. And if Wells won't come in himself, at least have him drop off the kid somewhere — Meshaal, isn't that his name? — so we can talk to him."

"Yes, suh. Soon as possible, suh."

"Prick."

"Takes one to know one."

The president of the United States was congenitally unsuited to express anger. Enemies called him icy, friends calm. For better or worse, he kept his usual tone at the press conference. He could have been reading recipe ingredients:

A crime against not just the United States but all the nations of the world . . . We are working alongside the Saudi government to find him. . . . The people of America will not rest until he is returned safely to his wife and family. . . . We call on his kidnappers to release him unharmed. . . . No religion sanctions this violence, not Christianity, not Judaism, and certainly not Islam. . . .

449

A man of peace, a diplomat, a husband, a father and grandfather . . . This evil and cowardly attack shall not stand. . . . These terrorists must know that any demands they make are pointless. The United States does not negotiate with murderers. . . . Let us all pray for his safe return.

He finished in twenty minutes and didn't take questions.

Saeed watched the speech from his giant palace in north Riyadh, a few kilometers from Abdullah's. Islamic calligraphy covered the walls of his study. Rare eighteenth-century copies of the Quran filled its shelves. Saeed never forgot that the House of Saud was Islam's ultimate protector. Besides, the clerics liked them.

When the president walked off the po-dium, Saeed stepped onto his terrace. He'd returned the president's call a few minutes before, during the conference, knowing that the man would be unreachable. He wanted to delay talking to the Americans as long as possible, until he had some idea what they knew, and if Abdullah had told them about the camp in Lebanon. They would have to let in the FBI, but Saeed hoped to keep the team as small as possible. His men needed to find Kurland before he was killed — or, even worse, tortured for the world to see. Saeed could only imagine how the United States would react to that kind of provocation. Arabs paid a high price when they underestimated America, as Saddam Hussein had learned.

During the day, a white umbrella bloomed automatically from a flagpole on the terrace to ward off the sun. The Saudis had installed thousands of similar umbrellas at Mecca, to protect worshippers. Now the sun had set and the flagpole was naked, giving Saeed a clear view south, toward central Riyadh. A dozen police helicopters buzzed over the concrete city, noisy and irritating as wasps. Without a target, they were useless. But the Americans at the embassy were surely reporting to Washington every few minutes, and Saeed and Mansour wanted their men to seem busy.

The overnight curfew was equally hopeless. The kidnappers had gotten a three-hour head start before the *muk* pieced together what had happened, easily enough time to shift Kurland into a fresh vehicle. From there they could have driven him into the desert or one of the smaller towns in the Najd. Searching the desert would be impossible. Saudi Arabia was a vast country, nearly as big as the United States east of the Mississippi. And if Kurland was still in Riyadh, he was no doubt locked in a safe house.

Meanwhile, crews were scraping the highway clean of the ambush, taking the broken and burned vehicles on flatbeds to an army base near the airport. Tonight the road would be repaved and repainted. Saeed knew they might be destroying forensic evidence. He didn't care. He wanted all trace of this madness gone. He wished he could erase it from his mind as easily. How had he allowed his son to lead him down this path? He didn't even know the name of the man running the operation, the man who must have betrayed them. Greed and age had made him a fool. Now, too late, his mind was sharp. He was fully awake. *If you don't test the depth of the water before you dive, you won't get to test it once you've drowned,* the fishermen on the Red Sea said. He and Mansour were in deep now.

He heard steps and turned to see his son. An idiotic smile creased Mansour's face, as though he still believed he could charm Saeed into accepting his reassurances. "Father. Are you sure you wouldn't rather be inside? We can sit —"

"Tell me the name of the man behind this."

Mansour hesitated.

"Now."

"Ahmad Bakr. He was a major in the National Guard. He was living in Suwaidi, but he's gone."

"You're sure it was him and not Ibrahim." This was General Walid Ibrahim, the man who had recruited Bakr and served as the cutout for Mansour.

"I think so."

"You *think* so."

"I'm sure."

"Did you ever meet Bakr?"

"Of course not. I told Ibrahim what I wanted him to do, and Ibrahim told him."

"It seems he didn't listen. Where he's from?"

"Tathlith. I've sent three men down to talk to his family. But they haven't seen him in years. Ibrahim and I knew of two of his hideouts in Suwaidi, but we've raided them already, and they're empty. Obviously, he's planned this for a very long time."

"Obviously. And your stupidity and your royal arrogance obviously blinded you to the obvious." Saeed raised a hand, pinched his son's cheek —

"Father —"

Pinched harder now, twisting and digging into the soft flesh until half-moons of blood boiled up. Mansour raised a hand to grab his father's wrist but pulled back. When Saeed finally let go, Mansour bowed his head and licked his lips.

"Where's he gone, this man Bakr?"

"I don't know yet. He must have put together a new safe house, skimmed the money I sent to put this together."

"How much money?"

"About eleven million dollars."

"You gave this man eleven million dollars."

"I thought Ibrahim was tracking it —"

"Forget it. Did Bakr know you were behind the orders?"

"No. I'm sure. Ibrahim never told him. And the money was untraceable. I tell you, father, we'll be all right. We'll find him."

"You tell me?" Fury had come easily to Saeed his whole life. "I let you do this because I thought you were man enough. But Abdullah was right. You're a child. I never should have let you play with men. You understand, if the United States sends in its army, it will be a catastrophe. For us and the Americans both. And if this man Bakr betrays us publicly, we'll lose everything. If that happens, I'll take you into the desert and shoot you in the head myself, leave your corpse to bake. Or perhaps Abdullah will pull the trigger. His last act as king. Do you understand?"

"Yes, father."

"Do you understand?"

"Yes."

"Good. Now start again. Tell me what you know. Everything."

But Mansour didn't know enough. All along, his main concerns had been secrecy and deniability. He had never taken seriously the possibility that Bakr might betray them, that Bakr might have a will of his own. Classic royal arrogance. He knew the names of Bakr's senior lieutenants, but he'd never met or spoken to any of them.

"Call Ibrahim. Tell him he's needed tonight. And then have the Second Directorate pick up his family. His father, brothers, sons."

"The Second Directorate." The Second Directorate was the *mukhabarat* arm that dealt with internal subversion. Saudis sometimes called it the "Torture Directorate." Though never loudly.

"Bring them to *muk* headquarters. I'll tell Ibrahim where they are. Then he'll give us the answers we need. If he has them."

Mansour turned to leave. "There's one

last thing, father. The camp in the Bekaa that Bakr ran was attacked three days ago." Mansour spoke quickly now, as if he feared another eruption. "I only learned about it this morning. I was going to tell you this afternoon, but then the ambush —"

"What happened?"

"Everyone in it was killed."

Saeed tried to process this new disaster. "Could this man Bakr have done it himself? To cover his tracks?"

"It's possible, but I don't know why he would. He could have closed the camp himself, dismissed everyone quietly, if he didn't need them. This attack made a lot of noise. The Lebanese police are investigating, and they have suspects. Two Americans."

"John Wells."

"I'm not sure, but one of the photos looks like him."

"They haven't released it publicly?"

"No. I think the Americans are pressing them to keep it quiet."

"For the first time in my life, I'm glad I'm old," Saeed said. "If I were young, I couldn't keep myself from hurting you, Mansour. I warned you about Wells."

"Yes, father."

"Do you see what this means? If this man

Bakr is as big a fool as you, the Americans may already have connected the camp to the attack on Kurland, and us to the camp. Or Bakr may be waiting to tell the world that we're paying him. What would you like me to tell the president, then? Yes, we financed this bombing in Bahrain and assassinated the princess, but of course we didn't attack your ambassador. We would never do that. *Even though the same man is behind all the attacks.* And he's a former officer in our own army. Do you think the Americans will believe that?"

"I understand, father." Mansour had called Saeed *father* more in the last ten minutes than he had in the last ten years.

"I'm so glad you do, my son."

"What should —"

"Give me some time. Maybe I'll find a solution. Anything else you've forgotten to tell me?"

Mansour shook his head.

"Call Ibrahim, then. And leave me. I need to think."

Bakr's Hezbollah general had told him about the attack in Lebanon the morning after it happened. The news worried Bakr greatly, especially when he heard that Americans were involved. How had they found him? He wished he could go back to the Bekaa and see for himself what had happened, but he had no time.

He reminded himself that no one important was still in Lebanon, and that as far as he knew, he'd removed any information that might point to his safe houses in Saudi Arabia. The camp didn't even have computers anymore. He communicated with Talib only by cell phone. When he learned of the attack, he switched to a new prepaid phone and made his men do the same.

Bakr figured he would be safe for a few days at a minimum, probably weeks or months. The Americans wouldn't attack inside Saudi Arabia without asking permission, or at least telling the Saudi government in advance. He could count on General Ibrahim — and Ibrahim's hidden masters — to warn him if the Americans got close. After all, until now he'd done everything they'd asked. And they had no idea of what he was planning next.

So he went ahead with his preparations for the ambush, positioning men and vehicles, finishing his safe house, making sure his lieutenants understood every detail. From his years in the National Guard, he had a good idea how the *muk,* the army, and the Guard would react. Since the terrorist attacks of 2003, the Sauds had invested tens of billions of dollars improving their police and Special Forces. They would begin by closing roads and imposing a curfew. Within a few days, they would be searching entire cities house to house.

Still, government bureaucracy and mutual distrust between the Interior Ministry and the National Guard would slow the initial response. Bakr figured they would need several hours before it shut the highways and airports. By then, he'd have Kurland hidden.

His enemies had a huge advantage, though. Mansour knew who he was, knew about the Bekaa and about the safe houses in Suwaidi. They would quickly track the vehicles and explosives and weapons he'd used in the ambush. They even knew the names of some of his men. And they would respond with overwhelming force. As carefully as he'd hidden his connection to the house he planned to use as a prison, as carefully as he'd built the cell inside, Bakr knew he wouldn't have long before the *muk* found him.

But he didn't plan to wait.

The call from the Diplomatic Quarter came sooner than Bakr had expected. He briefly

459

wondered if he should let this chance go, wait until all the pieces were in place. But he realized that he'd be worse than foolish to pass up this opportunity. He might never have another. So he'd ordered his men into battle.

Thanks be to Allah, he'd succeeded. Of course, the attack hadn't gone perfectly. Once they'd recovered from their initial shock, the Americans had fought hard. One of the ambassador's guards had killed his best lieutenant. But the bombs had done their work, and Bakr would always remember the shock on the ambassador's face as he realized that the police who'd come to save him weren't police at all.

After he bundled the ambassador in the back of his Tahoe, he drove north from Riyadh. He'd passed the turnoff to the king's palace and watched Jeeps and Humvees flood south onto the highway, sirens screaming. He couldn't help but smile. All those reinforcements for a battle that had already ended. Two booms tore the air behind them, two pillars of black smoke reached the sky, the last of Bakr's bombs, the two panel trucks that had blocked the road. They would add to the confusion.

Forty kilometers north of Riyadh he turned off the highway, headed west, and reached a wadi between dried, crumbling hills. A small aquifer ran beneath the land here. Recently, wealthy Riyadhis had bought plots in this valley and become gentleman farmers, installing wells to feed plots of cucumbers and oranges that loved the winter and hated the summer. Before Riyadh's bourgeois had found it, the valley had been home to a brick factory, now abandoned.

Bakr and his men left the Tahoes in the factory's garage and moved the ambassador to the trunk of a white Mercedes sedan. Then they drove southwest to an abandoned date farm in a wadi deep in the Saudi desert and waited for nightfall. Now Bakr was about to make his final move. The transfer was risky, and arguably unnecessary. But the police would never expect it. And Bakr believed with all his heart that Allah wouldn't let him fail in this mission. "Come on," he said to the pilot. "It's time."

Together they carried the ambassador's limp body to the helicopter.

At first Kurland wasn't sure he was awake at all. He opened his eyes, but the world around him didn't change. He couldn't find a hint of light. Then the day came back to him, scene by scene, as though he was watching a slideshow in his mind. The meeting with Abdullah. The ambush. The car bombs. The men grabbing him. Maybe he was having a nightmare. Once or twice he'd dreamed of attacks on the embassy.

"Wake up," he whispered.

But he was awake, he knew. He felt the chair under him and the bite of the cuffs on his wrists. His mouth was dry and clotted from the sedative they'd given him. He thought he'd been unconscious for at least twelve hours, probably longer. His body ached, as though he'd been handled and moved roughly and repeatedly.

He tilted his head left and right, trying to make sense of his surroundings. The walls were several feet away. The air was cool, not too stuffy, and he heard the faint hum of ventilation. Despite its darkness, this was a cell, not a tomb.

Time went by, he wasn't sure how much. The darkness terrified him, the darkness and the anticipation. His heart thumped wildly, and he warned himself to relax. He concentrated on controlling his breathing and pulse. *Pretty ironic if I die before they can kill me. Though it might be for the best.*

He heard the grind of metal on metal. A hatch above slid back. An overhead bulb flicked on, and Kurland saw the cell around

462

him, maybe fifteen feet square and nearly as deep. It had a concrete floor and walls, and in place of a ceiling were big metal plates, one with a hatch cut into it. He was chained to a chair near the back. In place of a ladder, simple steel rungs had been mounted on the front wall.

A man climbed down, a bag over his shoulder, his face unhooded. He was Saudi, early thirties, short, with brown eyes and the thick legs of a baseball player.

Kurland remembered a lesson from the cursory survival training that State provided its ambassadors, cursory because no one believed an ambassador could be kidnapped. *Don't panic if your captors are hooded. Hoods may mean they don't want you to see their faces because they plan to free you and don't want you to recognize them later.* Until now, Kurland hadn't understood the corollary of that proposition: *If they're not wearing hoods, they don't care if you see their faces. Because they're not planning to free you.*

Kurland thought back to the hour of advice he'd gotten in that conference room in Foggy Bottom: *Build a rapport. Establish your common humanity. Don't panic. Don't make threats. Don't push them for personally identifying details. Answer whatever questions*

463

they have. Don't lie. Try not to give up classi-fied information, but don't worry if you do. Look for clues to where you are. Consider possible escape routes. The tips struck him as worse than useless. His captors, whoever they were, had destroyed a convoy of ma-rines to get him. They were going to do what they liked.

But he was going to follow one rule, no matter what: *Don't beg.* Begging was coun-terproductive, the survival expert said. It widened the gap between captive and cap-tor by reminding the captor of his power. Kurland promised himself that even if he had an ironclad guarantee that begging would save his life, he wouldn't. He wouldn't give these murderers the pleasure.

Easy enough to say now.

The Saudi brought out a camera and a tripod. Seeing the camera loosened Kurland's bowels. Nothing good would hap-pen on camera. The man set up the camera, taking his time, and then reached again into his bag —

And pulled out bottles of Coca-Cola and water, and two pieces of pita bread. Despite his fear, Kurland felt a tremor of anticipa-tion. He hadn't realized until now that he was famished. The man uncuffed Kurland's hands and gave him the water bottle. He left the Coke and the food against the wall behind him. Kurland wondered if the water might be spiked with something but couldn't keep himself from drinking.

He had never tasted anything so good. He sipped slowly, trying to savor each mouthful. He wasn't sure whether to drink it all at once or save some, but the question answered itself. Before he could stop himself, he'd finished. He carefully put the empty bottle down next to his chair. "Thank you."

To Kurland's surprise, the man responded. His voice was soft, his accent vaguely English. "You're welcome."

"What's your name?"

"Don't be silly."

Kurland could have asked any number of questions: *Where am I? How long have I been here?* And, of course, *What do you plan to do with me?* But the cool way the man had said "Don't be silly" stopped him. He felt as if his captor had warned him with those three words that the ground rules were obvious, that if he pressed too hard he would be mistreated, and that if he behaved they'd be fair. The warning was a lie, of course. By definition, these men could change the rules on him anytime, treat him however they wanted for any reason or no reason at all. Still, Kurland felt better than if the man hadn't spoken at all.

"We have a speech we want you to make."

"I can't do that."

"Please don't argue. We just want you to say a few words, and then you can eat. I'm sure you're hungry."

"No."

"Your wife will want to see you're all right."

Barbara. Kurland was ashamed to realize that he'd forgotten her these last few minutes. She must be terrified. A place beyond panic. Even if he was already dead, he had to hang on as long as possible for her.

"What is it you want me to say?"

CHAPTER 20

JEDDAH, SAUDI ARABIA

Even from five miles offshore, the crisis was unmistakable. Graham Kurland had been kidnapped a day earlier. Now police and National Guard helicopters circled low and slow over downtown. A Saudi navy destroyer sat at anchor outside the harbor, broadside to the city, its radar winding slowly. Wells wasn't sure what good the destroyer would do in finding Kurland, but he didn't have to worry about it. He and Gaffan had their own escort, two Saudi National Guard speedboats armed with .50-caliber machine guns. They were bound for Abdullah's giant palace on the Red Sea.

Gaffan steered the boat between two jetties and into a basin outside the palace's high gray walls. An officer in a khaki dress uniform waved them toward a pier, as a machine gun tracked their progress from a turret atop the wall.

"Happy to see us," Gaffan said. He

467

brought the boat to a bobbing halt by the pier, and Wells hopped out.

"Good to be back on solid ground."

"Is that where we are?" Gaffan said.

The officer stepped toward them. *"Salaam aleikum."*

"Aleikum salaam."

"I'm Colonel Gharib. Your passports, please."

Wells handed them over. Gharib flipped through them, nodded at Meshaal.

"Who's this?"

"We found him in Lebanon. We're bringing him home." Meshaal shrank backward, toward the cruiser.

Gharib shook his head at the explanation, but all he said was, "This way." They followed him into the compound through heavy black gates. A golf cart waited. Gharib waved them in and motored south, past date palms and the largest swimming pool Wells had ever seen. The southern edge of the compound held buildings that looked to be staff quarters and infrastructure. Wells picked up the faint odor of a sewage treatment plant. Gharib stopped outside a windowless one-story building, unlocked the door, motioned for them to go inside. "You wait here —"

"There's no time —" But the door had

already closed, and the dead bolt thunked shut from the outside.

They'd sailed from Cyprus two afternoons before, less than two days after reaching the island. Within twelve hours of their landing, Wells knew they couldn't stay long. The local papers reported that the police were investigating three men who had attacked a couple on a deserted beach and stolen their car. And the boat they'd ditched had a Lebanese flag and registration. The cops had no doubt already asked the police in Beirut for help in tracking it down.

Soon enough, the Lebanese would discover Gaffan's name on their ship registry and connect the boat to the attack in the Bekaa. Then the Cyprus police would be after them for murder. Cyprus wasn't big enough to hide them from a full-scale manhunt. As the Mossad agents who had recently assassinated a Palestinian guerrilla leader in a hotel in Dubai had learned, international passports, databases, security cameras, and facial matching software had made black ops harder and harder to pull off cleanly.

The Dubai police had now issued bulletins for the Israelis involved in the hotel killing, including photos, aliases, and in

469

many cases real names. Of course, the Mossad agents had carried out the assassination on Israeli government orders. They were safe from extradition as long as they stayed in Israel. They could even travel on diplomatic passports without too much hassle, though they would be wise to avoid connecting through Dubai.

But Wells and Gaffan couldn't count on government protection. So far, the CIA hadn't stepped up for them. "Still waiting," Shafer said, when Wells called him the night after they landed.

"Ellis. Maybe I haven't been clear enough about what we found." In fact, Wells had told Shafer exactly what he'd discovered, the passports, manuals, and fake uniforms. Even "42 Aziz 3," the mysterious code he'd found in the notebook. "You need to get it in the system so you and the NSA can look it over."

"Then leave it at the embassy. And the kid, too."

But doing that would cost Wells his only leverage. He needed a guarantee that the CIA would provide clean papers for him and Gaffan, or even a presidential finding that would backstop the killings as acts of war justified under U.S. law — no different than drone strikes in Pakistan.

"You know I can't. Not until we have a deal."

"It'll happen, John."

"When?"

"Soon. I don't know."

"Duto's enjoying letting me twist, isn't he? Never gets old for him."

Shafer's silence was answer enough.

They couldn't count on Abdullah for help, either. Wells had hoped that in a worst-case scenario they could stay in the king's palace in France while they planned their next move. The morning after they landed, Wells called Kowalski.

"Tell him we found the place we were looking for."

"I hate to tell you. I don't think he cares. Our mutual acquaintance" — Kowalski meant Miteb — "says that when his granddaughter died, it knocked the fight out of him."

Wells thought of the way Abdullah had acted in Nice. The king had been furious, desperate to put his son on the throne. Alia's killing should have made him angrier. Not broken him. "That's not possible."

"Our friend was surprised, too. Said he expected the opposite. But you know, a man who's nearly ninety, a shock like this —

471

nature takes its course. Even the tallest tree falls eventually."

"Spare me the circle-of-life wisdom. Just give me Miteb's number so I can talk to him directly. I should have had it from the get-go."

Wells couldn't help feeling personally betrayed. He'd risked his life and Gaffan's for the king. Now Abdullah was dismissing Wells like a servant who had outlived his usefulness.

Wells told Gaffan what Kowalski and Shafer had said, their legal limbo.

"You think it would get this messy?" Gaffan said.

"Truth. I wouldn't have gotten you involved if I had. I thought we'd be okay, even without Abdullah. Or without the agency. Didn't count on us losing both. Guess I'm too used to having janitors."

"So we're looking at murder charges dogging us forever?"

"I don't think so. In the end, Duto'll thank us for hitting these guys." Wells wished he was as certain as he sounded.

"I'll have to make space in my cabinet for all the medals we get."

"Exactly. But it may take a couple days. And I don't think we want to be stuck here while we wait."

The next question was where to go. And how to get there. Wells could use his last clean passport to fly out. But Gaffan and Meshaal couldn't count on clearing airport security. Their best answer looked like another cruise. At noon on their second day in Cyprus, they went shopping. Money wasn't a problem. They still had the million dollars that Wells had left for Gaffan in the safe-deposit box, and Cypriot boat dealers were as friendly as the Lebanese to cash buyers.

For three hundred thousand dollars, they picked a forty-nine-foot cruiser with all the trimmings, satellite television and phone, a fancy autopilot, and enough fuel tanks to get them to Cape Verde and then across the Atlantic. The boat was new, so they didn't have to worry about the air-conditioning. It even had three cabins, so they wouldn't have to share.

The Saudi money greased everything. By late afternoon, the cruiser was fueled, insured, titled, and ready to go. It even had a name inked on its hull in six-inch black letters: *Judge Wapner.* Gaffan had insisted. Wells could almost hear the announcer's stern warning: *Don't take the law into your own hands. . . .*

"Very nice," Meshaal said, as they boarded.

"Glad you approve."

"Are we going to Gaza? Finally?"

"Maybe not right away." Wells could not imagine what the kid had made of the last seventy-two hours.

They headed south, toward the Suez Canal, at a steady twenty knots. They couldn't get through the canal until morning, so they had no need to speed. The cruiser more or less steered itself. As the Cyprus coast disappeared behind them, Wells decided to take another look at the stuff he'd found at the farmhouse. He spread the passport and manuals and notebook on a teak table in the rear of the cabin. He and Gaffan read in silence. Meshaal joined them a few minutes later. "What's this?"

"From your camp. Any of it look familiar?"

Meshaal flipped through the passports. "We had to give them in. Is mine here?"

"Yes. I've got it. For safekeeping. What about this?" Wells held up the green notebook from Talib's bedroom. Meshaal shook his head. "Does the phrase *forty-two Aziz three* mean anything? Some kind of code?"

"Not to me."

"But your leader called himself Aziz."

"But the way you say it, it sounds more like an address. In Buraydah, the town near where I grew up, there's King Abdul-Aziz Boulevard."

The kid might have just paid his freight. Wells had been thinking of the phrase as a code. But every village in the Kingdom must have had a road named after Aziz. "Do you know where it might be?"

"The three at the end . . . Some Saudi cities have a system where the numbers start again in each district. Or it could be a city with three different roads named after Aziz. Or even a building with three floors."

"That's good. Thank you, Meshaal."

They leafed through the papers as the boat chugged south but found nothing more of consequence. Around midnight, Gaffan and Meshaal headed to their bunks. Wells turned out the cabin lights and called Anne. They hadn't spoken in a week, since he left Cyprus for Lebanon.

"John."

"Lovely lady."

" 'Lovely Rita, meter maid.' "

"You're way too young for that song."

"I'm on a Beatles kick. Very retro. Though to be honest, I don't get why everybody thought they were so great."

"Once upon a time, they were bigger than

Jesus. John Lennon said so himself."

"We'll find out in a couple thousand years. I don't even think they're bigger than The National anymore."

"The who?"

"Not The Who, either. Those guys fill stadiums."

Wells smiled in the dark. He'd missed talking to her. "Who's on first."

"They came to see me, John."

"I hate to start this again, but who?"

"They said they were FBI, but I'm not sure. They wanted to know if I'd heard from you, if I knew where you were."

"I hope you told them the truth. On both counts."

"I did. Yes and no."

"Then it's fine. If they're agency or FBI, they can't hurt you as long as you're honest."

"I wish I could see you."

"I wish I could see you, too. I wish you were here. You'd be having fun with this." *Parts of it, anyway,* Wells didn't say. *Maybe not the part where I killed the six guys.*

"Are you in trouble, John?"

"The usual."

"These guys said you were in serious trouble."

"I'd call it the usual. Maybe a little more.

476

How are you?"

"I'm fine. Pulled over a drunk on Main Street two nights ago —"

"You're never going to let me live that down —"

"No, wait. And I swear, by the time I got him in the back of the cruiser, he told me I looked great in the uniform, and that if there were more girls in the bar like me he wouldn't have gotten himself arrested, because he'd still be there."

"Sounds like a real charmer. You give him your number?"

"I tried, but I couldn't remember it. I have so many phones now. He was cute, though."

"I'd better get home soon."

"You'd better."

By six a.m. they had docked at Port Said, the northern entrance to the Suez Canal. While Egyptian land surrounded the canal on both sides, they didn't need Egyptian visas to pass through it. According to international law, the Suez was open to vessels of any nationality, even during wartime — a rule meant to discourage any country from blockading or bombing it.

Normally, boats had to wait at Port Said for at least twenty-four hours, but thanks to a liberal application of Saudi cash, the *Judge*

Wapner avoided the usual delays and hitched onto the morning's southbound convoy. An Egyptian pilot came aboard to steer them behind a half-dozen ships stacked high with containers. The canal had no locks. But to keep the big ships from damaging its banks, the convoy crawled along at eight knots. Traveling a hundred twenty miles would take fourteen hours. They would reach Suez, the city that marked the southern end of the canal, around midnight.

The pilot spent his time sipping tea and smoking. He asked no questions about them or what they were doing, and Wells didn't volunteer. The canal was as flat as a lake and smelled stale, almost fetid. Desert spread endlessly on both sides, its monotony broken only by low concrete pillboxes on the west side, defenses against the increasingly unlikely possibility of an Israeli attack. Egyptian soldiers popped out to wave as the cruiser passed.

"They don't see too many ships like this?" Wells said.

"No."

Just after sunset, the desert fading from gold to black, the Egyptian's cell phone beeped. He listened for a moment, hung up. "Turn on the television," he said. "There's been a big terrorist attack in Saudi

Arabia. The president of the United States is talking."

They watched the press conference in silence until it ended. Wells didn't understand why Shafer hadn't called already, until he remembered Shafer didn't have his new phone.

Wells motioned for Gaffan to go downstairs.

"We have to go in."

"To Cairo? The embassy?"

"Jeddah. The Kingdom. If Abdullah helps us, we can get in without the Defense Ministry knowing. The agency will give us stuff they won't give the Saudis."

"How can you be sure they'll work with us at all?"

Because when a crisis hits this hard, guys like Duto know they have to try everything to fix it. Or at least look like they're trying. If that means bailing us out of a few murder charges, they will. Especially since they should have already.

Aloud, Wells said only: "I know. Trust me."

"It's worked great so far."

Wells called Shafer.

"Where are you?"

"The Suez Canal. Heading for Jeddah." Unfortunately, Jeddah was seven hundred miles south of the southern end of the

479

canal. With the ship at full throttle, they'd arrive sometime the next afternoon.

"The Saudis have closed their borders."

"I think we can get in. Abdullah has a palace on the Red Sea."

"So what's your plan?"

"Did the NSA find anything that matches forty-two Aziz three?"

"No."

"Have them run it again. And the NGA, too. This time for a street address." Wells explained what Meshaal had said.

"So it could be anywhere in the country? That narrows it down."

"Do it, Ellis."

"All right."

"What's happening back there?"

"Nothing good. They're moving two Ranger companies from Baghdad to Kuwait tomorrow. On your side, there's an Airborne battalion on its way to Incirlik" — an air base in Turkey.

"A battalion, Ellis?" An Airborne battalion meant seven hundred soldiers and armored vehicles delivered by parachute. An Airborne battalion meant an invasion, more or less.

"The feeling is that if we have to go in, we better go in hard."

"Please tell me you're sending in a team

480

to check out the camp. Even if it is three days late."

"Yes. But remember Kurland only got hit six hours ago. We're sorting through a lot of moving parts. We can't even be a hundred percent sure it's the same guys. Not yet."

"You're right, Ellis. This has nothing to do with the terrorists Gaffan and I just found. Another highly trained jihadi squad just started operating inside the KSA. A coincidence."

"All I'm saying is the stakes are too high not to check everything."

"While you're checking everything, how about you and the NSA run the names and passport numbers I'm about to give you, see if they go anywhere?" Wells read off the names from the camp.

"We will," Shafer said. "There is one problem with your theory that the guys from the camp are behind this. Especially if Saeed is funding them. It makes no sense. It's suicide for the Sauds if we connect them to the kidnappers."

"I think the jihadis took Saeed money and got ambitious. The camp looked like it was running pretty much on its own. And if I'm right, and this is a rogue op, Saeed isn't in control. If you were playing Red Team" — the enemy force — "how would you cause

481

maximum chaos?"

A long pause. Then Shafer said, "I think I'd take my hostage to a place where trying to rescue him would start a religious war."

"Mecca."

The theoretical ban on non-Muslims in Saudi Arabia was real in Mecca. The Saudi government enforced an exclusion zone that extended past the city's borders. Driving from Riyadh to Jeddah, non-Muslims had to take a highway around the city.

"Or Medina" — which had a similar ban — "but especially Mecca, sure."

"The kid we captured, he told me that some men in the camp went to Mecca."

"But how would they get Kurland past the roadblocks?"

"Helicopter. They fly him in tonight, low, the Saudis will think it's one of their own patrols."

"Clever, John. We're picking up a lot of confusion right now, lot of birds in the air. And then, if I were playing Red Team, I'd make it ugly. Do something terrible to Kurland. Unforgivable. The Staties say he's a nice guy, by the way. Maybe I'd even make it clear he's in Mecca. Almost dare the United States to come after him."

Wells thought of the way that the man called Aziz had tortured Meshaal's friend.

Imagining him doing something unforgivable to an American ambassador was easy.

"So we're heading for Jeddah. If Abdullah okays it, we'll land at his palace. If Kurland is in Mecca, we've got as good a chance of finding him as anyone. We can blend, speak the language, and Mecca's only forty miles away."

"Let us pick you up, chopper you in, save you some time."

"I'd rather get in quietly."

"Your choice. By the way, Duto said your problem with those murder charges, it's solved. Out of the goodness of his heart, he said."

"Nice of him. You hear anything, let me know. Otherwise, we'll call you from Jeddah."

Wells hung up, called the number that Kowalski had given him for Miteb. The phone was silent for several seconds, beeped as if it were being forwarded, fell silent. Wells was about to hang up when a man answered.

"Hello." The voice unmistakably Miteb's.

"Prince. This is John Wells."

"Mr. Wells. Thanks be to God that you called. It's a terrible thing that's happened to this man. I met him twice, you know —"

Wells needed to keep the old man focused. "Prince. I'm arriving tomorrow in Jeddah. With another American. It's important your brother send someone to meet us so that we can dock at his palace and come into the Kingdom directly."

"I don't understand."

"I don't want Prince Saeed to know we're here."

"Right. Of course." Miteb coughed, the sound as faint as a bare branch creaking.

"Promise me you'll do that."

"I promise. I'll tell my brother."

"How is he?"

"After Alia died, I thought he'd given up. Now he's angry again. It's Bedouin tradition" — Miteb coughed again, harder — "you open your tent to a stranger, and he's safe. Always. Once he leaves, he can be your enemy, you fight, kill him, but while he's inside, he's a guest. Mr. Kurland was our guest."

"We'll find him."

Inshallah —

"*Inshallah.* But first you have to let us in. And arrange a car and weapons."

"Give me until tomorrow morning, and I will."

And Miteb had. Wells didn't know if Abdul-

484

lah had ultimately okayed the decision to let them in — or even if Abdullah knew they were coming. Miteb hadn't said. Wells wondered if he'd have the chance to speak with the old king again. Abdullah deserved a more dignified exit than the one he was facing, but then the men who'd kidnapped Kurland weren't much interested in the king's dignity.

Just past noon, with the boat still one hundred fifty miles north of Jeddah, the voice of the Al Jazeera anchor quickened. "We've just learned that Ambassador Kurland's kidnappers have released a video. We're going to review it" — by which she meant *make sure nobody's chopped off his head* — "and then screen it for you."

Less than a minute later, the screen cut to Kurland. "My name is Graham Kurland." His face was pale, his voice weak. But he appeared unharmed. He sat on a wooden chair, his legs chained but his arms free. Behind him was a black banner with the Islamic creed, the *shahada,* embroidered in gold.

"Until yesterday, I mistakenly believed I was the American ambassador to the Kingdom of Saudi Arabia. I now understand that relations between the United States and the people of Arabia are impossible. My country is imperialist and filled with Zionists and infidels. It is time for the United States to free the people of the Arabian peninsula. I call on America to take five steps. First, it must ban its citizens from coming to Arabia, with the sole exception of Muslims completing the *hajj*. Second, it must no longer buy any product from Arabia, including oil. Third, it must immediately withdraw its soldiers from Iraq, Afghanistan, and all other Muslim lands. Fourth, it must end all aid to Israel. And fifth, it must close the concentration camp at Guantánamo Bay. Only then can the United States reach a pure and lasting peace with Islam."

Kurland coughed, wiped his mouth. "An ambassador is supposed to understand the place he lives. I wasn't a very good ambassador. I hid in my embassy. Now I see the true anger that the people of Arabia feel toward the United States. I wish I had known before." He shook his head slightly, as though he wanted the world to know that he didn't believe a word he'd said. "Barbara, I love you. Good-bye." The camera closed on him, on his weary face and terrified eyes. *We all know I'm going to die,* they said. *Let's just make it quick.*

The screen faded to black and, after a moment, lit again. Kurland was gone. A masked man stood before the banner. "As you can see, the ambassador remains unhurt. We call on the United States and the Kingdom of Saudi Arabia to respond to all five of our requirements by noon tomorrow. If they do not, action will be taken."

Wells muted the television. The kidnappers' strategy was clear. Asking the United States to impose an embargo on Saudi Arabia and stop supporting Israel? The demands were deliberately absurd. If the kidnappers had asked — for example — that all Saudi prisoners be released from Guantánamo, a face-saving compromise might theoretically have been possible. But these conditions left no room for discussion.

Of course, the kidnappers knew that. They didn't want drawn-out negotiations. They didn't know how long they could hide Kurland. They would milk the situation for a few days, get as much publicity as possible, then murder him. After that, most likely, they'd say that they were acting on the orders of senior members of the House of Saud. And they'd have the evidence to prove it. How could the United States allow them to stay in power? It had attacked Iraq for much less.

"It's crap, isn't it?" Gaffan said. "This is

just an excuse for them to do what they want. What they're going to do anyway. Cut him up."

Wells's phone rang.

"You saw?" Shafer said.

"I saw."

"Believe it or not, I have good news. The NSA may have a hit on forty-two Aziz three. They say it could be an address in southern Jeddah."

Thank you, Meshaal. "Why?"

"They checked every address matching forty-two Aziz, looking for phone or e-mail contact between the numbers that you gave them as well as other numbers and e-mail addresses they've developed. They said there's a suspicious pattern between cell tower sites around an Aziz street in south Jeddah. Also an Internet node there. But before you get too excited —"

"Yes?"

"The pattern is weak. The house numbers are messy, and they estimate only a forty percent probability of a match. But nowhere else in the country is even close to that."

" 'Messy'?"

"Their word."

"We land in four hours. We'll take a look."

"I'll call you when I get more."

"Ellis. If we find him —"

"You have carte blanche. And assume no backup. There's two Delta squads in Riyadh, but they're confined to the embassy. If that changes, I'll let you know."

Now they were stuck in limbo at Abdullah's palace. Wells wondered if they'd been betrayed even before they arrived, if Saeed's hold over Abdullah ran this deeply. But surely Abdullah controlled his own palace security.

An hour passed. The front door of the house was locked from the outside. The back door had a push-bar alarm like those that blocked fire stairs in office buildings. They could get out, but they'd be stuck on the palace grounds, with no car or weapons or identification. Wells figured they were better off waiting. His handset required a line-of-sight connection to the satellite, and the house had no windows. So they watched Al Jazeera, which had nothing new to report.

"This is Saudi Arabia," Meshaal said. "Why did you bring me here? You're not from Sheikh bin Laden."

"True."

"Let me out of here."

"That's not possible."

"I need to use the bathroom." Meshaal ran for the back door. Wells vaulted over the

489

couch, grabbed him, dragged him back.

"You have my word, Meshaal. No one will hurt you."

"Why would I believe you? You only lie to me."

"If we wanted to hurt you, we would have. But we're going to go very soon, and you're going to wait here and do what you're told. Yes?"

"I don't suppose I have a choice."

"No."

Another half hour passed before the door swung open and Gharib walked in. "He stays," the colonel said, nodding at Meshaal. "You come."

Gharib led them to an unmarked two-story building, unlocked a door, waved them into an empty office. Gowns and leather sandals were spread across a table. A smaller table held their passports, two cell phones, a paper bag stacked with riyals, and car keys. Glock pistols, two M-16s, bullet-resistant vests, and extra ammunition filled an open gun cabinet.

"Take what you need," Gharib said. "There's a Jeep outside. It's clean. Civilian registration. Once you leave, you won't be allowed back." He handed them two identity cards. "These say you're Egyptian, not Saudi. That seemed safer. They'll work for hotels and police checkpoints." He nodded at the phones. "Those have my numbers pre-programmed. If you bump into Guard soldiers and there's trouble, have them call me. The *muk,* too, though that'll take longer to get sorted out."

"And if we run into trouble with the other side?"

"Then I guess you'll be making videos, too. Anything else you need?"

"Silencers. Handcuffs or flex-cuffs. A bunch of plastic bags, just simple ones from grocery stores or places like that. A roll of electrical tape. And maps of Jeddah and Mecca."

"The Jeep has a GPS."

"I'm not sure how accurately I can program it in Arabic." Wells also wasn't sure he wanted the National Guard to know where he and Gaffan were going.

"Most of my maps are in Arabic."

"Even so."

Gharib disappeared, returned with everything Wells had asked for.

"What about Meshaal?" Wells said.

"He's our problem now."

"Go easy on him. He doesn't know anything."

"We'll take care of him." Gharib's hard, black eyes weren't reassuring. He could

491

have meant almost anything, and Wells didn't have time to ask.

"Thank you for your help."

"You're Muslim, Mr. Wells."

"Yes, colonel."

"Then God be with you. I hope you can see the Kaaba when all this is done."

"Inshallah."

"Inshallah."

CHAPTER 21

After Kurland made the video, the kidnapper let him piss in a bowl and then cuffed him to the chair and left. Kurland thought about his speech. The demands were too outlandish to be meaningful. This was political theater, meant to lead inexorably to a bullet in his head. Or worse, a knife to his neck.

His hands were locked together behind his back. He shrugged his shoulders and squeezed his hands together, trying to loosen the cuffs. After five minutes, he gave up. He'd done nothing but pull a muscle in his forearm. The cuffs around his ankles were even tighter. But he was no escape artist. He was a sixty-two-year-old man who shot ninety from the middle tees on a good day. Maybe when they moved him, *if* they moved him . . . He wasn't being defeatist. He wasn't resigned to his own death. More than anything, he wanted to get out of this room alive. But he couldn't, not on his own.

Kurland had always grounded himself in reality, one reason that his company had avoided the worst of the housing bust. During the bubble, his competitors marched west on I-88 into Kane County and even De Kalb, bidding wildly for Illinois farmland. Their land costs doubled and tripled, and they found themselves having to charge three and then four hundred thousand dollars for houses that a few years before had cost half as much. Kurland asked himself, *when the three-percent-down loans stop, who's going to buy these prairie palaces?* In 2005, he'd cut way back on new land purchases. His managers had howled. No new lots meant no new houses. They were putting themselves out of business. But he'd been right. Since the crash, Kurland Construction had picked up plenty of cheap land at bankruptcy auctions. The business was just waiting for him to come home.

If he ever did.

Enough. He didn't want to think about his own doom. He wasn't very religious, never had been, but he appreciated the Serenity Prayer. Cheesy but effective. *The wisdom to know the difference.* He closed his eyes and saw his wife playing tennis, her long brown legs under her skirt. She smiled sideways at him as he walked across the court for a kiss and a coffee. If he could keep her beside him, he'd be all right, whatever they did to him.

Abdullah rested on his bed, propped up against overstuffed pillows, his swollen stomach ballooning out of a white silk robe. He couldn't keep his temperature right anymore. Hour by hour, his flesh was ignoring his protests and leading him away.

But not yet. Not until this abomination was settled.

The Bedouin were renowned for their hospitality. The desert was a foe more lethal than any man. So a tribesman's tent was a place of peace, an escape from the sands. Centuries of custom dictated that hosts treat visitors with honor. *Only a dog snarls at a guest,* the tribesmen said. The fact that Kurland had been taken while traveling back from Abdullah's palace made matters worse. When Miteb gave Abdullah the news, the king's face flushed with shame.

Abdullah had spoken briefly to the president early that afternoon, expressing his condolences, promising that he and his men would do whatever they could to find Kurland. The two men agreed that the kidnappers' demands didn't bear discussion. But the conversation was strained. "Terrorism is a scourge of us all," Abdullah said.

"Yes," the president said, speaking through a translator. "Especially state-sponsored terrorism." A warning, deliberately vague.

Neither man mentioned the camp in Lebanon. John Wells must have told the Americans about it, Abdullah thought. But he didn't know if they'd raided the camp, or what evidence they'd found, if they'd tied the kidnappers to Saeed and Mansour. Abdullah couldn't ask, and the president had no reason to say. No doubt he wanted to reveal as little as possible, keep his options open.

"The FBI director tells me that visas for all our agents will reach Dubai within the hour," the president said.

"Yes. Dubai's only two hours by air from Riyadh. They'll be here before sunset."

"As far as I'm concerned, it's already taken too long. There can't be any more delays. We'll need full access to any evidence you develop. And we want the right to interrogate witnesses on our own if necessary."

"I understand."

"So can I count on your cooperation?"

"Yes." Under other circumstances, Abdullah might have objected. But he was done

496

helping Saeed and Mansour defend themselves from the Americans. If Saeed didn't
want these agents poking around on their
own, he would have to tell the president
himself. Most likely, Saeed would offer his
full cooperation and then Mansour would
make sure that the agents saw only what he
wanted.

"Good. Please understand, whether you
cooperate with us or not, we're going to find
the truth."

"We have nothing to hide." The king
couldn't remember the last time he'd told
such an obvious lie. But it was for his
country. He didn't know what else to do.

"And when we capture these men, we
intend to try them in the United States."

Now Abdullah had to object. "If they're
Saudi citizens and they're arrested here,
they're subject to our justice system. My
own people died in these attacks, too. And
believe me, we're perfectly capable of
enforcing our laws against these men."

The president was silent for few seconds.
"Let's say that the issue of trials can wait
until we capture these men."

"Agreed. And now I have a request for
you. Can you promise me that these soldiers
in Kuwait and Turkey won't be used in my
nation?"

"They won't be used against *you,* King. I can't promise they won't be used against the kidnappers."

"That's what those men want, Mr. President. For the world to see American soldiers marching through our cities, blowing up houses with tanks and helicopters."

"It'll be our last alternative."

"At least tell me you won't send them to Mecca or Medina. You must know —"

"I understand the sensitivities. So do our generals. We'll do our very best to avoid unnecessary provocation." The president had gone out of his way not to make any promises, Abdullah thought. "But *you* must know that we will do everything necessary to bring this man home alive."

"So will we."

"Good. Then we agree. I hope the next time we speak, the circumstances are happier." Without waiting to hear Abdullah's answer, the president hung up.

Since then, the hours had dragged interminably. Miteb reported that the *muk* had found two abandoned Chevy Tahoes painted with police logos northwest of here. They had traced the vehicles to a giant auto auction held east of Riyadh three months before. The name on their registrations corresponded to a man who had died a year before. Another dead end, for now.

Tomorrow the Guard would begin patrolling Riyadh and other major cities. But Abdullah knew better than to expect a miracle. The Guard was an army, not a police force. Unless its soldiers happened to see something unusual at a checkpoint or on patrol, they wouldn't find Kurland on their own. So once again, Abdullah found himself dependent on Saeed and Mansour and the *mukhabarat.* He still hadn't spoken with Saeed since the ambush. He dreaded the idea.

And as if Saeed were monitoring his very thoughts, at that moment his phone rang. "It's time for us to talk. Alone."

The brothers hadn't been alone in the same room for eight years, since the other princes anointed Abdullah as King Fahad's successor. Even two years ago, Abdullah would have relished this confrontation. But he was no longer sure he had the strength. "What do you want?"

"Not on this phone."

"Come to my palace, then."

Abdullah wanted nothing more than to close his eyes and sleep. Instead he called Hamoud and asked for a pot of strong black coffee and his robes.

■ ■ ■ ■

An hour later, they stood face-to-face in Abdullah's study. Saeed and Abdullah, Abdullah and Saeed, the twin foundations of the House of Saud. The king forswore the kisses and hugs and greetings: "What have you done?"

"I didn't order this, Abdullah."

"These men belong to you." Abdullah sat down heavily.

"I tell you I don't know the men who did this. Attacking Americans, it's suicide."

"Mansour, then."

"Mansour wants to be king. Not to live in a cave with Osama bin Laden."

"Then who?"

"They acted on their own. But I have good news. Progress. We've found the name of the man in charge —"

"Of course you've found it. You were behind him all along."

Saeed laughed, the sound tight and gravelly. As if the laugh had reminded him of his habits, he pulled a shiny red packet of Dunhills and a gold lighter from his pocket. He lit up a dose of cancer and sucked in deep.

"Don't you know we're the same, Abdullah?"

"Not even the same blood."

"Fool yourself, then. Two old men who can never give way. If you hadn't been so pigheaded, demanded Khalid as king, this would never have happened."

"Is this why you came here? To blame me?"

"Don't you want to hear where the investigation stands?"

"I want to hear that you've found this ambassador alive. Then we'll figure out how to deal with the men who kidnapped him."

"It's not so simple."

And we come to the real reason for your visit, Abdullah thought. Saeed sat beside Abdullah on a plush green silk couch. The brothers stared at each other in silence, the only sound Abdullah's breathing, heavy as a steam engine.

"My brother," Saeed said. "When you met with Kurland before he was attacked that day, what did you tell him?"

"Of you. What a snake you were. He didn't need convincing. I told him I suspected you in the attack on Alia. Our own blood, and you slaughtered her."

"I tell you I didn't know Alia was going to die."

Abdullah would have dealt whatever life he had left, months or years, for one day of strength. One day to squeeze the truth from his brother. But Allah didn't offer such trades. "Sit beside me and lie to my face."

"I need you to see our position."

"I see. If we don't save Kurland, we can't survive."

"And if we do save Kurland, what then? He'll go home and tell them everything."

"Good. The Americans can have you. And Mansour into the bargain."

"And what happens then? You think the Americans say to the world, 'Saeed bin Abdul-Aziz, he's behind this. But his brother King Abdullah and the rest of the princes, the rest of these billionaires in their palaces, we love them. More than ever.' No. We're all together now, my brother."

"You've brought this on us."

"And I am trying to *save* us."

Finally, Abdullah saw what Saeed was planning.

"You want to let Kurland die? Let the kidnappers kill him?"

"I want to find him."

"But he'll die in the rescue."

"Along with the kidnappers."

"Graham Kurland was my *guest*. Our guest."

502

"These stupid rules. We don't live in the desert anymore, Abdullah."

Everything that Abdullah hated about Saeed in two sentences.

"*Snake, scorpion,* those words are too fair for you. There's nothing living in you."

"Insult me all you wish, Abdullah. The situation doesn't change."

"Even if I agreed with your plan. And I don't. It's too late. He probably called the secretary of state as soon as he got in his car."

"No. He'd have waited to get back to the embassy. That kind of conversation, he would have wanted a secure line."

"Even if you're right, the Americans must know already. I told someone else."

Saeed stubbed out his cigarette. "John Wells."

How do you know about that? Abdullah almost said. But of course Saeed knew. He had moles everywhere, including in Abdullah's security detail. His spies were the reason that Abdullah had gone to Wells in the first place.

"Where is he now?"

"I don't know." Abdullah wondered if Saeed knew he was lying, if Saeed knew that Wells was inside the Kingdom. "But again, it doesn't matter. I'm sure Wells told the

Americans of my suspicions. He needed their help to attack that camp in Lebanon where your man trained his assassins."

"I tell you he wasn't my man —"

"One day to squeeze you," Abdullah murmured.

"What?"

"You'll kill Wells, too, then? If you come across him."

Saeed shrugged, as if Wells's fate was beneath his notice.

"You can't control this, Saeed. That simpering son of yours left a trail a thousand feet wide. The Americans will find it. Even if Kurland and Wells are dead. Our only chance, God willing, is to find the ambassador and give him back and kill the terrorists. And plead for mercy."

"No."

And then Abdullah understood the final piece. Saeed knew he couldn't escape if Kurland got out alive. This argument that Kurland could give them evidence they didn't have was only half true. If Kurland lived, the Americans would be relieved. They might even be willing to take Saeed in payment for the kidnapping instead of demanding the entire family. But if Kurland died, it would be all or nothing. The family would have to stand as one and hope that the Americans couldn't put together the evidence. Saeed was trying to expand his crime, make it so great that he couldn't be brought to account without bringing down the entire House of Saud.

"You'd risk us all to protect yourself and Mansour. Three hundred years of our family."

"It's the only way."

"And you expect me to abet your crime."

"Make sure that if the National Guard finds the ambassador, my men are notified. Immediately."

"Go, Saeed. Take your poison from my house."

Every ball Barbara hit went over the embassy wall. Kurland watched from the baseline. He told her to relax, but she wouldn't listen, didn't seem to hear him at all. And then Roberto began to instruct her, in Arabic, his voice low and guttural —

All at once Kurland realized where he was. He couldn't believe he'd fallen asleep. Maybe an after-effect of the sedative they'd given him. Maybe sleep was the only sensible response to this place.

The light above clicked on. The hatch pulled back. Two men climbed down the metal rungs, both carrying bags, the second also holding a steel stepladder. The first was the one he'd seen before, the one who'd made him read the speech. The second had broad shoulders and deep-set unsmiling eyes and a nose that had been badly broken many years before. Kurland pegged him as a commander. Maybe *the* commander.

The second man said something in Arabic. "The major wants me to ask how you're feeling," the first man said.

"I've been better. Have you had any word about your demands?" Kurland figured he might as well humor these men, pretend they had a chance of getting what they'd asked for.

"I'm sorry to tell you that it appears they've been rejected."

"Already?" *You're lying,* Kurland thought. He didn't have a good sense of time in here, but he knew he'd been asleep only four or five hours at most. He'd made the video an hour before he fell asleep. So a full day couldn't have passed since the release of the video. And however insane the demands were, the White House wouldn't reject them until the last moment of the deadline. Probably not even then. The president would delay as long as he could, to give the CIA and the Pentagon the most possible time to find him.

A bilious dread rose up Kurland's throat. These men had only one reason to lie. And that was to justify — to themselves, to him, to Allah — whatever they were about to do.

The translator unzipped his bag, took out the tripod and camera he'd used earlier, along with another bottle of Coke. "Would you like?"

"No, thank you."

"You should drink. You'll need your strength."

The fear crept out of Kurland's throat and into his mouth, as real and bitter as month-old milk. He thought of Barbara sitting with him at Wrigley Field. She didn't like base-ball, but she humored him a couple of times a year, the same way he humored her at the Art Institute galas. She wouldn't let him beg. *He wouldn't beg.*

The translator set up the tripod and camera as the commander put the steplad-der beside Kurland's chair. Now that the ladder was next to him, Kurland noticed that it had some unusual features. Its feet were welded to heavy metal plates. And two notches were cut into its top step.

Despite, or because of, his fear, Kurland found himself semi-calmly puzzling over the ladder's purpose. Its meaning. *I'll take Obscure Torture Devices for one thousand dollars, Mr. Trebek.* Were they planning a poor man's hanging? What was a poor man's hanging, anyway? He felt his breathing get shallow. No. He couldn't lose his cool. They hadn't even touched him yet.

Then the commander spread the contents of his bag on the cell's concrete floor. He turned toward Kurland and waved his hand over them like a magician unveiling his best trick. Six items lay on the ground. Five were merely frightening. The sixth was terrifying.

A fat hypodermic needle. A thick gauze bandage. Two sturdy steel clamps. A tourniquet.

And a circular saw, big and mean, its steel teeth shining brightly under the overhead bulb.

"You don't want to do this." Kurland kept his voice even. "You don't have to do this. Let's talk about this."

The commander answered in a long stream of Arabic.

"Would you like to know what he's saying?"

"Okay. Yes." *I'll buy every second I can.*

"He says that for two generations the United States has stolen the oil that belongs to the people of the Arabian Peninsula —"

"We haven't stolen it, we *paid* for it —"

508

The translator slapped Kurland's face with five stinging fingers, ending the argument. "Again. He says that for two generations the United States has stolen the oil that belongs to the people of the Arabian Peninsula. He says that the whole world knows this crime, and that the only reason no one stopped you is your army and your air force and all your tanks and bombs. He says that America is a thief."

The commander pulled latex gloves from his pocket and tugged them on his strong, brown hands. When he was satisfied with their fit, he spoke again.

"He asks if you know the penalty in *sharia*" — Muslim law — "for theft.

"No." Though Kurland did.

"It is amputation of the hand of the thief."

"I'm not a thief."

"Your country is. This is the law. This is justice."

Kurland nodded, as if they were in the middle of the sanest conversation he'd ever had. "Justice. So I'm to have my hand amputated. For the sins of the United States. He's going to do it. And you're going to videotape it. And then you're going to upload it or FedEx it or whatever to Al Jazeera so the whole world can watch."

"Correct. Are you left-handed or right-?"

509

"Right."

"Then the major will take your left."

"Kind of you."

The translator either didn't recognize the sarcasm or ignored it. He and the commander had a rapid-fire conversation in Arabic. "We're going to give you morphine to make you sleepy and make the operation easier."

"I don't want any morphine."

"You do. Believe me." He reached down, picked up the needle.

Behind his back, Kurland squeezed his hands together, clenched and unclenched his fingers. His left hand. He'd better get as much use of it as he could. "At least wait for the deadline to pass." He couldn't believe he was negotiating this way, as if the end of the deadline would somehow justify what they were planning to do to him. But those extra hours sounded more than pretty good about now.

"We both know your country won't agree. This way, the next video will be ready as soon as the deadline passes."

"I applaud your understanding of the demands of the twenty-four-hour news cycle. Though I guess I won't be applauding anything much longer."

If the translator understood the joke, he

didn't smile. He uncuffed Kurland's arms and recuffed his right hand to the chair leg. The commander grabbed Kurland's left arm with his thick gloved hands and pulled it around the chair and slapped it against the ladder's top step, the metal cool under his forearm.

Kurland didn't resist. He'd wondered sometimes when he saw the brief announcements that a death-row prisoner had been executed, why didn't the guy resist? Why didn't he fight instead of walking to his fate like a sheep? But now he knew. His own dignity was all he had left. And his voice.

"No religion justifies this. No law. You know that, right? You're just a couple of psychopaths with a saw. And whatever your plan is, whatever you're hoping to accomplish, it won't work, it's going to end with both of you dead, sooner, not later —"

The translator put a hand over Kurland's mouth, squeezed his nose shut. "Keep talking and there won't be any morphine. You won't like that."

The commander moved Kurland's arm until his wrist was dangling just off the edge of the ladder. With the translator's help, he slid the vises into the notches and wound them tight around Kurland's forearm, squeezing the muscles and the bone against the ladder's top step. And then squeezed tighter still, pinching the skin, immobilizing Kurland's arm well and truly.

The commander tied the tourniquet around Kurland's biceps and tapped the crook of Kurland's elbow until the vein rose. He aspirated the needle to make sure the morphine was free of air bubbles and slid it deep into Kurland's vein and sank the plunger. After the prick of the needle, pleasure flowed into Kurland's arm. Despite his knowledge of what was about to happen, he couldn't help but ride away on the rush that filled his body, as if the room and the very air he breathed were warm and liquid. His head lolled forward, and he sighed, and all the pressure left him. He hoped for an overdose. Better to die this way than from a bullet.

He didn't die, though. And the peace didn't last. The translator put the camera on the commander, and he spoke for a minute in Arabic. No doubt the same justifications he'd just given Kurland. Then he pulled on a surgical mask and goggles — goggles, as if he were about to prune a tree — and picked up the saw.

Its scream filled the room, and tears streamed down Kurland's cheeks. *No,* Kurland said. *Don't.* It was time for the cavalry, time for men in American uniforms to burst in and end this madness. Time and past time. He wouldn't complain at their tardiness —

But the cavalry didn't come. Only the commander, crossing the room in four slow steps. Kneeling beside the ladder. Lining up the protective housing around the saw's blade with the edge of the top step. Sliding the saw forward and backward, making sure the blade was where he wanted it. All the morphine in the world couldn't help Kurland now. His fear and adrenaline had burned through it. Even in the commander's tight grip, the saw was vibrating madly, shaking the ladder, shaking Kurland's poor left arm.

Kurland clenched his tongue — *Don't beg* — and closed his eyes —

And the commander pushed the saw forward and cut.

CHAPTER 22

JEDDAH

Wells drove along the blast-proof wall of Abdullah's palace, slabs of concrete fitted together as closely as a starlet's capped teeth. When the wall ended, he and Gaffan found themselves on the coastal cornice, the Red Sea to their right, flat and black. They were headed for a seedy neighborhood in south Jeddah, near the port.

The police had put Jeddah under an eleven p.m. to five a.m. curfew. But the deadline was more than three hours away. For now, traffic was heavy. They passed a half-dozen hotels before the road swung inland to accommodate another palace. Near its entrance, four police cars blocked traffic. A cop waved Wells over. Another put a flashlight in his eyes. "Identification?"

Wells handed over their identity cards. The cop looked them over, shined a light through the Jeep. "Make sure you're home by the curfew."

"Yes, sir."

They turned left, onto a wide avenue that ran through an upscale commercial district, big-box electronic stores and BMW and Mercedes dealerships. Wells made a block-long loop, four straight right turns, the quickest way to pick up surveillance. But they seemed to be alone. "We have any friends?"

"Not that I can see."

"Me either." Wells drove on, to the elevated highway along Jeddah's east side. At first glance the road could have passed for the 405 in Los Angeles or the 10 in Houston, four smoothly paved lanes in each direction, sometimes five, surrounded by brightly lit office buildings and industrial parks and oversized malls. Yet the traffic had a strangely caffeinated quality that Wells had never seen in the United States. He didn't think it was related to the kidnapping. Nearly everyone tailgated. *Everyone* sped. All the drivers were men, of course, mostly in their teens and twenties. They had nothing to do and nowhere to go except drive in circles burning cheap gas, hamsters on an asphalt wheel. The House of Saud stifled their creative and political and sexual energy. Islam was their only outlet. No wonder they blew themselves up so often.

After fifteen minutes, Wells turned right at a massive cloverleaf, passing a soccer stadium as he headed west, toward downtown. Soccer qualified as an acceptable public activity in the Kingdom, even if it did expose the players' legs. The highway ran through miles of empty lots waiting to be developed and a sign for a "Psychic Disease Hospital," which somehow sounded gentler to Wells than a psychiatric hospital. A mile southeast of downtown, Wells pulled off. After another roadblock, he drove under the highway into a grim warren of concrete and brick.

In Saudi Arabia, as in the United States, the poorest urban neighborhoods lay on the fringes of downtowns. They'd left the opulence of Abdullah's palace behind. The streets were potholed, narrow, and dark, the overhead lights burned out. The stench of sewage filled the Jeep, and some of the houses sat on concrete blocks. The Saudi government had budgeted billions of dollars to build a proper drainage system for Jeddah, but the money had mysteriously disappeared into the pockets of the men who ran the city. Not for the first time, Wells wondered about Abdullah. The king's concern for his subjects wasn't obvious in this part of town.

For now, though, the Kingdom's problems ran deeper than succession. If Kurland's kidnappers began to torture him in public, the United States and Saudi Arabia would be hard-pressed to avoid war. Time was short. Wells pulled over, called Shafer. "We're in."

"And free of unwanted baggage?"

"Think so. What have we missed?"

"The *muk* found the fake cop cars that took Kurland. The betting now is they're hiding him in the desert. Most of the passports you gave us are from guys in the Najd. Those families are getting their doors kicked in tonight."

"Any word on the helicopter?"

"I passed your theory to NSA and NGA, but they didn't get anything. The Saudis haven't let us put up drones. We're stuck with satellites and AWACS" — air force radar jets. "Tough to find one helicopter in a million square miles."

"So it's still in play. They could have brought him this way."

"Yes, but unless you get some evidence, it's not a priority. We have eighty FBI agents in Riyadh now. They're mainly trying to keep an eye on the *muk*. Theoretically, they can chase their own leads, but it hasn't happened yet."

"What about Lebanon?"

"We hit the camp this afternoon. Burned to the ground. Actual words of the Delta major in charge were: 'Like a nuke hit it.' We're asking the Syrians to lean on Hezbollah, get them to open up, but our leverage there is limited. To put it mildly."

Wells understood. No doubt the attack on Kurland had thrilled Hezbollah, along with its backers in Syria and Iran. Those two countries would love nothing more than for the United States to invade Saudi Arabia.

"Meantime, the Airborne and the Rangers are sitting tight," Shafer said. "Treasury and the NSA are trying to follow the money, looking to connect the camp with, how do I put this nicely, government sources in Saudi Arabia. So far they haven't found anything. Until they do that, the president has ordered that official policy is to assume that this attack is the work of independent non-state actors. His words."

" 'Independent non-state actors.' "

"Think Brad Pitt."

"You know what I like about you, Ellis? You always make time for a joke, brighten my day. And if we do connect the princes to the kidnappers?"

"No decision yet."

"We'll burn that bridge when we come to it."

"Exactly right."

"So. Summing up. The FBI's in Riyadh. The Airborne's in Turkey. The *muk* are knocking heads five hundred miles from here. No useful intel since yesterday."

"Correct, correct, correct, and correct."

"And we're still on our own in beautiful Jeddah, the jewel of the Red Sea."

"Just the way you like it." Shafer clicked off.

Wells was about to drive on when a police helicopter swung low overhead, its spotlight slicing left to right, catching a mosque's minaret before finding the Jeep. The light held them for fifteen seconds, filling the windshield with its dead white glare before moving on. When it was gone, Wells eased the Jeep back onto the road.

As he did, the cell phone that Wells had gotten at the palace trilled.

"This is Miteb." The prince's voice was low, hard to hear. "My brother asked me to call. He says you must be careful. He says the *muk* aren't to be trusted."

Tell me something I don't know, Wells didn't say. "He have anything specific? Do they know the names we're using?"

"I'm sorry. I don't understand."

"The names on our ID cards. Do the *muk* know them?"

A long pause, as if the prince was struggling to comprehend the concept of the national identity cards his family made its subjects carry. "I don't think so. I think it's more a general warning to do with Saeed. That he sees you as a problem. But I don't think he knows you're here, not yet. The place where you came in, that's a good place."

"All right. If anything changes, let me know."

"Please find our friend."

"We're trying." Wells hung up.

"What was that?" Gaffan said.

"Nothing good," Wells said, and explained.

"This keeps getting messier, doesn't it?"

"Quickest way to solve it is to find Kurland."

"True dat." Words that earned Gaffan a sidelong look from Wells.

But even finding 42 Aziz proved more difficult than Wells expected. The street grid was as sloppy as an undercooked waffle, and Gaffan had trouble with the map. They doubled back twice before Wells spotted "Aziz Street" painted crudely on a black sign screwed into a brick wall. To the left, toward downtown, a mosque sat beside three barred storefronts.

Wells turned right, deeper into the slum. The houses were small and mean, their lights peeking through barred windows. Concrete blocks, a rough parody of the walls protecting Abdullah's palace, hid their front yards. A stray dog trotted into the Jeep's headlights before turning tail and disappearing between two oil drums that overflowed with trash.

Wells didn't see anyone on the street or in the yards, but he did spot a couple of small groups of men on rooftops, talking and smoking. Many of these houses didn't have air-conditioning. After a day baking under the Saudi sun, they could be unbearable. The rooftops were like front porches in the nineteenth-century South, a way to escape the worst of the heat. But the curfew and the helicopters were keeping most people inside tonight.

"If I were Aziz, I'd be mad they named such a lousy street after me," Gaffan said.

"He's got plenty of others to choose from. Anyway, he's dead."

"You think they could be keeping Kurland here? Seems almost too quiet."

Wells understood what Gaffan meant. The

neighborhood was poor but not chaotic. Wells guessed most of these houses were filled with the migrant laborers who did the menial jobs the Saudis wouldn't. In times of crisis, they would buckle down and hope to be ignored. Armed men would stand out. Apparently, the police were making a similar calculation and focusing their attention on neighborhoods where jihadis had a stronger presence.

Six blocks on, Aziz Street dead-ended at an electrical substation. Wells made a U-turn, pulled over beside a house better lit than its neighbors, knocked heavily on the front gate. A man stepped out. He was too dark to be Saudi. Indian, probably. *"Salaam aleikum."*

"Aleikum salaam."

"I'm looking for number thirty-eight Aziz."

"This is number eighty-one. Thirty-eight is that way" — the man pointed toward downtown. "And on the other side. Near the mosque."

The location made sense. The mosque would draw traffic, helping to hide the jihadis' coming and going. "Is the mosque number forty-two?"

"No, maybe thirty-two, thirty-four."

"Do you go there?"

The man was no longer interested in the conversation. He backed away with slow, careful steps. "Good luck, mister."

Wells rolled toward the mosque's narrow minaret. Four buildings down from the mosque, a twentysomething man sat on the flat roof of a two-story house, his legs dangling over the front. He could have been trying to cool off. But he didn't seem relaxed. He shifted his attention up and down, from the helicopters to the Jeep and back. To the northwest, the center of the city, a shot clipped the night, a big high-caliber round. Then another. The kid popped up, looked toward the downtown office buildings.

Wells drove without slowing, past the house, the mosque, and the storefronts. Three blocks on, the street hooked right, then merged into a grimy avenue. "You think it's the one with the guy on the roof?" Gaffan said.

"I think we need to find out." Wells swung onto the avenue, past a long, low warehouse, and then turned right and right again, circling the warehouse. Aziz Street was three blocks down.

A police helicopter picked them up again. Wells slowed. It slowed, too. It was barely two hundred feet up, its rotor wash rattling the Jeep's windshield. Wells didn't see how they could get close to the house with the helicopter on them.

Then he had an idea. He drove past the mosque, didn't turn onto Aziz. Halfway down the next block, he pulled over. The chopper stayed on them.

"I'm getting out. I'll walk to the next corner, go left. You loop past the warehouse again, come back, park a block past the house on Aziz. Don't rush it. Let the chopper stay with you. If he follows me instead, I'll keep walking this way. In that case, make the loop, come back, pick me up a couple blocks down."

"You want to use the copter to distract the kid?"

"I'll go in the back of the house. He'll be focusing it. Give me a couple minutes, let the chopper get bored and peel off, then come in the front."

"What if it doesn't get bored?"

"Come in the front anyway. Worst case, we'll go out the back, ditch the Jeep."

"Worst case, they close off the neighborhood and trap us."

"They're spread thin. They're running roadblocks all over the city and they have no reason to focus on us in particular."

Gaffan shrugged, conceding the point. "You gonna take your rifle?" They'd stowed their vests and M-16s in the spare tire compartment but kept their Glocks under their seats.

"No." Wells reached under his seat for his pistol and silencer, slipped them in a white plastic bag imprinted with a cartoon chicken and the logo of Al Baik, a chain of popular fast-food restaurants in Jeddah. "Nobody ever thinks the guy holding a bag of chicken is a threat."

Wells stepped onto the street. The spotlight fell on him with almost physical force. Gaffan shifted into the driver's seat, and the Jeep rolled off. Wells shuffled along the curb, as if he had nowhere to be — *I'm just a guy heading home to eat some fried chicken in my concrete living room.* The helicopter hesitated, its light shifting between Wells and the Jeep. It decided on the Jeep and moved away.

As the helicopter's noise faded, Wells heard another half-dozen shots echoing from downtown. The police were busy tonight. No doubt the roadblocks had snared more than one unlucky criminal. Wells turned left on the nameless street just past Aziz. The chopper circled away, following Gaffan. Wells had a partial view of 42

Aziz, enough to see that the sentry on the roof was watching the helicopter. He walked past an alley that dead-ended at the back-right corner of the house. Two blocks up, he turned, paced back, timing his steps against the slow rotation of the spotlight tracing Gaffan. His window was narrow at best. In a few minutes, the police in the helicopter would either call in cars to stop the Jeep or find another target.

Then the spotlight twisted away, toward downtown. A problem. Either the helicopter had broken off contact or Gaffan had gotten lost somehow. Either way, Wells had to go in now, while the sentry was still distracted.

He jogged into the alley, the gown bunching around his legs. A step before the wall, he jumped up. In one motion, he laid the Al Baik bag atop the wall and wrapped his hands around the rough concrete. He dug in, pulled himself higher, all those push-ups paying off, and crawled on top of the wall. A dog barked from somewhere across the street, but the rest of the neighborhood stayed quiet.

The house had a small concrete yard littered with plastic water bottles. A Honda motorcycle was parked in the corner, hidden from the street. Heavy shades covered the windows, allowing only faint light into the yard. A television inside played what sounded like an Arabic news channel. Wells pulled the Glock from the bag and jumped down. He landed on a plastic bottle and pitched forward, his fingertips grazing the concrete before he pulled himself up as nimbly as a running back keeping his knee off the turf. The bottle skittered behind him. The television muted. A man inside the house said, "What was that? Go check." Then yelled, "Usman? Did you see anything back there?" From the roof, a voice yelled, "No, Hassan!"

"Check again. Make sure."

Wells had a problem now. Killing these men wouldn't be difficult. But he still didn't know if they were the right targets. He had no proof that 42 Aziz Street was connected to the kidnappers — or even that this house was actually 42 Aziz.

Narrow alleys ran along the sides of the house. Wells picked his way to the back-right corner and flattened himself against the rough concrete. The house was twenty feet high, and the guy on the roof, Usman, would have to lean almost straight over the corner to see him. Wells unscrewed the silencer and slipped it into the front-right pocket of his gown. He shifted the Glock to his left hand, holding it by the barrel now, high across his chest. The footsteps on the roof creaked closer. The back door snapped open and scraped against concrete. Wells pulled back his head and listened as the man in the house stepped into the yard. On the roof, Usman paced.

"I don't see anything," the man in the yard said.

"Me either," Usman said.

The man in the yard walked toward the corner where Wells was hiding. Wells waited, waited, then spun left, popping out from the alley. He swung the Glock with his left arm, a downward clubbing backhand, quicker than a looping right hook and nearly as powerful. The man's eyes opened wide, and he tried to raise his own pistol —

But Wells drove the corner of the Glock into the left side of the man's temple, the soft spot just above the eye. The man grunted and sagged sideways. Wells stepped up and swung his right fist into the man's belly. The man grunted again, his breath rushing out of him, giving Wells a whiff of the curried chicken he'd eaten that day. He dropped his pistol and toppled forward. Wells got under him and held him and hit him once more with the butt of the Glock to be sure he was out. He was skinny, maybe one hundred fifty pounds. Wells lowered him easily and laid him on the ground. In a couple hours, he'd wake up feeling like a car had run him over. But he would wake up.

The guy on the roof, Usman, yelled, "Is everything okay?" Wells shifted the pistol to his right hand, ran inside, found himself in the kitchen, a small, tidy room that also smelled like curried chicken. "What's going on?" someone at the front of the house said. Hassan, the third jihadi. Wells ducked toward the refrigerator. Hassan lumbered through the house and stepped into the kitchen holding a big black pistol in a two-handed grip.

Wells grabbed Hassan's hands and forced up the pistol. Hassan pulled the trigger, and the gun fired uselessly into the ceiling. Wells lifted his right leg and stomped down on Hassan's foot. Wells was wearing ankle-high black motorcycle boots. Hassan was barefoot. Three of his metatarsals snapped with a crack nearly as loud as the pistol shot a moment before. He dropped the gun and fell sideways and screamed. Wells let Hassan hit the floor and then kicked him in the chin to shut him up. His eyes rolled back in his head and two teeth popped out, sticky red with candy-cane blood. This one would wake up feeling like a *truck* had run him over.

Usman, the guy on the roof, was left. "Hey. What's happening?" he yelled down. Wells waited to be sure no one else was coming, then stepped through two stifling rooms and strode up the stairs. He stopped at the top step. A corridor ran the length of the second floor. At the back of the house, a rickety spiral staircase led to the roof.

Wells moved down the corridor as the door to the roof opened. He hid himself in a foul-smelling bathroom as Usman ran down the spiral stairs and into the hall. When Usman had passed, Wells stepped out. "Raise your hands."

Usman stopped, looked over his shoulder at Wells. Wells raised the pistol and Usman stretched his arms over his head. His hands were empty.

"On your knees." Usman hestitated, then ran for the front stairs. Wells aimed low, at his ass, and squeezed the Glock's trigger. The pistol's silenced shot was no louder than a gassy belch. Usman screamed and stumbled forward, sliding onto his knees.

"Hands up."

Again Usman raised them.

"Where's the ambassador?"

"What ambassador?"

The answer was a confession. Everyone in Saudi Arabia knew what had happened to Kurland. "Where is he?"

"I don't know." Usman braced himself, stood, stumbled for the stairs. Wells lifted the pistol and shot him again twice, high and lethal in the back. Usman grunted and flopped against the wall and slid down, a slow, ungainly death. Blood dripped out of his mouth when Wells flipped him over. He tried to speak, but Wells couldn't understand his mumbles. Already Wells regretted the fury that had made him pull the trigger. *Dead men tell no tales.*

Wells left him, searched the upstairs rooms. In the front bedroom, he found two AKs, a Quran, a week of Saudi newspapers, and a tattered Victoria's Secret catalog tucked under a mattress, the saddest piece of not-quite-pornography Wells had ever seen. A closet held a half-dozen *thobe*s in various sizes and jeans and long-sleeved shirts neatly folded on top of a hard orange plastic case. Wells swept the clothes aside, picked up the case, and carried it into the bedroom. It wasn't heavy. He clicked open its oversized black latches. He found a basic medical kit, the kind a paramedic might carry — gauze and bandages and scissors, latex gloves, masks, bottles of pills and tubes of antibiotic, a thermometer, and a stetho-scope. The supplies all appeared a couple years old. Wells wondered if something more interesting was hidden inside. He turned the case over, emptied it, but didn't find anything.

In the bathroom, he found three passports hidden in a plastic bag taped to the back of the toilet. Wells relaxed slightly when he found that they all had recent Lebanese entry and exit visas — near-certain proof that these men were jihadis who had trained at Aziz's camp.

"Ambassador? Ambassador Kurland? Can you hear me?" he yelled in English. But the house was silent. When he returned to the front steps, Usman was dead. Wells checked his pockets, found only a cheap disposable Nokia. A burner. He turned it on, flipped through it, but the registry was empty. Either the call logs had been deleted or it had never been used. He stood up as he heard a woman singing downstairs in Arabic, the voice startling him until he realized it was a ringtone.

Inside Hassan's gown, Wells found another phone, a disposable Nokia identical to the one he'd taken from Usman. Hassan grumbled semiconsciously as Wells took it. Its monochrome screen showed a 966 number, the Saudi area code. Wells let it ring until the call went to voicemail. A few seconds later, the mailbox icon lit up. Wells pushed 1, listened to a man saying, "Hassan. No package tonight. We're not finished yet, and it's too close to curfew. I'll bring it tomorrow. You'll have plenty of time. Peace be with you, brother." Wells riffed through Hassan's pockets but found only a Honda motorcycle key, presumably for the bike behind the house.

Footsteps in the alley pulled him up. He drew his pistol, hid himself against the wall beside the kitchen door. "John," Gaffan whispered. "You there?"

"Yeah. Long time no see."

Gaffan walked in. "I'm sorry. I got lost." Gaffan nudged Hassan's broken foot. "Looks like you handled things."

"Let's get the other one inside, shut the door."

Wells and Gaffan put the two jihadis Wells had immobilized on their stomachs, cuffed their hands and legs. The first jihadi, the one whom Wells had pistol-whipped, breathed slowly and unevenly. Wells filled a plastic jug with lukewarm water from the tap, poured it over the guy's head, got only a few guttural mumbles. He peeled back the guy's eyelids. His pupils constricted slowly. Wells had hit him in just the wrong spot, and he had a very severe concussion or slow bleed from a skull fracture. Skull fractures were becoming a specialty for Wells. Either way, the guy was useless to them. He needed real medical care, and it would be days before he could answer any questions. Only Hassan was left.

Wells refilled the jug, poured water over Hassan's head. Hassan shifted uncomfortably, opened his eyes, closed them quickly. Wells nudged his right foot. Hassan groaned and scrabbled sideways and stared up hatefully. Wells pushed him up so he was braced against the cabinets, and pulled over a chair and sat beside him. He hoped that a mighty helping of fear would do the trick. He didn't want to have to hurt this man. The Midnight House was fresh in his mind.

"Hassan. You need help. For your foot. We can get you help."

Hassan said nothing. Wells showed him the phone, the missed call. Hassan shook his head. "Who's this? Who called you?"

"Water. Please."

Wells got him a glass, tilted it to his lips. Hassan drank, cleared his throat in a low growl — and spat a runny mix of drool and phlegm and blood. It barely escaped his lips, slid slowly down on his chin. A tooth rolled out of his mouth and down his gown. "It was your mother. She wanted to screw. I said no."

Wells grabbed Hassan's cheeks, squeezed his ruined face. "Tell us where he is."

"He's in hell. Where he belongs."

Wells knelt beside him, reached for his foot. Hassan looked away. "What's in the package?"

"Your father's balls."

"You're going to make us hurt you."

"Do whatever you like."

But Wells found he couldn't do anything. He wasn't sure he could break this man with pain, and even if he could, he didn't want to try. He reached into his pocket for his pistol, put the silencer to Hassan's head. "I'm going to give you three seconds."

Hassan closed his eyes and mumbled the *shahada*, and Wells put the pistol away without even starting to count. Mock executions might not be physically painful, but they were still torture.

"I'm Muslim, too," Wells said. "And this is wrong. This isn't what Muhammad would have wanted."

"Now you tell me what it's like to be Muslim. You find a hundred ways to be a fool." Hassan grinned crooked and bloody. "Dance for me now. Dance for me and I'll tell you where he is."

Wells squeezed his fists and fought his very strong urge to shoot Hassan in the head. "We're going to find him. And you're going to die." Hassan shook his head, and Wells punched him in the stomach. Hassan slumped down onto the floor of the kitchen. Even so, Wells couldn't help but feel that Hassan had bested him. He reached for electrical tape and slapped it over Hassan's mouth so that he wouldn't have to hear the contempt in the man's voice anymore.

A tug on his shoulder pulled him up. Gaffan. Wells had been so focused on Hassan he'd forgotten Gaffan. "Forget it," Gaffan murmured. "Nobody can break a guy like that in ten minutes. Not you, not anyone. Now what?"

"Go over the house, find what I missed."

But they didn't find anything. The place seemed to be a cutout, a depot for men and messages to pass. Wells wondered if the "package" in the voicemail referred to Kurland himself.

Wells listened to the message again, realized something else. It was just ten p.m. now. The curfew didn't take effect for another hour. So the caller wasn't in Jeddah. He was somewhere nearby but not close enough to come here with only a few

536

minutes before curfew. One city, forty miles east, fit that profile better than any other. "Is the Jeep close?"

"Just up the block."

"Then let's go." Wells took one last look around the kitchen, opened the back door.

"Where to?"

Wells pulled the door shut behind them and they left 42 Aziz behind. "Mecca."

CHAPTER 23

Mecca. Under other circumstances, Wells would have been excited at the chance to see the heart of Islam. Christianity and Judaism had holy sites, of course — the Wailing Wall, Mount Sinai, Bethlehem. But no faith was as closely tied to a single spiritual center as Islam was to Mecca.

Muhammad had been born in Mecca, lived in Mecca when he received the prophecies that led him to preach, been forced from Mecca in fear and returned in triumph. Five times a day, 1.5 billion Muslims turned toward the Kaaba, the black stone at the heart of the Grand Mosque, to pray. The *hajj*, the spiritual journey to Mecca, was a central tenet of Islam. Millions of Muslims came each year. Their numbers would have been even greater if the Saudi government had not limited the size of the pilgrimage to control stampedes. Meanwhile, non-Muslims were barred even from setting foot in Mecca. "Oh you who believe! The idolaters are nothing but unclean, so they shall not approach the Sacred Mosque," the Quran's ninth verse said.

Yes, it was true that Muhammad had once commanded his followers to pray toward Jerusalem. He'd changed the direction of prayer to Mecca after falling out with the Jewish tribes in Arabia. And yes, it was true that many scholars believed that Muhammad had made the *hajj* part of Islam mainly to placate Mecca's merchants. Even before Islam existed, Mecca had profited from pilgrims visiting the Kaaba.

No matter. Wells didn't have to believe in the literal truth of every word in the Quran to feel the pull of the place. When he faced the Kaaba to pray, he imagined a billion whispered prayers coming from all over the world, from every direction, from worshippers of every color. Pleas of fear, hope, redemption, and revenge, dreams great and small, vows to honor and to love, all melding at the Grand Mosque into one holy message that only God could hear.

Unfortunately, as a place to live, Mecca left much to be desired. Home to almost two million people, the city was dust-clogged and overcrowded. Most Saudi cities dealt with their rapid growth by spreading into the desert. Mecca didn't have that option. It lay in a valley ringed by low mountains. Unable to expand horizontally, it had occupied every square inch of space in the valley and then grown vertically. Office towers and apartment buildings now hemmed in the Grand Mosque from all sides.

The mosque itself looked very different than it had fifty years before. To handle the crush of *hajj* pilgrims, the Saudi government had repeatedly rebuilt and expanded the structure. The mosque was now the world's largest, with gleaming white marble galleries surrounding a central plaza that held hundreds of thousands of worshippers. The Saudis had also expanded the city's network of walkways and pedestrian tunnels to ease the traffic jams that occurred every *hajj* as pilgrims traveled between the mosque and their temporary homes in tent cities outside Mecca.

Mecca's congestion offered endless hiding places for Graham Kurland and his kidnappers — assuming Wells's hunch was right and they were in the city. For now the call Hassan had received was his only clue. He grabbed his sat phone, called Shafer. "I have a number for you. Saudi. Probably a disposable phone. Used twenty minutes ago. Can

NSA do anything?"

"If it's on, probably. If not, I don't know. It may take a while. Depends on the carrier, how much cooperation we're getting."

"How long?"

"I don't know. How hot's the number?"

"Maybe very."

"Those two words don't go together. What happened at the house?"

"One KIA, two WIA."

"One *what* KIA?"

"I'm reasonably certain he was hostile."

Shafer was silent.

"He wasn't friendly, that's for sure."

"If you're wrong, you'd better hope the king likes you. Not much we can do if you killed a Saudi civ on Saudi soil."

"Just tell the FBI to get a team to the house. Tonight. One of the wounded is in bad shape."

"Sounds like you had yourself a fun time."

"It was unavoidable." *Aside from the guy I shot in the back.* "I need that trace, Ellis. While I was there, somebody called, left a message. I think it's related."

"Give me the number. And the number of the phone that received the call."

Wells did.

"I'll let you know soon as I hear."

The Jeep slowed as they approached a

541

roadblock at the entrance to Highway 5, the road connecting Jeddah and Mecca. The cops running the roadblock weren't cops. Half of them carried M-16s and wore Special Forces uniforms. The others were *muk* in black shirts and pants. They waved Gaffan over, put a floodlight on the Jeep. Wells kept his arms low by his sides. He'd noticed flecks of blood on the cuffs of his gown. On a close search, they'd be obvious.

Gaffan handed their identity cards to a Special Forces officer. He looked them over, then called the *muk* to check them out. Wells wondered whether Mansour had already learned the names on their cards.

"You should be home," the *muk* barked. "Where are you going?"

"Mecca."

"Mecca? Why tonight?"

"We have a job tomorrow. Cleaning a house. We didn't want to get caught in the traffic in the morning."

The *muk* shined a flashlight over the Jeep. "I don't see any supplies for cleaning."

"They're all at the house."

"Where are you staying?"

"The owner lets us sleep on his roof."

"Where?"

"It's on Abdul-Aziz Road. Two kilometers from the Grand Mosque."

542

The *muk* handed back their identity cards. "Drive fast, then. You only have thirty minutes, and if you get stopped at the western roadblock, they may make you sleep in the car and wait until the morning. Or they may arrest you." He handed back their identity cards, waved them on.

"Thank you, officer."

"Next —"

Gaffan sped off. "Abdul-Aziz Road," Wells said.

"Figured it was a safe bet."

The desert took over, the land as dark and flat as an ocean. If not for the glow of Jeddah behind them, Wells would hardly have believed he was traveling between two multimillion-person cities less than fifty miles apart.

His sat phone rang. "Our friends say the number traces to western Mecca," Shafer said.

"You have a street? An address?"

"They're still working that. They may need you to call it again."

"I thought —"

"It's not Verizon. They can't just ask nicely and get the location. And these disposables are tricky. Believe me when I tell you they're pulling out the stops. They're basically giv-

543

ing the Saudi telecom system an enema as we speak."

Five minutes later, Shafer called back. "They're ready. They say if you can get that phone up, they can get to the specific tower."

"How long do they need?"

"Thirty seconds. A minute would be better. But do it soon. They say that the way they're spooning data, they could take down the whole system."

" 'Spooning.' "

"It's a technical term."

Wells reached for Hassan's cell. *Thirty seconds.* If he screwed up, he'd not only blow his chance at finding the house, he might provoke the kidnappers into killing Kurland. Could he sound enough like a native Saudi to fool them? He murmured phrases to himself, smoothing his accent. They were halfway between Jeddah and Mecca now, rolling east at ninety miles an hour. As he watched, the cell's reception shrank to a single bar.

"Pull over."

"What about the curfew?"

"Just do it."

Gaffan slowed down, edged to the side of the highway. Wells called the 966 number, keeping his hand over the microphone. After three rings, a man picked up.

"I got your voicemail," Wells said quietly. "But we may have a problem —"

"Hassan. I can't hear you —"

Wells took his fingers off the microphone. "Better?"

"A little."

"Usman says a helicopter's circling."

"For how long?"

"I don't know. Hold on —" Wells covered the microphone. "Usman —" He imagined himself on the first floor of the house, running to the roof. He waited, watched the call timer move past forty-five seconds, fifty . . . "I'll call you back." He hung up. He'd stretched a handful of sentences into a fifty-eight-second conversation. In a few minutes he'd send a calming text to the man on the other end. *False alarm. Everything's fine. See you tomorrow.*

"Let's go."

They flew under the signs for the bypass highway that non-Muslims were required to take around Mecca. Wells wondered what would happen if they were arrested inside the city's borders. Gaffan wasn't Muslim at all, and a Wahhabi judge might find Wells's commitment to the faith lacking. So they had the *muk* and the kidnappers against

545

them, and now the religious police, too.

The highway was nearly empty now, three lanes of freshly paved asphalt. Gaffan pinned the Jeep's speedometer at an even one hundred sixty kilometers — one hundred miles — an hour. The land around them was still featureless, but ahead a halo of city lights rose behind a low mountain range. Then the road turned, and through a gap in the hills Wells saw a massive skyscraper towering over the city and the hills around it.

"What is that?" Gaffan said.

Incredibly, the Saudi government had built a massive office and hotel complex beside the Grand Mosque. The development was centered on a two-thousand-foot skyscraper, the second-largest in the world, topped by a gigantic clock modeled on London's Big Ben. Each of the clock's four faces was one hundred fifty feet high — the size of a midsized office building — and had at its center the Saudi palm-and-crossed-swords logo. On its face, the complex was an awful idea, a giant commercial center on top of a sacred religious site. And architecture critics agreed that the buildings were ugly and ponderous, much too big for the site, their bulk worsened by their lack of glass. The Burj Khalifa in Dubai, the world's

546

largest skyscraper, was a more-than-two-thousand-five-hundred-foot needle into the sky, a soaring monument to modern design and engineering. The Mecca tower was an overgrown Lego block.

But the Saudis weren't fools. And despite their wealth, they weren't inclined to build skyscrapers. The tallest buildings in Riyadh were less than half the size of this building. The princes had placed the complex where they did to remind the world that the glory of Islam and the glory of the House of Saud could not be separated. They'd knocked down a historic Ottoman Empire fortress to build it, ignoring the protests of the Turkish government, delivering the message that Mecca would never again belong to the Turks. From its heights, the skyscraper flashed the call to prayer five times a day, its green and white lights glowing over Mecca and the desert. It was a gift from the princes to proclaim the might and majesty of Islam. The symbolism was as simple and over-whelming as the Saudi flag.

Wells was starting to explain all this to Gaffan when his sat phone rang. "I have something for you."

"Please tell me it's an address."

"Not quite. But we have it down to two blocks in a neighborhood called Hindaw-

iyyah. Good news is there aren't any apartment buildings. It's all residential. Medium
to big houses. A good place to hide someone."

"What's the street?"

"It's called Shahab. The expressway turns
into a road called Umm al Qura" — Mother
of Villages, Mecca's historic title — "which
goes right to the mosque. Shahab's off
Umm al Qura, about twelve hundred meters
after the expressway ends. Right-hand side.
The hot zone is four hundred meters down,
give or take."

" 'Give or take.' "

"There's a radius around the cell towers.
Our friends played some games with the
signal to triangulate, but they could only
get to within about a hundred meters. A
circle with a two-block diameter. Maybe
thirty houses in all."

"Ellis. We can't start randomly kicking in
doors. If that's all you've got, you better call
the FBI."

"Mecca's out for the FBI. Unless somebody repeals the Quran."

"The *muk,* then."

"Bad idea for lots of reasons. Including
the fact that we'd have to tell them about
forty-two Aziz."

"So it's just us?"

"It's just you. But I have good news, too. Fresh overheads. You have Internet access?"

"No."

"Get someplace that does."

"Ellis. The curfew starts in ten minutes. If we're lucky, we'll get to town before they close the city. The *muk* are looking for us. Pretty soon they're gonna have the names on our identity cards. We don't have time to sit back, boot up, check Gmail —"

"Then I'll walk you through them."

"You want to describe satellite shots to me over the phone?"

"Unless you have a better idea."

The Jeep slowed. Wells looked up to see another roadblock, this one on the edge of the city. "I have no ideas at all." He hung up, stuffed the phone under the seat.

They cleared the roadblock, drove east on the Umm al Qura, toward the skyscraper that loomed over the Grand Mosque and the rest of the city. Like Jeddah, Mecca felt besieged, its streets empty, helicopters sweeping downtown and the ridges of the hills to the north and south.

"What now?" Gaffan said.

"Find this street, Shahab, and get deep into the neighborhood. Past the hot block. Find some place where we can pull over and

I can talk to Shafer without getting us arrested."

The streets in Mecca were better marked than those in the Jeddah slums. At 10:59 p.m., Gaffan turned into an empty lot and nosed the Jeep behind a dumpster. If the rest of the neighborhood was any guide, the lot would soon be home to yet another giant concrete mansion. They were two blocks from the hot zone the National Security Agency had found. If they stayed here too long, someone would call the police, but for now the helicopters were closer to downtown and most of the police were at roadblocks rather than on patrol. They had a few minutes. Wells called Shafer.

"You're there?"

"Yes. I don't see how this can work, but talk."

"First, make sure we're talking about the same place. Four blocks in, at the corner, there's a three-story house that reaches almost to the edge of the lot, with a green minibus parked in front —"

"Yes." They'd driven past that house maybe a minute before. Sitting in an office in Virginia, six thousand miles from these streets, Shafer could see over walls and into backyards invisible to Wells. The science-fiction writer Arthur C. Clarke had said it best: *"Any sufficiently advanced technology is indistinguishable from magic."*

For fifteen minutes, Shafer described cars, yards, fences, garages, trying to find the clue that Wells needed. "Next" — Wells would say when Shafer had exhausted a property's possibilities. "Next —"

And then Shafer said it.

"This one's not on Shahab. Half a block down, looks like new construction, a garage behind it. Parked in front of the garage, I see a motorbike, small, and what looks like an ambulance —"

"Say again, Ellis." Wells thought of the paramedic case he'd seen at 42 Aziz.

"In back. There's a vehicle, maybe five years old, you know, a cargo van, white, red stripes and the red crescent logo on the side and brackets for a light bar on top, but I don't actually see the light bar. Smaller than an American version, but an ambulance is pretty obvious, right?"

"Does it have a name, a hospital, anything like that?"

"I don't see one."

"What else?"

"The wall on this one is maybe eight feet, a little higher than the neighbors, nothing special. Nobody outside, nobody on the roof."

"Any pipes coming off the house or the garage, any signs of ventilation?"

A pause. "Could be a vent off the left side of the garage. I can't tell for sure."

"Ways in and out?"

"Nothing obvious. It's a fortress. The front gate's solid, and the top of the walls is studded with glass. You can't see it from the street, but it's there. There's no alley in back. You think this is it, John?"

"It's our best shot." By "best," Wells meant *only.*

" 'Cause it's gonna be tough. Too bad that ambulance isn't running. You could call nine-one-one, get them out of the house."

Nine-one-one. Get them out. The words triggered an idea. "Maybe we can."

Wells hung up, told Gaffan about the ambulance.

"You know, it's probably coincidence."

"What if I can prove it's not?" Wells explained his plan.

"That's the best idea anybody's had since this whole thing started."

So Wells reached down for the cell phone he'd taken from Usman.

CHAPTER 24

Cutting off Kurland's hand had taken less than a minute. After hitting bone twice, Bakr found the groove of Kurland's wrist and pressed the saw forward. Kurland tore at the vises, but their grip held him tight. He screamed, but Bakr couldn't hear him over the shriek of the blade. After the first surge of blood coated the floor, Bakr was surprised how slowly it came, thin, unsteady dribbles.

When the operation — as Bakr thought of it — was done, Bakr picked Kurland's hand off the floor and stuffed it into a plastic bag. He wanted it for a keepsake, if nothing more. He wrapped Kurland's stump in cotton gauze and strapped it to Kurland's chest. Then he tugged Kurland's mouth open and poured a half-dozen Cipro pills down his throat. Bakr didn't know if Cipro would help, but he didn't much care. Kurland had only two or at most three more days to live, anyway. Probably for the best. His eyes were dead already.

Before Bakr left the cell, he gave Kurland another hit of morphine to calm him. Still, Bakr had to be careful. Between the shock and the pain, too much morphine might send Kurland over. Bakr intended a messier and more public death for Kurland, an on-camera beheading. When he was done, Bakr would tell America and the world how the Saudi government had supported him. He'd have dates and bank accounts, evidence that the United States couldn't ignore. He imagined the response in Washington. The Americans had already invaded Afghanistan and Iraq. Now they would do the same to Saudi Arabia. In turn, the Muslim world would rise against them. And Bakr would lead the battle. This was his destiny, the reason Allah had saved him that day on the dune.

After watching the digital video of the amputation on his laptop, Bakr decided he needed to make two versions of his propaganda tape. The raw footage was too graphic. Even his stomach turned as he watched Kurland's hand hanging half off the stepladder with the saw digging in. He wanted to enrage the Americans, not sicken them. He would post the uncut video only to a few jihadi websites.

With the help of Abdul, his translator, Bakr recut the video to focus on the minutes before and after the cutting. He included a glimpse of Kurland's face and a longer cut to the gauze-covered stump to prove the tape was real. At the end of the video, he made an explicit threat to execute Kurland in twenty-four hours if his demands weren't met — and explained that the Saudi government had sponsored him, with the details to be revealed after Kurland's death.

Bakr planned to get this video to the world's news channels the same way he had delivered the first tape. Abdul would drive a freshly burned DVD to Hassan's safe house in Jeddah. From there, Hassan would copy it and upload it to a site run by a Finnish company that specialized in anonymous Internet hosting. They'd used a Russian company for the first video. Then they'd call Al Jazeera and CNN and give them a link to download the video. Bakr knew that the Americans had amazing abilities to monitor the Internet. He wanted to be sure that they couldn't track these transfers anywhere near him.

But he took too long cutting the second video. The curfew turned into a problem.

So he told Abdul to let Hassan know that they'd deliver the video in the morning. Technically, the deadline for Bakr's demands wouldn't pass until noon, and Bakr wanted to wait until after the deadline to post the video. Of course, the United States would never agree to his demands, but waiting would look better. In any case, the video would be online by late tomorrow afternoon, and the United States and Saudi Arabia would be on the edge of war.

Abdul called Hassan. "He's not answering."

"Leave a message, then." Bakr wasn't worried. Hassan might have been on the roof, watching the neighborhood. Or even on the toilet. "If we don't hear from him, we'll call back later." From a different cell. Since the raid on his camp, Bakr had become even more cautious about his phones and e-mail accounts. He never used the same phone twice in a row, and he turned them off whenever he wasn't using them. E-mail he tried to avoid entirely, although he couldn't always.

Sure enough, a half hour later, with the video finally finished, Hassan called Abdul back. But Abdul spent most of the call shouting into the phone. "What did he say?" Bakr asked after Abdul hung up.

"I couldn't hear very well. Something about a helicopter. He's worried. I asked him for details, and he said he'd get Usman, and after a few seconds the phone disconnected."

"Lots of helicopters out tonight."

"I tell you, he sounded upset. Not like himself."

There were only four of them in the house: Bakr, Abdul, Ramzi, and Marwan. The last two were in their mid-twenties and did the menial work, running errands and cooking and watching Kurland's cell. Bakr wasn't worried about Kurland escaping, but he did fear that Kurland might try to hurt himself, stop him from making the video.

"Come on," Bakr said. "Let's talk to the infidel."

A minute later, they stood beside Kurland. The ambassador's skin was pale and slack. His breaths came fast and shallow. Bakr put a thumb into Kurland's right nostril and tugged until Kurland came awake.

"Did you tell them where we are?" Bakr said, Abdul translating. Kurland shook his head. Bakr moved his hands up Kurland's face. "Tell me. Or I'll put out your eyes."

Now Kurland giggled quietly. The sound he made was not noise as much as the *idea* of noise. "I believe you might. Wouldn't even need the saw. Just get your thumbs in and push. You fool. How could I tell anyone anything? I don't know where we are."

"He says no," Abdul said. "He says he doesn't know where he is, anyway."

"Is that all he said?"

"Yes." Abdul didn't want to translate exactly what Kurland had said. He had no wish to see Kurland's eyes rolling loose, staring up at him from the floor of the cell.

"Fine, then."

"They coming for you?" Kurland said. "Is that it? Coming to get you?"

"Tell him I'm going to cut his throat. The next time I see him," Bakr said. Abdul hesitated. "Tell him," Bakr repeated. So Abdul did.

"Good," Kurland said. "It'll be a relief."

They had just left the cell when Abdul's phone buzzed with a text from Hassan. "False alarm. All clear." Yet Bakr wasn't relieved. The message should have had the code "66" at the end to prove it was real. It didn't. Maybe the stress had caused Hassan to forget, though Bakr had drummed the necessity for the codes into his commanders.

Bakr stepped outside, paced slowly around

the house. Could the *muk* or the Americans be on their way? Bakr couldn't imagine how. Hassan didn't know the house's exact location. No one did, except the four men inside it. And nothing connected Bakr to it. He'd rented it months before, paying cash, from a man who owned a dozen houses in Mecca. Anyway, the announcers on Saudi 1, the official television network, had said that the *muk* were focusing their search on the Najd and Riyadh. The announcers might be lying, trying to hide the truth about the search. But Bakr didn't think so. He had been very careful. And the neighborhood was quiet. The streets were empty, and the helicopters well away.

He was safe. They were safe. He was sure. Almost.

Inside, he picked up another phone, called Hassan. But the call went directly to voicemail. Hassan's cell was off. What was happening in Jeddah? He wished he could send Abdul to check, but the curfew made travel impossible. They would have to wait until the morning.

Ten minutes later, Abdul's phone buzzed again. This time the message came from Usman, not Hassan. "At Ramada Shubaika. Room 401. Come soon. No more messages." The Shubaika was a neighborhood in north-central Mecca, a couple of kilometers away, reachable on back roads. Even with the curfew, Abdul or Ramzi could probably get there on a scooter. But Bakr didn't understand how Usman had gotten to Mecca. Barely fifteen minutes before the curfew, Hassan had said that Usman was on the roof in Jeddah. And if something was really wrong, why had Hassan texted the all-clear?

Nothing made sense. Unless Hassan had already been captured when he called, and Usman had somehow escaped and gotten here. Bakr stared at the Nokia's screen: "Come soon. No more messages." He didn't fully believe the words, but he was afraid to ignore them. He couldn't go himself, and he couldn't chance losing Abdul. But Ramzi . . . and if something went wrong, if this turned out to be a trap, Bakr was certain that Ramzi wouldn't be afraid to martyr himself.

"Ramzi," Bakr called. "Come here."

Chapter 25

Wells lay prone beside a concrete wall, watching the house where he hoped Kurland was hidden, waiting to see whether his bait would draw the jihadis. He was just a few feet off the road but well hidden from the houses on both sides, thanks to the high, unbroken walls that lined the street. And he'd hardly heard a car since the curfew started. The *muk* were in a mood, and no sane Saudi wanted to anger them.

Glass scratched at Wells through his thin gown. Dust coated his mouth and throat. Yet Wells couldn't pretend that he didn't enjoy this hunt. Growing up, he'd spent more than one November Saturday sitting with his dad on the forested flanks of the mountains outside Hamilton, waiting for deer and elk to bring their brimming bodies close. Hunting was as close as they came to bonding. Though his father hadn't talked much, on those hunts or anywhere else.

Most surgeons didn't. A noisy operation was a troubled operation. Surgery was a strange way to spend a life. Surgeons saw the hidden damage time wreaked, blocked arteries and collapsed lungs. Inevitably, they grew to think of their fellow humans as broken machines. They cultivated their own inhumanity to cut with perfect dispassion. Yet a successful surgery was a kind of miracle. While Wells, whatever his philosophical musings, was a kind of anti-doctor, bringing death wherever he went, a one-man appointment in Samarra. Not for the first time, he wondered what his father would make of him.

So he lay on his stomach, staring at a gate two hundred feet away, in a hunt exactly like and exactly unlike the ones he'd known as a boy. Gaffan was a block back. Wells hoped someone came out in the next few minutes and made going in easy. He was tired of playing hunches. In Lebanon and again in Jeddah, they'd been forced to attack without knowing if they had the right target. This time, he wanted to be sure.

Somewhere behind the gate, an engine croaked to life. It was gas-powered and no more than a couple hundred CCs. It had to be the motorbike that Shafer had seen on the overheads. Wells stood, held his pistol loose. He'd left the M-16 in the car, figuring on silence and speed instead of maximum firepower. He was flush with the wall and certain that no one in the houses could see him.

The bike rumbled around the house, stopped at the gate. Two men murmured in Arabic, and the gate squeaked open sideways. Wells crossed a driveway, one house between him and the scooter. Behind him he heard the Jeep's engine turn over and crank up. He silently cursed Gaffan. *No.* Noise could only hurt them.

Behind the gate, a man said, "What's that?" and another said, "Should I go, then?" and the first said, "Hold on," and the gate stopped squeaking. Wells ran, ran as best he could with his blood-spattered gown bunching around his legs. He heard the gate squeak again, only now it sounded as though it was closing —

He got to the corner of the house. The gate was rolling forward, two feet between its front edge and the wall. Wells angled toward the wall and spun nimbly inside the gate —

Which slammed closed behind him as he got inside. He saw two men. One sat on a motorbike five feet from Wells. The other stood at the far end of the gate, maybe twelve feet away. "Hey," the man on the bike said. Wells lifted the Glock and shot him twice in the chest. The silenced rounds sounded like distant fireworks. The man's mouth opened, and his hands came up and he fell off the back of the bike, his legs still squeezing the saddle —

Wells turned toward the second man, who was coming at him, running, and got one shot off too high and missed. Now the guy was on him, four feet away, and Wells saw the knife in his hand. Wells pulled the trigger again, and the round caught the guy in the left shoulder and twisted him sideways. The guy stumbled, and Wells stepped aside and arched his back like a toreador and let the knife slide by. When the guy had fallen into the wall, Wells raised his arm until the tip of the silencer was almost touching the back of his head and shot him twice, even though once would have worked just fine. The top of his skull exploded, and his brains and blood splattered onto the concrete.

From the house, a voice yelled, "Ramzi! Marwan! What's happening?"

Bakr was in the kitchen, making a pot of tea, when he heard the commotion, the unmistakable puff of a silenced pistol. Even before he asked the question, he knew. They'd gotten here somehow, the *muk* or the Americans. He didn't understand how they had tracked him, but the answer no longer mattered. He still had time to kill Kurland. And then to escape with his video camera and lay out the evidence that proved the princes had supported him. "Come," he said to Abdul. The camera and knife were on the kitchen counter. He grabbed them and ran.

Wells heard the Jeep outside the gate. He didn't have time to open it. Gaffan would have to get in on his own. Wells ran for the front door and then changed his mind and angled toward the driveway in back. He ducked low as he passed two barred windows. At the back-right corner of the house, he stopped. The ambulance was parked across a short apron of asphalt, in front of a big windowless garage.

He stepped into the yard between the house and garage. Through a barred window, he saw the kitchen. A pot of tea steamed on the stove, but the room was empty. The back door into the house was open a few inches. Wells listened for footsteps but heard nothing. Had they gone upstairs? They wouldn't keep Kurland on the first floor. But Arab houses rarely had basements.

Then Wells remembered the cell in Lebanon that Meshaal had described. He ran for the garage, fearing that he was already too late.

Bakr and Abdul climbed into the cell. They wouldn't have time to make a proper video, but they could still put the camera on the stepladder and record the moment when Bakr cut off Kurland's head.

Kurland stirred as they reached him. His skin was gray, his eyes red and inflamed, as if his body had responded to the amputation by giving up its defenses against infection. He said something Bakr didn't understand and stuck out his tongue. He smelled like an open sewer, his insides rotting. Bakr didn't understand how Kurland had gotten so sick so quickly. But no matter. Bakr set up the camera on the stepladder, its top step now coated with dried blood. "Tell him the Americans haven't met our demands and the time for his execution has come," he said to Abdul.

"Do we have time?"

"Do it."

Abdul spoke. Kurland responded with two words that needed no translation.

"Ask him if he wants to convert to Islam."

This time the answer was three words.

"Fine, then. Tell him that by coming to the Arabian Peninsula, he's broken Islamic law, and that he's rejected the opportunity to save himself by converting. Tell him the penalty is death."

The garage was a big concrete shed, three car-sized bays wide. Wells tried to lift the front doors, found them locked. He ran to the windowless door on the side of the garage, pressed on its steel handle. It, too, was locked. He wondered if the men inside were waiting, standing inside the door with their rifles poised. Forcing your way into a room without covering fire was an all-time no-no. But he needed to keep coming. So far, the sirens weren't any closer. Help — if the Saudi police qualified as help — was a ways off.

Wells put the tip of the silencer to the edge of the door, just above the handle. He angled it diagonally down and squeezed the trigger twice. By his count, he'd fired seven rounds here, and three at the house in Jeddah. He still had nine rounds left. Which ought to be enough.

From somewhere inside the garage, a man shrieked.

■ ■ ■ ■

Kurland opened his eyes. They were back.
They were talking. The big one talked in
Arabic, and the little one translated. That
was how it went. But whatever language
they spoke, they were beasts. They'd taken
his *hand.* His left hand, with his wedding
ring. Too late, he'd realized his ring was
gone. He wished they'd taken his right. If
he was going to die in this little room, he
wanted to die wearing his ring.

Now they were back for the rest of him.
He knew even before they spoke. They
didn't offer him water or Coke or anything
else. No fake courtesies. Not that he wanted
any. They seemed rushed. They made their
speeches, their psychotic justifications, and
ignored his curses and came at him. The
big one holding a knife that must have been
a foot long, with a black handle and a
gleaming serrated edge. Kurland was afraid
now, more afraid than he'd ever been, but
angry, too. He wanted to see Barbara again.
His kids. And grandkids. *I don't deserve this.
I don't deserve to die.* Though no one ever
did.

Fine, then. He would die. But he didn't
plan to make it easy. Dignity didn't matter

to him anymore. His skin burned and his skull throbbed and his swollen tongue filled his mouth like a loaf of bread. They'd taken his dignity when they took his hand. So when they got close he shook his arm free of its sling and pushed the tip of the stump against the wall behind him — *the pain* —

He screamed. And dug his heels into the floor to rock the chair off its back legs, and leaned forward and toppled over, feeling a ridiculous surge of triumph as the floor rose toward him —

The shriek broke off. Then started again, this time resolving into a man's voice, words in English: "No, you don't, you bastards —" Wells pushed open the door and came into the garage in three big sideways steps, holding the Glock in a two-hand grip, keeping his shoulders forward and down to make himself a smaller target. All useless if someone was waiting inside, but he had to try. He looked side to side —

A Toyota Camry, a shovel, a pick, a humming electrical generator, empty water bottles, an orange first-aid kit that looked like the twin of the one he'd found in Jeddah. No jihadis. He ran around the Camry and saw two flat metal plates, big, the ones that utility workers used to cover the holes they made when they dug up streets. A crude hinged hatch had been cut into the front plate. The hatch, two feet square, was unlocked. And open.

The hole was about twelve feet deep. Wells peeked down, saw metal rods embedded in the wall that seemed to serve as a crude ladder. But the hatch was too narrow and the cell too deep to allow him to glimpse the entire space below. Unless he squatted down and put his face to the hatch, he couldn't see Kurland or the kidnappers.

Bakr couldn't believe that Kurland had knocked over his chair. *Crazy American.* He and Abdul flipped it up, ignoring Kurland, who was yelling and waving his stump, blood leaking from the gauze. Bakr reached for his knife, but Kurland thrashed his head sideways so he couldn't get a clean stroke. Bakr tried to grab his chin, but Kurland snapped his jaw like a wild dog. "Get the morphine," Bakr said to Abdul. The syringes were in the first-aid kit, in the garage.

"We don't have time —"

"I want the video to be clean, not this screaming —"

"The video, the video, you're insane —"

"Do it!"

■ ■ ■ ■

Wells heard them yelling and backed away from the hatch and dropped onto his hands and knees. They didn't know he was here. For the first time, he thought he might succeed. He was far enough from the hatch that the jihadi climbing out wouldn't see him, close enough to be able to kill the guy cleanly. "This is stupid," the man below said. His feet pounded on the metal rungs, rising step by step —

The man's hands emerged and the top of his head, thick black hair. He rose through the hatch as if he were materializing from empty space, a magic trick. He swung his head around, defenseless. His eyes widened and his eyebrows rose as he saw Wells, and Wells leaned forward and put the tip of the silencer to his forehead and pulled the trigger and blew off the top of his head with a 9-millimeter kiss —

And gravity had its way with his corpse and sucked him back into the cell. Wells stood up, knowing he had only one chance. He stepped toward the hatch, and without hesitating put his hands at his sides and stepped through the hole like a kid jumping off the high dive —

He fell through. Halfway down he caught his shoulder on one of the rungs embedded in the wall. He twisted sideways and wrenched a knee as he landed. He stumbled forward over the legs of the man he'd killed. He braced himself against the wall, without a shot —

Abdul fell through the hatch, dead, and before Bakr could fully register what was happening, another man plunged into the cell, wearing a bloodstained gown, a pistol in his hand. The man landed awkwardly and fell forward, toward the side of the cell, and Bakr looked at him and then at Kurland, and knew what he needed to do —

Wells turned himself and raised the pistol, but he was late, too late —

Bakr screamed *"Allahu Akbar!"* and drove the knife into Kurland's belly, a killing stroke, Bakr knew, even as the man in the corner finally got his pistol up and the rounds tore at him, two in his arm and two more in his chest and a marvelous black warmth filled him —

Wells fired until he had no ammunition left and pushed himself up and hobbled across the cell. The blood splashed out of Kurland and pooled on the concrete. Bakr had torn through the big arteries in his stomach. Wells knew he couldn't do anything, but he knelt before Kurland and pressed his hands to the wound and tried to stanch the flow. "I'm sorry," he said. Kurland's eyes were closing, but he locked on Wells when he heard the English.

"American?"

"Yes." The blood seeped around the knife blade, around Wells's hands.

Kurland's eyes drooped. "Stay with me," Wells said. He pushed harder. Kurland groaned.

"My ring. My wife. Ring."

Wells saw the stump, the left hand missing, and understood. "Your wedding ring."

"Tell her —" Kurland's breath came fast. His voice was a whisper.

"Tell her —" Wells said.

"Tell her I fought." His head slumped forward, and he was gone.

Wells closed his own eyes and leaned against the wall in a room with two men he'd killed and a third he'd failed to save. He would have world enough and time to consider how he could have saved Kurland. What he should have done differently. What his next move would be. Whether Saeed or someone else needed to pay for this atrocity. For now, he closed his eyes and sat in silence for eternity, or a minute or two. Until he heard someone in the garage above.

"John," Gaffan yelled. "You in here?"

"Down here."

"We clear?"

"Clear."

Gaffan's footsteps clanked over the plates. "Everything okay?"

"No," Wells said quietly. "It's not even close."

EPILOGUE

The Saudis could be very charming when they had to be.

And they had to be to calm the fury after Graham Kurland's death. After ten years and two frustrating wars, Americans had lost patience with Islamic terror — and with Saudi Arabia, which seemed to be its biggest backer. The fact that the kidnappers had mutilated Kurland became a closely guarded secret; the national security adviser called it "the kind of detail that could start a war." Plenty of Americans wanted war anyway. The day after Kurland's death, protestors surrounded the Saudi embassy, and polls showed that forty-six percent of Americans wanted to invade the Kingdom. The president asked for calm, saying that the United States needed to investigate. Blaming the Saudi government would be premature, especially since the government's forces had nearly rescued Kurland, he said.

Abdullah and Saeed also spoke out. In carefully managed interviews on CNN two days after Kurland's death, the men expressed sorrow for his killing and vowed to punish the perpetrators.

"Un-Islamic," Abdullah said. "A tragedy."

"Terrorists," Saeed said. "A crime."

The next day, Abdullah flew to Chicago for Kurland's funeral. The service and burial were closed to the public, but the reports that the king would be attending sparked promises of protests. Despite pleas from the Kurland family, the president, and the archbishop of Chicago, hundreds of demonstrators tried to reach Holy Name Cathedral, but police in riot gear faced them down.

At the funeral, the president was cool as ever. "Graham could have chosen to serve anywhere. He was that big a donor," the president said in his eulogy, and the mourners laughed politely, as they were meant to do. "But he wanted to go somewhere difficult. He wanted to make a difference. I hope that the way he died isn't all we remember about him. That would be the truest tragedy."

When it was Barbara's turn to speak, she

stood blankly before the mourners, shaking her head until her children came and led her down. Afterward, though, she found her voice. With a dozen Secret Service officers and FBI agents around her, she led Abdullah outside the cathedral to the makeshift pen where reporters and camera crews waited. In her long black dress and mourning gloves, she stood awkwardly next to the king, not quite touching him.

"I know in my heart that this is a good man," she said. "He's suffered, too. They killed his granddaughter two weeks ago. Graham liked him. Graham believed in diplomacy. Graham wouldn't have wanted war."

Graham wouldn't have wanted war. The whispered words were played over and over. A week after the funeral, only twenty-seven percent of Americans wanted to invade. The Saudis did their part, too, arresting dozens of men, and making sure that every arrest was reported. "We won't rest until all these criminals are in prison or dead," Mansour said. "We'll do whatever's necessary to prove we're a faithful ally."

The role Wells and Gaffan had played was never disclosed. Officially, a Saudi task force had tracked down Kurland with the help of tips from Saudis appalled by the kidnapping. Off the record, Duto told his favorite scribblers at the *Times* and the *Post* that the CIA and NSA had provided crucial tips. Duto explained that the rescue had failed because the first man into the underground cell in Mecca, a Saudi Special Forces soldier named Jalal, fell as he entered and didn't get a clean shot at Ahmad Bakr. The agency trusted the Saudi account of the rescue, because CIA operatives had interviewed Jalal and found him credible. His story also matched the physical evidence, Duto said.

Internally, the CIA and White House had a much darker view, of course. Once Bakr was identified, rolling up the remains of his network was easy. Finding his bosses proved more difficult. After four days of tracing bank accounts and wire transfers, the NSA and Treasury Department discovered Bakr's paymaster: Walid Ibrahim, a previously unknown brigadier general in the Saudi National Guard. The real question was whether Ibrahim had acted on his own or on the orders of someone more senior. The even more real question was what the United States should do if a top royal was involved.

Despite the public's anger, for once the CIA and Pentagon and State Department and White House were in agreement. A full-scale invasion was impossible. The sight of American soldiers occupying Mecca and Medina would infuriate Muslims everywhere. If the Saudis blew their oil fields, oil would go to at least two hundred dollars a barrel. And the princes had ruled their country so tightly that a viable opposition party didn't exist. If they fell, Saudi Arabia would fall into the hands of radical Islamists — or into outright anarchy.

But allowing the perpetrators to escape was equally unacceptable. After two days of meetings, the president issued a secret finding that anyone who had supported Bakr's group would be considered an "unlawful enemy combatant" subject to arrest and extradition. The finding continued: "If judicial remedies are found to be impossible to apply, I hereby authorize extrajudicial measures to penalize any and all conspirators. Such penalties shall apply whether conspirators had prior awareness of all Bakr's plans."

In plain English, anyone included would have to give himself up or face assassination, even if he didn't know that Bakr had planned to kidnap Kurland. But the money trail stopped at Walid Ibrahim, and the NSA couldn't find any intercepts connecting

Ibrahim or Bakr to senior royals. Under interrogation, lower-ranking members of Bakr's group admitted that Bakr had said his money had come from within the Saudi government. But he'd never mentioned specific princes. In fact, Bakr had regularly expressed his hate of the House of Saud.

Walid Ibrahim could have definitively answered the question. But Ibrahim had put a bullet in his brain two days after Kurland's death, even before the United States learned who he was. The Saudis told the White House that Ibrahim must have known he'd be caught and wanted to spare his family the embarrassment of a trial. No one in Washington believed them, but since Ibrahim's body had been cremated, the story was impossible to challenge.

A week into their investigation, the agency and the White House had more or less come around to Wells's theory. Senior princes, probably Saeed and Mansour, had supported Bakr, using him as a chip in their succession struggle with Abdullah. At some point, Bakr decided on his own to attack Kurland, hoping to provoke a war between the United States and Saudi Arabia.

The theory fit the available evidence. But a theory, even a plausible one, wasn't the same as proof. What if another prince had funded Bakr? What if Ibrahim had somehow run the group by himself? The United States simply didn't have enough evidence to arrest Saeed or Mansour, much less assassinate them.

Which left Wells. But Wells preferred to keep his own counsel. "He's not talking while the flavor lasts," Shafer told Duto, stealing a line from an old gum ad. "Says he's already told you as much as he can."

"Unacceptable."

"You should tell him so. Want to guess what he'll say? If I were in his position, I'd tell you I'd be glad to talk — first to you, then CNN. He probably won't be that subtle, though. He'll probably just tell you to come and get him."

"He ought to *want* us to get these guys."

"Maybe he's telling the truth, Vinny. I realize that's so far from your personal experience that you can't even imagine it, but it is technically possible. Maybe he doesn't know anything else. Or maybe he thinks we'll blow it. Our record isn't so great lately."

"Neither is his."

"Be sure to tell him so when you guys chat."

Two weeks after Kurland's death, the White

581

House press secretary announced that Walid Ibrahim, a Saudi general who was a prime suspect as a funder of the network that kidnapped Kurland, had committed suicide. The United States so far had not found proof that the conspiracy extended past Ibrahim, but the investigation was continuing. The press secretary added that the White House was "extremely disappointed" that the Saudi government hadn't arrested Ibrahim before his suicide.

The same night, the secretary of state flew to Riyadh for a secret meeting with Abdullah and Saeed. Security wasn't a problem. She never left her jet. Her speech to the brothers was straightforward.

"I came here to tell you the United States will not accept you" — she looked at Saeed — "or your sons as king. Not as Abdullah's successor, or ever. And you, Saeed, will resign as defense minister, and your son will give up the *mukhabarat.*"

"You dare interfere in our family's offices?"

"Should I tell you why we dare? Could be an unpleasant conversation. The consensus in Washington is that you're getting off easy."

"What proof do I have that you'll stick to this bargain?"

"This isn't a bargain. It doesn't guarantee anything. It's a minimum penalty, not a maximum. Do we understand each other?"

"You know," Abdullah said. "You know what's happened, everything. You know you know. And so does he, and so do I, and we all sit here knowing and not knowing at the same time. It makes my mind ache."

"My brother's become a philosopher in his old age," Saeed said.

Saeed looked at his brother and at the secretary, that foolish woman. He had no choice. "All right," he said. But still in his head he heard the voice, defiant, maddening: *Mine. Mine. Mine.*

Alia's speech in Jeddah had been taped. Against Miteb's advice, Abdullah had watched. The video didn't end when the bomb blew. A dozen times, Abdullah had seen his granddaughter bleed to death. Now, in the secretary's jet, Alia visited him. She asked him how Saeed and Mansour could escape so easily. The United States hadn't demanded their exile. They would live untouched in their palaces.

Abdullah knew he could bring Saeed and Mansour to justice simply by telling the Americans what Saeed had said on the night after Kurland was kidnapped. The words were as good as a confession. Yet Abdullah couldn't make himself speak. To speak was to condemn his brother and nephew to death. To stay silent was to allow them their murders. And either course might jeopardize his nation. He couldn't decide what to do, couldn't even imagine how to make a choice. The Americans, with all their toys and tools. Why couldn't they find proof on their own? Why did they need him? And if they couldn't or wouldn't act, should he try to reach out to Wells? Plot his own revenge? He no longer cared if Khalid succeeded him. He simply wanted justice, but he knew that his own decisions had torn justice from him, put it on the other side of the sun.

Every night Abdullah looked for answers and found none. And every night before his eyes closed, he prayed for an honorable escape from his dilemma. He prayed to die. Yet he felt stronger than he had in years. Allah's final joke. Abdullah wouldn't be allowed death's easy escape from these decisions.

Wells watched all of this, and none of it, from North Conway. He and Gaffan had left Mecca a few hours after the failed rescue. Wells figured he'd leave the Grand

Mosque and the Kaaba for another trip. A proper *hajj,* one that didn't drench him in another man's blood. The next day, he and Gaffan flew out on an air force jet, stopping briefly in Cyprus on their way to New York. They mostly slept, didn't talk much.

Meshaal had come with them, too, Wells's only request of Abdullah. The kid's life expectancy in Saudi Arabia could be measured in weeks. Wells figured Meshaal had earned the chance to sort himself out in the United States. If he wasn't happy, he could always go to Gaza.

When they landed in New York, Gaffan took his bag and the briefcase with what was left of his million dollars and gave Wells a manly half-hug. "It's been real, it's been fun," Gaffan said. "You want to do it again, let me know."

"I'll do that," Wells said. He didn't know yet if he'd go after Saeed, or if Saeed would come after him. Though he had a feeling that their dance wasn't finished.

He'd thought a lot about Kurland's last words. *"Tell her I fought."* He had seen Barbara in Chicago the day before the funeral. She sat alone in her study, her eyes half closed, grief etched in her cheeks. Wells silently reached into his pocket, gave her

585

the ring. It was in a plastic bag. He hadn't wanted to touch it. It belonged to her, no one else. She shook it out and slipped it onto her finger beside her own wedding band. It was much too big. Its yellow gold caught the light as she twirled it loosely.

"He asked me to be sure you got it."

"Thank you."

"I'm sorry." Wells didn't know what to say next. *I tried? I wanted to save him? If I'd had just a few more seconds?* Like he'd been caught in traffic and missed his flight. "He wasn't scared. At the end. He was lucid. And he wasn't in pain. He asked me to tell you something."

He told her. She listened and nodded, and then their conversation seemed to be over.

Wells wanted to go to the funeral, but someone might recognize him and wonder. There were too many unanswered questions already. So he stayed away.

He didn't tell Anne about Abdullah and Saeed, or what had happened in Lebanon. But — two weeks on, the same night the secretary of state made her trip to Riyadh — he told her about Kurland. They sat in her kitchen, eating dinner, homemade lasagna. Tonka lay curled under his feet, chewing happily on a piece.

"I should have shot through the hatch. But I couldn't see the setup inside —"

"The whole world was looking for him, and you almost saved him by yourself."

"Only I didn't."

She didn't say anything, just stood, walked behind him, wrapped her arms around him.

"Something else that's bothering me." He told her Kurland's last words. "What I don't understand, why wouldn't he say he loved her instead? He did, too, even in those few seconds I could tell. And it was the same when I met her."

"You really don't see?"

He tilted his head so he was looking over his shoulder, into her eyes. "No."

"Saying it would have dishonored what they had. He didn't have to, John. She already knew."

ACKNOWLEDGMENTS

One problem with writing a book a year is that the acknowledgments can get stale. But the crew at Putnam never does. They're as hardworking as ever. Thanks to Neil, Ivan, Leslie, Tom, Marilyn, and everyone else who makes these novels more than a Word file. Thanks to Heather and Matthew, agents extraordinaire. Thanks to Susan Buckley and Dev for watching my back. Thanks to Deirdre and Jess for those close first reads, and for not being afraid to say what doesn't work, and what does. Thanks to my parents and brother for your support and suggestions. Most of all, thanks to Jackie, my wife, who always finds the time and energy to be a great friend and partner.

And — this part never gets stale either — thanks to everyone who took the time to read this far. Without you, John Wells would have retired a long time ago. I appreciate your feedback, and you can always reach me at alexbersonauthor@gmail.com and follow me on Facebook and Twitter. I can't promise to respond (though until now I've managed to write back to just about everyone), but I pledge to read every note I get.

ABOUT THE AUTHOR

As a reporter for the *New York Times*, **Alex Berenson** has covered topics ranging from the occupation of Iraq to the flooding of New Orleans to the financial crimes of Bernie Madoff. His previous novels include *The Faithful Spy*, winner of the 2007 Edgar Award, *The Ghost War, The Silent Man,* and *The Midnight House. The Number* is a work of nonfiction. He lives in New York City.

PERMISSIONS

The House of Saud, which is the ruling family of Saudi Arabia, provides a central structure to fictional events in this novel. The descriptions of the rise of the House of Saud and its relationship to Wahhabi Islam are factually accurate, to the best of the author's knowledge, and based on reliable nonfiction histories. However, imaginary people are intermingled freely with real ones, so, for example, Princes Saced and Mansour are wholly fictional characters, and are not, of course, the defense minister and the director of the *mukhabarat*, respectively, of the present-day Saudi Arabian government. Similarly, although King Abdullah is real, his plan to install his son on the throne—along with all other dialogue, action, and motives attributed to him or other members of the ruling family whether real or fictional—is a product of the author's imagination and is not based upon actual events. Finally, references to unidentified members of the Saud ruling family are also fictional and bear no resemblances to any real person, living or dead.